I0891453

Praise for

THE GLASS HOUSE

Book One in the Menzies Mental Health Series

'Stunning . . . [A] unique novel that's so timely' *DAILY TELEGRAPH*

'Contains all the comforting trappings of a fast-paced medical procedural' *SYDNEY MORNING HERALD*

'Casts a non-judgemental but candid, informed and astute eye on the system . . . It arouses our sympathy and empathy, develops our understanding and increases our knowledge in areas long kept hidden or decreed taboo. And it's a darn good read' LIVING ARTS CANBERRA

'A racy, pacy ride through heartbreak and the occasional breathtaking miracle' *COUNTRY STYLE*

'An absorbing read that you'll want to stay up late to finish' *INSTYLE AUSTRALIA*

'A remarkable exposé . . . told with an engaging, light touch reminiscent of *Eleanor Oliphant is Completely Fine* and Simsion's *The Rosie Project*' BOOKS+PUBLISHING

'Highly engaging. Brings alive the frontline of mental health care' PROFESSOR PATRICK McGORRY AO, Australian of the Year 2010

'Entertaining, enlightening, it embraces the complexity of what it means to be human' MEREDITH JAFFÉ

'A great read that combines laugh-out-loud moments with those that bring tears to your eyes. Anne Buist skilfully writes from her own experiences and co-author Graeme Simsion adds his inimitable *Rosie Project* style. An honest, sensitive look into mental health care in Australia' PROFESSOR JAYASHRI KULKARNI AM, psychiatrist, Monash University

'Gripping, rich and insightful, and brimming with compassion. Shines a light on the grit and dedication of frontline workers, while giving a voice to everyone impacted by mental illness' ARIANE BEESTON, author of *Because I'm Not Myself, You See*

'Sensitive, respectful, enjoyable' YENN PURKIS, mental health and autism self-advocate and author

ANNE BUIST &
GRAEME SIMSION

THE OASIS

hachette AUSTRALIA

hachette AUSTRALIA

Published in Australia and New Zealand in 2025
by Hachette Australia
(an imprint of Hachette Australia Pty Limited)
Gadigal Country, Level 17, 207 Kent Street, Sydney, NSW 2000
www.hachette.com.au

Hachette Australia acknowledges and pays our respects to the past, present and future Traditional Owners and Custodians of Country throughout Australia and recognises the continuation of cultural, spiritual and educational practices of Aboriginal and Torres Strait Islander peoples. Our head office is located on the lands of the Gadigal people of the Eora Nation.

Copyright © Anne Buist and Graeme Simsion 2025

This book is copyright. Apart from any fair dealing for the purposes of private study, research, criticism or review permitted under the *Copyright Act 1968*, no part may be stored or reproduced by any process without prior written permission. Enquiries should be made to the publisher.

A catalogue record for this book is available from the National Library of Australia

ISBN: 978 0 7336 5150 2 (paperback)

Cover design and illustration by Alex Ross
Cover image courtesy of Shutterstock
Author photographs courtesy of Max Deliopoulos
Typeset in 11.7/18.2 pt Sabon LT Pro by Bookhouse, Sydney
Printed and bound in Australia by McPherson's Printing Group

MIX Paper | Supporting responsible forestry FSC® C001695

The paper this book is printed on is certified against the Forest Stewardship Council® Standards. McPherson's Printing Group holds FSC® chain of custody certification SA-COC-005379. FSC® promotes environmentally responsible, socially beneficial and economically viable management of the world's forests.

To the many people whose stories and struggles inspired this series

ONE

FLIGHT TO HEALTH

The guy getting out of the battered hatchback has tried to strike a balance between fitting in and hiding his identity. His orange safety vest and the extension ladder protruding from the back of the vehicle – red briefs tied to the last rung – give a fair impression of a tradie or cleaner. The hoodie, head torch and the bag of rope he's unpacking suggest a burglar, or someone breaking out a prisoner. The latter is pretty much what he's aiming to do.

Inside the Menzies Mental Health Service's Extended Care Unit, dance-music producer and inpatient DJ Voices is pulling the top off a piano stool. It arrived a few days ago, along with the new keyboard that she'd been permitted to accept as a gift.

In the stool's storage cavity, beneath a false bottom, are two small audio players packed in bubble wrap. DJ's accomplice – the guy outside with the ladder and rope – visited earlier in the week and they scoped out where to put them: a fist-sized hole in the wall of the common room, and a gap at the back of the bench in the tearoom.

DJ is thirty-two with green hair, dressed more neatly than the other patients in jeans and long-sleeved t-shirt: street clothes for the street outside. She's significantly overweight – a side effect of the antipsychotics. They also have a sedating effect, but right now the adrenaline is cutting through, giving her clarity, as it does when she performs.

Her accomplice is wired too, but he's struggling to get the ladder extended and propped against the courtyard wall. And now, the tricky part: the other side, where DJ Voices will have to climb up. No way could he get a second ladder over. And no way could she pull herself up a rope. His solution is a rope ladder, anchored to the hatchback's bumper.

After three trips up the regular ladder, he gets the length of the securing rope right. A helicopter might have been simpler.

DJ has hit play on the audio units and dropped them into place, and is waiting in the common room for the fun to begin. It doesn't take long. 'Help, let me out. I'm trapped! I can't breathe!'

Nice clean sound and surprisingly loud. She can barely suppress her laughter. Let *them* be freaked out by voices for a change. And they are.

Commotion, then a code yellow over the PA system. People arriving. She waits for the confusion to build, then heads for the courtyard . . . only to find that's where the staff are shooing her fellow inmates, clearing the building. No chance for her to get to the ladder before they see it.

'I'm dying in here,' screams the audio player in the tearoom as security guys tear a cupboard apart.

More responders are coming through the main door. Unfamiliar faces. They don't know her either.

She grabs a student nurse's jacket – complete with name badge: Tom – from the back of a chair, steps aside as a security guy barges in, then walks out through the open door.

'There's a weird guy insisting he sees you. Like, right away.'

The gum-chewing temp standing in the doorway of my office apparently hasn't done the respect-is-expected module.

In a mental health service, 'weird' is normal, though we avoid both of those words when we're talking about patients. But here, at the outpatient clinic, walk-ins aren't so normal. However, my 9 am appointment hasn't turned up – *that's* normal – so 'right away' isn't actually a problem.

Gum Chewer adds that Weird Guy won't give his real name: calls himself Frodo.

'Does he look –' I stop. She said weird. Anything more specific than that is my job.

I've been in the clinic for three days and I'm already loving it. While I learned heaps in the Acute Unit, the work I'm doing here is closer to how I see my future. And my future is finally looking secure. *I'm in the psychiatry training program.* Hard to explain what a big deal that is.

My mum: 'I thought you were already a trainee.' (No, I was a *registrar,* working in a psych ward but without my work counting toward qualifying as a full-fledged consultant psychiatrist.)

My brother, Lennon: 'Trainee? How long does it take?' (Still five years of six-month placements plus a lot of boxes to tick.)

My sister, Mel: 'I just tell people you're already a psychologist.' (Screams in frustration. *Psychiatrist.* I know the words are similar. But I'm a *doctor,* I deal with *serious mental illness*, I prescribe *drugs . . .*)

My dad: '"Registrar" sounds like someone at the council. Good to put that behind you.' (I'm still a registrar – that's the term for *all* doctors once they're past the intern and house medical officer stages but before they qualify as consultants.)

My dad, laughing: 'Clear as mud, Hanny.'

I get where Mel was coming from. Psychologists and psychiatrists are confused in the public mind, and there is some overlap, but things are changing. Psychiatry has been moving from lie-on-the-couch psychotherapy toward 'real', physical medicine – the biological approach. Scan the brain, see what lights up, prescribe the appropriate drug. Leave the talking to the psychologists.

That's the goal, for some at least, but diagnostic tools and medication aren't there yet, by a long way. As for leaving the talking to the psychologists, it's not always possible.

Often, we're the guys on the spot, no psychologist in sight, with the patient unlikely to be able to afford one anyway. So they get someone whose training in the psychological therapies is pretty much what every doctor gets taught about bedside manner. By the time I qualify, I'll have done a bit more, but it will be measured in hours rather than years.

Even in the Acute Unit, where we were dealing with the hard end of mental illness, the biological approach by itself wasn't always enough, or even much good at all. My boss in Acute, Nash Sharma, resisted admitting an anorexia nervosa patient essentially because we had no drug to treat her. It was our psychologist who finally made some headway, at least with the family.

Then there was our patient with postpartum psychosis. Medication and electroconvulsive therapy did miracles for her illness, but they didn't address her troubles bonding with her baby, rejection by her husband, and fending off the mother-in-law from hell.

And Xavier, the politician. My fellow trainee, Alex, who was seeing him as a psychotherapy training case, bore most of the blame when he suicided. But there was no criticism of him being discharged from Acute with a prescription for antidepressants when his problems were way more complicated.

Now I'm seeing patients who are living in the community. Most are on medication and my first job is to review that. It's usually straightforward, and I can use the rest of the thirty minutes – fifty for a new patient – to talk about issues arising from their mental health and its treatment, and sometimes even the causes. We don't have as long as I'd like, and I don't have the skills of an expert psychotherapist, but they're not going to see an expert psychotherapist.

I feel I'll be able to do some good and I'm planning to get better at it. I've got space to breathe: to extend a session if the next patient doesn't show up; to plan my appointments. After working as a doctor for almost three years, I'm finally being treated as a grown-up.

I follow Gum Chewer to reception, where plate-glass screens give us a view into the waiting room. It's empty apart from Mr Frodo. He's standing – hobbit height and a ball of nervous energy. Wearing sunglasses inside. I've seen him somewhere before.

I push the speaker button so he can hear me through the screen. 'Ah, Frodo?'

He smiles – possibly relieved that I don't look too intimidating. Psychiatrists – including trainees like me – don't wear scrubs. I'm in my usual short skirt and Doc Martens. Female, twenty-eight, medium height – just, glasses, fringe: a human welcome mat.

'I'm Dr Hannah Wright. You wanted to see me?'

'Yes. Urgently.'

'Are you a clinic patient?'

'No, but it's about a patient.' He lowers his voice. 'Confidential. Matter of life and death.'

I've had a minute to assess him. Possibly paranoid but I don't see him as dangerous. I have a duress alarm under my desk.

I let him into the labyrinth. The building was originally the stables and barn of a colonial house – the clinic's official name is the Stables. What used to be the main house is now a hotel. On the other side there's a shopping mall and we're hidden behind a red-brick wall and a huge gum tree. Inside, the 1870s-meets-1980s-reno look is patchy and you need a GPS to navigate the corridors.

Frodo follows me to my office. According to the heritage note beside the door, it was once a dog kennel. Apparently for a small dog that had an aversion to sunlight. It's basic: desk, computer, three green upholstered upright chairs and a Toulouse-Lautrec print.

'So, er . . . Frodo, can I have your legal name and the name of the patient?'

I smile, trying to put him at ease. He looks mid to late thirties. A little shabby. He takes his sunglasses off and his eyes are pale blue.

'No. You only need to know I'm Frodo. It's my identity and you have to respect that.' I don't think that's how it's supposed to work, but Frodo continues before I can push it. 'I guess you need to know the patient's real name for the prescription.'

'It'd be a start.'

'Celeste Boyce.'

'Okay. Why isn't she here?'

'She's in hiding. But she needs her medication. If she misses her clozapine, it's dangerous, right? I wasn't messing with you: life and death.'

'It's certainly problematic. Are you telling me she's not been taking it?'

'She's had it for the last two nights but she needs two hundred grams tonight.'

'I'm hoping you mean milligrams.'

'Yep. And a few weeks' supply after that.'

'Then I need to see her. Does she usually come here for her meds?'

'She used to,' says Frodo. 'Before they locked her up.'

I look hard at Frodo. I *have* seen him before. 'Does Celeste have another name?'

'Yes,' says Frodo, looking at the door.

'And would that name be DJ Voices?'

He nods.

Shit. DJ was, until two days ago, a patient in our Extended Care Unit – officially the *Secure* Extended Care Unit. Not so secure, because she walked out of it while somebody, possibly Frodo, was creating a diversion by throwing a rope ladder over the wall and enabling other patients to abscond. All but DJ were found pretty quickly.

Inevitably the media got onto it. After starting with the danger-to-the-public angle, they switched to the human-interest story. DJ had been a rising star of the electronic music scene before being hit with schizoaffective disorder. She still performed on day leave but was apparently not well enough to live independently.

I'd gone to one of her gigs. She'd seemed to be doing okay, though watching her from a few metres away wasn't exactly a clinical assessment. At one point she'd needed a time-out. A guy had come on and reassured us she was okay – the guy sitting in front of me now.

DJ had apparently been 'grounded' – the media's word – because she'd returned to the hospital late from a gig. A nice fit with the narrative of *sane person locked up and treated paternalistically* that was supposed to belong to the bad old days. Unfortunately, Keith Barnard, the head of Extended Care, is a relic of those days, according to Jon Homann, another of my fellow trainees, who's just finished a rotation with him.

'It says in the paperwork she needs to be treated in the least restrictive environment,' Frodo says. 'My place may not be a mansion, but it's not an *asylum* with no sex, no . . . privacy, nowhere to practise. We had to crowdfund her a new keyboard; the old one got wrecked by one of the patients – how can you call that a safe place? Then they punish her for being back an hour late.'

He's barely taken a breath, and if this wasn't so obviously something he's passionate about, I'd be thinking manic. No; just anxious and on a mission.

'I need to check this out,' I say. 'If she came back and presented her case to the Mental Health Tribunal . . .'

Frodo lets out a snort that shakes his entire body. 'If we're talking legal shit, what if you don't give me a prescription and something happens?'

I put my hand up, and Frodo goes quiet while I check DJ's record on the system. It confirms that she is – or was – on two hundred milligrams of clozapine a day, a solid dose for a female.

I tell Frodo I need to refer to a consultant, and he attempts a threatening look. 'Don't fuck with us.'

I smile and lead him back to the waiting room. And then go for help.

Louis the Locum (pronounced the French way with a Scottish accent – Lou-*eh*), brown hair in a ponytail, is the latest in a long line of acting heads. He gives me more freedom than Nash did – his welcoming message was basically, 'Call me if you're in trouble, but don't expect much.'

I find him with his feet up in the tearoom, and explain the problem.

'Mmm,' he says. 'Cannae be sure about the ins and outs of it all. Best ask the prof.'

Rather than hassling Professor Gordon, clinical director of the whole Service, I ring Extended Care.

Alex, my occasional date during our time in Acute, answers. His placement in Extended Care was a late change, probably to give him some recovery time after his psychotherapy patient suicided. That was six weeks ago and he's basically ghosted me since.

I don't know if it's because he needs time out, blames me for discouraging him from phoning Xavier the night he died or wasn't comfortable with me seeing his vulnerability and distress. Or just took the opportunity to bail.

'Alex? Hi. It's Hannah.'

There's a pause. 'Are you after me?'

'Actually, I'm after Dr Barnard.' The aforementioned head of Extended Care – a dinosaur in an untucked white shirt.

'He's in his office with the door closed. Which means *do not disturb*. Unless patients are climbing the wall on a rope ladder.'

There's a flash of the old Alex there. I miss seeing him every day with his untidy brown hair and slightly retro fashion sense, taking the piss with the senior nurse and giving a running commentary when Nash sparred with management. And his intense belief in psychotherapy, which is also slightly retro. I want to ask him how he is, but I keep it professional.

'Can you just say to me that you've seen the patient recently and that continuing her clozapine is appropriate?'

'Lucky you're speaking to me, not Keith. He'd tell you to call the police. But you were only asking about medication, right?' He puts on a voice. 'I believe that continuing clozapine would be appropriate.'

'Do *you* think I should call the police?'

The formal voice again: 'I believe that continuing clozapine would be appropriate.'

I laugh and ask the question. 'How are you doing?'

There's a long pause. Then, 'I'm a lot better. Sorry I've been a bit remote, but I needed to regroup. I'd like to talk.'

'I guess that's what you do.'

'So?'

'I'll see if I can find a slot.'

I call Jon. He was DJ's treating doctor until the changeover of rotations this week; he's now working in the Mother Baby Unit.

'She's mainly a danger to herself,' he says. 'Non-compliance, drug usage, risky behaviour.'

Frodo's pacing in the waiting room. I really should check with a consultant. Which brings me back to Prof Gordon. He and I have some history. For a while he blocked my entry to the psychiatry training program, until I basically agreed I'd see a therapist myself. In hindsight, I guess it was a backhanded way of supporting my interest in psychotherapy; I doubt he'd have cared if I was planning to go down the biological–medication path.

At some point, I'll organise that therapy. With any luck, Prof has forgotten about it.

His secretary puts me through.

'Ah, Hannah,' Prof says. 'Have you found a therapist yet?'

Shit. 'Everyone appears to be fully booked.' So I'm told.

'Did you tell them you're a trainee psychiatrist? We look after each other. Try Isaac Sandler. Very experienced.'

'I know the name,' I say. 'We admitted one of his patients last term. She . . .' I stop. Nash had been unimpressed; she'd got better in two weeks on an antidepressant – after five years in therapy with the guy Prof's now recommending.

'Ah yes. Young Sophie. I believe you patched her up after a crisis,' says Prof. 'Don't confuse that with solving the underlying problem. Issy tells me that losing her job was the trigger, but he's treating the results of years of childhood sexual abuse.'

Prof has a point – the point that makes me want to learn more about psychotherapy. I explain my problem with Frodo and DJ.

'DJ?' says Prof. 'The . . .' He's fishing for the word to describe what she does.

'DJ.'

'Right. Ask Nash.' He hangs up.

He seems to have forgotten that I'm no longer working for Nash, who, last I heard, was on holiday in India. Looks like it's my call.

I write DJ a script for five days' clozapine. When I give it to Frodo, I tell him to bring her in on Monday.

'Nope,' he says. 'The longer she's out, the less anyone will be chasing her.'

'Then you'll have to come in.'

I give him my number; not something I'd normally do, but it's in my interests to give him every chance to do the right thing. I'm already feeling uncertain: why did Frodo choose sex as the example of something DJ couldn't have in hospital? He presents like everybody's idea of an incel.

As he leaves, I call after him, 'Why did you ask to see me?' There are two other trainees at the Stables.

'I didn't. I asked for the youngest doctor.'

An hour later Keith Barnard calls me from Extended Care. 'Where is she?'

'I don't know.'

'What do you mean you don't know?'

'Frodo wouldn't tell me.'

Silence, then: 'Frodo?'

'Er, it's his . . . identity.'

'His what? Did you call the police?'

'Um, no.'

'What *did* you do?'

'I gave him five days' worth of clozapine.'

'Who told you to do that?'

'I couldn't reach anyone. I had to make a call.'

'Well, you made the wrong call. If he comes in again, ring the police.'

I don't hear him slam the phone down but . . . yeah.

—

There's a meeting to announce the new organisational structure for the Menzies Mental Health Service and now I'm going to be late.

I jog the kilometre from the Stables to the main hospital campus with its steel-and-glass towers for the surgery, obstetric, general medicine, cardiac and oncology units, and the run-down original buildings which house the central mental health services. It's late winter and bitterly cold.

A trolley with an unconscious patient, IV fluids attached, rolls past as I enter the lecture theatre. Everyone's still taking their seats. There's maybe a hundred of us: doctors, psychologists, social workers, one occupational therapist, senior nurses and a few admin staff.

Nicole Ogilvy, short, even in her regulation high heels, hair in a neat twist, is tapping her toe beside the podium. She's in a slim-legged suit today – a poster woman for power dressing. She's the admin director and it's her meeting.

I spot Alex and Jon near the front. Alex is in a turtleneck and jacket, hair now over his collar but swept back. He looks thinner, less boyish. Jon is in chunky boots, sports jacket and baggy jeans, shaggy hair now almost as long as Alex's. A Bilinarra man, three thousand kilometres from his family in Darwin. I'm not sure he's settled into Melbourne yet.

'Nicole's been in the job six months,' says Alex when I join them. 'She's ready to make big changes. Take out some enemies.'

'You're thinking Nash and Prof?' I say.

It turns out Nash is back from India, after being forced by Nicole to take his accumulated leave and by his wife to take it in the country of their birth. He and Nicole regularly butt heads, but I think she respects his competence. Prof Gordon was meant to retire when Nicole was appointed, but managed to hold on to half of his old job.

Prof finally arrives: suit, tie, clipped Freudian beard. He glances at Alex. Some of the responsibility for Xavier's suicide has stuck to Prof, who was Alex's supervisor.

Unexpectedly, it's he, rather than Nicole, who steps up to the podium and clears his throat theatrically.

'As I'm sure you're aware,' he says, 'this is a time of change in mental health. We are under pressure to implement the initiatives arising from the Mental Health Commission review . . .'

'. . . while continuing to provide the high-quality . . .' It's Alex in my ear: not quite the words Prof's saying, but near enough.

I manage not to laugh. But I'm watching Prof's body language – waiting for him to blink twice to tell us he's being held hostage.

'Nor can we afford to neglect the development of the next generation of psychiatrists. Accordingly, I have decided that my current roles should be split. I will continue to lead research and training . . .'

'Shafted,' says Alex, still in my ear. I've missed the closeness.

'Dr Sharma will take over the operational aspects of my role. I will remain at arm's length, except in the event that an issue of overall governance arises.'

So, half right. Prof has been sidelined, but Nash has been promoted. Which, I guess, makes him ultimately my boss, but I'm thinking – hoping – Nicole's plan is to load him with so much work that he won't have time to get in her way. Or mine.

Prof hands over to Nash. I can't tell if the break has done him any good. He looks just the same. Same open-neck white shirt, dark trousers and jacket. Same movie-star eyes and smile.

Nash thanks everyone for the vote of confidence, tells us he'll be open to suggestions, and the meeting breaks up. Back to work.

I'm about to suggest a coffee to Alex, but Nash collars me. Keith Barnard is with him, ill-fitting trousers belted below his gut. Only he and Prof wear ties, but Keith's is loose around his neck, top button undone.

We huddle in a corner of the lecture theatre while doctors in scrubs are coming in to replace the psych staff in street clothes.

'What happened with Celeste Boyce?' Nash asks me.

I explain carefully: Frodo's visit, the time pressure, putting the patient's needs first.

'Why didn't you talk to Keith?'

'He was in a meeting.'

Nash raises an eyebrow. 'Keith?'

'My registrar should have interrupted me. Alex Ashwood. Not the finest judge of a situation. He apparently knew the patient was planning to abscond but didn't report it.'

Keith is watching Nash's response. I get the sense that they don't actually know each other well. Nash doesn't say anything.

Keith crosses his arms. 'We'd just got her on an even keel. Her weekends out were destabilising and I'm concerned that she was – and now is – being taken advantage of. She's with a group of heavy drug users.'

'You know this?' says Nash.

'Let's not be naive. She's in the electronic music scene. Which is all about drugs. And I know this because I'm the one who gets to see them after they've fried their brains with methamphetamines.'

Keith leans into me. 'But we're talking about Celeste specifically, who's a shining example. Schizoaffective – possibly triggered by so-called party drugs, but definitely exacerbated by them. Sexually transmitted diseases. Termination that nearly killed her. She's not safe.'

Now he's lecturing me.

'Nobody's disagreeing that we needed to get patients – *some* patients – out of the long-stay wards. Government saved a lot of money. But it hasn't gone back into supporting them in the community. You only have to walk down the street to see where they're ending up. If the Stables was doing what it's supposed to do –'

Nash interrupts, turns to me. 'Do you have a plan to review her?'

'In five days, I'll speak to . . . her friend again.'

'Right,' says Keith. 'Frodo the Frog.'

Nash raises a hand. Enough already.

'Wait,' says Keith, addressing Nash. 'I want us to be very clear that Dr Wright has taken it upon herself to disregard what people senior to her, who have assessed the patient over an extended period, have decided in the past and would have wanted her to continue. If anything happens to Ms Boyce –'

'This is the case that's been in the media?' It's Nicole, who has apparently been listening to us while talking with the hospital medical director.

Nash nods.

'Correct me if I'm wrong, but I'm hearing that, not for the first time, a junior doctor has been left without support to make a consequential and, in this case, visible decision – in part, because we're still relying on locums to run the Stables. Am I right?'

Nash nods again. 'Louis –'

'I want you to make it a priority to fill that role. In the meantime, I'm going to ask you to take responsibility for this case.' She pauses. 'And the Stables.'

And, just like that, Nash is now my direct boss.

Keith looks at us smugly.

Nash looks right back. 'Keith, I take your point about needing to do a better job of transitioning long-term patients to the community. Would you like to schedule two sessions a week in the clinic to help me with that?'

It's not a question and Nash doesn't wait for an answer, instead accompanying me on my walk back to the Stables.

I'm a bit shaken, and he does his best to make light of it. 'First half-hour in my new job and I freed up a long-term bed.'

We walk for a while in silence, then he adds, 'Not ideal you being supervised by a locum. If I'm going to be running the clinic, I'll take over that role.' He smiles. 'If you'd asked me about Celeste, I'd have said "make sure she gets her meds".'

—

Alex texts me: *Quick drink 6pm?*

I text back: *Does it have to be quick?*

No point playing games: I get how he must have needed space, and it looks like he's ready to resume normal programming. Maybe starting with the kiss that didn't get a chance to go anywhere.

He texts back: *Can't stay long tonight. But I want to see you.*

I head straight from work to the place we used to go regularly, behind an unmarked door and up a steep staircase, opening into a modern rooftop bar with views of the city.

Alex is there already. Early means anxious, but he's used the time to order margaritas. This is a guy who knows what I like to drink better than I do, who understands what I spend most of my life doing and worrying about. Whose only real fault is that he's a colleague. I can live with that.

We pass a few minutes sipping the cocktails and talking about work. There's something I want to ask him about DJ Voices. And about the person supposed to represent the interests of patients and advocate for them.

'Do you know what the consumer rep said about DJ being grounded?'

'She didn't say anything. She's been on sick leave for six weeks. Stress. You can guess what Keith says about that.'

'I'm doing too much guessing.'

'*If you specify lived experience as a job requirement, don't be surprised when you get someone with mental health issues.*'

'Nice. Speaking of guessing: you wanted to talk?'

'I did. And do.' He takes a breath and a drink. 'To say sorry for not being in touch, but I didn't want to bring you down with me. I'm a lot better now.'

'Just needed time?'

'That, and . . . I wanted to tell you face to face. It's actually why I can't stay. I've started seeing someone.'

Shit. I just nod.

'She wasn't involved in what happened, like you were, so she can see it from the outside. She's smart; she gets how I've been feeling. I'm not sure she's the one for me long-term, but . . .'

Next thing he's going to tell me I'd like her.

'You'd like her.'

'I'll take your word for it. I'm happy for you. Guess I'll see you around.' Awkward, but accurate. I get up.

'I hope so,' says Alex. 'And, Hannah . . . I thought, a couple of months ago, there was something . . .'

I put him out of his misery. 'Things change. It wasn't going anywhere.' Obviously.

He nods, slowly, like he's the one being dumped.

—

Nash is in the Stables' meeting room – the Barn – when I show up Monday morning for the daily handover.

The Crisis Assessment and Treatment Team, the Mobile Support Team, and the Continuing Care Team are all sitting around the long table. The CATT guys are relaxed and joking, drinking coffee, though beer would better fit their image. I recognise Grace, a lithe and energetic CATT nurse with a high-cut jet-black bob and the straightest fringe I've ever seen – way shorter than mine. The gum-chewing temp is apparently staying on at reception; her name is Mia and the gum is for nicotine withdrawal.

Nash introduces himself, tells us he wants to hear ideas as to how the Stables can be improved, then moves straight on to the weekend dramas. He asks one of the case managers for a summary of Celeste Boyce's case.

Jan 'I've been here forever' Paterson – jeans and flats, hair at number-one length from supporting a shave for cancer, eyes of a basset hound – looks at Nash without any expression. 'I haven't looked after DJ for two years.'

Nash turns to me.

I've brought a summary of the notes from our not-so-secure Secure Extended Care Unit. Jon's were the only ones that felt like they were about another human being: they mention her music and her reason for dyeing her hair green (it was purple until it got wet in a chlorinated swimming pool, and DJ decided the new colour was more distinctive). I slip into my case-presentation persona, the one I use in tribunals and will use in my exams.

'Celeste Boyce – known professionally as DJ Voices – is a thirty-two-year-old single woman first diagnosed with schizoaffective disorder ten years ago. She had nine admissions in the following eight years, three of them in the year prior to being admitted to the Extended Care Unit.'

I look at my summary. 'Her key symptoms were delusions about having an unspecified special mission. She is also a successful composer and performer of electronic music.'

'Also?' says Grace. 'She's awesome. Heard her play at a festival.'

'When I saw her,' says Jan, 'she was too disorganised to get herself to gigs.'

'Mood?' says Nash.

Schizoaffective disorder, unlike schizophrenia, comes with depression and/or hypomania, though the mood swings aren't as dramatic as in bipolar disorder. DJ has had periods of both.

I continue: 'Non-compliant and using illicit drugs for the few years before admission. Recent drug tests when she's been on leave have been negative apart from one for marijuana.'

'Other risks?' Nash asks.

'One overdose way back,' I say. 'There's a suggestion that she was persuaded to give her income to the people she was with. She was in a house with lots of transients. Had sex indiscriminately.'

'Treated for at least two sexually transmitted infections,' says Jan.

'And three terminations,' I add. 'Last time she got an infection which wasn't spotted until late and she ended up in intensive care.'

Nash frowns. 'Family?'

'Anxious mother,' says Jan, who two minutes ago couldn't give a summary. 'Both parents were relieved she was admitted to Extended Care and visit her regularly.'

'We've been to her parents' house,' says Grace. 'Not there. GP hasn't seen her either.'

'And the boyfriend? Frodo?'

'He said DJ was at his place,' I say.

'Bag End,' says Grace.

I can see we're in for a lot of hobbit references. My image of Frodo is more of a guy in his parents' basement. On the internet with a bunch of other incels, sharing stories and photos of the famous performer he's kidnapped and is having sex with in exchange for the drugs she needs. Because a trainee psychiatrist, a *young female* trainee psychiatrist, didn't call the cops.

'They'll run out of meds tonight,' I say.

—

There's a call from a blocked number while I'm in my first supervision meeting with Nash, and he nods for me to take it. Frodo.

I put my phone on speaker. Nash's expression says, *Bad idea to give your phone number out*, but it's more amused than critical.

'I really need you to bring DJ in,' I tell Frodo.

'Not happening. Police were at her parents' asking where I live after I spoke to you.'

'I didn't call them.' No prizes for guessing who did.

'She's doing fine. I just need a prescription,' says Frodo.

Nash is doing sign language.

'Frodo. The consultant here would like to speak to you.'

'No way.'

'Dr Sharma isn't Dr Barnard. If he sees DJ and she's okay, like you say, then he'll put her onto a community treatment order so she can stay with you and the police will stop hassling you.'

'He can do that? No tribunal?'

'He has that power.' Any consultant does.

There's silence. Nash winks at me.

'Okay,' says Frodo. 'But you've got to come to us.'

A few minutes later we're at Nash's car. I clear the junk from the passenger seat and we head for the less affluent part of our catchment area, across the river.

Nash is focused on the mid-morning traffic and we don't speak much. Which gives me time to think beyond the scenario I have in my head of Nash putting DJ on a community treatment order and everything being just peachy forever after.

If Nash thinks DJ's at risk of not taking her medication, or from Frodo, from anything, he won't be issuing a community treatment order. He'll ask her to return to Extended Care, and if she refuses, he'll do what Keith Barnard wanted me to do: call the police. I feel I've promised Frodo that won't happen. Backed Frodo's wishful thinking against the judgement of a senior clinician.

When we get to the address, it's a vacant block of land.

Nash raises an eyebrow. 'Have you read *The Collector*?'

'Sorry, no.'

He gives me a summary of the plot: man kidnaps woman and abuses her. Basically, the scenario I've been worried about.

'Apparently most serial killers have read it,' he says. 'And yes, I'm concerned by this guy's behaviour.'

We get out of the car. It's a suburban street, a mix of neat weatherboards with mown lawns, and dumps with verandahs crowded with pushers and dead appliances. My phone buzzes: *2 mins.*

And two minutes later, Frodo emerges from the house three doors down. It's a bit run-down but there's no rubbish on the verandah. There are gnomes in the garden. I want to take a photo for the team. Bag End.

He looks suspiciously at Nash, who towers over him. To me he says, 'I'm trusting you.'

'Like you, we want what's best for DJ,' says Nash.

'Yeah, well, you need to accept that your idea of best isn't everyone's,' says Frodo. 'There's more than one way to live.'

Frodo leads us inside to DJ, who's standing in front of an electronic keyboard with headphones on. In the basement.

'Her studio,' says Frodo.

No windows, but a sofa, bookcase and a wedge-shaped sculpture create an ambience that fits what she's doing. And there's a big portable radiator keeping the place warm.

DJ hasn't noticed us. She's moving an arm rhythmically as if hitting a drum. Frodo taps her on the arm and she looks up. Sighs. Takes off the headphones.

We introduce ourselves.

'I'm not going back,' she says.

Nash convinces her that he understands and just wants to talk to her. Upstairs, as the light in the basement is on the darker side of dim.

DJ follows us up to a cluttered living room where we sit on an assortment of chairs. Nash nods to me to take a history. Just like old times.

I start tentatively. 'I understand you weren't very happy in Extended Care.'

DJ isn't really looking at me. She seems distracted. 'I couldn't practise,' she says. 'It's not like I was bothering anyone. I had headphones, but they took them off me. Because I was an hour late back from leave.'

I catch Nash's expression. He'll follow that up.

'Can I ask how you came to be in there in the first place?' I ask.

DJ leans her head back and her arm does the drum-playing action again. She's humming.

'Um, DJ?'

'Yeah, I'm just . . .' She sighs. 'I was doing my parents' heads in, okay? They don't get the music. They don't get *me*.'

'Do you think you were unwell?'

She seems to be paying attention now. 'Unwell. You mean mentally ill. Meaning what exactly?'

Frodo interrupts. 'Your diagnostic criteria have no basis in science. Collection of symptoms without a nosological base.'

My medical degree versus Dr Google. DJ ignores the comment.

'My parents don't approve of any kind of drugs. Or sex unless you're basically married.' She looks at my hand – no ring – and then at me. Winks. 'Bet you have sex when you want it, and no-one's locking you up, are they?'

No to both, but I'm the one supposed to be asking the questions.

'I get that the system seems unfair,' I say. 'But at the moment, to get you out of it, we have to work with it.'

'I'm not going back,' says DJ.

In case I missed it the first and second times, Frodo adds, 'She's not going back.'

'DJ,' I say, 'can we run through some questions?'

'Sure.'

I go through the mood and psychosis checklist. Mood is stable, better since leaving Extended Care. She isn't paranoid; the only thing on her mind is her next gig; and, yes, she hears voices.

'Where do you think the name came from?' she says. For the first time, she smiles at me. She's quite pretty, in a girlie way, though there's nothing girlie about the overalls and cap she's wearing, or the spiky green hair poking out from beneath. 'The clozapine dulls them, but they don't go away, not altogether.'

'What do they say?'

'That I've got to save the world. And that I'm fat. Half right.' She smiles again. 'I tell them to fuck off.'

Seems that her illness is symptomatic but well controlled. Now for risk assessment. No suicidal thoughts? Thoughts to harm others?

'Only if I ever see that cunt Barnard again.'

I write down *animosity* rather than *homicidal intent.*

'Drugs?'

'Nah. Unless you count marijuana.'

'Alcohol?'

'Yeah. Bet you drink too.'

She's a whisky drinker – about three standard drinks at a gig. She says. I'd bet on five. Everyone lies about their drinking. Now to the tricky bit.

'In the past, you were in ICU. Intensive care. Do you recall?'

'Being there?' She shakes her head.

'You've had a number of terminations. I'm wondering, are you . . . er, I mean are you on contraception?'

'I don't do hormones,' DJ says. 'The pill sends me loopy.'

'There are other options. I can make an appointment if you need –'

'He uses condoms,' she says. 'He' is Frodo, who's looking uncomfortable.

Now the *really* tricky bit, but she's given me a lead.

'Frodo, I need to speak with DJ alone.'

DJ jumps in before he can object. 'Let's get this over.'

Frodo drags himself out of the chair and leaves the room. He won't be far away.

'DJ, who manages your money?' I say. 'Pays the bills?'

She looks puzzled. 'Frodo does all that.'

'Do you . . . feel he's controlling it? Or you?'

'He can do what he likes as long as I can play music.' She smiles. 'Called him Fanboy for ages. But he kept turning up and offered me a good deal.'

'What sort of deal?'

'Place to live and he gets me to gigs. Even if he's got to break me out of prison.'

She stops for a moment, as if unsure how much to share. 'I wouldn't have got out without him. He did the recordings and everything. Then, I get to his car and there's patients climbing over the wall like I was meant to. Frodo's tied the rope ladder to his bumper bar, and there's too much tension on the rope for him to untie it. I'm saying, just go, drive, get out of here, but if he takes off there's going to be guys flying through the air. So he waits till everyone who wants to get out has got over the wall. Like, I'm saying, he's a kind sort of guy.'

'And the sex?'

'I can take or leave it. I don't get horny – it's the pills. But . . . he does all this stuff for me and that's what he wants.' She laughs. 'So I take it.'

I look to Nash. Seems to me she's making rational decisions, not driven by psychotic thoughts, delusions or voices. But Nash is the one who'll have to sign the form.

He leans forward. 'If you said you didn't feel like it, would he push you? Has he ever pushed you to be intimate when you didn't want it?'

'I don't ever really want it. Though with you, I might.' She turns and winks at me again.

That hasn't helped. I can see Nash is worried about the situation with Frodo.

'Are you having sex with anyone else?' he asks.

'Maybe. It's a free world.'

Nash leans back. 'DJ, what I can't understand is why you didn't just ask to be discharged. Frodo could have worked with the case manager, and we could have avoided all this drama.'

'You might have, but that cunt Barnard said I had to prove I was okay on weekend leave. I come back an hour late – which isn't a sign of not being okay. It's a sign of being fucking normal. And then he stops me going to a gig.'

'You're happy to keep taking the clozapine?' Nash asks.

'I don't like it, but I know I need it.'

'You'd see us at the Stables? Maybe have the Mobile Support Team drop in?'

'If that's what I have to do.'

Nash looks at me. *What do you think, Hannah?*

He's not asking my advice: just interested in what decision I'd make – something to discuss in supervision. We don't have to agree with DJ's choices, just be satisfied that she isn't a risk to herself or others. Risk to herself, particularly around the relationship with Frodo, will be the issue in Nash's mind, as it is in mine, but I think, on balance, autonomy wins. I nod.

Nash calls Frodo back and tells them both the conditions of the community treatment order. Looks like he's come to the same conclusion as me.

'But she stays here, right?' says Frodo.

'As long as she keeps well, which means taking her medication,' says Nash. 'And comes into the Stables for check-ups.'

DJ nods. 'As long as I don't have to see that cunt Barnard.'

Nash all but rolls his eyes and Frodo sees it.

'You've got to understand,' he says. 'DJ did something that pissed him off and he's been on her case forever.'

'You'll see Dr Wright,' says Nash to DJ.

DJ returns to the basement. Frodo shows us out, not looking as relieved as he should be.

'You look worried,' I say.

'Yeah,' he says, opening the front door. 'Not sure what I'm going to tell them.'

Two guys – one with a TV camera, the other holding a microphone – are waiting for us.

Nash signals for me to stop and walks out alone. 'Nothing to see here,' he says. 'If you're expecting a story about someone being locked up . . . not happening.'

Frodo follows him out. 'All good. Thanks for being here. Hang on.' He dashes inside and emerges with something he gives to the microphone guy.

'Tickets for DJ Voices. Everybody wins.'

Everybody except Keith Barnard. I've probably pissed him off.

TWO

COUNTERTRANSFERENCE

Naomi Disch does not take shit from anyone. Especially men who, having failed to persuade her to do what they want, ask to speak to her husband. Phone in hand, she's pacing around the living room while the husband in question, pleased to avoid the confrontation with someone he's likely to meet at a parent–teacher evening, encourages her with two thumbs up. The girls aren't in the room, but she imagines they're listening.

'No, David. We're quite firm about this. Brianna will come home when she's ready and feels safe doing so.'

David's voice is less calm. 'She'll come home when I say so. That's now. And what do you mean "safe"?'

'I'm talking about emotional safety.'

'What's that supposed to mean? I'm getting in the car and coming over right now.'

'You'll find the door shut.'

'Then I'll get the police.'

'I'm afraid, David, this is what I'm talking about. Bullying. And, while I have you, Brianna's told us that she wants some outside support. A psychologist or some kind of counsellor.'

'That's not going to happen. We're a family and we deal with our own problems.'

Naomi breathes in. Holds it till she's hung up the phone.

'Like that worked well with her sister,' she says.

Elena Karras, the Acute Unit psychologist, looks out of place in my dog box. Patients usually show up in tracksuits or something less formal. Though yesterday I had a manic woman in a ball gown. In contrast, Elena is understatedly elegant. I think I have a girl crush, though I won't be copying her style. Boho shift dresses make me feel like I'm wearing a tent and chunky jewellery like I'm playing a grown-up. On Elena, they look almost regal.

'I've had a call about Brianna Young,' Elena says.

Brianna's sister, Chloe, was my patient: a woman in her late twenties dying from anorexia nervosa. Fifteen-year-old Brianna was struggling with Chloe's condition and her parents' response.

In a last-ditch attempt to slow the progression, which the parents were unintentionally abetting, Elena saw the family in therapy and took a radical, confrontational approach. She broke through, but not without some drama. Watching from behind the one-way glass, Alex and I were close to calling Security when the father – David – lost it with Elena.

Afterward, Elena suggested that I could work with her to help Brianna, but I'd heard nothing more. Until now.

Elena gives one of her signature sighs. 'She ran away.'

'Brianna? Is she okay?'

'As far as I can tell. The family she's staying with want me to see her.'

'Are you going to?'

'I said I'd do one session – they're paying. But it isn't a long-term solution unless her parents change their mind.'

'They don't want her to see you?'

Elena laughs. 'Chloe's doing better, but I don't think they're ready to thank me for it. I assume they don't know Brianna's seeing me.'

'I could see her.'

Elena shakes her head. 'Solo? I couldn't approve that. It's a training issue, so you'd have to talk to Prof, but . . . are you free tomorrow afternoon to see her with me?'

I'll make sure I have the time. An opportunity to do – or see – psychotherapy in public psychiatry, where most patients are treated solely with medication, is gold.

I've sat in with Elena on a few sessions of cognitive behavioural therapy, which is a mainstay of psychology, but her work with the Young family was like watching an Olympic ice skater: amazing, and definitely not for beginners. As demonstrated by Alex, who was inspired to get adventurous with his own psychotherapy patient. Alex will never know whether it was a factor in Xavier's suicide. But Brianna is an ordinary fifteen-year-old dealing with some family shit. I can relate to that. And helping her feels like something I can do. I'll get Mia to reschedule tomorrow's patients into my lunchbreaks.

'Tomorrow afternoon's good,' I say.

—

I'm reflecting on Brianna, hoping I'll be able to see her beyond a single session with Elena, when my phone rings: it's Goldie the Goth, Prof's PA. 'Putting Prof through.'

Has Elena already asked him for permission for Brianna to be my psychotherapy patient? It's not about that.

'Just letting you know I've spoken to Isaac Sandler, the therapist I mentioned, and he can make room to see you,' says Prof, like he's doing me a favour.

No point arguing. 'Thank you,' I say. 'I appreciate that it'll be important if I'm going to do psychotherapy with patients. Actually, Elena has one for me. Younger sister of a woman with severe anorexia nervosa.'

'You don't think it's a bit early for you to be taking on a psychotherapy case?'

'Well, I know her. She's not high-risk, more in need of a mentor.'

'Therapists are not mentors.' There's a pause, then, 'Make sure the family is given all the options. And my approval is on the basis that Elena will be supervising you.'

'Thank you –'

'And make sure you get in touch with Isaac.'

I don't need to see Isaac to know I'm already identifying way too much with Brianna. Which means I do need to see Isaac.

I remind myself that my situation was completely different from Brianna's. When I was fifteen, I had to deal with finding one of the foster kids that our family took in – Foster Kid Fifty-Three – after he hanged himself. It's only in the last couple of months that I've felt ready to say his name – *Aaron* – and spoken about it with my study group.

What I haven't spoken about is Foster Kid Fifty-Two. Or faced who my anger – when I allow it to surface – is directed at. I guess I'm going to need a therapist for moving forward in that space.

But for Brianna?

I'm overthinking it. I remember what it was like to be fifteen and I know what I needed then. I can be that for her.

—

Nash has called a 'future directions' meeting for the Stables. Nicole is invited or has invited herself. In fact, she's probably the reason for the meeting – Nash isn't much for meetings that aren't strictly clinical.

If Nash was busy before, now he's frantic, pulled between two sites and juggling a management role that doesn't come naturally. The increased contact with Nicole can't be good for his stress levels.

He's on time, a rare event. Nicole is not, which is unheard of. And we have an addition: Keith Barnard, looking like he's been dragged to a party he didn't want to go to.

Nash introduces him: 'a familiar face for patients transitioning from Extended Care to the community'. I assume that won't include DJ Voices.

When Nicole does walk in, almost half an hour late, she looks like shit. I've only ever seen her with perfect make-up and hair. And the stilettos. She's wearing them today, but no make-up. Her hair's down, no jacket, and her look is pure shattered. She forces a smile. 'Sorry to be late. Something unexpected came up.'

Nash looks concerned, and doesn't actually have a lot to say besides repeating that he's interested in our thoughts on how the Stables could be improved.

He's rewarded with a flood of complaints about everything from the coffee machine to a patient having a meltdown because the clinic wasn't autism-friendly. He says he'll think about them. *For god's sake, Nash, delegate.*

Nicole leaves before the meeting is over.

Nash decides it's supervision time and I follow him into his office, which once housed a horse. It now has wide windows where the stable doors must have been, looking onto the car park.

Nicole is out there, on the phone, shouting. Her car is stacked with clothes.

—

I arrive at Elena's private rooms, right next to the hospital, with two minutes to spare. Her office is bright with comfy modern armchairs and prints from around the world.

Brianna is waiting. Her purple hair has black roots, and there's more silver in her ears as well as her lip and nose than when I last saw her. Heaps of make-up. Black-lined eyes. Having seen her parents in family therapy, I'd bet they never let up about the way she looks, and she keeps pushing their limits.

Brianna goes straight to Elena and gives her a hug. Elena suggests she take a seat opposite and I sit to one side. Brianna's eyes gravitate to a picture of a woman and teenager standing on a mountain peak.

'I think you know Dr Wright from the ward,' says Elena. 'She was looking after Chloe. I've asked her to sit in because she was part of the team behind the one-way glass in the family sessions.'

I've seen more of Brianna than she has of me.

She half-smiles. 'Bet you won't be forgetting my family any time soon.'

'A lot happened,' I say carefully.

Brianna holds my gaze and something passes between us. Have I signalled that she was the one I identified with in the therapy sessions? Because she's looking at me as if I said that out loud.

I *know* I can be the mentor she needs. The one I wished I'd had at her age.

'Now, Brianna,' says Elena, 'we have to work out how we can help you. I've agreed to today so we can do that, but I don't think it's going to be possible for me to continue seeing you.'

'But I want to see you. I don't care what my parents think.'

'Unfortunately, it's not that simple.'

Brianna isn't a patient of the Service, which means Elena would need to see her privately. Elena almost certainly charges more than the Medicare scheduled fee and would bill Brianna for the difference. Awkward.

Elena leans forward and squeezes Brianna's hand. 'How about you tell us what's happening and then we can talk about the options.'

'Home is horrible,' says Brianna. 'I mean, my parents should be pleased. Chloe's eating, kind of.' She lapses into silence.

'It sounds like they – and you . . . aren't happy though.'

'Chloe's okay. But she's not totally on the planet. Talking about becoming a social worker.'

'You don't think that's realistic?'

'You've seen her.'

'And your parents?'

'Dad's on his computer all the time and it's like we're not there. Like it's all my fault.'

'Your fault for what?'

Brianna shrugs. Looking miserable – and young under all the camouflage.

'And your mum?'

'I think she's depressed. They should be the ones getting help, not me.'

Elena nods slowly. 'I guess you're the advance guard for your family when it comes to understanding their feelings. How are *you* feeling?'

Brianna gives a theatrical sigh – an exaggerated Elena-style sigh. 'Sad. Confused. Angry, I suppose. I need to get my shit together if I want to start the IB – that's the International Baccalaureate – next year. I want to get into Veterinary Science but . . . I can't concentrate. Didn't get my homework in for like the first time ever.' She's still got a way to go to qualify for a conduct-disorder diagnosis. 'I'm staying with my friend's parents. I just wish my parents could be like them.'

Elena explores her situation and it's clear that Brianna left home so her parents would pay her attention; she knows she has to go back. Wants to, but also wants her parents to change. Wishful thinking from what I saw of them.

'Here's what I think,' Elena says. 'You're smart, but you need some help to make sense of your family and sort out your relationship with them.'

Brianna nods.

'What I would usually suggest is six to twelve sessions, once a week for fifty minutes, then see if we need to do any more.'

Brianna nods again.

'If I were to offer that to you though, there's a cost,' says Elena.

'I could get a job at McDonald's,' says Brianna. 'I've been thinking about doing that anyway.'

'You could,' says Elena. 'But even if I waived the cost, given your parents have made it clear they don't want you to see me, I wonder what impact attending appointments with me would have.'

'It's my choice.'

'It is,' agrees Elena. 'Which is why I want you to make it considering the consequences and not just because you're angry.'

Brianna opens her mouth and closes it. Elena waits.

Finally Brianna fills the space. 'It'll annoy them.'

'I guess there's quite a lot of anger already simmering in your household.'

A tear tracks down Brianna's cheek. 'What am I supposed to do then? Just suck it up?'

'There are options other than me.'

'Right. I'll see the school chaplain who's about ninety. Or the pastor, who's my dad's best buddy.' She takes a breath. 'You know my family. You know me.'

I want to interrupt. Elena doesn't know Prof has – kind of – given me the okay to see Brianna. I try meaningful stares.

Elena ignores them. 'One option is that I find another psychologist and word them up. Get your friend's parents to emphasise how important it is you see someone.'

'My dad won't pay for anyone,' Brianna says, looking at me.

'Seeing me might be a possibility,' I say before I can stop myself.

Brianna smiles. Elena doesn't.

'I've spoken to Prof,' I say quietly to Elena. 'If you could supervise.'

That did not help.

Elena addresses Brianna. 'Is it okay if we talk with your mum and dad and let you know?'

'Whatever.' Brianna grabs her bag and leaves. She's fighting tears and doesn't want us to see.

'I'm sorry,' I say, as soon as she's gone. 'I just thought . . .'

Elena shakes her head. 'I hope you've asked Nash. He's your manager, right? And as she's technically under Child and Adolescent you'll need their okay as well. And I shouldn't need to tell you that we don't discuss supervision arrangements in front of a patient.'

Now I'm the one feeling like a fifteen-year-old being told off. Still, I'm looking like Brianna's only option. And Elena's my only option.

—

It's my turn to host our study group, which has been going for six months now, and will hopefully continue until we all qualify. The other three first-year trainees plus Carey, who's not yet in the program, and I get together for exam preparation, case discussion and general peer support. And most of my social life.

I share my garden apartment in a converted Edwardian mansion close to the Menzies with Jess, paramedic-in-training. She's cooking – as she always does when the group meets here. She's in leopard-print overalls that are baggy everywhere except the chest and show a lot of boob – the pale, freckled kind that goes with her curly red hair. We've known each other since school in Horsham, a country town three and a half hours northwest of Melbourne, and for a while she dated my brother, Lennon.

The others will insist that she join us for dinner. She'll talk more than the rest of us combined, ask awkward questions, and afterward everyone will tell me how great she is.

I've done some thinking about how to deal with Alex: basically, forget we were ever more than colleagues. That should work for him too. Except he's been my most supportive colleague, the one

I can talk to about psychotherapy – and about my own stuff. I'm not sure how much of that we can keep, but I'll let him take the lead.

I run my plan past Jess.

'You're still in love with him,' she says.

'We never got that far.'

'If you think you were going to be in love with him, then you were already. And you still want to see him. You're clinging to a dream.'

Alex arrives first, with a bottle of wine. Pinot gris. He knows what I drink.

Carey is right behind him. Carey has taken the exact role that I had six months ago – working in the Acute Unit, hanging out for a position in the training program. They're proudly autistic and non-binary. Not sure how those attributes are going to play with the selection committee.

Ndidi and Jon turn up together, fifteen minutes late, Jon in his usual baggy jeans and boots, Ndidi in her signature pantsuit. She has new hair extensions with red and purple ribbon woven into her long braids.

Jess emerges from the kitchen and spots Jon. 'How's the Mother Baby Unit?'

Jon smiles. 'A bit challenging at times.'

'I thought it would be. I mean, mothers and babies being separated. Must bring up some issues for you. Being Aboriginal.'

Shit, Jess. Just straight in.

But Jon nods: 'Thanks for asking.' And follows her to the kitchen.

It's a good half-hour before we get ourselves seated around the small dining table in the living room with dips, wine and beer. Jon,

Alex and I give our takes on DJ's story, and it's apparent I'm not the only one who has issues with Keith Barnard.

'Relevance deprivation syndrome,' says Ndidi. 'Back in the day, Keith would have been king of the asylum. House on the grounds, hundreds of beds –'

'One thousand, two hundred and forty,' says Alex. 'Three specialist mental hospitals –'

'You've researched this?' asks Carey.

'Work for Keith and he'll tell you,' says Jon. 'It's partly nostalgia. But he's got a thing about DJ trash-talking him, having sex with the other patients. And with all the disability she has to deal with, she's still bigger in her world than he is in his.'

'Wish you'd told me before,' says Alex. 'After she absconded, Keith asked for my input, because I actually see patients. I told him that she was keen to be discharged and had some reasonably coherent thoughts about how she might live outside.'

'He had a problem with that?' I ask.

'Possibly. He definitely had a problem with me suggesting that she might benefit – when she returned – from some supportive –'

'Psychotherapy?' Ndidi finishes the sentence for him and shakes her head. 'For schizophrenia?'

Here we go.

'Schizoaffective disorder,' says Alex. 'Yeah, he reacted the same way you just did. I wasn't suggesting Lacanian analysis. But we're talking about a creative artist. Anyway, he brought up what happened with Xavier. It's not like I was going to do the therapy with DJ Voices myself.'

Jon nods. 'He's a dick. But try not to piss him off. He can be vindictive.'

That's pretty much what DJ said. I may have some recovery work to do with Keith, especially if he's going to be working in the Stables.

'Tell me about it,' says Alex. 'He just rejected my application for a psychotherapy conference. Should have just been a formality. Wrote: *Inappropriate for this trainee at this time.*'

'Let me know if he does anything we can nail him for,' says Ndidi. She's the first-year rep for the College of Psychiatrists. Our union, more or less.

Jess brings in the chicken and I share my news about Brianna and the possibility of doing some supervised psychotherapy. Everyone's supportive; they know where my interests lie.

But later, as he's leaving, Alex gives me a knowing smile: 'Remember to fit your own mask first.'

'Meaning?'

'You've got issues with your family. You need to start sorting them out if you want to do the best work with Brianna.'

—

Alex is right – and I need to see my family anyway. Mum's been bugging me about Lennon, like I can magically make him return home. They're struggling with the empty nest and being unable to help him with his drinking problem.

Friday after work, Jess and I fight the peak-hour traffic heading out of the city. I'll drop her off at her parents' place on the way. She's bundled up in a bright pink beanie and scarf and barely takes a breath as she tells me about her day. And week. And, as she did when she was trying to get into the paramedic course, she picks my brain about emergency medicine.

We hit the highway and head north, with a stop for fuel and burgers. I need to eat, but I know that my mother will have something bubbling on the stove and insist on feeding me again.

When I've finished explaining to Jess how I'd handle a breech-presentation birth with prolapsed umbilical cord in the desert with only the water from the radiator, she moves to Favourite Topic Number Two.

'He's still in love with you,' she says, feet on the dashboard, practising to be an accident victim. 'Why else would he have brought your favourite wine?'

'Maybe he likes pinot gris. Jess, he's seeing *someone else*.'

'To deal with the pain of losing you.'

'Jess. It's over.'

'Okay, move on. Have you thought about Jon?'

'*What?*'

'Just an idea.'

'A really bad idea. It was bad enough dating a colleague, and now you're suggesting I switch to the one other guy in my study group.'

'If he's The One, nothing else would matter.'

'He's not. He's a really nice guy, but . . . how about you fit your own face mask before helping others?'

—

I drop Jess in town. The unlit dirt road to my parents' feels foreign. It *has* been a while. Last time I drove up, it was still light. As I'm approaching their driveway, a roo jumps into my headlights. I brake in time, but it spooks me.

Coming up to the house, the feeling of displacement is still there; not quite *something's wrong*, but *something's changed.* My dad – Big Merv – isn't on the verandah waiting to squeeze the life out of me, and I don't have the sense of being surrounded by caravans and wrecked cars, and . . .

Because it's late and dark and they're probably inside playing music. *Get a grip, Hannah.*

I let myself in and they're not playing music. They're watching TV. It's just my parents in the living room, sitting together on the sofa, a single lamp on. I weave a path between chairs and side tables stacked with books.

'Hi, Hanny,' says Dad, pausing the movie. He stands and I get the belated bear hug. He's getting older. Creases deeper around his eyes and mouth, beard mostly grey and his hair too.

I say the obvious out loud: 'It's so quiet.'

The home of my memories was all noise and chaos. Growing up, we had the carousel of foster kids, but even after that the house had always seemed full – of friends, musos, ex-foster kids who've kept in touch, my sister's family and, of course, Lennon.

'We won't stay up late,' says Dad.

Mum insists I take Lennon's room. I'm happy to; it's too cold for the caravan and my old room is full of junk.

The house is a rambling weatherboard with peeling paint, common spaces that spill into each other, and doors always open. Except, back in the day, Mel's, Lennon's and my bedrooms. We put locks on those doors ourselves.

'Have you heard from Lennon?' asks my mother as soon as I'm seated.

'A few weeks ago. When he moved to the Northern Territory.'

He's working in a pub. Not ideal for a guy with an alcohol problem. He's estranged himself from our parents for no reason that he or I could explain to them, beyond 'needing space'.

'I just don't understand why he –'

'Now, Gen,' says Dad, putting his arm around my mother. 'We've been through it.'

I know I have issues with my parents, but with which version of them? The one that brought foster kids into our lives? The one that didn't reflect on the impact that choice had on us? The empty-nesters trying to hold on to us?

Mum, on cue, gets up and heads for the kitchen. She's going to ladle a big serve of whatever stew she's kept warm into a bowl and watch to make sure I eat it. It's 10 pm.

Dad waits till Mum is gone before asking me: 'Doing okay?'

'All good. Busy at work.'

'You still seeing the surgeon's son?'

Shit. I'm sure I never told them I was dating Alex. 'Mmm. He's a colleague. It's complicated.'

I can hear Isaac Sandler, my therapist who I haven't met, saying, 'Why do you find it difficult to be open with your father?'

And the answer would be: 'Because I want my family to believe that any issues in my life have been resolved, because . . .' I guess that's the next level.

Mum calls from the kitchen. 'I'm making a camomile tea. Would you like one?'

'Just tea?'

'Bit late for anything heavier, but if you want to eat, I can find something.'

'Thanks,' I say. 'That'd be nice.'

—

I lie awake for ages. I feel Lennon's absence starkly here in his bedroom. There's still his collection of sci-fi novels crammed into bookshelves, and though the walls are blank I can picture the *Star Wars* poster signed by Ewan McGregor. Lennon had saved up for it forever and one of the foster kids drew over it with marker pen.

Lennon and I used to plot here late at night about how to survive whichever kid was giving us grief. I'm reminded of the yearning I had to escape, and I feel as guilty now as I did then. They are good people, my parents.

When I do sleep, I dream of the last two foster kids. Again.

Dad's an early riser, and on Saturday morning I thread my way through the clutter in the main shed to join him at the workbench. He's sitting on a stool, tinkering with a breadmaker. Three more are lined up for his attention or for spare parts.

'Something on your mind, Hannah?' he asks, undoing a screw.

'I want to ask you something.' I take a breath. 'Fifty-Two.'

'The poor boy who took his own –'

'No, Fifty-*Two*. Simon.'

I think I know all I need to about Aaron – Fifty-Three. But I need to understand more about Fifty-Two if I'm going to make sense of the fragments and feelings I have. Preparation for seeing a therapist.

My father sits perfectly still for a few moments, then continues tinkering without saying anything.

'What happened to him?' I ask.

'Simon was moved on after what happened. Not sure it's healthy thinking about him. Can't change the past.'

No, but the past affects the present.

'I know he went to juvey,' I say. 'Stole a car, I think.' He sent me a card from there – the last contact I had.

'Could be.'

I sigh in frustration. 'Do you remember what his surname was?'

Dad shakes his head. 'To be frank with you, I've got more important things to occupy me. You told your mother you spoke to Lennon.'

'I did. He's doing okay.'

'He won't answer our calls.'

'He just needs some space.'

'I can't understand that,' says my father, who spends his weekends out in the workshop by himself. 'This is your trade – you tell me what's going on.'

'Dad, he's got a drinking problem. That's not what I do – it's a whole other thing. But maybe he doesn't want to see you till he's right.'

'That's . . . Tell him we love him no matter what problems he might have. He shouldn't be ashamed.'

I can't tell Dad that I think it's the other way round. Lennon needs to be right before he can deal with our family.

—

My sister, Mel, arrives at lunchtime with her three children – but not her partner – and I ask her about Simon. She's three years older than me and had gone off to agricultural college before Fifty-Three – *Aaron* – died. She used the death as an excuse to return home and never went back to study. Another life changed. But she remembers Simon.

'Fifty-Two, right? Smart kid – might have been gay?'

'You think?'

That's what time does to memory. On this one, I trust mine more than hers.

She can't recall his surname either. 'Got into trouble with the police after he left, right? Shame. I thought he was okay.'

That leaves The Book. Mum kept a record of every foster kid. Name and number. Not that Mum and Dad called them by number. Each kid had a photo, a small watercolour Mum painted of them and a few words.

I've been avoiding The Book because it will be hard to miss Aaron's page and I'm not sure I want to see what Mum put there. She wears her heart on her sleeve and isn't too subtle about what's in it.

I go looking in what was once the playroom. It's now the 'library', full of books and files. After half an hour of searching, feeling like I'm a kid doing something sneaky, I find two volumes of it; the last is missing.

No way Mum's disposed of it. My family wouldn't throw away a broken printer. And they're not into gestures.

Mum is busy with my niece, so I slip into her studio. Her work on the easel is for the grandchildren: fairies in the garden in pinks and greens. The fairy queen has Mel's face. The cupboards are full of paints. I'm about to give up when I remember Lennon convinced Dad to put a secret panel behind his bedhead to keep his stuff safe.

I go back to Lennon's old room, move the bed, pull off the panel and . . . there it is. Which I guess means it was Lennon who hid it. An arm's length from where my head was last night.

The Book is A4-size, with gold patterns on the front and back. I flip to the end and try to turn the pages back without looking at the last entry, but I'm compelled.

Aaron's pimply grin stares at me. He looks younger than thirteen. My mother's painting of him has rose petals on the ground. And her likeness of him is an angel ascending. He looks more girl than boy.

I turn to the previous page. *Simon Trevallyan.* Staring right at the camera, cocky grin. Good-looking and knew it. My stomach drops and I take a breath.

My mother's picture is of some sort of animal but I have no idea what. And in small letters she's printed: *He lives down in a ribcage in the dry leaves of a heart.* It doesn't sound like her.

I figure I have all I'm going to get from my family. We have a quiet dinner – just the three of us. I don't mention Simon and my parents don't mention Lennon.

The next morning, it's more like the home I recall. Mel and her brood are back and Foster Kid Forty-Eight – Kayla – visits with two of her children. She's a fostering success story, more or less: her substance-abusing parents got their act together after joining a religious sect. But she's still talking about what a bastard her ex is when I leave to pick up Jess.

I ask Jess about Simon as we're driving home and get a dark look.

'Dickhead. Got chucked out of school. Went to jail.'

'Juvey. For stealing a car. Not exactly a . . .' I stop myself before I say 'hanging offence'.

'You don't go to juvey for stealing one car. And he was obsessed with Ms Tits.'

'Who? What are you talking about?'

'Ms Pitts, the drama teacher. Everyone called her Ms Tits because –'

'You don't have to explain.' Except I can't recall hearing her being called that. I was disconnected from the social life of the school. To my classmates I was an unappealing combination of nerdy and scary: scary, because dealing with the foster kids had given me a *don't mess with me* aura. Mel had it too; Lennon didn't.

'He sent her flowers,' says Jess. 'Irises from someone's garden. She didn't know who they were from but she totally loved them. Still weird though.'

'Kids do weird things.'

'Anyway, why are you so interested?'

I don't have an answer I can give her. I wonder where the experience of seeing his image is going to take my memories and dreams.

—

Monday morning, I ring the intake team in Child Psych, angling to get Brianna on their books so I can see her. How much of my life do I have to spend on this admin shit?

They sound like they feel the same way.

'Attending school?'

'Yes.'

'Homeless?'

'Well, she was staying with a friend . . .'

'That's a no. Being abused?'

'Not physically . . .'

'So, no unless you can convince me otherwise. Suicidal thoughts?'

'I'm not aware –'

'Then no. No. Do you know how many troubled teenagers we have on our waiting list?'

They don't seem interested in hearing that it's me who'd be seeing Brianna, not them.

I go back to Elena's office.

'I'm not saying this is a good idea,' she says, 'but if Prof is onside I'll see what I can do.' She smiles. Seems I'm forgiven for being pushy. 'You have to know the system.'

At lunchtime, I'm summoned to see Daniela Popa. She's the consultant in charge of the Eating Disorder Unit – and famously work-shy. The only connection I can think of is that she's seeing Brianna's sister, Chloe, for her anorexia nervosa. Elena is with her.

'Chloe is doing reasonably well,' says Daniela. 'Bloods stable and thirty-six kilograms. Elena tells me Brianna wants someone to talk to.'

I nod. 'Her parents aren't offering much support.'

'As you know, you need a psychiatrist to oversee your work if it's to count for your qualification. I'm prepared to do that.' She gives me a hard smile. 'I'm *obliged* to do it under my contract.'

Daniela turns to Elena. 'You will actually supervise her, yes?'

Elena pauses, then nods. 'After each session.'

'Fine.' Daniela looks at me. 'Keep me up to date with anything major. By email.'

And we are both dismissed.

'How can Daniela be Brianna's doctor?' I ask Elena. 'Brianna can't be put under the Eating Disorder Unit, can she?'

'Daniela also works in Child and Adolescent,' says Elena. 'Brianna's friend's mother's a tough cookie. She wasn't going to let Brianna return home if her parents didn't agree to letting her see someone.'

I'm mentally punching the air when she adds, 'It still needs to be approved by Nash.'

I catch Nash at the coffee machine in the afternoon. I figure I'll suss out his mood before asking permission to spend time on psychotherapy.

'Missing the excitement of Acute?' I ask.

He presses the double-espresso button. 'What's this about seeing Brianna Young?'

I tell him the story: she needs support and her parents won't pay for it. *And I can help.*

'You're a first-year, Hannah,' says Nash. 'You've got a big job already and plenty of time ahead of you to do your cases. And you'll do them better with more experience.'

He probably sees the psychotherapy cases as boxes to tick on the way to qualification, rather than training for what I see as a central part of my job. And it's only a few months since he let Alex, another first-year, take on Xavier as a psychotherapy case. He'll likely regret that for the rest of his life.

'It's only a short case,' I say. 'Not my long-psychotherapy patient.'

Nash raises an eyebrow. 'You think you're going to sort her out in a few weeks? You're not in Acute anymore.'

I argue for longer than I should: there's no suggestion Brianna's a suicide risk; I've had nearly a year's psych experience if you count the rotation I did as a house medical officer; I've watched Elena; I've read up; I'll learn so much from this experience . . .

Nash shakes his head. 'She doesn't need medication. A psychologist can do all this.' He finishes his coffee and puts the cup in the dishwasher. 'Do it in your study afternoon.'

I call by to tell Elena that I've jumped all the hurdles.

'One to go,' she says, deadpan, and gives me Brianna's parents' phone numbers.

Brianna's mother, Sue, answers when I call the landline. Predictably, she tells me that I'll need to speak with her husband when he gets home.

—

I don't want to speak to David Young from home – don't want the slightest feeling of him being in my personal space – so I stay back in the Stables. At 6.15 pm, it's deserted, except for a nurse on call with the CATT team at the other end of the building and Keith Barnard, working back with his door closed. I guess he's doing online medico-legal work, which is apparently his side hustle.

I've spent half an hour twisting myself into a knot of anger and defensiveness, all of it directed at Brianna's father, and am trying to distract myself with a dating app when Alex walks in.

'Elena said you might be working late. She told me she'd set you a bit of a challenge.'

'Don't you have somewhere to be?'

He plonks himself on one of the chairs. 'Thought you might need some moral support. I haven't forgotten what it was like watching the family through the glass. The father was pretty angry. Threatening to sue.'

'We all say stuff when we're angry.'

'Sounds like a good place to start with him. And his anger's never been directed at you, right?'

I'm about to protest but . . . it's true. The experience of watching David Young explode with fury was so visceral that my memory is of being in the room, rather than invisible behind the glass. And I guess I took his anger at Elena on myself. But when I did talk to David, on his visits to see Chloe, I didn't pick up any issue with me. Beyond his general arseholeness. Good point, Alex.

'How's everything else?' he says.

It's a thinly disguised version of the therapist's *Why did you come to see me?* – except he's come to see me.

But it works. Without thinking, I start telling him about my weekend at Mum and Dad's. And when I *do* think, I realise I don't want to tell him about my fixation with what happened when I was fifteen. Instead, I fill him in on my parents' worries about Lennon.

'Not much you can – or should – do,' says Alex.

'Agreed. Try telling that to my father.'

'Seems like he's the one who's suffering. Who needed someone to talk to.'

'Not sure I did much of a job there.'

'You listened. Be grateful – be honoured – your dad asked you for advice on something so important.'

I look at my watch and Alex gets the message. He puts his hand briefly on my shoulder, then disappears. I turn to see Keith on his way out and his smile tells me he saw the moment of intimacy.

I start to dial, then stop. I think a bit about my dad, struggling with his wayward child. I think he'd be kinder to a therapist than David's been, but he's nothing if not fiercely protective of his family. Including the foster kids. Was he any gentler and more reasonable with Child Protection when they came to visit than David was with Elena? Well, yes, but I dial with less anger than I had a few minutes ago.

I introduce myself as the junior doctor who cared for Chloe on the ward, and that's a good start. David goes for reasonableness rather than bullying.

'You need to understand I'm being held over a barrel by Mrs Disch – her friend's mother. If Brianna's got problems she should talk about them with her family or our pastor, who's a qualified therapist. And who we can trust to tell us what's going on.'

I don't say anything, and he talks himself into it.

'If she has to see someone outside our community, at least we know you. I believe you did the best you could for Chloe under the circumstances you were in.'

'Well, thank –'

'And I know someone who knows your family. I understand they've done a lot of good work. So, I'm trusting you to share our values.'

At some level, possibly. I don't think we'd need to dig too deeply to find differences. The reference to my family is creepy – perhaps meant to be.

'It's not my job to impose my values on Brianna,' I say. 'Or even to advise her. I won't get in your way there. I'm primarily a person she can talk to.' I take a breath. 'But one of my values – it's actually a legal obligation – is that I can't share anything Brianna tells me, not without her permission, unless she's threatening to harm herself or someone else.'

Meaning: *I'm not going to tell you 'what's going on', as your 'qualified-therapist' pastor apparently does.*

David's turn to take a breath. 'Very well. If Brianna wants to avail herself of the offer, I'll let you know.'

'She's welcome to call me herself.'

'We'll decide that. One more thing. I'm assuming you don't report to Dr Karras?'

I'm glad he framed it that way. 'No, she's a psychologist, I'm a doctor. I report to Dr Sharma, the consultant who was in charge of Chloe's care. And I'll be consulting with Dr Popa, who you know.'

'Good. You may or may not be aware that Dr Karras behaved . . . very inappropriately with our family. I hope I don't have to say this, but if something like that was to happen with Brianna, I wouldn't hesitate to make a complaint to the health regulator. AHPRA. As I've done with Dr Karras.'

—

I walk out of the Stables to find Alex waiting for me.

'Thought you'd need a drink,' he says. And then: 'I know what we said. But just work stuff? It'd be a shame to lose that.'

It's exactly what I've decided myself. There's really no-one else at my level who's interested in psychotherapy. He's keener than I am, in the sense that it's ultimately all he wants to do – fifty-minute sessions with long-term patients – while I'm looking to find a balance, probably in public psychiatry rather than private.

I still feel like pushing back: *You don't get to dump me and then call the shots*. But I also need a drink. And a debrief.

On the way to the bar, I call Elena.

She picks up. 'Did something happen with David?'

'Why didn't you tell me he'd reported you?'

'Reported me?'

Oh shit. She didn't know. Maybe complaints take a while to get processed.

She doesn't sound shattered, but she's definitely rattled. The approach she used wasn't standard; it was always going to be hard to prove if it was effective or destructive. Whatever happens with the complaint, it'll be a hassle. Even for an established professional.

—

Alex and I spend an hour talking at our usual bar. He reminds me that I'm not going to have David in the room when I'm doing therapy; Brianna isn't any more likely to lodge a complaint herself than any other patient; and I'll be working under supervision.

'Have you got yourself a therapist yet?' he asks.

'I'm thinking Isaac Sandler. Prof's suggestion.'

'I wouldn't have thought it was Nash's.' He remembers Sandler's patient in Acute and Nash's view that a week of medication was worth five years of psychotherapy. More or less. I fill him in on Prof's take.

'Okay,' he says. 'But . . . you sure Sandler's a good choice?'

'Prof thinks so.'

'That's the point,' says Alex. 'The issue isn't whether Sandler managed your patient well, but what he told Prof.'

'Sorry?'

'What I'm saying is that he told his mate, Prof, the patient's history. Fired from her job. Sexual abuse. And now you're telling me. So much for confidentiality.'

I let the implications sink in. Maybe Prof and Isaac Sandler are in a peer-review group together. But do I want my therapist talking to Prof about my issues? And Prof talking to . . . who else?

'What excuse do I give Prof for not seeing Sandler?'

Alex smiles. 'Leave it with me.'

—

When I get home, I give in to the temptation that's been bugging me since my trip to my parents' and google Simon Trevallyan.

There's a company and a person with that name. Click – and there he is. Foster Kid Fifty-Two. Twenty-eight – same as me. Single. Lots of photos on social media – some with attractive women – without any context. He's a financial advisor.

I stare at his photo for a long time, try to picture his journey from foster care to juvenile detention to owning his own company. And before that . . . I don't think I ever knew anything about his earlier life.

A minute later, without thinking about it, I've messaged him.

THREE

MULTIPLE PERSONALITIES

As she gets out of the car, Taylah catches the guy next door checking her out. She gives him the finger, but she's smiling – on the inside. There were a couple of guys at the mall too, looking at her while she was looking at the pots of flowers outside the florist.

The idea of working in a flower shop pops into her head, and she lets the feeling sit for a few moments. Not the idea, just the feeling.

Then she steps into her house and it's like someone has thrown a switch. From sunshine to the sort of shitty grey day that might turn into a storm or just stay shitty.

Her mother – Kelly – is on the sofa. Kelly's new boyfriend, Ivan, is beside her, one hand holding a beer, the other halfway up her bare thigh.

Taylah's sister, Aleesha, is in an armchair, scrolling her phone. The dog is sprawled on the recliner and the TV's showing a documentary about abuse in the Catholic Church. Taylah stands watching for a minute.

'This is shit,' she says.

'I dunno,' says Ivan, 'some of those nuns are pretty hot. Wouldn't mind being abused by one of them.'

Kelly laughs, loudly. 'Ivan, you're terrible.'

Taylah picks up the remote from the floor.

'Leave it,' says Aleesha. 'Where are you going to sit anyway?'

'You can sit on my lap,' says Ivan.

'Better fucking not,' says Kelly. 'You can sit on my lap if you want. Who wants to sit on Mummy's lap?'

Where Ivan's hand is.

If a therapist, or hypothetical well-meaning family member, or a journalist of the kind that thrusts a camera in the face of a grieving relative, were to ask Taylah at this moment 'How are you feeling?', she'd tell them to go fuck themselves. Not just because she's learned that people asking about her wellbeing give fuck-all back, but because she couldn't answer the question. Not in any coherent way.

Her head is a slurry of anger, sadness, disgust, shame, loathing, envy, anxiety, confusion, emptiness and despair. Worse than despair: hopelessness. If her emotions were a lake, hopelessness would float to the top. But they're not: they're a cesspool of pain, whirling, pulling her in.

Drowning her in her own shit.

Thursday morning I'm walking to work, taking time to reflect on the day ahead, when my phone buzzes. It's a text from Jon: *Sorry*. And a wink emoji.

I call him. He's walking too – heading home from a rough night on call. He had to get Lian, one of our clinic trainees, to come in and help with the load in the Emergency Department.

'On a Wednesday night?'

'Full moon. Plus South Eastern is full and telling everyone to go to us.'

'They can't –'

'Try finding someone to tell that to in the middle of the night.'

'How does it make work for me?' I ask.

'Taylah Keane came in. With her mother.'

'No sister? You got off lightly.'

Everyone knows the Keane family. We have some frequent flyers, but the Keanes are platinum class.

'Let me guess,' I say. 'Taylah overdosed and her mother brought her in and wanted Valium for the stress. Taylah wanted to be admitted into Short Stay –'

'Acute.'

'Must have seen you were under pressure and thought you might cave.'

He laughs. 'I might have if we'd had any beds. What made me cave was the mother – Kelly – complaining about not getting priority over the out-of-area patients. You know those signs we have up about being abusive –'

'But you didn't have any beds. What could you . . . ?'

Silence.

Now I get the *sorry*. 'You've referred them to the Stables.'

'Just Taylah,' says Jon. 'I gave Kelly a packet of Valium.'

—

Sure enough, Taylah's on our waitlist. Only Lian and I have space in our diaries – and Lian will be at home after spending the night helping Jon in ED.

'No harm in a quick review,' Nash says at the morning handover meeting. 'Just check she's safe.'

Just.

If Nash has seen my reluctance, he'll probably put it down to Taylah having a borderline personality disorder. There's a negative connotation in *borderline* along with the other common personality disorders: *narcissistic*, *antisocial*, *histrionic*, *dependent* . . . I suspect it's as much about the lack of effective treatments as the behaviours associated with them. We – and the law – hold the patients responsible in a way we don't with disorders that respond to medication.

But my issue with Taylah is more specific than that. She's at risk of suicide, and thanks to what happened with Aaron, Foster Kid Fifty-Three, I'm uncomfortable with patients like her. It was the main reason I agreed to having my own therapy.

Earlier in the year, I sent Taylah home from ED when she was threatening suicide. It was the right choice, but how much was that decision affected by my need to prove something? A few weeks later, I helped Alex make a similar call – and Xavier died. Once with Taylah was enough. She'd pick up and exploit any anxiety on my part.

'It's just a one-off?' I say to Nash, and he nods. 'So, what's the plan beyond that?'

'She turns up at ED again,' says Jan the case manager. 'If there's a bed in Short Stay, she gets it. If not . . . well, here we are.'

So, no plan.

Jan sees my look. 'She doesn't stick with anything.'

Which, I guess, is part of the problem we're supposed to be treating. A catch-22. Like Grace from the CATT team complaining that she doesn't have the energy to make coffee until she's had one.

—

Taylah shows up – on time. She's in jeans and a tight, low-necked top, wearing a lot of make-up (in the notes I'll say *fully made-up* to highlight her self-care) and looking nervous. Oddly sweet. Her hair's no longer platinum blonde with dark roots – it's all dark. It suits her.

The bad news is that she's accompanied by her mother, Kelly. How to describe her? She's not just annoyed: there's a sense of entitlement about her – a Karen insisting on speaking to the manager. I'm hoping she doesn't remember me.

'I remember you,' she says, as soon as I step into the waiting room. 'The Valium nazi. My daughter takes an overdose, her boyfriend cuts his head open, my other daughter calls the police, I'm trying to look after all of them – not to mention my own issues – and you reckon that's worth two Valium.'

I don't engage; just beckon Taylah to follow me, but Kelly stays on her tail. As we pass reception, Louis is talking to Mia, and Kelly realises she has an audience.

'Hello? *Customer* here,' she says to Mia. 'Doing what you tell us to do – check if people are okay. If not, get help, right? My daughter is *not* okay, so I try to get help. You'd agree with that, wouldn't you? If it was your daughter?'

She waits until Mia nods.

'I wait half the night in the Emergency Department . . .' Right on cue, Lian walks in. Kelly hesitates just a moment before backing her memory. 'You were there. Too busy with that woman off her meds. I saw the dark bloke.' She turns to me. 'I'm not being racist. You could take some lessons from him. I'm –'

'I'll ask you to sit in the waiting room while Dr Wright talks to your daughter, Mrs Keane,' Louis says, finally getting involved. And copping Kelly's stare on high beam.

'You're the consultant, are you? You don't look like you're busy. Where did you get that coffee?'

I head down the corridor to my kennel, Taylah following. I close the door and we sit in two chairs away from the desk. Closer than is comfortable for me, and probably for her, but better than the seeing-the-principal set-up.

'Taylah, can I ask why you're here?'

'I was told to come.'

'I'm guessing you don't always do what you're told.'

Taylah grins. 'I suppose not. But I really want help.'

'I'm not sure that we can offer what you need.'

Instantly, she's angry. 'Right. Too hard. Don't worry about it then – I'll just go and take a fucking overdose. Solve everyone's problem.'

She's already up and at the door. Because I rejected her. That's what she heard, and she heard right. *Fix it, Hannah.*

'Do you want to keep doing that for the rest of your life?' I ask.

Door open, she pauses. 'Doing what?'

'Overdosing. Going from calm to furious in a split second? It must be exhausting.'

Taylah starts to tear up. 'Well, it's not like anybody's offering to help, are they? I *went* for help' – she's echoing her mother – 'and they sent me here. Now you say you can't help.'

'Can we at least talk about what you want, what you need and what the options are?'

'No point, you've said you can't help. Or you'll send me to someone else who says they can't help. Right?'

I feel like I'm in quicksand.

'Maybe I can show you some techniques to help manage your emotions.' Even as I say it, I'm wondering if it's a good idea. Taylah has been dealing with the mental health system a lot longer than I've been dealing with patients, and if I make a mistake she'll be all over it.

'What sort of techniques?'

'Anxiety management. Want to give it a go? If it helps, you could get your GP to give you a referral to see a psychologist.'

'See? You put it back on me. You think I haven't tried to see someone? You say "psychologist" like they're free. They charge shitloads more than you get back. Then you miss a couple of appointments because your life has gone to shit and maybe you need the money to eat, and they don't want to see you anymore.'

But something brought her here and whatever that is, it sits her back down. I get up and close the door.

Maybe Short Stay has anxiety management groups – but I'd guess she would have been too busy sabotaging herself to attend them. And what can you do in three days?

What can *I* do in what's left of thirty minutes?

I tap into my experience of yoga, an app I tried to help me sleep and principles I've read up on, some of them at least in psych texts. I get Taylah to close her eyes, think about waves coming in and out on a beach, breathing . . . the usual stuff.

Afterward, she's calmer, and I finally do what Nash asked me to do and run her through the suicide checklist. The thing that I thought would bother me hasn't. My training and instincts are telling me that she's not at risk right now, and the formal assessment gives me the same answer.

At the end of the session, I suggest she could practise the relaxation exercise. Maybe join a yoga class if she can't see a psychologist.

'You think pretending I'm in Queensland is going to help when my mum starts on me?'

Time's up and I'm out of answers. Frustratingly, just about everything she's said is right. Just about everything *Kelly* said is right.

We supposedly have universal health care in Australia. I guess many people would take that to mean that if they had a life-threatening illness, they'd get to see someone with expertise in that illness and then receive the established best treatment for it.

That's a million miles away from what I've been able to offer Taylah: a mixture of common sense and beginner yoga that has about zero to do with my medical studies. And the reason? Maybe the word 'mental' in front of Taylah's illness is the problem.

I walk her back to reception, where Kelly is waiting. Drinking coffee from Keith's drug-company mug.

—

Carey's eating alone in the cafe at lunchtime and I join them. Kelly's rant about customer service has reminded me of the complaint about the Stables not being autism-friendly and I hit Carey up for some advice.

They have plenty. 'I imagine the waiting room is loud and visually intrusive, too many people, lack of clear process, poor communication about steps and outcomes . . .'

Jon, looking jaded from his night on call, joins us at the table. He listens for a minute before interrupting.

'No offence, Hannah, but why should Carey have to be the go-to person for questions about autism? It's like why should I be the guy to explain all the time whether we should be doing an acknowledgement of traditional owners or a welcome to country? And whether I'd be willing to do it? For what it's worth, I'm as much a visitor as you are; it needs to be a Wurundjeri person.'

Carey smiles. 'Excellent point, Jon. However, I need to earn some emotional-bank-account credits with Hannah, so I'll do an assessment of the Stables. When do you need it?'

'A few days ago.'

'I'll interpret that as ASAP.'

—

My first patient after lunch is DJ Voices. I'm relieved. I wasn't looking forward to telling Keith Barnard he was right if she didn't come for her medication. Frodo is with her. I leave him in the waiting room and call her in.

DJ says she's fine, doing gigs and making music. I'm about to give her a prescription and a time for the next appointment when she adds, 'But my legs are starting to slow me down.'

She moves to unzip her baggy pants. I steer her to the tack room – now the examination room – and get her up on the table. I've never seen anything like what she shows me. She's overweight, but her legs look like they belong to a sumo wrestler.

I indent her flesh. It stays indented. Pitting oedema, more extreme than I've ever seen, even in terminal heart failure.

I locate a stethoscope. It's broken, as shared-use stethoscopes often are. No-one in psych wears one around their neck: we've all been traumatised by the simulated strangling in the aggression-management module. It takes me ten minutes to find another.

DJ's lungs are clear. *I* breathe easier. Check her chest X-ray – a few months old, but no sign of heart enlargement.

'How long have your legs looked like this?' I ask.

'Since I got out, I guess.'

She assures me she's taking her clozapine regularly, denies using any other drugs.

I'm stumped.

I call Frodo into the examination room and tell them she needs a medical review, urgently. Frodo promises me he'll make it happen.

'Anything else worrying either of you?' I ask.

Frodo nods immediately. 'She won't come to bed.'

'Frodo, if DJ doesn't want to have sex –'

He's already shaking his head. 'We have sex on the sex wedge in the basement. She doesn't come to bed *to sleep*.'

Sex wedge? Focus. 'DJ . . . where do you sleep?'

'Wherever.'

'She goes to sleep at the synthesiser,' says Frodo. 'But if I wake her, she just starts playing music and *never comes to bed*.'

Got it. The fluid in her legs is lymph, the clear stuff that nourishes tissue and carries off waste. The lymphatic system doesn't have a pump: we need to sleep horizontal for it to work.

'DJ, you have to lie down to sleep, or your legs will keep ballooning. And you'll end up very sick.'

She's not registering. No eye contact – schizophrenic illness doing its thing.

'You'd have to come back into Extended Care,' I say.

'I'm not going back.'

'I don't want that to happen either. So promise me: you have to lie down for at least six hours every day.'

I turn to Frodo. 'Call me if she doesn't. Remember what you said when you came here for the medication: a matter of life and death?'

He nods.

'That's what this is.'

—

Carey's put a new patient – an hour appointment – in my diary: Zelda Sayre. But I can't find a discharge summary. Annoying, as she's my last for the day. I leave a message for Carey and ask Mia to hold Zelda until the summary arrives.

'She's been here for forty minutes,' says Mia. 'Walking around. I'm picking OCD. Or ADHD.'

A message comes back from Carey: *Can't find it. Give her two weeks of methylenedioxymethamphetamine.*

What? MDMA. Ecstasy.

I walk to the waiting room, and standing there is someone I've seen before. It takes me a moment to realise it's Carey's friend Amy – a patient of Prof's who Carey diagnosed as autistic with the certainty of *it takes one to know one*. She's holding a tablet computer.

'I'm Zelda,' she says when she spots me. She laughs. 'Actually, I'm Amy, your mystery shopper. Checking for autism-friendliness, as you requested. I'm scoring the Stables three out of ten, which is relatively good.'

I almost laugh myself, partly at Amy's manner, partly because what she's saying is surely true, then realise how inappropriate my reaction is. I didn't laugh at Kelly or Taylah when they pointed out deficiencies in the system. It actually takes an effort to do a mental reset and say what I'd say if it was Alex or Ndidi or Jon – someone non-autistic – putting so much effort into doing something I'd asked for as a favour.

'Hey, thanks for doing this, and please thank Carey too. I guess Zelda's going to be a no-show.'

'There is no Zelda, so you can finish early. You didn't think autistic people were capable of deception, did you?'

I laugh. Awkwardly. She's right.

'Actually, the idea came from Alex. The name too. We asked him, because you and he have a special relationship. Is that the right term?'

If Carey could see it, everybody must have been able to.

'Actually, things have changed. I only see him at study group now.'

'Okay. Shall I say, "colleague you once had a special relationship with"?'

'Only if that information's absolutely necessary.'

Amy smiles. 'Oh, and there was a message from him. *Since you now have some spare time, you shouldn't have to work late. Meet you at 6 pm at the usual place.*'

—

Thanks to Zelda, I have time to finish my paperwork and still get away at 5:45 pm. Keith and I walk out at the same time and he intercepts me.

'How was Mrs Fitzgerald?' he asks.

'I'm sorry?'

'You don't know the name of F Scott Fitzgerald's wife?' He smiles. 'I don't imagine most people of your generation would. Unless they fancy themselves as intellectuals.'

He smiles and walks off. I have no idea what point he's making, but I google F Scott Fitzgerald on the way to the bar to meet Alex. His wife's name was Zelda. I think I knew that. Didn't know her maiden name was Sayre.

The weather is bone-chilling cold and no-one's on the rooftop deck. There's a room inside with an open fire going and it's dark and cosy. Alex has snaffled the big chairs by the fireplace and ordered old fashioneds for us both.

I'm wondering if his girlfriend knows that we're continuing the conversations that were once about more than work. At least, their subtext was. But I've got used to debriefing with him and I guess we've set the boundaries. The ones we didn't need before.

Drinks come. We have snacks. He tells me he's got somewhere to be for dinner. I tell him that Keith spotted the fake patient, and he laughs.

'Wouldn't worry about it. Watch the appointment book. He'll start doing the same so he can do tele-psych on the clinic's time, and he'll know you won't be able to call him out. And vice versa.'

Except Keith's a consultant, a friend of Prof, and I'm a trainee.

Alex asks about Lennon and my dad – have I spoken to them? – and I find myself talking through why I'm avoiding my family, which is essentially for the same reason I've been slow to find a therapist. Not being prepared to do what we ask our patients to do.

I've been thinking about Taylah, and I want to see what he has to say about borderline personality disorder. I already know there's no medication for it, unless you count mood stabilisers and antidepressants.

Alex smiles. 'Meds are good for symptomatic relief. For us. Makes us feel like we're doing something. Which leaves . . . wait for it . . . psychotherapy.'

'Why do you think I asked you? Not responsive to meds: call Alex. But I can't see . . . this patient . . . lying on Prof's couch.'

'That's psychodynamic or analytical psychotherapy. Dialectical behaviour therapy is the treatment of choice for borderline personality. Supposedly.'

'Why "supposedly"?'

'According to the psychologists. It's an academic question, because she can't afford a psychologist and we're not set up to do it.'

'So . . . she's screwed?'

'Not at all. I said *treatment of choice*, not *only* treatment. Your patient's struggling with complex issues. She probably doesn't have anyone she can trust, any relationship that isn't under threat, anyone who isn't telling her what choices to make instead of helping her make the right ones . . .'

'You're telling me she needs a friend.'

'It's more – and different. Someone who won't dump their own stuff on her. Someone who can try to understand what's led her to become how she is, how that plays out, what she might be able to do to change –'

I'm laughing at his intensity. It's a serious matter, but we've talked about this kind of supportive therapy a million times. It's more than bedside manner, less than full-on psychotherapy – and we need it every day with just about every patient. And their families.

'But,' says Alex, 'if you do it well, you'll make a difference for your patient.'

I shake my head. 'Not *my* patient.'

—

Spring has officially arrived but Saturday morning is still cold. I've finally convinced Ndidi to do a parkrun after a lot of excuses on her part. Which is a turnaround, because she was the one who got me started on them. She has a slow day, and I'm the one waiting with coffees at the finish line.

'That's what taking a break does,' I say.

'That's what taking hormones does.'

I've been hoping Ndidi would bring it up. She and Torben have been trying for a family for a while.

'Only for a short time, hopefully,' I say.

We head for a bench in the sun and I wait while she sips her coffee and, I guess, thinks about how much to share.

'If this doesn't work . . . I don't want to do IVF. Don't ask why. And I'll have to do some rethinking. Torben and I have different priorities.' Then she changes topic. 'Are you free tonight? I've got a friend you should meet.'

'Right . . . Male, about my age?'

'As it happens. Friend of Torben who's doing a documentary on foster kids, and I guess you know something about that. You'll like him. Smart, but not in a medical way. Cute and looking for a girlfriend, not just sex. But that too.'

—

After an afternoon studying and wondering what to wear, I get an Uber to Ndidi's. I've ended up in jeans, jumper and coat – didn't want to be trying too hard. I've got nothing to lose, except the imbalance of Alex having a girlfriend and me being single.

Hannah, that is not *the point.*

Ndidi doesn't cook much; with luck her mother will have been around with a feast. Nup. When I arrive, Torben's at the barbecue, despite the cold.

'Mum's gone to Canada,' says Ndidi. 'My sister's having a baby.'

That'll be hurting.

Jason, the director, is only a bit taller than me, with shoulder-length red–brown hair and a matching untidy beard. I join him and Torben at the barbecue. He's excited about his documentary. Getting anything made is hard, but his Sudanese co-producer is a darling of the funding bodies.

He breaks off enthusing to Torben and turns to me. 'Ndidi says your family fostered kids?'

I try to give him a balanced picture without saying, *On the plus side, I think we really helped some of the kids. On the minus side, one of them hanged himself.*

'Would your family speak to me?' he asks.

'On camera?'

'It's pretty non-threatening.'

'I doubt my parents would,' I say. 'But they're in touch with some of the ex-foster kids.'

Kayla would jump over dead bodies to dump on all the people who let her down. Or just to be on-screen.

'What message are you trying to send?'

'No message. I just want to show it: the good and the bad; when things work; when things don't. As powerfully and beautifully as I can. How about you? You'd be great on camera.'

'No, thanks.' If I were to speak honestly about my own experience, my parents would be hurt. I'll save it for the therapist. But I'm feeling less self-conscious about the match-up. Jason's a straightforward guy who's passionate about what he's doing. But there's no chemistry. I don't think.

—

Over the weekend, Taylah demonstrates – again – the ineffectiveness of our ad hoc interventions and, more specifically, unqualified yoga instruction as treatment for borderline personality disorder. She presents at the Emergency Department following another overdose.

I hear all about it at Monday's handover in the Barn. So does Nicole, who, externally at least, is back to normal after her meltdown. She's come to this morning's meeting specifically because of the Keane family's repeat attendances at ED.

I'm in two minds about Nicole's practice of keeping a close eye on a few selected cases. She gets up everyone's noses, but if her intention is to get a sense of the challenges we face – well, meet the Keanes.

'Taylah had a fight with her sister,' says Grace. 'Still no Short Stay beds so we're supposed to be visiting her, but we can't see her every day. Plus she's not exactly welcoming.'

Grace is relaxed in her summary: seems this was a cry for help rather than a serious suicide attempt. I breathe a sigh of relief – for Taylah and for me. I'm starting to feel I've got Taylah's number.

Nicole is looking at the notes, toe tapping impatiently. 'What follow-up did you organise, Hannah?'

I glance at Nash. 'The hospital doesn't have the resources for extended therapy, and she wasn't prepared to pay for a psychologist.' I'm not going to mention the yoga option.

Nicole turns to Nash. 'Do you have any idea what this family has cost us over the years? For what seems to be zero progress.'

'Unless you count saving her life multiple times,' says Nash. 'Paracetamol overdoses don't fix themselves.'

'I said zero *progress*. What happened last night is going to keep happening. If nothing changes, nothing changes.'

'What KPI is going to measure whether whatever resources we throw at this do any good?' he says. 'We've been trying to minimise their use of the system . . .'

'Fewer emergencies. Keep them out of ED. That's your KPI. And, you know, just as a bonus, maybe we can make life a bit better for a family that's been struggling for a long time.'

'We don't have the resources, the expertise –'

Nicole interrupts, looks to Jan. 'What's your title?'

'I'm a case manager.'

'Then you have a case to manage.'

As soon as Nicole's gone, Nash hauls us all back in: 'Let's get it sorted now. Big-picture ideas. We're talking about three people. We have, theoretically, all the resources of the Service.'

'Separate accommodation,' says Grace. She laughs. 'In different states.'

Jan shakes her head. 'They're in government housing. The only way they'll get separate accommodation is if Taylah or Aleesha gets a partner and child. And then they'll have to wait five years.'

'Still probably cheaper than what we're doing,' says Nash. 'But when I said "big picture" I meant the world that I control.'

'Group therapy?' says George, one of the CATT nurses.

'For ourselves?' says Louis.

There's laughter, but Nash nods. 'We see them individually but coordinate and debrief regularly. Don't let them play us off against each other. Volunteers?'

'Taylah's the immediate issue,' says Louis.

'She comes into ED wanting to get into Short Stay,' I say. 'Could we schedule some short stays for her? Without the ED drama?'

Louis nods. 'Good thinking. Give her something to look forward to.'

Taylah's life in a sentence.

'Plus some follow-up between admissions,' says Nash.

'I'll take the mother,' says Louis. 'I had a wee chat with her and she seemed prepared to make a connection.'

Louis's contract has been renewed, so he'll be around to do it.

'I could take Aleesha,' I say. The one I haven't met and with the fewest admissions. The one who isn't Taylah.

'Thanks, Hannah,' says Jan, 'but she's a handful. I'll take her.'

Now they're all looking at me.

'You've seen Taylah,' says Nash. 'Twice? And you came up with the Short Stay idea.'

I clear my throat. 'I'm only here for six months. Handing her over when my term at the Stables is up just repeats the pattern of rejection.'

'Good point,' says Nash. 'You could take her on as your long-psychotherapy case . . . and see her as long as she needs. Right into private practice. A patient for life.'

—

Rather than grab Nash after the meeting, I wait till my regular supervision session in his office that afternoon But it's the first item on my agenda.

'I have some real issues with suicide.'

'I'm aware of that,' says Nash. 'But you're going to get your own therapy, right? Have to deal with it sometime.' He smiles. 'You made such a strong argument about seeing Brianna.'

'But I'd need a supervisor.'

'I'm your supervisor.'

Right. For a case that can't be treated with meds. At least until she overdoses.

'At the end of the day, you're training to be a psychiatrist,' he says. 'Brianna could go to a private psychologist, but Taylah's one for us. People who regularly present at Emergency, drug overdoses – that's our domain.'

Having won, he sits back for a few moments. Then: 'We know she makes suicide attempts but they're cries for help. Doesn't mean she won't miscalculate, but that's what it would be – a miscalculation, an accident. And you think you'll learn a lot from Brianna? Wait till you've done some work with Taylah before you decide what path you want to take.'

Because Taylah will show you the futility of psychotherapy.

—

I see Elena for an update on Brianna. Nothing to report – the family hasn't been in touch – so I use the time to pick her brain on borderline personality disorder.

She tells me what I know already: people with borderline personality disorder are difficult and not ideal for a first long-psychotherapy case. But I'll be doing supportive therapy, not digging into Taylah's past.

'They don't trust people,' says Elena, 'and will interpret your intentions in the worst light.'

'Any suggestions as to how to deal with that?'

Elena gives me a look that I've become familiar with: *Why do I have to advise junior doctors who are probably paid more than I am on how to do their jobs?* Or: *Why don't you just stick to medication and stay off my patch?*

I'm sure she knows the answer, which is basically: The system.

'No easy solutions,' she says. 'You'll need to be mindful of fractures in your relationship with her in every interaction, and bolster her skill set to manage them.'

'And, I guess, avoid being sucked into making it personal.'

'Yes. I imagine Prof has advised you to see a therapist yourself, so you'll have another sounding board.'

'I'm still looking for one.'

'I'll ask around,' says Elena. 'Don't see Egard Ryner.'

I don't recognise the name. 'Why?'

'The usual. Boundaries.' Code for sex with patients.

'How do you know?'

'Everyone – well, every *therapist* – knows.'

'How come he's still practising?'

'Probably never been reported. Patients tell us, but a legal setting's a different thing. None of us are going to stick our necks out.'

'And I get the warning because I'm an insider.'

Elena nods. 'Not ideal. But if a psychiatrist has plenty of availability, it's like an empty taverna. Keep walking.'

'Maybe I'll find a busy one and wait for a table to come free.'

Elena laughs, then stops. 'Now that you mention it . . . One of my ex-patients passed away a week or so ago. She was seeing Joan Drinkwater forever. And Joan's been seeing patients longer than forever.'

—

Friday at 11 am we're all set for the Keane family – three appointments with three therapists – and the waiting room is empty. A part of me is disappointed. Taylah wouldn't be easy, but maybe she is the gold – or the brittle quartz – that would make me a better therapist. And I'm starting to feel that I might be able to help her.

I've spent the previous evening on the sofa reading up about borderline personality disorders and dialectical behaviour therapy. In an ideal world, Taylah would come in for one to three individual sessions a week with a dialectical behavioural therapy specialist, and at least one cognitive anxiety management group. In the real world, she's got me once a week for non-judgemental support.

DBT uses a combination of cognitive behavioural anxiety management techniques with a psychodynamic underpinning. Says my book. It could include the relaxation I did in the last session with Taylah. I got that right, at least.

Mia buzzes me. Taylah's finally here, smoking in the waiting room.

'Be kind to the receptionist,' I say as we navigate the labyrinth. 'She's on nicotine patches and you're taunting her with the smell of tobacco.'

'Her problem.' Taylah's lateness may be a sign of anger. She's got a Sephora bag poking out of her handbag and I figure she dropped into the mall to kill time. And send a message to me that this appointment isn't important to her.

'They told me to come back here, but you aren't going to help me,' she says. 'I want a Short Stay admission.'

'Let's talk about that.'

Taylah looks briefly hopeful and then suspicious.

I recognise the look and make an unexpected connection. Foster Kid Twenty. I think she was eight. Followed me around like a cocker-spaniel puppy and I found it kind of amusing. I probably exploited her, sending her to get me things, but I'd been, what, thirteen? When she left, she was so excited about finally getting to live with her mum. Six months later, she was back with us. Her mum had ditched her for a boyfriend. The cocker spaniel had become a Doberman with the look Taylah is giving me now: *Don't trust anyone – they'll kick you in the teeth.* If you can't trust your mum, who can you trust? I have a rush of anger that I squash. It's not toward Taylah.

Remembering Foster Kid Twenty helps. I'll try to hold on to it.

'First, tell me again what you want help with, Taylah. Because we need to be on the same page.'

Taylor looks at the ceiling. 'I want to not feel like shit.'

'Do you feel like shit all the time or just some of the time?'

'It's up and down.'

I type *mood issues* then delete it and write *affective instability.*

'The only thing that helps is cutting. Takes away some of the pain.'

I type *self-harm as a way of managing emotional pain.*

'And then I just want peace and I take an overdose.'

Overdose – overwhelmed?

I ask, 'How is being alone for you?'

'Shit.'

Fear of abandonment. Probably enough for now. The computer is putting distance between us. I push the keyboard aside.

'What helps other than self-harm? Anything?'

'Short Stay.' She's aiming low – not even trying for a longer admission. 'I mean, three days gives me time to de-escalate, you know?'

De-escalate. Right. Taylah really has been at this longer than me.

'Okay, let's accept that for now,' I say. 'But you go to ED too – does that help?'

'Not unless I get to go to Short Stay.'

'From the outside,' I say, 'it looks like a lot of stress – and potential real physical harm – for the chance of getting admitted to Short Stay. Which has stopped happening, right?'

'That's your lot's fault.'

'In an ideal world,' I ask, 'what would your life look like?'

I'm not following any protocol, but we need to establish a goal for therapy. Taylah doesn't look like she's thought beyond the next half-hour and which of us is going to come out on top.

'Boyfriend who isn't a dick,' she finally says. 'Place of my own up north where it's warmer.'

No mention of a better relationship with her mother or sister, but it's something.

'Any thoughts as to what gets in the way of that happening?'

'My mother and sister.'

'So would . . . understanding why they push your buttons help, do you think?'

Taylah shrugs. I'm being too ambitious.

'How about I offer you a deal?'

The suspicion, never far away, is back.

'How about we try weekly therapy? We can review how it's going, before the end of January.' When my rotation ends. 'Once a week. Call the CATT team if you're in a crisis instead of going to ED.'

'That won't help.'

'I'm hoping it will, but I hear you. If you can stick to that part of the bargain, you get four Short Stay admissions a year. Four. No more. Planned admissions.'

I can see Taylah calculating if this will get her more admissions than she'd get otherwise; the same calculation Nash did when he gave me the number. It will, because she's had a lot of direct discharges from ED. But it also means saved time for ED staff – and less risk to her. Some control in her hands; some need to show restraint.

'Can I go to Short Stay now?'

'Let's plan one at a time. Are you sure now is when you need it most?'

Taylah pauses for a few moments. 'Okay, maybe in a couple of weeks.'

She's on board.

'It will only happen if you stay out of ED between now and then,' I say. 'Can you do that?'

Another shrug.

'You can use the breathing techniques we did last week. Do you have any meds that help?'

'Valium.'

We talk about things she can do when she's feeling overwhelmed. Take a bath, walk the dog, phone a friend. Simple things, but not things she thinks about when, without warning, she feels her life's falling apart.

'And I get to go to Short Stay in two weeks, right?'

I nod. 'I'll give you some Valium, but put it where your mother won't find it. I'm not going to replace it if you lose it.'

I think there's a better than even chance it might work – at least for a couple of weeks.

—

Sunday evening, I drop into the Stables to do a little overdue redecorating. Nash's car is in the car park, though there's no sign of him.

Mum calls, and I mention the documentary. She calls me back as I'm walking home. She and Dad are both up for it.

'And Kayla's here and she's willing to tell her story.'

Brave Kayla.

While I'm clearing my to-do list, I call Lennon, thinking that I can report to Alex that I've been in touch with both my parents and my brother.

Lennon answers. 'At work. Have to keep it short.'

I tell him about the documentary.

'They'll feel they're doing something good,' he says.

'You don't think . . .' I pause. 'That we should talk to them before –'

'No. What's the point? It's their truth.'

'But –'

'Sorry, Hanny, gotta go. Busy, busy.'

—

Monday, the Stables feels different. Calmer. It's my own – or rather Carey's and Amy's – doing: no boomer music, three cheap lamps from the op shop providing lighting in the waiting room in place of the overhead fluoros, which have tape over their switches. A one-page flowchart, *What To Expect From Your Visit*, next to the poster about us not tolerating aggressive behaviour.

Some of Amy's and Carey's recommendations are about staff behaviour, which I'll have to raise with Nash, and it'll probably take an Act of Parliament to get paper towels in the bathrooms as an alternative to the noisy air blowers. As for changing the name from the Stables to something more patient-centric – I'd need to overturn a century of history.

It's been a busy weekend – as usual – and sure enough, the Keane family get a mention at the morning handover.

'It was Aleesha this weekend,' says Grace.

Jan nods. 'I spoke to her on the phone last week, and she told me to shove my appointment.'

'Kelly rescheduled,' says Louis. 'We had a long natter. Thinks her kids resent the new man in her life.'

I wasn't far off when I compared Taylah to Foster Kid Twenty. Except Taylah's mother has prioritised her partner over her children not once but again and again.

'What they need is a nunnery,' says Jan. 'Support, boundaries and no men.'

'Taylah saw me last week,' I say. 'Any word on how she got on over the weekend?'

Grace grins. 'She grabbed me when I dropped in on Sunday. Wanted me to tell you she let them go to ED without her.'

I allow myself a small fist pump.

'Don't get too excited,' says Grace. 'She's still cutting. Her thigh now.'

Forgot to include that in the deal.

After the meeting, Nash pats me on the shoulder and says, 'Well done.'

Whether through luck or skill, we've taken a step in the right direction. We've demonstrated that Taylah has the capacity to delay gratification and to plan, at least in a small way.

I'm still reflecting on my success with Taylah later that afternoon when Mia puts a call through.

'Brianna Young for you.'

Brianna sounds like she's been crying.

'Are you okay?' I ask.

'No. I need to see you. I'm back home.'

'Okay. You know I've spoken with your dad?'

'Whatever. I want to see you.'

'Next Wednesday? After school?'

'I need to see you now.'

'Are you safe?'

'Yes. But . . .'

I look in the diary. 'Tomorrow? Four thirty?'

'You can't do earlier?'

'I've got space at eleven, but don't you have school –'

'Forget about school,' says the girl who wants to do her International Baccalaureate and be a vet.

FOUR

AUTONOMY

It's the soap-opera version of childbirth. No grunts, no screams, no blood, the mother radiant, the new father bursting with love and pride. Even the bundled newborn is smiling. It's a dramatic life these beautiful people lead: family feuds, friendships betrayed, medical crises, lots of medical crises. But all that is forgotten in this special moment.

The light of the television barely illuminates the couple watching, transfixed by the emotional climax to weeks of anticipation and suspense.

Capeka takes her husband's hand and squeezes. He squeezes back.

The notes for my first patient of the day don't quite add up.

Capeka Dulka is a thirty-five-year-old long-term Stables patient with chronic schizophrenia. She's one of the third of sufferers who have ongoing disability. Medication only dampens the symptoms. Married. A bit unusual for those with the more serious forms of schizophrenia, but more common for women, partly because their illness often starts at a later age, when they might already have a partner, but also because women in general have better social skills to begin with. And if they're passive, they might find a partner who's looking for that.

Capeka was with the Mobile Support Team until she got a disability package. Does she also have a physical disability? And there's reference to two admissions to the Mother Baby Unit. I wonder how much of the childcare she's able to do.

She comes in with her husband, Jozef, and I have to do a complete recalibration. He walks with a stick and has one leg in a calliper. There's a large scar down one side of his head and his left eye is partially closed. The disability package is likely his.

Capeka is medium height, significantly overweight, facial expression blank – her affect dulled by both schizophrenia and medication.

I introduce myself, get them seated in my office, and ask Capeka how she is.

'I'm good,' she says. Not much in the way of expression or discernible emotion. A light accent – I guess Slavic.

'Tell me a bit about your life at the moment.'

'Is same as always.'

I rattle off the usual questions and find they mostly stay home. The disability package provides someone to help plan their meals, clean and shop, and some speech therapy and physio for Jozef. They see family on weekends 'sometimes'. They watch a lot of television.

I turn to Jozef, who hasn't said anything. 'I don't have any information here about your disability.'

'Wazzz a a a car *car* accident,' he says slowly, muscles tense, face grimacing with the effort. 'Tennnn yyyyears ago.'

It seems he has an acquired brain injury. But he's managed to continue a life with Capeka.

I get back to Capeka, find she no longer has any so-called positive symptoms: voices and delusions. Instead, she's been left with the negative symptoms: lack of motivation, poverty of thought, withdrawal and lack of expressed emotion. Her spark has gone.

The strong instinctive reactions I have to Brianna and Taylah aren't in play here; I'm not getting the usual social cues – eye contact, nodding, smiling – that people ordinarily rely on in forming connections.

'How are the medications?' I ask Capeka, checking the computer. 'I see you were changed from risperidone to aripiprazole a long time ago.'

She nods. 'On the other one, the risperidone, I couldn't get pregnant.'

'You have . . . two children?'

Capeka nods.

'Rrrruben and Mmmmaria,' says Jozef. 'Mmmmaria is Capekaaa's mmmmother's nnname too.'

'How old are they?'

'Six and four,' says Capeka.

'And . . . how are they?'

How does this couple manage two young children? I think of my sister's kids, running everywhere, constantly needing attention. How does it work if Mum and Dad are watching television and not conversing much? How do children learn about emotion from a mother who's struggling with feeling, or at least with expressing any emotions?

'Children are good,' says Capeka. 'We do not see them much. My mother says we upset them.'

'I'm sorry to hear that . . . They're with your mother?'

Capeka nods. 'I bought Ruben a backpack for school. He started this year.'

This has to be hard for them. But we have limited time, and there's other stuff I need to cover.

'How's your physical health? We might need to check your weight and do some blood tests.'

'No need,' says Capeka. 'They weigh me yesterday. Eighty-eight kilograms. Also lots of tests.'

Her GP sounds very proactive, which they need to be as long-term antipsychotic use puts on weight and the two combined often lead to diabetes.

Capeka seems to have read my mind. 'My sugar is high so I will take insulin in the pregnancy.'

'Pregnancy?' I falter.

'I have had the hormones,' she says. 'The embryo is Friday.'

I hope I don't look as horrified as I feel. 'Capeka, I'm sorry but I'm a bit confused. Why are your older children with your mother?'

'I think, because she is closer to Ruben's school.'

I'm trying to be neutral. The maternal grandmother might be overly interfering, overriding this couple's autonomy, possibly based on ableist assumptions. Before I knew they had kids, I was right behind them; now I'm starting to worry about the children's rights. And those of the child they're planning.

'Were Child Protection involved?' I ask.

Capeka doesn't respond.

Jozef says, 'They kkkkept ccccoming to the house. Wwwweee had a nnnnannnny bbbut shshshe dddidn't like us.'

'Does the IVF clinic know Ruben and Maria are with their grandmother?'

Blank looks from them both.

'Is . . . is this a public IVF service?' I'm thinking about financial stress.

'Private,' says Capeka. 'Koala Fertility.'

'Expensive,' says Jozef, but he's beaming. 'Mmmmy accident payout.'

'Do you think this new baby might also need to be cared for by your mother?' I ask.

I see Capeka zone out. Not going there.

But Jozef gives me the look a man gives someone who has deliberately hurt his wife.

'We only come here for her medication.'

—

Brianna arrives with time to spare. I'm wondering if there's anything to her urgency beyond testing whether I care enough – or am manipulable enough – to bring her appointment forward. Maybe some crisis with her sister, Chloe, which is what her family has been all about.

She's in the waiting room in school uniform, all the silver removed, no make-up. It makes her seem more vulnerable and out of place. She's ignoring the guy pacing around in pants so low you can see his bum crack, and the anxious young woman with a baby in a pram.

I read up last night about IPT – interpersonal psychotherapy – at Elena's suggestion. It's about feelings and how those feelings are triggered by the people in the patient's life. It sounds perfect for Brianna.

Elena also suggested I focus on defining the boundaries between me and Brianna. Being predictable and reliable. Caring but no pushover. A lot of things to focus on. Even though this isn't full-on psychodynamic therapy – even though I won't be exploring Brianna's past and how it defines her; even though I won't be helping her make sense of who she is or wants to be, what defences she uses or why her family is the way it is – the relationship between patient and therapist will inevitably be part of the process.

I've reminded Nash that it would be nice if I could get the guidance I need as part of my training rather than relying on our busy psychologist and Dr Google. I'd half-forgotten that I'd pushed him to let me take Brianna on. He hadn't.

Only when I've closed my office door behind her do I realise that Brianna is looking . . . *wretched*. I go with my gut, forget the boundaries I'm meant to be focusing on, and give her a hug.

I feel her begin to cry.

'Take your time,' I say.

I let her cry for a few minutes, then sit her down and give her a box of tissues.

Finally she takes a deep breath, looks at me and says, 'I'm pregnant.'

IPT, CBT, DBT and psychodynamic theory evaporate in my mind space.

'Are you sure?' I ask. 'Just the test from the chemist?'

Brianna nods miserably.

'We're going to work this through, okay? Facts, then feelings, then actions.'

She nods again, visibly relieved. A problem shared.

'When was your last period?'

We determine that she's over ten weeks into the pregnancy. Too late for a pill. I order a blood test to confirm.

As I'm writing out the request, Brianna asks, 'You don't have to tell my parents, do you?'

'No.' Legally, Brianna just needs to be capable of making responsible decisions. 'But I'll need to tell my supervising psychiatrist and Elena – we're a team.'

Brianna is back to looking miserable.

'How are you feeling?' I ask.

'How do you expect?' There's a little of her sassiness in the tone but not much. 'I don't want to be a mother. Not now. I've got my whole life ahead of me.' Her voice breaks as she says it.

My immediate reaction is: *Of course. Let's get this sorted right now.* But I'm her therapist, not her friend. And I have no idea of her values beyond her coming from what seems to be a hard-line religious family. Which she's rebelling against. *Has been* rebelling against.

'Lots of options,' I say. 'And we've got a week or so to decide.'

'Nothing to decide. I want an abortion.'

'Which I can help you with,' I say. 'But can we talk about it? To make sure it's the right choice for the right reasons? Lots of people have terminations and don't regret them. But some people do. If you don't want to risk being one of those, let's talk about your feelings and how you want to manage this. You're sounding scared.'

'Bathroom,' says Brianna, and races out. I'm thinking the blood test is a formality.

I take the opportunity to call Elena. She picks up and I give her a quick summary.

'Holy Mother of God, what was she thinking?'

'I guess I'm going to find out.'

I hear her take a breath. 'I need you to think about something.'

'Brianna will be back in a minute.'

'Chloe . . . her older sister, as you know, has anorexia. Sometimes it's associated with sexual abuse; the theory is that the abuse can trigger a desire to remain childlike in appearance. I've seen no direct evidence of that, but . . . if someone abused *Chloe* in the past . . .'

She doesn't have to say who she's thinking about. My stomach actually heaves. I take a few deep breaths.

'Just keep it in mind,' says Elena. 'Take control without taking away her right to make her decisions.'

Brianna is back.

'Sick?' I ask.

She nods. 'Not going to be for long.' She shakes her head angrily. 'I . . . I thought I was so . . . I can't believe I didn't make him use a condom.'

Through the tears she looks very young. My countertransference – my feelings for the patient based on my own experience – is in overdrive. I've never been pregnant but I'm identifying way too closely with her. I can almost taste the fear I felt when I saw Aaron's body hanging from a rope. And the feeling I had in the aftermath, when a line had been crossed and the hollow in my stomach told me that my childhood was over.

I take another breath, blow away the memories. It's back to just me and Brianna. I'm the adult in the room.

I squeeze her hand. 'All fifteen-year-olds think they can handle things they can't. If we're lucky, we escape without getting hurt too much. If not, then we get help so we can work through it and come out the other end older but wiser. You're here, that's what you're doing, and older and wiser is how you will be in a few weeks or months.'

I want to say, *It may take a lot longer if you change your mind and have the baby*, but I'm not going to advocate. If she makes the choice for the right reasons, eyes open, then she will be able to live with the decision no matter what it is.

'I'm not going to *make* you tell me anything,' I say. 'But can you tell me . . . do you know the father of the baby?'

She nods.

'Was it consensual?'

'Did he rape me? No.'

She might say that about her father.

'I kind of came onto him,' she says.

I wait.

'He's a student. A uni student.'

I'm pretty sure she's telling the truth. Good news – not her dad. Bad news – he's likely more than two years older than her, which makes it sexual assault. I'll worry about that later.

'You seemed angry earlier. Who at?'

'My parents. They treat me like I'm a kid.'

She's thrown a toddler-type tantrum, but, thanks to her age and options, has ended up with adult consequences. It's amazing anyone survives their teenage years unscathed. There's some uneasiness in the back of my mind that I squash before I can grasp whether it's about Brianna or myself at fifteen.

'If you were to tell them,' I say, 'what would happen?'

'You've seen them,' says Brianna. 'Dad would throw me out.' She adds with barely concealed anger, 'And Mum will do what she's told.'

My identification with Brianna has given me some insight. Subconsciously, she wanted to do something awful and have her parents still love her. But the reality is now staring her in the face.

Beyond this, I'm out of my depth. She's saying her father is the more likely to have strong views based on his moral or religious position, and she's probably right. But she appears more angry at her mother. Does that mean she needs her mother more?

'What if you just told your mother? Brought her to an appointment?'

'You'd end up with another patient.' She manages a small laugh.

'Which we could deal with.'

'She'd tell my dad anyway.'

'Are your parents religiously opposed to terminations?'

'It's like the worst sin. It's okay – I don't believe in it.'

But it's a complication we could do without.

'Okay, this is what we're going to do,' I say. 'You're going to get the blood test. Come back and see me tomorrow. I can have an appointment organised for you to be assessed and then, if you want, the termination can be in the following few days.'

Brianna looks down into her lap, starts picking at the skin on the side of her thumb. 'I can't. We've got a camp leaving on Friday. It's like super important if I want to do the IB next year. I won't be back till Friday next week. Like, late.'

Her manner has changed and my mind is racing. She'll be twelve weeks by then.

'You want to go on the camp? You can wait until after it?' I say slowly.

Brianna looks unsure but finally nods. How critical can school camp be? She's giving herself time to think, which is what I've encouraged her to do.

Have I tried so hard to be neutral that I've ended up pushing a fifteen-year-old in the wrong direction? Or has my reassurance freed her to think beyond her panicked urge to make the problem go away?

'I'd like to examine you,' I say. 'Just to be sure you're not further along than we think.'

Brianna nods. I hope my skills are up to it. Brianna is thin, which will help.

I commandeer the tack room. No uterus above the pelvic rim, so less than twelve weeks now.

We head back to my office.

'Do you want to tell anyone?' I ask. 'A friend? Or, the er ... uni student?'

'Him? No way!'

That makes it easier. She's feeling bad enough without having to manage someone else's issues. Including her father's. Who will surely see me as an accessory to killing an unborn child and find a way to report me.

'But,' she says, 'maybe Maddy. Her mum is amazing.'

'If you change your mind about telling your parents, you might want to talk to me first, and we can think about creating a safe space for you to do it.'

Brianna starts to shake. 'I can't.'

'*You don't have to tell them*, okay?' I say, putting a hand on her arm. 'But you want to be an adult? Then we need to think this through. Deal?'

She nods.

'I want you to write down every positive and negative you can think of about having this baby or not. How you would feel about each – having the baby with and without your parents' support; having a termination, with and without their support. When I next see you, you should be making a final decision. If you're going to have a termination, we don't want to leave it too long.'

Brianna nods again.

'And if you do tell a friend, make sure she doesn't tell anyone, okay? You've mentioned your friend's mum, and she might feel she has a responsibility to tell your parents. If you're not a hundred per cent certain you can trust someone, don't tell them.'

I give her my number and tell her to call me if she's in crisis. And ask her to text me an emoji every day to keep me up to date. I remember how long a week was at fifteen.

'Do you . . . think it's a sin?' she asks. 'I mean, morally wrong.'

'A lot of people think it is, but a lot – most – don't,' I say.

'But what do you think?'

'I think this is going to be a tough decision and I'm here to help.' We've come a way since *Nothing to decide. I want an abortion.*

She's still miserable when she leaves. But she gives me a hug.

—

I head straight to the Acute Unit, where Elena is based, forgetting to put on my coat. It's mid-September, with a touch of green on the trees, but the temperature is still winter. While I'm waiting for her in the glass house – the staff base – I tap out an email to Dr Popa. I figure pregnancy counts as 'major' and she'd want an update.

Elena and I grab an interview room, and I go through the session with her. Where I went off script because I had no script. Where I started saying 'we'. Where I hugged Brianna. Where I gave her my phone number.

Elena listens, as she does. When I'm finished, I'm half-expecting her to lose it with me: *What was I thinking letting you do this? What were* you *thinking?*

Instead, she says, 'Sounds like you did what we talked about: took control without taking over her right to make the decision. That's actually all you needed to get right, but you did better than that.'

She lets me sit with that before going on. 'The "we" is a moot point. Prof would probably say it was unwise, but you likely forged a stronger link by doing it. He would definitely tell you not to give out your phone number.'

Like I did to Frodo. Need to watch that one.

She sees my expression. 'Speaking of professional behaviour, David Young did lodge a complaint. No-one thinks it'll go anywhere but I have to deal with two sets of lawyers – my insurance and the hospital. And the regulator. Your situation is completely different and nothing you've done is an issue.'

I'm sure we're both thinking, *David may not agree.*

And there's a question I don't feel I've answered about Brianna. 'What *was* she thinking? Why is her family so fucked?'

'That might take years of analysis they won't have,' says Elena. 'Families are complicated.'

'Nash said the family therapy risked making things worse.'

Elena's lips purse. I've hit a nerve.

'Like he had a better plan,' she says. 'He was going to send Chloe home to die. She was the sickest, and the paradoxical therapy has given her at least a few more months or years.' *So screw you, Nash.*

Elena's tone softens a bit. 'Now we have to see if we can help Brianna. She's not the first fifteen-year-old to get pregnant. She's fortunate to have a therapist: most wouldn't.'

'But she still needs her parents.'

'I agree. Maybe we can get them back into another family session.'

'Maybe,' I say. 'But you know which side of the glass I'm going to be on.'

We talk through the next steps.

'Brianna trusts you,' says Elena. 'I don't need to be there. But the questions that you evaded?'

I nod. Evasion was exactly how it felt.

'She was looking for your permission. As a parental figure.'

'Do I give it?'

'You know your role isn't to make the decision for her. But this is about learning to trust. Her and you. Go with your instinct,' she says.

Fine, as long as Brianna's father doesn't find out.

—

The next day I brief Nash about Capeka and Jozef, and their plans to have a baby which will likely end up with her mother again. 'I'm thinking we should call Child Protection and get them to intervene. Or should I ring her mother and see what she thinks about another child?'

Nash considers for a moment. 'Child Protection won't do anything until she's actually pregnant, and even then they won't intervene until she delivers. Call the mother if you like. She may have some sway with her daughter.'

'Surely there's some legal avenue?'

'Not sure,' says Nash. 'You said she's been in the Mother Baby Unit?'

'Four years ago.'

'Ask Sandra Byrd. This is her world.'

—

I start with Capeka's mother, Maria. Over the phone, she sounds caring. Maybe tired. A heavy accent.

'Ruben is doing well at school,' she says. 'Already reading. And little Masha is always smiling.'

'Can I ask how they are with their parents?'

Maria lets out a long sigh. 'My daughter and her husband . . . they love their children, I know. But they have no patience. No understanding that perhaps they need to be quiet. Ruben is scared of his father and they do not understand this. Little Masha does not want to play with Capeka because there is no joy there.'

'Do you know . . . What if Capeka were to have IVF again?'

Maria shrieks. 'No, this cannot happen. The Child Protection told them they could not have more. She has something to stop this.'

Not anymore, she doesn't.

'Um . . . yes . . . Look, I understand your concern.'

'I am sixty-seven. Already I have no retirement like my friends. Another baby will kill me.'

I might use that line.

I call the IVF clinic and leave an urgent message for Capeka's doctor to call me, then make an appointment to see Sandra Byrd, head of the Mother Baby Unit.

—

Joan Drinkwater, the therapist Elena has suggested for me, *looks* like she's been doing it forever. I'd guess she's in her early eighties: small, grey, careful. Reminds me of Queen Elizabeth II toward the end of her life.

We meet at her home – it's a few kilometres further from the city than mine. Her consulting rooms – a waiting room and an office, both warmly furnished – share the same entrance as her living space but are on the opposite side of the hallway.

I'm nervous and make a lame joke about swiping left or right. I've got a date after, which is probably what prompted my comment. But she doesn't get it. And wants me to explain. I sit opposite her in miniskirt, tight jumper and ankle boots, doing my best.

I can see that she's a bit shocked – not offended, just surprised – by modern dating rituals. Doesn't she have kids? Grandkids?

I'd like to talk about Brianna, but she needs to know my background first.

I've been thinking about the *Why did you come to see me?* question. *Trouble dealing with suicide* was my first thought, but I've broadened it to *Dealing with stuff that happened in my childhood.*

She asks how it's affecting me in the here and now.

'I've been having bad dreams . . . about the suicide I witnessed.'

She blanches, and I feel compelled to reassure her.

'But since I've been proactive, they haven't come as often.'

'Proactive?'

'Well, I messaged this guy who was there. I figure talking with him, someone who had the same experience, might help.'

'You had his address?'

'Actually, I found him on Facebook.'

Everybody knows what Facebook is. Apparently not.

'Let me tell you a little about how I work,' she says.

She sees patients from 8 am to 7 pm five days a week. *Winding down*, said her assistant, who comes in once a week to 'do the computer stuff'. On weekends, she reads. Mainly psychiatry. Her patients are all over sixty, most much older, navigating the later stages of ordinary lives.

'You might say I should get a life. But I'm very happy with the one I have. And with the kind of patients I'm seeing.'

I really like her. But she's clearly found her happy place, and I don't belong there. I don't want to be talking about my issues with someone who doesn't understand the world I live in.

—

While I'm waiting for the tram outside Joan's, Alex texts me – the usual drink invitation. I'd love to talk with him about Joan and Brianna and life in general, but Jason the documentary maker has asked me out for Thai.

It was easier to say yes. It looks like he'll be dealing with my family; he seems nice and smart and interested; and it might stop Jess hassling me about what a great guy Jon is. And my brain hassling me about Alex.

I type *Sorry, busy*, to Alex, then change *busy* to *date*. That's what I want, isn't it? The equality of us both seeing someone? *Send.*

The tram takes me straight into the city. Jason's also made an effort. He's trimmed his beard and pulled his hair into a ponytail. It suits him. He's in all black, including a long coat.

Thai turns out to be a fusion restaurant with a young crowd, surprising flavours and lemongrass margaritas.

'I gather from Ndidi you're single. Obviously, I guess,' he says.

'Is that all she told you about me?'

He smiles. 'A bit serious, has a built-in emotions sensor, and you can take the girl out of the country but you can't take the country . . .'

I laugh – and file it away. Is that how my colleagues see me? 'Ndidi's calling *me* serious?' I say. 'She's *super*-serious: all work and politics.'

'Not always. You know she's great at paintball?'

'No way.'

Jason laughs. 'You're right.' Then he says more soberly, 'They're going through some stuff at the moment.' He seems to think I know about it. 'Torben's okay with the baby idea, but didn't realise it'd be such a process.'

I guess that's Torben's story. My built-in emotions sensor has been telling me that there are things they should've sorted before they hit the fertility drugs.

'Hopefully they'll work it out,' I say, because that's what you say to a friend of theirs who you don't really know yet. 'But . . . I'm trying hard to lose the country-girl tag.'

Jason takes a sip of his Mexican–Thai fusion drink. 'What did Ndidi say about me?'

'You're not a doctor. She thinks doctors with doctors is a bad thing – and it happens all the time. I lived with one for a while. She's probably right.'

Even as I say it, I'm thinking about Alex.

'I was with another director for two years,' says Jason. 'I ended it.'

I wait for him to tell me why.

'We didn't see eye to eye professionally and it really got in the way.' He pauses and I wait for him to explain. 'Directors have to direct the camera guy *and* the actors, which means the look and the performances. I'm stronger on the visuals, she was more into the acting. Maybe that sounds like a good combination, but . . . we argued all the time about what was good and what wasn't. Does that make sense?'

'I can see why you're doing documentaries.'

'Problem is to *stop* them acting.'

He's easy to talk to. I can relate to his passion for what he does, and it's nice hearing about someone else's world for a change.

'It's a constant battle to come up with something new that looks like something that's worked before,' he says. 'And I'm a straight white man.'

'You're telling me that's a problem?'

'I appreciate the advantages. But the funding bodies are looking for something else. I've had to promise that I'll find some foster families or kids that are from marginalised communities.'

'Do people with mental health problems count?'

Jason smiles and shakes his head. 'Sorry, race and gender diversity are what they're looking for. They don't see mentally ill people as a marginalised community in the same way. Do you?'

I do, and we have an intelligent conversation about it. I start to tell him about my dilemma with Capeka, and end up having to explain schizophrenia – should have expected that. But it's a good night.

We share an Uber. I don't invite him in, but as I'm getting out I almost change my mind – and I kiss him goodnight.

—

When I walk through the door, Jess is immediately after the details and isn't easily fobbed off. Except I'm distracted – Simon has replied to my message.

Hannah, you're a doctor! I can't believe it's been thirteen years! Lots happened. We have to have coffee. Or if it works for you, dinner. I'm in Melbourne.

I realise I'm holding my breath as I read. I let it out slowly. It's hard to get a handle on what my feelings are. Time hasn't sorted them out, probably because I've worked at burying them – and everything around them. There's still the original attraction from the first time I saw him, when teenage hormones were leading me into uncharted territory. But then there's Aaron's death, which has surely distorted my memory of Simon, just as it's affected my response to patients at risk of suicide.

I start to write a reply. Delete it.

Jess is sitting on the sofa with her laptop, legs tucked under her, still waiting. She gets up and comes over. 'I get it now. Really bad date.'

'Why do you say that?'

'You're back on the app.'

'What?'

'You *look* like you're on a dating app.'

I click on Simon's profile, and show her. It takes her a few seconds to recognise him.

'Shit. He messaged you? No, you messaged him first. I'm right, aren't I? You were asking me about him.'

'Just curious. Wanted to know what happened to him. Now I know. He's doing okay.'

'He looks like a real-estate agent.' It's not a compliment. 'Promise me you won't date him.'

'Hey. Slow down.'

'Show me the message.'

'No. You're being intrusive.'

'I'm trying to stop you doing something really wrong. Might even be illegal. He's basically your brother.'

'Jess, you're being ridiculous. He was a foster kid.'

'Right. Your foster brother.'

'Whatever you want to call him, it was for about three months. I didn't grow up with him.'

Jess shakes her head. 'We come from the country. That's what people think we do. You're not helping.'

'Stop. I'm not going to sleep with him. I'm not even going to date him. Okay?'

I pick up my laptop from the dining table and go to my room. From no man in my life to three . . . No, Simon is *not* a date. I need his help to pick through my childhood memories, nothing more. And I shouldn't be counting Alex.

I could do dinner. Friday next week?

Simon's response is immediate: *Great. Pick you up at 7:30?*

I'm about to give him my address when something stops me. Am I being paranoid? Rationally, probably yes; instinctively, no.

I'll be at work. Meet you outside the Menzies Hospital main entrance.

Looking forward to it. He's added a heart emoji.

My stomach flips. I'm not sure it's in a good way.

—

Next morning, I wake to a sad-panda emoji from Brianna. I respond with a flexed bicep. More than a week before I see her again. Will she last until then? I picture her telling Maddy, Maddy telling the teachers and next thing her father's there and all hell is breaking loose.

Brianna might be smart, but she's fifteen and hurting – and confused by the clash between the values she was raised with and what she wants to do. With stakes that could be life-changing.

Meanwhile, I've got a patient who *wants* a baby.

The IVF clinic hasn't returned my call. I call again on my walk to the Stables, and push till they look up Capeka.

'She's Dr Barker's patient. Is that who you're after?'

'I don't know. Who's in charge?'

Dr Barker. Who isn't in yet. After I get to work, I call back every half-hour and get him on the third try.

'I'm a psych reg at the Menzies clinic,' I start. 'It's about Capeka Dulka's mental health. I don't think she should have the implant that's due this week.'

'I'm busy,' says Dr Barker. 'Speak to my registrar.'

He hangs up. I can't believe it.

I ring the clinic back. 'Who's Dr Barker's registrar?'

'Dr Stockwell.'

'Bryce Stockwell?'

'Yes.'

'Put me through to him, please.' Bryce and I went through medicine together; he was one of the boys' club. A shrinking club, because it was never just a boys' club, but a white-boys-who-went-to-private-schools-or-wish-they-had club, and a big proportion of today's medical students are Asian, for a start.

Registrars used not to be placed in private practice, but there aren't enough public positions and plenty of private providers who can use some extra bodies. 'Hannah? How are you?' He sounds like he's talking to a slightly slow country cousin.

'I'm fine. Calling about a patient: Capeka Dulka.'

'She's booked in tomorrow morning. Is there a problem?'

'She's already had two children removed. Her mother can't manage another. Her husband isn't capable of caring for a child either.'

'And your involvement?'

'I'm part of her psych team. She has chronic schizophrenia.'

'Does she have a guardian?'

'No.'

'Does she have the money to pay for the treatment without starving?'

'Well, yes, but it's her husband's accident payout.'

'And their prerogative as to how they use it.'

'What about her medication and potential effects on the foetus? Do you have a perinatal psychiatrist looking after her pregnancy?'

'She's been fully informed and made her choices.'

My, ex, Marcus, was a trainee obstetrician. I shouldn't be surprised by the narrow-minded, uninformed disregard for psychological issues and consequences.

'So,' I say, 'you're going to implant another embryo, bring another baby into the world, even though these parents will have to endure having another child removed, even though the grandmother has said it will kill her? What about the child?'

'And what about anti-discrimination law? We do what our patients ask us to do. We inform them as well as we can, their GPs are involved, and I'm sure they do their own research.'

'And of course they pay you.'

'Listen, Hannah, if Mrs Dulka didn't need help to get pregnant, we wouldn't be having this discussion. I imagine where you grew up you knew quite a few girls who brought babies into less than ideal circumstances, without IVF.'

I take a breath. 'You're right. I imagine when you were growing up, you didn't know many girls at all.'

'Ooh, cutting.'

'Not really. If I was trying to be cutting, I'd ask why you chose a job where you have a chance to get women pregnant.'

—

I run into Alex making instant coffee in the registrars' room. Our work locations in the Menzies Mental Health Service change with our rotations every six months, but this small space with its chairs, fridge and kettle is a haven of stability and community.

I'm expecting him to ask about my date, but he doesn't, so I tell him about the call with Bryce. He loves my jibe about IVF work as a substitute for sex: you probably have to be a Freudian to appreciate it.

Then I tell him about Brianna.

He nods slowly. 'What happened in your life that's affecting your feelings for Brianna – your countertransference? And I'm not talking about the kid who suicided.' And, when I don't answer: 'I'm not expecting you to tell me. But you need to find yourself a therapist before you do much more of this.'

'Thanks, Professor Ashwood. I've been trying.' I tell him about Joan Drinkwater, the elderly therapist.

'She'd probably be a good choice if you were looking at long-term analysis.'

He sees my expression – Joan may not be the best choice for anything long-term – and we both laugh.

'I still haven't got an excuse to give Prof about why I didn't see his buddy Isaac Sandler,' I say. 'You were going to come up with one, remember?'

'Remembered and done. Conflict of interest. Tell him – imply to him – that a family member is already seeing Isaac. The subtext is that Prof has a conflict of interest in recommending him. He'll pick that up, but won't think you've done it deliberately. Or if he does, he'll be impressed with your subtlety.'

'*Your* subtlety. Since it was your idea.'

I am sort of impressed. But the family member seeing a psychotherapist? I try to picture my mother or Mel in therapy. Or Lennon, with whatever's behind his drinking problem. He could use it. They could all use it.

—

Professor Sandra Byrd, head of the Mother Baby Unit, and the Service's most flamboyant dresser since Carey retired the all-red outfits, is in a canary-yellow pantsuit with Joan Miró paintings across the front and back of the jacket. Jon's with her in her office; I'd forgotten how closely the registrars shadow their consultants on the wards.

She remembers Capeka. 'Not one of our success stories. The issue with chronic schizophrenia and parenting is the gap between what the infant needs and what the parent is capable of providing.'

'And it was a big gap with Capeka?'

'It was. We had the husband – Jozef? – in too. He's unable to pick up a baby safely. He made the bottles, but . . . Capeka doesn't appear to have much motivation or insight.'

'But surely losing her children would be traumatic.'

'When we have to separate mothers and babies, which isn't often, it's women with personality disorders who scream blue murder, not so much the women with chronic schizophrenia. Doesn't mean they don't feel it. But some of them are relieved because the effort to care for a baby is overwhelming.'

'So, what happened with her children?' asks Jon.

'Because of Jozef's disability package, they had around-the-clock support,' says Sandra. 'But it wasn't sustainable.'

'When did Capeka's mother get involved?' I ask.

'Her mother was there from the start. We recommended she have the child two days a week . . . we felt the grandmother was always going to be an important part of the child's life. Child Protection went for Grandma having primary custody after a couple of night shifts couldn't be filled, and Capeka and Jozef essentially failed their parenting assessment.'

'So how did a second child happen?'

'They went straight to IVF again,' says Sandra.

'Did the IVF clinic talk to you?' Jon asks her.

'No. Child Protection was informed eventually, and as soon as Capeka delivered she was back here.'

'And there had been no change in her capacity?' says Jon.

Sandra shakes her head. 'Worse. We observed her with the two-year-old.'

'So she never had the second child at home?' I ask.

Sandra nods.

'And now she's about to have another IVF implant. Could we get a guardian appointed to make the decision?'

'No. She's able to make her own decisions.' She's sounding like Bryce from the IVF clinic.

'Isn't anyone thinking of the consequences for the *baby*? Of the burden of care on Capeka's mother?'

Sandra takes a moment, then smiles at both Jon and me. 'When I was a trainee, I was totally focused on passing the exams, learning what I needed to know. And looking after patients, of course. I wouldn't have dreamed of arguing with a consultant or . . . redecorating a clinic.' She pauses. 'I think it's a change for the better, and I appreciate your concern in this case, but is this the hill you want to die on?'

Jon's been surprisingly quiet, given he's made it clear to us that he has an issue with the separation of mothers and babies. We've all assumed it's to do with the Stolen Generation but only Jess has actually asked. 'His mother,' was her summary.

When Sandra's gone, I say to him, 'Am I wrong in thinking this is . . .'

'. . . fucked up? It's not good, but I've seen heaps worse. At home it's white people fixing Black people's problems that the white people largely caused in the first place. In here, race isn't always the issue but you've still got culture, social class and education. It's not just separating mothers and babies. It's the bigger issue of people in power thinking they know what's best for others.'

—

Friday, Brianna's pregnancy test comes back positive, and I let her know – not sure if she's left for camp yet. She sends a pile of poo emoji.

I text back: *Is that how you're feeling about camp or do you have diarrhoea?*

She sends back: *Gross*. Then *lol.*

Next day it's an angry face; and *Told Maddy*. Her friend.

I spend the weekend wondering about Maddy and her mother, Naomi. I figure they're on Brianna's side so them knowing would be a positive. Most likely. But it distracts me enough during the parkrun that I forget to pick up my finish token and miss out on a time.

Ndidi isn't there; she's texted: *Fertility drugs didn't work. Not up to running. Hormone wave or just life being shit?*

I send her hugs. She'll accept them in a text message.

—

On Monday I update Nash on Capeka Dulka. I've reached some sort of acceptance from a combination of what Jon said, Sandra's advice to pick my battles and, begrudgingly, Bryce's *If she didn't need help to get pregnant, we wouldn't be having this discussion.* But I'm still convinced Capeka shouldn't be getting IVF.

'Something to learn early,' says Nash, when we discuss the case in supervision. 'Psychiatry is about sitting with things that are far from perfect. Our patients have often done that all their lives, long before the onset of mental illness. We are their role models. We do the best we can. But we're not going to win every battle.'

He smiles. 'You only had to give Mrs Dulka her meds.'

FIVE

CONFABULATION

The younger of the two men at the bar table is laughing. 'Bloody hell, mate, you had me until right at the end.'

'It's all true. Every word of it,' says the older guy.

He's in his sixties and looks exactly like the high-school history teacher he is, down to the checked jacket with the patches on the elbows. They've had a few drinks, but his expression is sober and straight-faced.

His colleague laughs again. 'Come on. You did a great job pulling me in. But give me a break. I'm not that gullible.'

'I told you, it all happened. You know that. You're only surprised it happened to someone you know.'

'Okay, okay, you've got me. Not believing you, but starting to wonder if you believe it yourself. So, better say you don't, or I'm going to have to get you to talk to someone.'

Ian Wilson is the oldest patient I've seen to date: sixty-four. Older patients – or at least those with age-related illness – would generally go to a specialist psychogeriatric clinic.

Skimming the referral, I'm not sure how he got in to see us. No past history in public mental health, according to the system. And his GP doesn't seem too worried. But Mia tells me that Ian's friend phoned with a compelling argument: *We don't want unsafe schoolteachers out there.*

The friend is in the waiting room with Ian. I guess he's early fifties and he looks like . . . a schoolteacher.

'Scott Glover,' he says, shaking my hand, holding on to it for dear life. 'Thanks so much for seeing Ian.' He flashes a look at the older man. 'We work together, private school. Ian doesn't really want to be here. I came here seven or eight years ago, not for myself, but . . .'

The mental health system is a mystery to most people, and Scott has taken the entry point he knows.

'Is the lady with the big brown eyes still working here?' he asks.

I feel safe saying, 'Probably not.' There's a lot of turnover in one year, let alone seven or eight.

Ian is standing a little apart from us. He gives me a grin. Casual but neat; looks after himself. Blue eyes that really fix on you.

'Ian's a great history teacher,' says Scott. 'One of the best.' He lowers his voice. 'I'm a bit worried he's starting to believe some of his own tales.'

'How about I see Ian,' I say. 'I'll call you in if I need some clarification.'

Scott gives me a theatrical wink. 'I'll wait.'

I take Ian into my office and prepare to hear something delusional. I'm already considering diagnoses.

If I'm to get through patients with the speed that Nash expects, I have to narrow the questions. Starting with the most likely diagnosis is a good strategy. With no past history, my go-to for 'making up stories' is an organic – biological – cause: brain tumour, primary or secondary to a cancer elsewhere; some neurological disorder; dementia.

My next option is delusional disorder. More common in older people. Schizophrenia tends to appear early. Bipolar should also have declared itself by now. Or maybe he's just got a dose of narcissism and relevance deprivation syndrome. My job: work it out in fifty minutes and write it up in ten.

It takes me only five to establish that I'm going to need the whole hour and maybe the next. I can't work out if he's got pressure of speech (suggests bipolar or organic cause) or if he just likes the sound of his own voice (suggests narcissism). And my attempts to cut him off are being sabotaged by the fact that I'm finding him fascinating.

'The thing is,' says Ian, looking relaxed in the chair opposite me, 'I might have been a bit indiscreet over a bottle of red, but I've said nothing that matters this late in the piece.' He nods to the computer I'm typing into. 'Happy for you to put a summary in there, but I need you to keep mum about the specifics. As your profession requires.'

As long as he's not planning to harm somebody, including himself.

'How much do you want to know?' he says.

'Maybe start with what worried your friend.'

Ian laughs. 'It's a long story. Don't write down the details, no recording, and then I can tell you what I couldn't tell Scott, help you see that what seems fantastic to him is actually true. And, to reiterate, strictly confidential.'

'Okay,' I say slowly. I've stopped typing.

'Firstly – and Scott doesn't know this – my name isn't Ian Wilson. Growing up, I was called Grisha. You don't need to know the full name. Later I was Greg Solway.'

Grisha? Can I picture Ian as Eastern European? Maybe.

'Grew up in Russia – the USSR – in the sixties and it was a bloody miserable place. My mother worked for the ballet. Not a dancer, a seamstress.'

He proceeds to tell me what it was like backstage at the Kirov Ballet as a young boy; the dancers he met, including Mikhail Baryshnikov and Rudolf Nureyev – 'after he defected'. He spins a good yarn – I almost feel I'm there watching Baryshnikov dance 'the most emotional Albrecht in *Giselle* the world has ever seen'.

I check my watch and Ian takes it as a cue to speak faster.

'My mother and I got out. Long story, but the ballet returned home without us and the Russians didn't care as much about us as the dancers. We had distant family in Brisbane and the Australian government was more welcoming back then.'

I can tell he wants to tell me about the defection and I'd like to hear it, but I pull him back on track. 'And this worried Scott?'

'No, no, I think he's happy to humour me on this one. So, I finish school here, lose the accent. Change my name. Get a job in the public service.' He winks at me. 'This is where it gets murky, but let's say I was very welcome. I speak French, Chinese and Russian. And I chose to leave Russia and live in this country, or at least my mother did.'

'You were a spy?' I say.

'We were called diplomats. When things turned ugly, I was still a junior one, but officially a diplomat.'

'And what did ugly look like?'

'I was, to use the modern vernacular, sprung. There's books on it. Even a movie. Having the Russians unhappy with you makes life interesting.'

I can see why Scott thought Ian was a little over the top. But this sort of thing did happen. Just not to people in my world.

'But this is all in the past, right?' I say.

'It was, until ASIO started bugging the house.'

'Why?'

'I went into hiding, obviously,' says Ian. 'Been Ian Wilson longer than I was Grisha or Greg. But there are Russian sleeper agents I know the names of.'

'Surely you divulged those to our . . . um . . . intel years ago?'

'Of course. But people have started talking over the years, and, as it happens, I was talking to the Russians too.'

'A double agent?'

'You build trust. Sometimes you have to cross the line. ASIO took a long time to work it out. But I read the news. You see who's been arrested, who's defected. They know. Nobody likes to be made a fool of.'

He's right about that. I've stopped trying to follow the details.

'So, is the bugging worrying you? What do you think they'll do?'

'Not particularly, though it's tempting to give them some false leads.' He sighs. 'It bothers my wife though.'

'She believes you're being monitored?'

'Of course. She knows everything. If you don't believe me, I'm happy to bring her in.'

Might be a good idea.

'So, what's Scott worried about – other than you telling a few tall tales?'

Ian laughs. 'Man's led a limited life. And, to be fair, he doesn't have the background information I've given you. In strict confidence.'

I pull my thoughts together and do a quick screen of other possible symptoms. None, other than an affinity for alcohol, which is sufficient to earn him an alcohol abuse disorder diagnosis. It also increases his risk of early dementia.

I run him through a mini mental state examination. He gets full points on the language questions, does okay spelling *world* backward, and makes a single mistake counting backward in sevens. He easily registers three items: *apple, table, happiness*. But he can't remember them three minutes later. His score is high enough to avoid a diagnosis of significant cognitive impairment, but I doubt he'd qualify for spy school.

'I'll get my consultant to see you before you go, and maybe some tests and an appointment with your wife,' I say. 'We may not find anything. I'll let Scott know the plan, okay?'

'As long as you don't tell anyone my former name.' Ian smiles. 'Okay?'

I nod and leave him in my office, where Nash will want to see him. But Mia tells me he's been called away and will have to catch Ian at his next appointment.

I find Scott in animated conversation with Jan. The woman with the big brown eyes. I guess that's one way of describing her.

'Is he okay?' Scott asks me.

'I can't say yet. We need to do some follow-up. I'm wondering if you can clarify what you were worried about.'

'He's told you his story? Look, sorry, but he swore me to secrecy. He's para— Sorry, I don't mean technically paranoid, that's for you to judge. But I can't . . .'

'He told me about the Cold War and changing his name.'

I feel Scott's relief. 'Right. He thinks he's a spy, for chrissake. And that ASIO . . . well, you've heard the story.'

'Has he said or done anything else odd?'

'No, he's a respected teacher. An excellent teacher. French as well as history. A few weeks ago we had a night for grandparents, and there's a Russian couple and I catch him chatting with them. They tell me his Russian's excellent. I had no idea, and I ask where he learned it and why he doesn't teach it. He says something like "loose lips sink ships". Then he takes me out and tells me this story.'

'I guess I'm wondering why you're so concerned? If he's just full of himself . . .'

'He works with children. If he's mentally ill, we need to know.'

I have to ask. 'You've heard the story in detail. No chance it's true? I mean, he speaks Russian . . .'

He laughs. 'I hope you're kidding me. No way.'

I assure Scott we'll make sure Ian's safe and get his mobile number.

I return to Ian, hand him a form for his blood tests and CT scan, and ask him to come back with his wife in two days. He's fine about it: medical workup's always a good idea and together we can set Scott's mind at ease.

I can't resist googling Greg Solway. I'm still thinking delusional, but I have to eliminate the possibility that he's telling the truth.

The internet lights up. A book called *Loose Lips* and a documentary of the same name. A Wikipedia entry. Newspaper articles from the eighties. Defector turned embassy employee turned spy turned fugitive. As per the story.

Question is, has Ian Wilson taken on this man's identity as his delusion? If so, it's the most elaborate delusion I've ever seen. On the other hand, my experience with delusions is in the context of schizophrenia. I've never dealt with a pure delusional disorder.

I do an image search. Most of the photos are of the same person; a few are of politicians talking about him. I get one that is clearly labelled *Greg Solway*. Younger, thinner. But no doubt. It's Ian Wilson.

—

DJ Voices and Frodo have been waiting to see me.

'No change,' says Frodo before we even get to my room.

We sit down and I look at DJ. 'Legs?'

She pulls up her tracksuit bottoms. Huge calves, the skin so stretched that it seems the fluid could be leaking out of them. Looks like she's still sleeping upright.

'They gave me stockings to wear but I figured you'd want to see my legs without them,' she says.

'Do you wear them most of the time?'

She shrugs.

'DJ, do you understand you might struggle to walk soon?'

She doesn't look fussed. 'Get distracted. Music is all I care about. I've been doing this really neat thing with delays and reverbs.'

Frodo is nodding enthusiastically. 'It's awesome,' he says. 'She's had a million hits on her online demo.'

That does sound awesome. Her physical state is not.

I take them through an average day. When DJ isn't performing, she's in the basement; Frodo delivers her meals down there. I've realised that the strange bit of furniture I saw there must be the sex wedge, so she doesn't even have to go upstairs for that. Maybe she takes a shower after, but her music seems to be all-consuming. It's amazing she doesn't have vitamin D deficiency from lack of sunlight.

Actually, she probably does. I add it to the list of tests I'll order. I need to check this swelling isn't destabilising her blood chemistry.

'Let's try this,' I say. 'Frodo, when you deliver food, find a stool. And DJ, put your feet on the stool while you eat. Can you do that?'

DJ shrugs again. I'm hoping she doesn't have some delusion about keeping her feet on the floor.

'I'll see if the Mobile Support Team can visit,' I say. 'And while they are there – a break from music and legs up.'

DJ is less enthusiastic about this. When I speak to the mobile team, they're similarly doubtful, but prepared to give it a try.

Keith seems to be reviewing her file – he's added a note: *Has anyone done a drug screen?*

—

Between appointments, a call with an unfamiliar number comes up. It's Naomi Disch, Brianna's friend's mother.

'You know Brianna is pregnant?' she says.

'Yes,' I say.

'What are you doing about it?'

'I can't really talk about confidential –'

'It's not very confidential if I know about it, is it?'

'Brianna wanted the week to think. She has another appointment after she's back from camp.'

'I presume her parents don't know? Her father's a religious nutter. He threatened me with the police.'

'I've met him.'

'You'll help her get a termination? If not, I will.'

'I'll help her do what she wants,' I say.

'She's fifteen. She doesn't have a clue what she wants. This idea that you have to go through hoops to get an abortion – it should be the other way around. It should be really hard for a fifteen-year-old to be allowed to have a baby.'

'If she does want a termination . . . she'll need someone to take her to the appointment.'

'That will be me,' says Naomi. 'I'm telling you, I don't believe in hell, but David Young . . .'

Naomi's call reminds me that Daniela Popa hasn't replied to my email. I call and persuade the ward clerk to put me through.

'You're telling me she got pregnant?' Dr Popa says, repeating what I've just told her and what was in my apparently unread email. I bring her up to date.

'I'd like her to tell her parents at some stage,' I say. 'But I can't do it alone.'

'Appropriate judgement. For a moment I was thinking we had another cowboy trainee.'

Another. Ouch.

'Elena has been holding my hand all the way,' I say. 'But . . . I wasn't really prepared for this.'

There's a pause. 'Without the tough cases, you don't learn.'

But no offer to actually help.

—

On Wednesday, Taylah shows up on time, all boobs and make-up in leggings and a tight top. We thread our way through to my office and she gets straight to the point.

'I can go to Short Stay in a week, right?'

'It's what we agreed.'

'Good, because I need a break.'

She's sounding assertive, confident – not like someone I'd admit under normal circumstances.

'Has something in particular happened?'

Taylah is silent.

'Grace mentioned you'd been cutting.'

The bravado is gone, just like that. 'Ivan . . . you know who Ivan is?'

'Your mother's boyfriend?'

Taylah nods and I can see I've scored a point with her. *Someone listened.*

'Yeah. Well, he's basically living with us now. I mean, he's got his own place, I think, but he's at ours just about every night, too pissed to drive home. Anyway, Mum goes out to get some smokes, and he comes and sits next to me, puts his arm around me.'

'How did that make you feel?' I ask.

The question is straight out of the interpersonal therapy playbook, and probably deserves a *How would YOU feel if your mother's boyfriend sexually assaulted you?* But Taylah is all about feelings and gives me a straight answer.

'Gross. He's old and fat and . . . I really hate him.'

She's shrunk back into the chair, more child than young adult, and is blinking back tears – demonstrating the flipping between emotional extremes that's at the core of borderline personality disorder. I wait, thinking about how I'd feel if I was in her shoes, and my feelings must be written on my face, because there's a moment of connection, a sense of an unguarded space opening up between us.

And into that space, Taylah puts four words: 'Ivan's not the first.'

Now I'm torn. My plan was to help her work on her current situation: her relationships with Ivan, her sister and particularly her mother. Supportive psychotherapy. That's what Elena would do, and what the staff in Short Stay will have done – at best. Along with any therapists she's seen, because government rebates run out after twelve sessions, which isn't enough time to look at and deal with the past traumas that may have led to the present problems.

The exception to the twelve-week session rule is psychiatrists. We're rebated for fifty a year. So, weirdly, even as we're supposedly moving away from the talking therapies, we've become the owners of the long-term psychotherapies, and have to see a patient for forty sessions as part of our qualification.

All of which is to say: I'm probably the only chance Taylah has to do a form of therapy that looks hard at what happened in her past. Except . . . it may not be effective. Borderline personality disorder is famously difficult to treat, and I'm a first-timer, with a biologically minded psychiatrist as supervisor. I don't know what we'd uncover, and if it would make her worse. *A patient for life*, said Nash. I really should bail.

'Tell me what happened before Ivan,' I say, and she nods then pauses for a while before starting.

Father left when she was two. Seen him a few times in recent years, lived with him briefly. He's up north with another partner and their own children.

And her mum, Kelly?

'Mum's never had much time for us. It was okay when we were looking cute or doing something for her. I won a beauty contest when I was six – she said I was taking after her. Weird I remember that.'

There were times when her mum was scary and locked her in the pantry and made her miss meals. Taylah was too afraid to eat the food in the pantry. There'd also been good times singing together, with Kelly playing guitar.

I suggest that part of continuing to be at home with Kelly is trying to recapture some moments like that, but it doesn't land.

'Mum's only interested in her fucking boyfriend.'

That, I suspect, is the heart of both Taylah's current problem and her past trauma. And I'm way out of my depth.

—

I raise Taylah at my next supervision session with Nash. And, no surprise I guess, he has a biological suggestion.

'There's some research linking borderline personality with autism spectrum disorder and ADHD. Mainly about misdiagnosis, especially in women. If you have someone diagnosed as borderline when in fact it's ADHD . . .'

I finish the thought for him. 'You want me to prescribe dexamphetamine for Taylah?'

I don't think I've done a good job of hiding my incredulity and he laughs.

'I don't think Taylah has ADHD. And I'm not encouraging you to send her home with Ritalin. Just keeping you up to date with what we can do with medication.'

Except that's not where I need help.

'Given we've agreed that's not going to work for Taylah,' I say, 'I'm thinking . . . You said that she's in our territory, not the psychologists', but then the best practice treatments are all psychological therapies . . .'

'From what you've told me, I think you're doing well with her. Probably better than she's had before.'

'You mean what she's had from other psych trainees. Who know hardly anything.' I'm getting agitated, and thinking of Sandra Byrd's gentle reprimand about rocking the boat. But this has been on my mind and matters to me. 'I'd just like to see more attention to psychotherapy in the training program.'

Nash smiles. 'I'll put it on my list. Now that I don't have to worry about making the clinic autism-friendly.'

—

Last appointment on Thursday is Ian Wilson. His CT scan has shown some age-related changes, compatible with early dementia or just plain ageing. Bloods are normal apart from some liver-function results which fit with his alcohol intake. The memory clinic hasn't seen him yet.

Time for a second opinion, and I've lined up Nash. I give him a summary beforehand, including the book and movie, but without revealing the real name. I finish with: 'It seems he's telling the truth, and maybe an early dementia is leading him to be a little less . . . well, less . . .'

'Spy-like?' I have a feeling Nash is on the edge of laughing.

'Well, less discreet at least.'

Beside Ian in the waiting room is a woman who I'm guessing is ethnically Chinese. His wife, Ling. I haven't asked anything about her. Is she a spy too?

Nash introduces himself and leads the way to his office.

Ling stares at us through large round glasses. Ian works his charm. Nash pulls him back to the ASIO bugs.

'They're in the television, and they're damn good ones,' Ian says.

'Have you thought of getting a new TV?' asks Nash.

Ian shakes his head. 'They'd know I was onto them. Better to be playing them.'

'So,' says Nash, 'if they're so good, how were you able to find them? Not meaning to be rude, but you've been out of the business a while by your account.'

'Training,' says Ian. 'You don't forget.'

'Fair enough,' says Nash. 'But how do you know they are there? What alerted you?'

'The light,' says Ian.

'Can you explain what you mean by "the light"?'

'Red glow at the bottom of the air conditioner. It's flashing, but not at a regular rate. Shows it's picking up the signal. Thought it was connecting with the radio but when I moved that, it kept going.'

Okay . . .

'Have you tried moving the TV?' Nash asks.

'No point. They're smart enough to have a backup. In the ceiling. I can feel the waves.' He taps his head.

Nash turns to Ling. 'What are your thoughts about all this?'

'Ian knows about these things,' she says.

'Have you actually seen one of these bugs?'

'Governments are too smart for that,' she says, nodding. 'I worry more than him about what will happen next. What will they do to us?'

'People do disappear,' adds Ian, without apparent concern.

Nash wraps it up, asks him to return when we have all the test results back.

When they're gone, he turns to me. 'Now what do you think?'

I let out a sigh. 'Delusional disorder.' I point out in my defence that he had a solid basis of fact to become delusional about.

'And Ling?'

'Folie à deux.' Meaning she is delusional too, and if we were able to separate them, the level of her conviction would fade.

'I don't think he'll take medication,' I say.

'And it's often not very effective, particularly if there are signs of his brain ageing, which is probably why he's got delusional disorder at this time.'

'So what do we do?'

'Try and get him through to retirement without making a fool of himself at school.'

'You think that's the only risk?' I say.

'Nothing's certain in this world – beyond the fact that humans can't sense radio waves – but delusional disorder tends to be quite focused. I can't see any way that thinking he's being monitored will translate into inappropriate behaviour with students – beyond talking about it.'

'Not sure how we break the news to him, and whether he'll let me talk to Scott about it.'

Nash just smiles. It seems that's my job.

—

Friday is crazy-busy. The CATT team wants me to see someone on their registrar's afternoon off and one of the clinic's long-termers has been thrown out of their accommodation and is camping with their stuff in our waiting room. Right on 5 pm, I leave him to Jan and run home. I have to change and return to the hospital for Simon – Foster Kid Fifty-Two turned financial wizard – to pick me up.

I'm glad Jess isn't home. I walk back to work, because I don't want to be out of breath and I'm in heels, which I haven't worn for a while. On the way to a meeting with my past. Doing what I'm asking Taylah to do.

When I get to the hospital, Simon's already there. There's a black Porsche in the no-parking zone and a lean guy standing beside it, talking on his phone. He sees me approaching and ends the call.

'Wow,' he says. 'You grew up.'

'You did too.' He looks older than twenty-eight. I feel a shiver go through me. Shit. And my heels are clearly some subconscious desire to please him.

I nod at the car. 'I remember you wanted one.'

'You'll be pleased to know this one was paid for.'

He's stylishly dressed, and a lot taller than me even with the heels. It's his eyes – on me – that I find unnerving. *Wolf*, I think, but then shake my head. Too much baggage clouding my judgement.

He opens the passenger-side door. As I'm about to slip into the front seat, Ndidi and Alex come out of the hospital. Alex spots us, and there's a flash of . . . at the very least *not happy*, before he shuts it down.

Ndidi catches my eye, mouths something that might be 'hot' and gives me a thumbs up.

'I hope that was your best friend giving me the seal of approval,' says Simon as he powers out of the driveway to get in front of a bus, earning a long horn blast.

'I think she was giving it to me, not you.'

Simon raises his eyebrows. 'You'll think I'm sexist if I agree with her, right?'

'That's far more self-aware than I was expecting.'

'Come on, I was fifteen when you last saw me. Give me a break.'

I realise how much on the defensive I am. *I am not fifteen now.* I take a breath, tell myself to chill. 'Sorry. It wasn't under the best circumstances that you left.'

'Or arrived. Being in foster care was not a high point in my life.'

'Or juvey, I imagine.'

'Actually, that was the best thing that could have happened to me.'

We accelerate through an orange light. He's relaxed, happy in his own skin. At fifteen, he was trying to achieve the same effect and it hadn't quite worked. But now he's filled in the holes that fifteen-year-old Simon Trevallyan couldn't, and I have to give him credit for that.

'Tell me about it,' I say.

Simon laughs. 'You're sounding like a shrink. I will, as long as you promise to tell me all about yourself.'

In the end we do talk a lot about our lives. He's a good listener and seems genuinely interested. He's booked dinner at a restaurant that's way too formal for me, but then asks if we can have a table in the bar.

'Trying too hard,' he says as we sit down. 'I'm sure you can work out why. Call me out if you catch me doing it.'

'Well,' I say, 'there's the car.'

'Goes with the territory. If you're going to give financial advice, you better look like you're doing okay yourself.'

'And you are?'

'I am. But I wouldn't tell you if I wasn't.'

The food is great, and Simon is best friends with our server by the second course.

'Juvey was a wake-up call,' he tells me. 'Some nasty people there – staff included. I decided I didn't want to spend my life in that world.'

'I don't remember much about your family. How you came to be with us.'

Simon leans right back, then forward again. 'My dad died. Then my mother . . . This guy, Paul . . . Can't blame her for moving on, but . . .' I see a tenseness in his jaw that may have been there all evening. 'Paul was an arsehole. And I started drinking. Drugs. Paul and Mum didn't handle it well.' He takes a sip of wine. 'I ended up with you and your family. They helped a lot.'

'What happened to your father?'

'Climbing accident. Annapurna. Snow blindness. Horrible way to go.'

'Shit.'

Simon pours me more wine. 'It was a long time ago.'

I read this as code for *It's still too hard to talk about.*

'So what did you do after juvey?'

'Went back to school and did a commerce degree.' He pauses, and I sense he's thinking *She's a doctor.* 'Then a master's. There was a merchant bank that looked out for the top students. Worked with them for a bit, then set out on my own. As I said, so far, so good.'

'Congratulations,' I say. 'Wife, kids?'

'Interested?' he says flippantly. 'Lots of girlfriends, but still waiting to meet the One. Someone I can talk to on the same level.'

He asks me about my job, but doesn't pepper me with the usual questions about mental health that laypeople ask. He's interested in the issues and my feelings and I find myself sharing more than I have with anyone outside my study group for quite a while. I barely notice what we're eating or drinking. When he smiles, he looks like he can see right into my inner thoughts. He did it back then too.

We've finished dessert before I ask *my* question. 'What happened with Aaron?'

Simon doesn't react beyond a faint crinkle in his forehead. 'You know more than I do.'

'I found him. Doesn't mean I know what led up – what happened before.'

Simon leans forward. 'Nothing we could have done would have made any difference. He was a mess.'

'He was just a kid,' I say. 'He . . . looked up to you.'

'I was fifteen,' says Simon. 'You too. I shouldn't have been drinking. Shouldn't have let him have any. But I was barely able to look after myself, let alone him.'

He's right. We were all kids. I'm looking for answers where there's no question.

'Sorry, it just haunts me,' I say. 'He didn't . . . he didn't say anything to you, before he went out and found the tree?'

As he sits there with his elbows on the table, there's a stillness about him which reminds me of someone or something. A lion about to pounce? No, it's something else, and the wine isn't helping me make sense of my feelings and fragments of memory.

He looks hard at me, then shakes his head. 'That's the part you're thinking about and not . . . after?' He smiles for a moment, and then he's serious again. 'It's still eating you up, isn't it? For what it's worth, it shook me up – I guess it still does. You had to be there, didn't you? To understand what it does to you. And what you do. Only you and I know that.'

'You want to talk about it?'

He takes my hand and says, 'We can talk about all of it. Okay? But let's have fun too. You up for that?'

If I don't think too hard, the answer is easy: *Yes.*

If I *do* think: he's smart, funny, ambitious, single. Tenacious, given where he's come from, and I can cut him a little slack for overcompensating with the fast car and flashy restaurant. There's complexity behind it. Interesting and interested. And he's not a doctor.

But in the mix – and no doubt clouding my judgement about everything else – is a big dose of sexual attraction that surely has its roots in our past, which means it comes from a bad place.

So, if I think as a *psychiatrist* . . . If I do hook up with him, get close to him, my past is going to come crashing back into my life. Sooner or later, I've got to deal with it, but that's the point of having a therapist.

I make myself a promise: *You will not have sex with Simon until you've got a therapist.* I smile. I may have been avoiding therapy, but I'm motivated now. Meantime, I need to buy a little space.

'I'm sort of seeing someone,' I say at last.

'I'm sort of seeing a lot of people. So shall we sort of see each other again?'

I laugh. 'In a couple of weeks maybe?'

'Sure. Can I give you a ride home?'

'Thank you, it's been lovely, but I'll Uber.'

Simon insists on paying and says if that worries me, I can pay next time when I choose the place. Sounds good.

In the Uber I see a text from Ndidi: *So, Jason's going to be disappointed?*

I text back: *If he's expecting an exclusive relationship after one date.*

In fact, we've been texting about the documentary and trying to find a time that works for a second date. But I don't need to keep Ndidi in the loop.

Nor Alex, with that look when he saw Simon. What does he expect when he's dating someone else?

—

Ian Wilson comes back to see me first thing Monday morning. Without Ling, but with his colleague Scott, who we leave in the waiting room.

Walking to my office, we pass Jan going the other way with two coffees. I wouldn't have clocked it, but Ian gives me an exaggerated wink. Right.

'So do I have the all-clear?' he asks as we sit down.

The memory clinic thinks there may be early signs of dementia and suggests he cuts out or at least reduces his alcohol.

'The thing is . . .' I begin.

The thing is, Nash, having said that drugs may not do any good, still wants Ian to try an antipsychotic to stop the delusions breaking into his day-to-day life – at work especially. Whether the medication helps or not, it will have a bunch of side effects.

I try an appeal to the big part of Ian that's still rational.

'It looks like your memory might not be as good as it once was. I think the memory clinic suggested you stop drinking?'

'I'll cut down. Ling doesn't drink with me, so she's going to move me on to herbal tea after dinner.'

He leans back in the chair, looks at the ceiling for a bit. I wait.

'You checked me out, didn't you? Checked my story.'

I nod.

'Rightly so. Probably not hard to do these days. And it was all as I told you?'

'As far as I could tell.'

'The filmmakers took some liberties, and I have to admit, I sometimes mix up their story with mine. But . . . you didn't find any holes?'

He's actually asking. Checking.

He looks me in the eye. 'I've lived a big life. I've been to places, met people, done some things that I think were important, at least at the time. Now, all I've got is the memories – that's a great cliché, isn't it? But I thought I'd have those . . . as long as I lived.'

I look at him: sixty-four years old, about the same age as my father. Smart enough to know that something's not right – and what the consequences might be.

'You know, I'm not an expert in memory,' I say. 'But I think those long-term memories are going to stay with you longer than the short-term stuff.'

'Like where I put my keys.' He laughs.

I see an opening. 'And remembering your craft.'

'What do you mean?'

'The memory thing, age, maybe the drinking . . . may have made you a bit too relaxed about telling people things.'

He nods slowly and I push on.

'I mean, would you have told me you were Greg Solway back in the eighties? Even with patient confidentiality?'

This time it's a shake of the head.

'If you're worried about the bugs, you could take a tablet that might make you worry less, but it's really more about not talking about it, isn't it? If you don't mention it to Scott or your students, do you think the government may be less worried too?'

Ian smiles. 'You've got a point. I'd got to the stage where I was thinking it didn't matter anymore, but you're right. If they think I'm worth bugging . . .'

'Do you think you could . . . ?' I mime a zip across my mouth. 'Particularly to protect the boys at the school? Mission . . . um . . . Closed Lips?'

'I don't think I'll need a codename for something I'm not going to communicate about. You can leave the spycraft to me. But the point you make is fair.'

'Maybe you should put it all down on paper,' I say. 'And remember it can't be published until . . . well, the bugging stops.'

Ian frowns, nods. 'So you can tell Scott I'm just getting older but fully sane?'

'You'd like me to talk to him?'

'That's fine, as long as there's no details. Don't tell anyone my real name.' He winks at me. 'I'd have to kill you if you did.'

SIX

STUCK

The man in the bathroom is tall and lean, but trouble is so deeply etched into his face that his age is hard to guess. He's fully dressed, which is a problem because he wants to take a shower. He's going to give it his best shot. One step at a time.

He counts to ten. Looks to each corner of the room in turn. Counts to ten again. Removes his watch. Repeats the count, then looks again to the corner of the room, does the count again and peels off his jumper.

This is going to take a while.

Taylah is on time for her appointment – again. And it's apparent that she's done some thinking in the past week.

'Remember I told you that Ivan wasn't the first – like not the first time one of Mum's boyfriends has hit on me?'

I remember. And I've done some thinking too, aided by some reading and, surprisingly, Nash. 'See borderline personality disorder, think childhood abuse,' he said. 'Not necessarily sexual abuse; not *necessarily* any abuse. But you've met the family.'

Taylah waits for me to ask.

'Do you want to tell me about the first?'

She snorts. 'Why just the first? Just about every boyfriend my mother's had has tried it. She hates that I'm hotter than her.'

'So she knows?'

'Pretends she doesn't.'

'Maybe start wherever makes sense to you.'

'Jimmy. He lived with us for years. So he was like our stepfather.'

'How old were you?'

'Eight.' She takes a breath. 'I was thirteen when I went to live with my dad. I didn't go back till Jimmy and Mum had split up.'

'Did you ever try to talk to her about it?'

Taylah shakes her head. 'Back then, no. Don't know why, not really.'

Probably because Kelly didn't want to hear – or couldn't deal with it. And however angry Taylah is at her mother, she is stuck, still hoping for unconditional love she never had.

Taylah works it out for herself. 'I was trying to protect her, I think. Or maybe myself.'

I stay quiet, and there's a stillness around Taylah now.

'I tried to protect Aleesha too. Got her to hide under the bed. And . . . yeah.' Whether I want her to go there or not, the floodgates have opened. 'He used to sit me on his lap to watch television. I thought it was special, because I got to stay up late and eat chocolate.'

Taylah and Foster Kid Twenty, the cocker spaniel turned Doberman, blur together in front of me. Children who had to grow up too early. I'm getting too close: my own unresolved issues, but also just being a newbie. If I feel for all my patients as much as I do Taylah – and, in spades, Brianna – I'll burn out.

'I'll never be able to eat a Mars bar ever again.' Taylah's in tears, reliving the experience with as much distance as she is able. Doing okay, but any moment I could be dealing with a smashed computer or slashed wrists.

'He touched me. It hurt. He had to have known that.'

'It's abuse, and it wasn't your fault in any way,' I say.

'I never said no.' Now she's whispering.

'You were a child – you couldn't give consent. And you're allowed to be angry,' I say, possibly too forcefully. 'I'm angry too. He broke the law. He didn't want anyone to know what he did because it was so wrong. You were a child. You did *nothing* wrong. It was not your responsibility to say no.'

I'm as much feminist – human being – as psychiatrist here. This is stuff we all should know; stuff we all should say to victims of abuse. In Taylah's case, she needs to identify the source of her anger rather than direct it inward, as she does when she cuts or overdoses, overwhelmed with self-loathing.

Taylah's eyes flicker. Surprise? That someone wants to stand up for her? When even her mother hasn't.

From what I know about the relationship that forms between patient and therapist – the *therapeutic alliance* – I might be seen by Brianna as an older-sister figure, but for Taylah all women are her mother, until she starts working through their relationship.

'I thought maybe I could talk to Aleesha,' she says. 'I'm sick of it. Sick of covering for arseholes like Ivan and Jimmy.'

'I understand that, and I agree you shouldn't have to cover for them or put up with them,' I say. 'But you need to protect yourself.' Now for some cognitive behavioural therapy. 'Remember the plan for dealing with these emotions?'

I go through the relaxation and distraction ideas for when she is overwhelmed.

'Yes, but I need Aleesha on board,' she says.

'I hear what you're saying. But what if she doesn't believe you?'

Taylah laughs. 'She'll believe me about Ivan. After he was done with me, he tried it on her. He won't be doing it again.' She sees my expression and smiles. 'Finger in the eye.'

I look at my watch. Taylah and I agreed on boundaries, and that includes strict timekeeping. The smile is a good thing to end on. That and the fact that she's going to Short Stay tomorrow.

—

Jan sticks her head into my office. 'Your one o'clock isn't coming in; we need to do a home visit.'

It isn't a question. She has her keys in her hand.

'We have to be back for my four o'clock,' I say. No way am I missing Brianna's appointment.

'Yuusuf Abdi,' she says as we drive. 'He's missed his last two appointments and his sister's called to say she's worried.'

'Why isn't the CATT team going?'

'It's not an emergency – this is chronic.'

'What about the Mobile Support Team?'

'He hasn't been referred. And he won't let them in. His sister is letting us in, but he knows me and I'm more likely than CATT or the mobile team to be able to get him out of his room. He's barricaded himself in.'

'Not taking his meds?'

'He's very compliant. Just treatment-resistant. We've thrown everything at him and nothing much works, sadly. Somali man. Used to be a professor of philosophy, but since COVID he can't leave the house. They let him work remotely for a while, but in the end . . .'

Jan needs me with her to review the medication. The medication that doesn't work.

'What's he on?'

'Clomipramine three hundred milligrams and lurasidone one hundred and sixty milligrams,' says Jan. She's hunched over the steering wheel and driving at forty kilometres an hour in a sixty zone.

'So he has schizoaffective disorder?' I ask, working backward from medication to diagnosis.

'No,' says Jan. 'OCD.'

Because we train on the job, our learning is driven by the cases we see. Obsessive-compulsive disorder is uncommon and I didn't see it in general medicine or in the Acute Unit. I've read a little, but not about the hard end, where Yuusuf seems to be.

The only person I've known with OCD was a colleague when I was an intern. The hand-cleaning training reinforced her fears about hospitals being full of germs. There's a requirement to wash your hands every time you touch a patient, after you've adjusted their drip, touched their bedclothes, handed them medication . . . She'd take ten to twenty minutes every time. She got dermatitis and had to work longer hours to make up for the time she lost each day. But she managed. Just.

Yuusuf's sister, Geedi, is dressed in a traditional guntiino in dark brown and yellow tones, tied over her shoulder, with matching headscarf.

'I have just arrived,' she tells us as she lets us into the suburban weatherboard. 'A neighbour does the garden. Inside is worse than I thought.'

It's worse than anything my imagination would have created, and, standing in the doorway looking at it, I'm not sure I want to go any further. There is a *lot* of rubbish. A month's worth of takeaways. Mostly in green bags that are stacked, but there are containers piled up near the closed door of a far room. The smell is pretty bad and, coming into October, the warmer weather isn't going to help. Aren't OCD sufferers supposed to be clean freaks?

'Yuusuf told me he was fine, and I was busy,' says Geedi. 'This will take me several days to clean.'

'I can organise some emergency funding to pay for a cleaner,' says Jan.

'Yuusuf would not be comfortable with strangers in his house,' says Geedi. 'I will move in. He is not eating well. I will cook for him also.'

Jan nods. 'Have you seen him?'

'No. He spoke to me though. I have a key. There are masks at the door you must put on before he will consider opening his bedroom.'

Jan and I weave our way through the rubbish bags to the locked door and don N95 surgical masks from the box. Jan knocks and says who we are, assures him we are masked.

The door is cautiously opened, only partly, because it hits a box. Geedi hangs back while Jan and I squeeze around in the hallway to see our patient. Yuusuf is a tall, thin man in baggy trousers and a loose-fitting top – which look like they haven't been washed in a while.

Jan is a social worker by training, a manager by role. And I'm a doctor, here for the drugs. Yuusuf has health insurance, but there's no chance of him visiting a private psychiatrist, and it looks like house calls wouldn't fly either. He tried tele-psychiatry for a while, but the psychologist he was seeing was worried about his safety and referred him to the public system. Jan and me.

'Yuusuf,' says Jan. 'Are the thoughts worse?'

He nods. 'Constantly I am worrying that I will be infected.' He extends his hands. 'I have no more cream. But I do not think I can get to the skin specialist.'

His hands and forearms are bleeding in places, with dark patches in others; he winces as his hand glides over one.

'Are you showering?' asks Jan.

If the waft of body odour is anything to go by, no.

Yuusuf looks embarrassed, hangs his head. 'At the thought of showering I panic. Before I can shower, for each step – each action – I must count to ten, check the four corners of the room, count again.'

'How many steps?' I ask.

'This depends on how many items of clothing I have. And I must count and check for each part of my body. Thirty perhaps. If I make it into the shower, I run out of hot water before I'm finished. I try . . . once every week or two. Perhaps.'

It makes no sense to me. Shouldn't his whole body be raw from scrubbing and exposure to soap, not just his hands?

'That doesn't worry you – not showering?' I ask. 'With germs I mean?'

Yuusuf shakes his head. 'I am keeping my hands clean. This is more important to me.'

'And you're concerned that if you don't, you'll get sick?'

'That I will get sick, make others sick. COVID is constantly on my mind. I stay in to protect everyone as much as myself. Though . . . it is mainly because of the time my compulsions take. I am exhausted by these.'

'You've tried cognitive behavioural techniques?' He's seen a psychologist, and that's their usual starting point.

'I've tried many kinds of therapies. And medications. They don't help. I am an academic, albeit not in the sciences. I understand, intellectually, that I am not at serious risk. But the anxiety is there and will not go.'

'Even after the counting and checking and washing?'

'They help sometimes. For a while. Then it starts again.'

Even with the mask, I can tell his expression is anxious. He is tortured. What he's saying is, in laypeople's words, as crazy as anything I've heard. Including from my patients with schizophrenia. There's a high level of intelligence here, and a good recognition of what he's doing. He knows it doesn't make sense.

He's been on the medication for six months. The doses are high: the maximum I'd be prepared to go to with the antipsychotic, and way above what I would prescribe for the antidepressant. I get the name of his hand cream.

'I need to talk to my consultant,' I say. 'And we'll come back with a treatment plan. I'll bring cream.'

'In the meantime, Geedi will stay and look after you,' says Jan. 'And get rid of the garbage.'

Yuusuf nods, though he isn't happy. 'I can't leave the house; it's too much. Last time I took the rubbish out, I spent all night checking and washing my hands – and half of that was standing outside.'

—

Back at the Stables, Nash is on the phone in his office, feet on the desk, animated.

'Of course,' he says, 'I'm not saying it's acceptable to have patients waiting in ED for twenty-four hours . . . We're meeting weekly and doing a Friday afternoon clear-out . . . You're the boss.'

He's laughing as he ends the call and turns to me. 'Nicole. Patients queued up in ED because Acute is full. But we're getting on top of it. Ndidi and Carey are less likely than you and Alex to spend hours doing psychotherapy on people with schizophrenia.'

He's just trying to wind me up. But *you're the boss* to Nicole?

I give him a summary of Yuusuf's situation.

'He's very debilitated,' I say. 'But I'm wondering why he's on an antipsychotic. OCD isn't a psychotic disorder, right?'

'It's not. Though we can get the diagnosis wrong, especially in smart people like this patient. In schizophrenia, the patient may spin a good tale about not believing their delusions, but they do. They can't be talked out of those beliefs, whatever they might pretend. And they may act on them. In OCD, the sufferer can genuinely know that their so-called beliefs are untrue, but it doesn't take away the need to complete the compulsion.'

'That's basically what he reported,' I say. 'And he was definitely anxious.'

'I've treated him in hospital,' says Nash. 'He has a very severe form of OCD. The usual starting point is psychological therapies: cognitive behavioural therapy and exposure therapy where the person delays giving into a compulsion and replaces it with anxiety management techniques. Combined with antidepressants. SSRIs then clomipramine. Then antipsychotics. We've tried all those with Yuusuf. At the end of the day, we have only so many tools in the box.'

'What now then?'

'I don't think he's had asenapine.'

'And if that doesn't work . . . which seems likely?'

'Psychosurgery is an option,' says Nash. 'Better than sixty per cent response.'

'Really?' I'm thinking of *One Flew Over the Cuckoo's Nest*. 'Doesn't it have massive side effects?'

'We're not going to give him a lobotomy. The only psychosurgery we do in Australia is deep brain stimulation and just a few of those a year. But it can make the difference between suffering every minute and having a life worth living.'

There's no doubt Yuusuf is suffering. Would he agree to something that radical?

'But before we get to that,' says Nash, 'he has private health insurance, doesn't he?'

'Jan seems to think so.'

'Then let's organise TMS. Transcranial magnetic stimulation.'

'I'm not familiar –'

'Like electroconvulsive therapy in that we're stimulating the brain, but no electrodes, just a magnetic coil held near the forehead. Patient remains awake and there are fewer memory side effects.'

'So it's the version of ECT you get if you can afford private health insurance?' I'm only half-joking.

'They're different. The data's inconclusive in OCD . . . but there have been some positive outcomes in trials.' Says Nash, who rejects psychotherapy because the evidence isn't strong enough.

He calls a friend of his at a large private clinic, who not only pulls some strings to get Yuusuf in quickly, but, when Nash enquires, offers to see me in therapy.

'Adrian said he had a slot for someone smart and stable,' says Nash.

'But he'll take me until he finds them?'

Nash grins. 'He's not the most organised guy in the room, but he likes his patients and likes a challenge.'

Not sure how to take that.

At my desk, I read up quickly on TMS – *deep* TMS – and its stimulation over the two specific brain regions. Sounds more new-age than psychiatric. It's administered daily for six weeks for around thirty minutes. I'm pleased with myself when I find Jan and tell her it's all set. But she looks worried.

'Do you think he'll say no?' I ask, realising I haven't actually asked Yuusuf.

'I'm sure he'll be okay with the idea. But how are we going to get him there?'

Yuusuf can't leave his room. He can't be given Valium to dull his anxiety because it will interfere with the TMS. And the TMS machine can't come to him.

Jan says she'll talk with Yuusuf and Geedi, and get him his cream in the meantime.

Nash thinks we could give him olanzapine, which is a sedative but won't mess with the treatment. Daily for six weeks.

None of us are optimistic.

—

Brianna's emoji this morning was a shrug. At 4 pm, sitting in the waiting room, she looks washed out.

In my office, she produces a piece of paper headed *Reasons for having a baby*. There's nothing else on it. She turns it over. The other side, headed *Why not to have a baby*, is covered in scrawls; at the bottom *A LIFE!* in capitals and underlined.

Brianna points to it. 'Maddy wrote that. I hate it. Being pregnant. And, yeah, I want a life. Maybe with kids, but not now.'

'I've written you a referral to take to the women's health clinic.' I push it toward her. 'And I've made an appointment for you tomorrow morning. They'll tell you about the process, make you sign a consent form and then make another appointment for the procedure. You'll need to take that day off school. Naomi will take you to the clinic if you ask. And I'll see you back here every week as long as you need.'

Brianna looks at her hands. 'I thought of all the possibilities. If I tell my parents, I mean. None of them are good.'

'And if you don't tell them?'

'Maybe I'll tell them one day.'

'In a perfect world, what would you like to happen?'

'That it disappears.' Brianna takes a breath, blinks back tears. 'That Mum and Dad say sorry they've been acting like I don't exist, that they realise I'm not a child.'

'And accept you having a termination?'

'In a perfect world, I wouldn't be pregnant. But if I have to be . . . Accept it's my choice, and Mum would go with me.'

'So is there anything that might make that happen?'

Brianna takes the tissue box. I hope there are some left.

'I can't take the risk,' she says. 'The one thing I'm totally sure of is that I don't want to be pregnant, and I don't want a baby. If I told them . . . maybe they'd find some way to make me have it. Mum would say she'd look after it. So she can fuck up another kid. It'd be there all the time, like a reminder, and my father would never let me forget it.'

I nod. Her decision is rational, thought through. She's maintained it for over a week.

'Mum wouldn't come with me unless Dad said she could. And he'd never do that.'

'Parents are . . . human,' I say. 'You might like them to be different but you're not in a position to change them.'

'Mum's so pathetic. Why won't she stand up to him?' Brianna has tears streaming down her face. 'I mean, we did this class at camp, about respect in relationships – real respect, not the shit my dad talks about. He doesn't respect her. Or me.'

I put my hand on hers. 'One day, maybe you can talk with your mum about that.'

Brianna wipes her nose and looks at me, eyes glistening. 'If I was your daughter, would you help me have a termination?'

That's the question that's been sitting waiting all along. It's been in my mind since David threatened me, and it's been in Brianna's mind since she had a positive pregnancy test.

I'm a therapist. I don't share my own views, and I don't tell my patients what to do. But Elena said Brianna would need my permission.

'You're not my daughter,' I say. 'But you are my patient and what I want is what's best for *you*. You don't need anyone's approval, Brianna. You've worked this out for yourself.'

Brianna takes the letter and leaves.

—

There's a study-group meeting tonight at Carey's – the first they've hosted. I pick Jon up on the way and he's unusually quiet. I ask how his photography is going – just to talk about something other than work. His house is full of photos he took back home.

'Haven't even unpacked the camera,' he says.

Carey's place is a townhouse without a garden. The front room is jammed with boxes and filing cabinets. The kitchen–living area has six straight-backed chairs and nothing on the walls. There's a laptop on the table along with wine and conspicuously classy glasses.

Carey has three bottles open – white, red and sparkling – and invites us to help ourselves. I wonder if they're conducting a research project on catering for us. Or just doing their best to be a good host.

'Jon,' they say, 'will you excuse me asking Hannah a question specifically for her while we wait for the others?'

Jon smiles. 'Can I listen in? In case I learn something?'

'Of course. I assumed you'd stay in the same room, which is why I asked your permission. I need help with an aspect of my clinical skills. In line with the purpose of our study group. But the immediate issue is getting through my training-program interview.'

I laugh. 'You know I didn't get in? The first time, at least.'

'Because Professor Gordon thought you had unresolved personal issues arising from childhood trauma and needed therapy.'

My reaction – mouthing *fuck* – is enough for even Carey to read.

'Working with Prof, you learn these things,' they say. 'Particularly as he's indiscreet. But even he conceded that you had excellent intuition. Which is my weak point.'

'If I could jump in,' says Jon, 'you might also want to work on tact. And –'

'Showing off,' says Carey, opening the door to Alex and Ndidi. 'I should have said *one of my* weak points. But I'm only asking Hannah for help with intuition.'

'I'm not sure I can teach intuition,' I say.

'Disagree,' says Alex. 'If you think of your intuition as an aspect of countertransference – essentially, the way you feel about the patient – then it's something you can reflect on and develop.'

'See,' says Jon, 'it just needed a technical word to make it legitimate.'

Ndidi shakes her head. 'Where's the research that supports going with your gut?'

'I just think it makes sense,' Alex says. 'I don't think you'll find a paper on it, because countertransference is supposed to be more about you, and what you bring to the therapeutic relationship.'

'In fact,' says Carey, 'there *is* research.' They get their phone out and find the reference – nice to see they don't remember *everything*. 'Tanzilli and Lingiardi, 2022. The subject was narcissistic personality disorder, but I think the findings can be generalised.'

I can see that Alex is a bit peeved. We trainees challenge and correct each other all the time, but psychotherapy is his space.

'Good point, Alex,' says Carey. 'I hadn't connected the paper to my own issues, but if I keep a record of feelings versus actual diagnoses, I may find myself becoming more conscious of my feelings and of using them as a first-line diagnostic indicator.' Carey looks at me: *see, I noticed Alex's reaction and responded tactfully*. Unfortunately, Alex also catches the look which undermines the good work a little. But he sits down, and the rest of us follow suit.

'I think what Alex and Carey are saying,' says Jon, 'is that we have feelings about patients who present with certain disorders – and when you get those feelings with a new patient, it's a clue that you may be dealing with that same disorder.' He stops and turns to me. 'We've all seen the Keane family – some of them, right?'

Nods all round.

'Good choice,' says Alex. 'The paper Carey read used personality disorders as the example, and Taylah's got an obvious borderline personality disorder.'

'How does she make you feel?' Jon asks me.

I take a moment to think about it before responding. I was originally worried about seeing Taylah because of the suicide issues, and she's triggered some feelings from my past, but I haven't reflected on how I feel about her.

'Taylah can be annoying and frustrating, but mainly I want to . . . help her fly. But I sense that no matter how much I give her it won't be enough.'

'Been there before?' says Jon.

I realise I have. I've seen a few patients with borderline personality disorder, especially when I've been on call, and had similar feelings to what I feel about Taylah. And Foster Kid Twenty. I bet if I saw her now, she'd come with a borderline diagnosis.

'What about Kelly, the mother?' says Jon.

'Totally different. She's manipulative too, but she's prickly. Out to get you before you get her.'

Ndidi smiles. 'It's not just you who feels that way.'

'Narcissistic personality disorder,' says Carey. 'According to Prof.'

Good to know.

'And Aleesha?' Jon asks.

'I haven't had so much to do with her. But there's something about her that's not genuine. This is totally intuition, but she makes me feel . . . uneasy.' I turn to Carey. 'So what's her diagnosis?'

'Sorry, no idea. I've never seen her, and I don't think Prof's told me.'

'But once you know,' says Ndidi, 'you can throw away the books, right?' She spots Carey's expression of disbelief. 'Sorry, just being sarcastic.'

I laugh. 'Saying, "I have this feeling that I've had before," isn't going to get me through the exams. Or get Carey through their interview.' But I wonder how many private psychiatrists end up relying on their well-honed instincts.

Carey has been taking notes on their laptop.

'We'll get lunch,' I say to them. 'Mondays are good.' For clarity, I add, 'Not just lunch. I'll do my best to help with the intuition.'

Amy, Carey's friend, has let herself in, her neat ponytail, shirt and skirt suggesting she's come straight from work. She begins distributing burgers and fries from a big bag, before joining us at the table.

As she gives me my burger, she asks, 'Did you read my report about the autism-friendliness – actually, since the score was less than five, I should say autism-*unfriendliness* – of the Stables?'

I give her a quick summary of the changes I've made: noise reduction, softer lighting, notices. I can see that Jon, in particular, is impressed.

'What about the name?' Amy says. 'Patients aren't horses.'

'Or coming to see horses,' says Jon. 'I mean, we're the ones who are based there. How do you think the patients see it?'

'I guess,' I say, 'we should be thinking about how we'd *like* them to see it.'

'Go on,' says Alex. 'Finish the thought.'

'I'd like them to see the clinic as a place for getting help, replenishment . . .'

'An oasis,' says Jon.

'Nice,' says Ndidi. 'What's the Aboriginal word?'

'Do you know the Kenyan word for oasis?'

Ndidi's Nigerian. And there's an edge to Jon's voice. 'I'm a Bilinarra man. How would I know? We're on Wurundjeri land.' He takes a breath and smiles. 'Oasis is good. One step at a time.'

I shake my head. 'If I suggest it to Nash, he'll agree and then it'll never happen. Too many other important things, and he won't be sympathetic to me for thinking otherwise.'

We shift to talking about patients, and Amy takes that as her cue to leave. I ask for bright ideas to help Yuusuf get to TMS.

Ndidi agrees with Nash: sedation seems to be the only real option.

'Every day for six weeks?' I ask. But maybe that would be no worse than his daily life.

'What about hypnosis?' suggests Jon.

Alex isn't excited. 'Too anxious. But I like that we're looking wider than medication for a change –'

'TMS is a physical intervention,' says Ndidi. 'Counts as medicine.'

'For fuck's sake,' says Alex. 'Sorry, but I get this all day from Keith and everybody else. Like it's all physical brain changes and you hit it with meds or maybe something else – anything but psychotherapy – and . . . where do you think the brain changes came from in the first place?'

Carey treats this as an exam question. 'Genetic predisposition, environmental factors –'

'Which includes psychological stuff. We were talking about Taylah Keane. Her childhood abuse, whether physical or psychological, will have changed the structure of her brain. There's no hard line between physical and psychological. And that's not Freud; it's the leading edge of psychiatric research.'

'Hazmat suit,' says Carey.

'What are you talking about?' says Alex.

'For the OCD patient. Worn properly, they offer a high level of protection, as he will know if he's been concerned about COVID.'

It takes me a moment to catch up with the change in topic, but . . . could it work? I promise Carey I'll take it up with Nash and Jan.

TMS, hazmat suits, countertransference as a diagnostic tool. Not exactly exam prep, but if we can find a way forward for Yuusuf, this evening will have been worthwhile for someone at least.

Alex is still having a tough time in Extended Care, though he tries to play down how it's affecting him. Not sure how much is the private schoolboy thing of not asking for help and how much it's still a performance for me. I'm starting to see that his script has been: *I can handle anything they throw at* me, *but* you *need my wise advice.*

'Just more of the same shit,' he says. 'DJ's parents have put in a complaint about me.'

'That's ridiculous,' I say. 'She was under your care for what, two minutes?'

'A day. But that was the day the breakout happened. They seem to think that I *knew* she was going to abscond. Because she told me she'd break out if they didn't reinstate her leave. If I reported every time a patient in Extended Care threatened to do something . . .'

'It's bullshit,' says Ndidi. 'It won't go anywhere.'

'It has already. Keith's sent the complaint to HR.'

'Have your union rep with you,' says Ndidi. 'I mean it.'

Alex answers by getting up. 'Thanks for dinner, Carey, and please thank Amy too. I'm heading off.'

—

Driving home, Jon's smile is there but it's superficial.

'Bit tense tonight,' I say. 'I mean, we were on each other's cases a bit . . .'

'Alex is hurting,' he says. 'Ndidi's struggling too. And Carey doesn't show it but they're really anxious about the interview for the program.'

'What about you? Work stressful?'

'I'm coping. Sandra's good. We've had a couple of First Nations women in, and I was a bit edgy at first, but there's a genuine desire not to repeat the mistakes of the past.'

'Is that all that's going on for you?'

Jon rests his head against the window. 'I miss my mob. Guy living with me went home and turns out I don't like living alone much.'

I wait for him to continue.

'There's a lot of stuff I wasn't expecting. I'm struggling to deal with things not being good enough. Including myself.'

'I guess it's better than it used to be,' I say.

Jon shakes his head. 'If you're talking about diagnosis and medications . . . but the human aspect? The pressure to clear beds? It's an issue in the Mother Baby Unit and that's probably the least pressured. There are just so many service gaps. Expecting people – professionals, I mean – to go above and beyond isn't reasonable. Yet so many of our patients need that.'

'And we do it,' I say.

'We do it. The nurses, even management. We're always saying the money should go to clinicians, not admin, but then they're left understaffed and we complain because the payroll gets stuffed up.'

He's right, but Sandra was probably right too about working within the limits of our power. I just let him go on.

'All the shit going on that's making mental illness worse? Drugs, racism, just the whole system. You felt it with that woman who was going to have IVF for a child she couldn't keep.'

'I did. You helped me see my limits there.'

'By suggesting you do nothing?'

'We can't fix everything.'

He takes a long breath. 'At least you gave it a shot.'

—

I raise the hazmat suit idea with Jan and Nash and they think it's worth trying.

Jan and I head out to see Yuusuf again. Jan's regrowth is creating a spiky halo; she looks like an echidna.

Yuusuf's sister opens the door to us. 'He is worse,' she says.

The house isn't – Geedi has performed miracles. No garbage and a smell of lemon.

Yuusuf's door is shut.

'He did not have time to eat yesterday,' Geedi says.

It takes some coaxing to get Yuusuf to open up.

'I have to protect my sister,' he says. 'Terrible, terrible new thoughts come to me. If I do not touch all of the walls each time I have this thought, I fear I may do some of these terrible things.'

'So here's what we're going to do,' says Jan with the authority of having been around forever and seen and done everything. 'The mobile team will be here first thing Friday morning with a hazmat suit, like they wear in the Infectious Disease Unit to keep staff safe. Works against Ebola, and that's far worse than COVID.'

Lucky she's got me and not Carey with her: they'd doubtless point out that COVID is more infectious. But Yuusuf is listening.

'You're going to put the suit on and they're going to take you to Northside Clinic for TMS, daily for six weeks, not on weekends. You'll be home by lunchtime.'

She gets out a bunch of plastic folders containing all the information, sprays them with disinfectant and puts them on the table.

'We think it's the best chance to get you functioning,' I say.

'Then yes, I will do this,' Yuusuf says.

Geedi appears in the hall. 'Would it be okay then for me to go home?'

Yuusuf nods. 'Please, yes.'

Geedi looks relieved. 'I have seven children to care for.'

—

Friday, Yuusuf gets to TMS in a hazmat suit. I see him at the private clinic because I've got a 9.30 am appointment to see Nash's therapist buddy, Adrian. It's awkward, and I let Yuusuf think I'm there for professional reasons. Which I am: therapy is about making me a better therapist.

Yuusuf goes straight in, so I guess I'll have to wait on feedback from the Mobile Support Team. But when he comes out forty minutes later, I'm still waiting. There's good news: having seen his level of disability, his psychiatrist is organising for him to be admitted for the duration of the treatment. Yuusuf's eyes are smiling. 'I think this was useful. I'm optimistic,' he says.

The receptionist is apologetic: Adrian has been held up, but is 'not far away'. I'm used to waiting at medical appointments and I tell myself off for being harder on my own profession. Except . . . psychotherapy sessions are fixed at fifty minutes, and it seems Adrian's delay is for some personal reason.

Finally, a full hour late, Adrian shows up. I like the look of him immediately – about forty, his clothes, hair and beard all untidy. He pulls off his helmet, parks his bike in a room off reception, checks his appointment book and spots me.

'Sorry I'm late. You must be Hannah. Crazy morning. Got behind and thought the bike'd be quicker but . . . Anyway, I'm just going to grab a coffee.'

He's looking at the door. He's going out to get one.

'I'm sorry, but I need to be back at work as soon as possible,' I say. 'If we could start now . . .'

He shakes his head. 'I'm the one who needs to apologise.' He points to a woman who's been waiting almost as long as I have.

'She's ahead of you,' he says.

—

I return to work to find a bright new sign at the entrance, screwed to the wall: *Welcome to the Oasis.*

It's a stylised picture of First Nations kids gathered at a waterhole – I'm guessing it's a Jon Homann original, and I'm sure he didn't get any kind of permission to put it up. But from now on, I'm working at the Oasis. And good luck to anyone who wants to pull down First Nations art from a mental health clinic.

SEVEN

CO-DEPENDENCY

Canned corn is on special, and a neat, slightly anxious woman in her late thirties is taking advantage of it, stacking her trolley.

A dishevelled elderly man sees what she's doing and follows suit, pulling cans off the supermarket shelf by the armful.

The woman increases her pace to keep up, as much as she can without looking desperate, and then a bit beyond that.

It only spurs the old man to greater effort, dropping cans in his panic.

A small woman, wearing a turban, comes up behind them and tries discreetly to access the corn herself. Discreetly isn't going to do it.

'Excuse me. Could you possibly save just one for me? I'm expecting visitors.'

The man ignores her, but the female shopper stops, pulled back into an awareness of what she's doing.

'I'm sorry.' She hands the turbaned woman a can. 'Is one enough?'

The woman laughs, not unkindly. 'For me, one is enough. You are having a party?'

The first woman looks at her trolley, stacked with corn and nothing else. She isn't having a party. Slowly, she starts replacing the cans on the shelf.

The turbaned woman turns to the man, who has slowed down, a little confused now. 'I'm thinking this might be too much of one thing for you too. Would you like me to help you choose some food?'

Today, for the first time since I started work at the clinic, I don't have any appointments booked. I'm covering the Crisis Assessment and Treatment Team – the CATT registrar is on study leave.

Jon and I meet for breakfast at one of the cafes near the clinic . . . *the Oasis*. I'm going to make an effort to connect with him more often now that he's been upfront about missing family and friends. But it's he who's invited me to breakfast this morning. And there's something I'd like his perspective on.

In medicine, you learn early that you need to create some space between yourself and your patients. You have to be objective, and you can't carry everyone's pain. I've struggled to maintain that space with Brianna and, to an extent, Taylah.

But I'm currently feeling distanced from my patients in a different way.

'Nash was talking about KPIs,' I tell Jon when our coffees arrive, 'and Nicole made a sarcastic remark about maybe doing some good for the patients as well.'

Jon laughs. 'Role reversal. Must have seen a chance to mess with Nash's head. She does that, in case you haven't noticed.'

'Maybe, but at the time I was wondering whether Taylah would make a good long-psychotherapy case for my qualification. When

I should be a hundred per cent focused on what's right for the patient, I'm thinking *What can I learn here?* or *Will I get points for doing this?*'

Jon nods. 'The problem of trying to do everything. We want to improve our skills, qualify . . .' He laughs. 'And do the paperwork, hit the KPIs, have a life. At least you're aware of it.'

I smile. 'The voice of reason. Even when you're unhappy with something. You realise we all envy how . . .' I'm looking for the word, and don't quite find it. 'How calm you are.'

Jon puts his hands behind his head and leans back. 'Try again. Try easygoing. Or accommodating. Or just gutless.'

'What are you talking about? You screwed a sign to the clinic wall. You call me out – more than anybody else in the group does.'

'You're a peer.'

He hasn't answered my question. I wait.

'We had a consumer rep in Extended Care,' he says.

'The one who's on sick leave?'

'Because of Keith. I guess you know that Keith spends half his day in his office doing private stuff – tribunals and legal reports.'

'I'd heard.'

'Everybody's heard and nobody rocks the boat. But the consumer rep had the . . . *guts* to tell him he needed to spend more time with the patients and talking with her. So, Keith basically drove her into a relapse.'

'Drove her? How?'

'He's her boss, a psychiatrist; she's vulnerable – he pushed her buttons. Nothing that'd play in court, but . . . gaslighting, subtle stuff.'

'Shit.'

'And I didn't stand up for her. I could have said something.'

He shakes his head, obviously disappointed in himself, even distressed, but . . .

'Listen, Jon. There's hardly a person on the planet who hasn't avoided a conflict with their boss. Especially when that boss's got form, like Keith.'

Jon shakes his head. 'Thanks for listening, Hannah. That actually wasn't what I wanted to talk to you about. Not consciously anyway.' He laughs. 'You know Ndidi pretty well?'

'I guess.' I'm probably closer to her than anyone else in the group is, but 'pretty well' is a stretch.

'What's with the matchmaking?'

Ndidi is having Jon over to dinner tonight. With a single girlfriend.

'Probably noticed you're a bit lonely. Or at least single.'

'Okay. But if you can get her to back off, that'd be good. I'm not looking.'

—

I wander into the CATT office, where Grace is making coffee. Her colleague George, beefy and red-cheeked, thin hair pulled back in a ponytail, is on the phone to Acute to get the bed-availability update.

The CATT registrar mostly stays at the clinic – the *Oasis* – and only goes out on visits when a review of medication is needed. But today the CATT team is down a nurse, and Nash thinks it'll be good experience for me to go out on the road.

Except I've organised lunch with Simon. I found a buzzy cafe nearby, checked it out in advance, made a booking even though they said they didn't really take bookings. I may have been over-functioning.

I text him: *Sorry – have to cancel – this is what my job's like.*

He's straight back to me: *Dinner next time.*

I'd suggested lunch because the question of going home with him wouldn't come up, and I wouldn't have to say no because I still haven't found a therapist. And not just because I've made that promise to myself. I'm still unsure about where Simon's coming from, what he wants, my feelings about him then and now.

'It won't be all drama and excitement,' Grace tells me, as if that's a bad thing. 'Couple of cases from last weekend we're following up. Checking they're still alive and taking their meds.'

'You might go through the whole day with nothing else,' George says.

'Unless there's a *crisis*,' says Grace. 'What's the team called again?'

Grace is going to be driving. She's wired at the best of times. I wonder if I'll get to find out if drama and excitement put her into chill mode – which they do with me – or feed the fire.

After another coffee – like Grace needs it – we start our rounds, leaving George on phone duty.

Between lane changes, Grace tells me the story of her life. 'ABC – you know what that means, right? Australian-born Chinese, though actually I was born in Hong Kong, but Hong Kong was under British rule, and anyway my family came out when I was young. Well, divided time between there and here. Now just here.' She has a brother who is 'a bit of a loser but my mother's little prince – usual Chinese shit'.

Grace can talk. Driving's another matter. I'd give her nine out of ten – if we had a siren. Without a siren, she's a two.

I get a break when we arrive at our first stop: a Sikh family. The seventeen-year-old son, Gurpreet, who was discharged after being treated in Acute for a first-episode psychosis, is quiet, but he's sleeping at night instead of roaming the house. Taking his meds.

CATT supported him while he was waiting for a bed, and they're now supporting him in the early recovery. Essential, because the target lengths of stay in Acute are shorter than the time it takes for the medication to start working.

'I wish all families were like this,' says Grace to me after the parents, Gurisha and Angad, have poured coffee and disappeared to get us something to eat. 'And I don't just mean because they're great cooks – Gurisha's a bit of an activist and there's an uncle who runs a restaurant. During the COVID lockdowns, the Sikh community provided food to the public-housing people. You know that, right?'

We're sampling vada – sweetcorn fritters – when George calls. We need to see a woman who's scared that her five-year-old might kill her. A *crisis*, as Grace points out to George. Grace promises to check in on Gurpreet in three days and we say a hasty goodbye.

'Are you sure that's what George said?' I ask when we're back in the car. 'Not that she was worried *she* might kill the five-year-old?'

'You don't know this five-year-old.' Grace's eyes are bright and she's driving faster.

In approximately no time, we pull into a permit-only parking spot in front of a two-storey public-housing complex and head upstairs. A woman in her mid-twenties is waiting outside a door, hugging herself. She looks relieved to see us.

'What's happening, Dana?' Grace asks.

'I only said he *should* drink all his milk. Didn't *tell* him to.' Dana is speaking softly and looks like a frightened child herself.

The apartment is a domestic version of *Apocalypse Now*. There's milk all over the kitchen table and what looks like peanut butter and bread ground into the floor and pasted to the wall. Holes in at least three of the walls – at five-year-old height.

I'm not sure what to expect, but we find Mason sitting quietly on his bed with an iPad and an angelic smile below spiky, jet-black hair. He's wearing Burberry – I can see the label as the top is inside out. Dana, I guess, is wearing vintage Kmart.

'Mason, have you been angry at your mum again?' asks Grace.

'Mum is stupid,' says the smiling cherub.

'I'm pretty sure you were asked not to say that about your mother,' Grace says.

Dana has retreated to the kitchen to clean up.

'If I'd thrown my sandwich on the floor when I was little,' I say, 'I would have gone hungry.'

Actually, someone would have given me some of their food, but I feel this kid might need a hard line that he's not getting from his mother.

'The sandwich was crap.' Mason returns to his tablet – finished with us.

We go back to the table – cleaned of milk – and wait while Dana boils the kettle.

'What happened?' asks Grace.

'He just went off his head. Like his dad.'

'Mason's father,' Grace tells me, 'is in prison for assault.'

'I didn't press charges,' Dana says quickly.

'No, but the police did.'

'He's still shitty at me. Thinks I shouldn't have gone to the hospital.'

'Dana had a broken arm,' says Grace.

'When does he get out?' I ask.

'Next month.'

'And he's coming back here?'

'Yeah.' Her hand goes to her hair, tidies it. She smiles. 'Mason listens to his dad.'

'Have you spoken to Orange Door?' I ask. 'Or any other of the family violence services?'

'They can't help. Mason's his kid, so of course he's going to want to see him. When he's not drinking, he's good.'

'By "drinking", she means ice,' says Grace, and Dana doesn't argue. She reaches for a mug.

'What do you think Mason makes of the violence?' I ask.

'He's his dad through and through,' Dana says.

Great. And by not standing firm and providing consequences for bad behaviour, she's contributing to the problem. Not the only factor, but she's all I've got to work with.

We get her another appointment with Child Psych – she won't see Orange Door.

'The kid's father,' says Grace, back in the car. 'Full-on thug. So was her father.'

'It makes me so mad.'

'Can't save the world. Just an occasional little portion. Child Psych will chip away. One day maybe she'll decide enough is enough.'

I scramble to put on the safety belt as we head off to the other recent discharge and Grace shares her thoughts on Attention Deficit Hyperactivity Disorder.

'That's what they think Mason has,' she says. 'What I think is that his mother's terrified of him and he's in control, and what little boy wouldn't go ape if you gave him that?' She doesn't wait for an answer. 'On the other hand, there's real ADHD. You're looking at it.'

I'm not surprised. She doesn't stay on topic, and the longest I've seen her sit is in the car. In team meetings, she's up and down getting coffee, eating and taking phone calls.

'What do you think of it as a diagnosis?' she asks. 'It's controversial in adults. To some people anyway.'

'Haven't dealt with it clinically,' I say.

'Yeah well, jury is out I reckon. I'm trying Ritalin. First cousin to ice, right? Buzz is good but it's screwing with my sleep.'

Buzz is not the intended effect.

She's telling me about sleep apps when the phone goes. She takes the call on hands-free.

'Family violence,' says George, giving us an address.

Grace is doing a U-turn as I ask for details. 'Isn't that a police problem?'

'Police are there. Waiting for you guys,' says George. 'The husband has convinced them his wife's unwell.'

Grace and I exchange glances. No words required.

The police are waiting on the garden path when we arrive. A female cop greets us.

'Neighbours called us,' she says. 'A lot of yelling.'

Ben and Andrea are the couple in question. Nothing physical toward *her*, says the cop – *she's* been pushing *him*. He's convinced she's 'not herself'. Air quotes and eye roll, which add up to *one for you guys*.

'How did she seem to you?' Grace asks.

The cop shrugs.

Her colleague – who looks too young for his job – says, 'Stressed. Like my mum on a bad day.'

The front door is open. We knock and the cops leave us to it.

Ben comes to the door. Late thirties, maybe early forties. Medium height and Henry Cavill looks – and smile.

He brings us into the kitchen. More coffee for Grace.

Andrea is with the children – I guess their ages at six and ten – who are looking distressed. She takes them to the living room, settles them in front of the television, and joins us at the kitchen table. She's my height and weight, casually dressed.

'We were fighting over money,' she says. 'Ben needs to go shopping and see how expensive food is.'

'It isn't that,' says Ben. 'It's because a lot of the food you're buying we'll never eat.' He opens the pantry. 'Take a look. Maybe we'll get through fifty cans of baked beans. But if you like anchovies – help yourself. None of us do and there's enough to stock a supermarket.'

I look to Andrea.

'The beans were on sale, so I was being *responsible*. And I've got a lamb recipe that uses anchovies – you don't taste them, but they add to the flavour according to Jamie . . . what's-his-name – and I'd forgotten we already had some.'

'It isn't just that,' Ben says earnestly. 'Andrea, you aren't yourself.'

'How are you feeling, Andrea?' I ask.

'I'd be fine if he wasn't always on my case.'

'Do you get depressed?'

'I'm not happy.' She waves her hand to indicate Ben. 'But things aren't good between us. Haven't been for a while.'

I wait for her to elaborate, but she seems to have trouble collecting her thoughts.

Ben pipes up that she's vague. I'm thinking coercive control.

He smiles his Henry Cavill smile. 'She got postnatal depression after the kids,' he adds. 'And her mother gets depression.'

'She's not my *biological* mother,' says Andrea and adds, 'I'm adopted.'

I resist the temptation to correct her simplistic take on nature versus nurture, and just ask, 'Do you think you could be depressed again?'

'Maybe. Doesn't feel like before, but, like I said, I'm not happy, so I guess.'

She was prescribed antidepressants for her postnatal depression and it would be easy to give her another script, but circumstances have changed, and I'm not in a position to take a detailed history. I suggest she sees her GP.

Ben's not impressed: *Been there, done that.*

I ask if they've thought about relationship counselling.

'I love her,' says Ben. 'If whatever's wrong is sorted out, the rest will be fine.'

I hope he's right. There's been something off about the conversation, but I can't put my finger on it.

—

I recognise the recently discharged patient we visit next. Warren Baker has schizophrenia, diagnosed relatively late in life following a marriage break-up in his thirties. He worked until his fifties, when his behaviour, including failure to wash, led to him being let go. I treated him in the Acute Ward last rotation. He's sixty-two and looks eighty.

'The ward social worker was tied up and didn't get to do a home visit,' says Grace. 'He's harmless and on a depot' – a long-acting antipsychotic that the clinic administers every few weeks – 'but she thought because he's just around the corner from young Gurpreet, we might as well go in. Which was the plan until the attack of the five-year-old. But . . . still not far out of our way.'

There's a reason that we do follow-up visits after discharge even if the patient is 'harmless and on a depot'. I'm amazed that the neighbours haven't reported Warren. Perhaps they have. He's got about the same amount of junk as my father, but in a suburban front garden rather than spread across hectares of land. No caravans, but a burnt-out car body, two old washing machines and the remains of a kayak. A kayak?

Grace offers an explanation. 'Once you start piling up shit, people think it's okay to put their own on top.'

Some sort of psych metaphor there.

The walls of the house are covered in spray paint and what I'm guessing is egg splatter. *Pedo* is written in large letters.

Warren, it turns out, is a hoarder. When he opens the front door to us, it's hard to see light behind him for the stacks of papers either side of the hallway. He shuffles back in and we follow. Two cats wander out, and I see three more on an interior window-sill. There are two supermarket bags on the bench: I glance inside and the contents look sensibly chosen. Someone's shopping for him. But not cleaning.

At first glance the place is like Yuusuf's, but it doesn't take too long to see the differences. Yuusuf didn't have all this junk, and the smell was confined to the rubbish bags. His house, in its own way, was clean. Warren's is oppressive and dark. I'm thinking the cats were locked in here at some stage, or else it's been a long time since the kitty litter was emptied. Grace doesn't ask for coffee.

'This isn't safe, Warren,' she says.

'Fine for me and the cats,' he says, brow furrowed.

I run through a checklist and confirm his psychosis is stable.

As we leave, I ask about the eggs and the graffiti.

Warren immediately becomes distressed. 'The kids do it. I've never touched them. Any kid.'

We tell him we'll be back when we've found a solution. Moving him would solve some of the problems, but likely at a cost – not just financial. In supported accommodation Warren will lose his freedom, and more than likely, his sense of self. It wouldn't be a simple process and he'd need a guardian to approve it – one he doesn't have currently.

'I reckon if we report the place, they'll have it torn down,' Grace says. 'At least take all his stuff.'

'Better than him burning to death. Or dying from . . .' Gastro, I guess.

In the car, I ring the ward social worker, Essy, who is new. Nicole's appointment as admin director has led to several new hires with the same background.

'What can we do?' I ask Essy.

'Does he own his house? Has the council given warnings?'

No idea.

'I can't be expected to do everything. He's been discharged, hasn't he? You guys need to deal with it.'

I try Jan. She doesn't want to be bothered with it either. 'Call the council.'

So I do. After being on hold, then misdirected, I am told the house is owned by Warren but he's going to be in trouble if he hasn't moved the rubbish on his lawn by the end of the week. I ask about a cleaner. They'll get back to me.

There won't be any exam questions about this part of my job.

—

The police are in touch again, via George.

'We get to visit a guy in lock-up,' says Grace. 'You'll love this one.'

I raise an eyebrow.

'Not his first rodeo. Dangerous driving.'

There's obviously something she's not telling me.

Grace's eyes twinkle. 'Let's say he's giving the cops an interesting experience – enough to call us.'

The police station is a large cream-brick relic of the eighties next to a suburban courthouse. Several police cars are parked in the street. Luckily, there's no-one in them because they'd book Grace for her high-speed parking attempt that narrowly misses one car – a *police* car – and finishes with ours on the kerb.

The sergeant – a red-haired woman with a mass of freckles – is delighted to see Grace. They have a coffee while the constable takes me to see 'Kingsize Pain in the Arse'.

I recognise him before I see him: the booming voice of Max Kennedy KC is unmistakable. He's a barrister with bipolar disorder who did a stint – a memorable stint – in Acute before transferring to a private hospital.

He's standing behind bars in a barren room: dishevelled, shirt inside out. His pants are missing a belt and sinking dangerously low below his substantial belly. There's a guy in the cell opposite who looks like he's trying to sleep off last night's bender – I think it's him I can smell, but I can't be sure Max's hygiene is up to scratch either.

'Good heavens!' says Max. 'It's the adorable Doctor Quatro!'

The name he gave me in Acute. Apparently I remind him of a rock singer from his teenage years.

'Max . . . have you stopped taking your lithium?'

I feel a moment of therapeutic nihilism. We thought we'd convinced him to stay on the drug that keeps him stable enough to hold on to his job and relationship.

'Dear doctor, don't despair! Devilishly difficult dilemma: damned if I do and damned if I don't.'

This could take a while.

'Definitely dreadful. Drug doing damage. Careering creatinine killing the kidneys!'

'You had to stop the lithium?' I interrupt Max's affirmative, alliterative – and annoyingly long – reply. 'What are you taking instead?'

'A cocktail, dear doctor, dear doctor, dear doctor. A lavishing of lamotrigine, a steady stream of Seroquel and a dash of diazepam.'

I wonder if he's amping it up to get off the driving charges.

'What were you doing when the police picked you up?'

'Followed the police car through the intersection. All those cars stopped and waiting – I'd have been a fool not to take advantage. Don't think the police liked me getting ahead of them. Malicious prosecution.' Max beams. 'Took the shortcut through the park.'

'I'm booking him,' says the red-haired sergeant when I return to the front desk. 'He's a menace. Could have killed a woman with a pram in the park.'

'Max is manic,' I say. 'Mental . . .' *Enough with the m's.* 'Psychiatric illness. And he's had to come off his meds for health reasons. We'll find him an inpatient bed.'

'And coming off meds accounts for him pinching my butt?'

'Maybe.' That's one he could be faking. 'There's a downside to the merriment,' I say. 'Among other things, he may have kidney damage – and he's unlikely to live a long life, regardless.'

The sergeant seems to think this wouldn't be a bad thing.

'You realise,' I say, 'that he had no control over getting bipolar disorder? It could happen just as easily to me or you. Out of nowhere.'

She's stopped smiling. 'Seriously?'

'The fickle finger of fate.'

—

George calls again as we're leaving. Carey turned up looking for me for their Monday interview coaching. Shit. I had expected they'd check which Monday. And we won't be heading back yet because there's a call-out to an address in the lower socioeconomic end of the catchment area.

Grace grins as she hits the end button. 'Keanes.'

I've picked the right day to be on the road. After dealing with the Keane family in ED, Taylah in therapy, and encountering all of them off and on at the Oasis, I'm actually excited about seeing them in their home. It might help me make some sense of the dynamics.

'Who's the identified patient?' I ask.

'Taylah. Just out of Short Stay and wants to go back.'

'At least she hasn't gone to ED.' Progress, I tell myself.

The Keane house is on a main road, with an unfenced lawn recently mown and a tired looking Commodore in the driveway. Grace nearly hits it as she squeezes our car in behind.

I recognise Kelly's raised voice as we get out and knock on the door.

Aleesha answers, wearing an oversized jumper and sweatpants, and waves us in. I catch a smirk when she thinks I'm not looking. She leans against the doorjamb to watch the fun.

An older guy who I figure must be Ivan is on a large vinyl chair, tilted back with the footrest out, watching television. He looks up briefly, then resumes watching. Just another visit from the mental health crisis people.

Ivan's in jeans and a collared shirt, with thinning hair and a gut. And a black eye, presumably caused by Aleesha's finger. On appearance at least, he's less of a slob than I was expecting. No worse than Keith Barnard. Kelly is standing beside him, in tight top and leggings, deep fake tan, long pink nails. Taylah is crying on the sofa. She looks up and is taken aback to see me.

'On CATT for the day,' I say. 'What's going on, Taylah?'

Taylah blows her nose. 'Every year, like I mean *every single year*, Aleesha's birthday is a fucking disaster. So is mine, but last year I went away with Trent and it was quiet at least.' She starts to cry again, pulling out a bunch of tissues from the box beside her.

'You were in the Short Stay Unit though?'

As requested – begged for. *Just give me time out from my family.* But my simple statement of reality triggers a wail.

'That's her problem,' says Aleesha. 'I got tickets to watch the finale of *Rich and Single*.'

'Rich and *thick*,' says Ivan. 'Like cream.'

'Like, live,' says Kelly. 'Aleesha did it as a surprise for everybody, the whole family, but then Taylah went into Short Stay.'

'I got three tickets,' says Aleesha.

I look at Ivan, and he shakes his head with something approaching disgust. At reality TV? At the three women he shares a house with? At himself?

Taylah answers the question. 'She and Mum went and they took *Trent*.'

Taylah's ex-boyfriend.

'How does he fit in?' I say.

'Aleesha invited him,' says Taylah.

'It was my birthday,' says Aleesha. 'I can do what I want, right? He and Taylah broke up ages ago. Anyway, I didn't realise it'd upset Taylah so I messaged him it was off, but he showed up because he didn't get the message.'

'Trent's a dick,' laughs Kelly.

Ivan grabs the TV remote and turns up the sound.

'How about I talk to Taylah in the kitchen?' I say.

Aleesha looks like she's going to follow us. I turn and add, 'Alone.'

We end up in Taylah's bedroom. I would have guessed boy-band posters, an unwashed pink bedspread half-off and clothes all over the floor. Instead, it's neat, with off-white walls and a large painting behind the bed – a beach scene. It has her name at the bottom and it's not bad.

Taylah sees me looking at it. 'Only subject I liked at school,' she says as she throws herself on the bed.

'And these?' I point to the shelves, which hold what must be a hundred exercise books.

'Just something I started doing when Mum was in the psych ward. For weeks when I was about six.'

She gives me permission to look and I find it hard not to react. The books are full of pressed dried flowers. Some tiny, all with a date and what I think is a description until I look more closely at one from a few years earlier. It's next to a daisy and reads: *Mum took me to Maccas today and I got a happy meal toy!* I flick a few pages. Next to a thistle: *Mum told Aleesha she was prettier than me.*

'It's kind of a diary,' says Taylah.

'It's also kind of like CBT,' I say. 'I mean you taught yourself some ways to distract yourself when bad things happen . . . and remember the good things.'

'I guess.'

It's a record of the bad things too, but she's put a lot of work into these books. Where her sister and mother have walled their emotions – vulnerable emotions – inside, Taylah is seeking love and warmth and acceptance, and resorting to flowers to find a semblance of something good.

'Sounds like the birthday wasn't anywhere you'd want to be, because it would have ended up like what's just happened, right?' I say.

This pulls Taylah up. 'Yeah, well, I guess. But I missed seeing Ella being thrown out on her butt, and Jarrod groping Fi and –'

'But you had time out.'

Taylah looks like she's going to continue her rant, but stops and smiles. 'It was too short, with finding out about Trent. When can I go again?'

The speed of her shift in affect is giving me whiplash.

'Three more times in the next year.' Should cover Kelly's and Taylah's birthdays as well as Christmas. 'In what ways *did* it help?'

'The Short Stay people listen,' says Taylah. 'And they're nice.'

About as close to unconditional love as Taylah gets to have. For three nights, four days. Sixteen days a year if she keeps to our deal.

'Did you have a chance to think about anything?' I say. 'Things that might help you manage those impulses to overdose?'

'They talked to me about that. After I found out about Trent. And it was good talking to Maeve.'

'She's one of the nurses?'

'No, she was there after an overdose.'

A fellow traveller.

'She came back to visit her family. They're fucked like mine,' says Taylah. 'So . . . Short Stay. But she's got a job on an island. A resort. Great weather, okay money. Says the people she's working with are really nice, supportive.'

'Ever thought of doing something like that?'

'Nah.'

'Why not?'

'I know people here. Mum needs me.'

For sport.

'I wonder . . . do you think you need your mum?'

'Well . . . she's always been there.'

'But not always in the way you need, would that be fair to say?'

'She does her best.'

'It sounds like Maeve is getting the support she needs from her work team,' I say.

No harm in inserting an idea. It'll probably take years before she'll be ready to cut the apron strings. Perhaps she'll never work out that Kelly isn't capable of giving her what she needs.

And Kelly? Isn't she just looking for what *she* needs?

I try not to feel too despondent. Not everyone is destined to repeat patterns, and Taylah has been trying. She did ask for help.

I find Grace with Ivan and Kelly, suggesting ways of dealing with Taylah's volatility. I figure she's wasting her breath. Unlike Taylah, Kelly needs to feel superior and is unlikely to concede anything to Grace. My instinct is that to get anywhere, you'd have to suck up to her.

I'm about to leave when Ivan calls out, 'You're a doctor, right? Can you take a look at my eye?'

Eyes are a whole specialist thing, but I shine my phone light in his.

'Has it been getting better or worse?'

'Probably better.'

'If that changes, get yourself to the Eye and Ear Hospital.'

He smiles, and I can see him giving exactly that look to Aleesha or Taylah.

I add, 'You were lucky. Whatever you did that caused that, don't do it again.'

—

Minor miracle: the council calls back. They'll look at organising a cleaner for Warren, but need photos first – health and safety considerations, blah blah.

I don't like Warren's chances of being clean enough to qualify for a cleaner, but we head back, to find two boys, mid-teens, on the porch, yelling obscenities. There's fresh graffiti on the wall.

'That kid is Gurpreet's younger brother,' says Grace. 'Wait.'

It takes me a moment to remember the young man with schizophrenia we visited earlier. Meanwhile, Grace is calling his parents.

Then she's out of the car and barring the narrow exit path through the junk. 'You're in deep shit now, both of you. What are your parents going to say?'

The Sikh boy looks ashamed – like he might cry. The other teen – red-headed and the instigator I'm thinking – isn't going to let some little Asian woman intimidate him.

'Fuck off,' he says. 'The guy's a pedo, a psycho. Should be locked up. Reckon I might set a match to him and the whole place.'

'Really?' Grace pulls out her phone, waves it at him and starts taking video. 'Got that on audio, mate. Reckon with a picture the police won't have too much trouble tracking you down. And it's Mandeep, isn't it?' She's looking at the Sikh boy.

It seems so. He cringes.

She turns back to Redhead. 'He'll do a deal and you'll be doing jail time.'

I've got my answer to whether she fires up under stress. But Redhead's taken a step toward her, eyeing the phone.

'Don't even think about it,' she says. 'I'm a black belt in tae kwon do.'

I feel like I'm in a *Karate Kid* movie – a badly acted version. If I wasn't worried about Grace, I'd be laughing.

A middle-aged woman who I guess is a neighbour – or maybe just an interested passer-by – has stopped on the footpath to watch. At least we'll have a witness.

Mandeep grabs Redhead's arm. 'You can't hit a lady.'

Redhead takes a few steps back, lining up a spectacular leap from the porch over the burnt-out car body. He starts his run and Mandeep grabs his arm again, just as he commits to the jump. He falls between the porch and the car body and ends up on the ground, screaming.

I run over and see right away what he's done. I shout to Grace: 'Call an ambulance – tell them we've got a dislocated shoulder.'

I've never put one back, and I figure I'll leave it to someone who knows what they're doing.

'Doing it now,' calls the neighbour. 'And the police.'

The ambulance arrives first, and the paramedics do a swift, effective and apparently painful job on Redhead's shoulder.

Then the police pull up, just in time to stop Redhead hightailing it out of here.

Next come Mandeep's parents, who, after the shock of police cars, ambulance and a growing gallery of spectators, don't take long to work out what's been happening. The two of them tear strips off the boys, and it's interesting to see Redhead's bravado disappear in the face of parental admonishment.

'Pity Dana can't do a bit of that,' I say to Grace.

Grace points to the kid whose parents I've just cited as a model of good parenting and then to the graffiti he's just sprayed. 'Who's to say what works?'

She's right. I'm just going off what my parents did – and what I thought they should have done.

Grace grins. 'But I think you're right. Maybe if Dana took a job in their restaurant she'd pick up some good habits.'

Mandeep's mother turns to the police. 'I am Gurisha Devi and this is my husband, Angad. We will pay for any damage.'

One of the cops points to the front garden. 'I reckon it'd be impossible to damage this place beyond where it is already.'

Warren is now on the front porch, looking at the mayhem in bewilderment. Then he sees the graffiti. 'Why do they do this?'

Angad looks mortified. He's up the steps talking to Warren, and they disappear inside. I hope he has a strong stomach.

The police give Redhead a telling-off and let him go. When they aren't looking, he flips Grace the bird and takes off.

Gurisha turns to me. 'On the weekend, the community will come – you especially, Mandeep – and we will clean the house. The boy with the red hair will be here too. I know his parents.'

'Good people,' I say to Grace as we weave through the afternoon traffic.

'Most people are,' she says. 'You have to believe that to do this job.'

EIGHT

TURNING POINTS

Rosalie hates the ice. Because it's the ice that makes her life miserable and frightening and, yes, dangerous. The hulking man, three times her size, standing in the doorway of the living room threatening to kill her if she doesn't get him a fucking pizza *now* is a victim of it. He's mentally ill too, but mentally ill people aren't supposed to be any more violent than anyone else. So they keep saying. But if he wasn't mentally ill, maybe he wouldn't have started on the ice. Or would be able to get off it.

She's not sure if his anger is from the drug or the withdrawal or the schizophrenia. One thing she is sure about is that it's her problem to deal with. She doesn't want him locked up in jail or the loony bin.

But tonight she's tired. She wants to see the end of the program. Then she can get her phone off the charger and order the damn pizza. And because of that she makes a mistake. A bad mistake.

'Just give me a couple of minutes, love.'

The look in her son's eyes tells her that wasn't the right answer.

'Luka is here,' says Mia.

I was about to have lunch. Which means eating a sandwich from the mall while typing letters to GPs and making calls. Luka's a serious methamphetamine user who I met in the Emergency Department. It was my first on-call shift as a psych registrar, and everything was a bit heightened that night. I saw him last week for his depot. He doesn't have an appointment for today.

Mia sounds anxious. 'He doesn't look good.'

When I started at the clinic, I wouldn't have given much weight to a receptionist's assessment. I know better now. If they're worried, there's usually something to be worried about.

There is. I watch through the toughened glass and am glad there's no-one else in the waiting room. Luka is a big guy – big-boned, tall, muscle and lard. And he's agitated. Scratching at the tattoos on his arms. Is he high or withdrawing?

I ask Mia to lock the front door: she's got a remote switch.

'Luka,' I say through the intercom. 'When did you last sleep?'

Luka looks at me, eyes darting. 'Don't remember.'

He keeps pacing, in front of the glass now. I can see facial tics and his movements are jerky. Skin sores he's digging at, and I think he's lost weight. Still huge. Definitely high.

'Been tweaking. Wasn't working, you know? So took some more shards.'

At least he's coherent. In ED he was swearing and punching anyone in range. But the wrong person coming into the waiting room now could provoke him.

'Get someone from CATT,' I tell Mia. I'd have liked to say, *Get me the largest male*, but I know Grace, the smallest woman, would take offence.

'Will you take some olanzapine?' I ask Luka as Mia disappears.

'Yeah, anything,' he says. 'Got to slow my head down. Feels bad.'

Sure enough, it's Grace who shows up. Wearing a mobile alarm, which is something.

We have a small pharmacy trolley on site, but Grace has to find someone with the key. When she's back I make up a twenty-milligram syringe – works faster via the intramuscular route – and a ten-milligram tablet of Valium. He'll probably need another, but I don't want him passing out on the floor.

We cautiously join Luka. He lets Grace jab him and swallows the tablet.

'Will you stay here while we see if you settle down?' I say.

'Yeah, yeah,' he says, back to pacing and mumbling. 'Not good, not good.'

'Worried about people after you?' asks Grace. Ice can make you paranoid, even with the depot.

'Not thinking right.' He shakes his head as if hoping the action will make things fall into place. 'It's Mum. That's what it is. Mum.'

'Your *mum* is after you?' asks Grace.

'Nah, you need to help her.'

'With what?' I say.

'Not good, she's not good.'

Grace and I retire to behind the barrier. George from CATT – big but not as big as Luka – joins us, now that the risky stuff has been done.

I call Luka's home number – he lives with his mother, Rosalie – but no-one answers.

'How about you keep an eye on Tinkerbell here,' says Grace to George, 'while Hannah and I check out his mum?'

'You sure you need me?' I ask.

'She might need a doctor and the CATT registrar's still on study leave.'

I leave another ten milligrams of Valium with George and we hit the road.

'This is what we live for,' Grace says, as a red-light camera flashes.

The front door of the flat is locked, and no-one answers. Grace bangs loudly enough that an elderly neighbour sticks her head out. I tell her who we are.

'Do you know if Rosalie is in there?' Grace asks.

'I don't know, dear,' says the neighbour. 'But there was a bit of noise last night before I turned my hearing aids off.'

'We'll have to get the police to break in,' says Grace.

'No need,' says the neighbour. 'I'll show you where she hides the key.'

Rosalie is on the sofa. She's maybe fifties, slight. In pyjamas and cardigan. Conscious but only just. There's a lump on her head and her hair is matted with blood.

We call an ambulance and sit with her.

'You've got concussion,' I say. 'You need to be checked out.'

'I'll be okay,' Rosalie mumbles.

'You need an X-ray – you might have an internal bleed. Can you tell us what happened?'

Rosalie pulls her cardigan around herself. It's blue with grey sharks. 'Luka's been doing it tough,' she says.

'I think he's been using,' I say. 'A lot.'

'He gets depressed.'

Luka gets depressed because that's how it feels coming off ice. He either gets through that phase with the help of Valium, or, as on this occasion, he just takes more. And gets worse. The depot seems to have stopped him becoming psychotic. But it hasn't protected his mother.

'Did he hit you?' I ask.

'He didn't mean to. He just pushed and I fell over. It was an accident.'

'You need to have him charged,' says Grace. 'Otherwise, this will keep happening.'

'No.' Rosalie's been softly spoken until now. This 'no' is determined.

'He could kill you,' says Grace.

'Even unintentionally,' I add.

'No. No police, no charges.'

The ambulance arrives, and the paramedics take a handover from me and help Rosalie hobble out. Grace and I lock up and we're back on the race track.

At the Oasis, Luka has had his second Valium and is more settled. He looks distressed when we tell him his mother's in hospital, but we send him home with some more olanzapine, telling him she's likely to be back later today.

'And no more ice,' says Grace – like he'd take any notice of her. 'We'll stop by later and check you out.'

'Any ideas on stopping it happening again?' I ask Grace, once Luka's shuffled out.

'There's only one idea that's going to stop it happening again and I already said it. No more ice.'

—

I come into work the next day to find DJ Voices and Frodo waiting for me. DJ has a tribunal hearing starting in twenty minutes – a review of her community treatment order. It has four months left to run, but she's applied to have it lifted. She wants to see me before the hearing starts. Without Frodo.

We go to the tack room, and she pulls her tracksuit bottoms up. Her fluid-filled legs aren't great but there's some improvement.

'Putting them up when I eat,' she says. 'Like you told me to.'

'Be better if you slept in bed.'

'I don't love Frodo.'

'You don't have to –'

'That's not what I want to talk about.'

'So . . .'

'I might not want to stay with him. Can I do that? Leave?'

'No-one wants you living somewhere or with someone you don't want to be with.'

'But the community treatment order? Does it have to be Frodo's address?'

'Is there another place you have in mind for the CTO?'

'Yes.'

'And . . . any timeline?'

'Forget it. I'll let my lawyer argue it.'

We head to the Barn, where Jan and Frodo are sitting at the meeting table, waiting, the large screen switched on for the video conference. DJ greets a couple in their sixties sitting in the corner, both short, round and bespectacled. Her parents.

The room is cluttered with chairs, mostly empty. A large screen displays a notice saying the Mental Health Tribunal will start soon.

Five minutes before we're due to start, the door opens. It's Alex. He beckons me outside and answers the question before I ask it.

'Fucking Keith sent me. To get her back into Extended Care.'

'What? No chance. She's –'

'He said, "You fucked it, you fix it."'

'Meaning?'

'What I said. He's decided to blame me for her absconding, and he wants her back – I don't know for how long, but to prove a point. He says nobody comes to a tribunal pushing to get a patient back into hospital, so they'll take notice. And the patient's lawyer will be the same. Everybody just being nice; no match for Dr Alex fucking Ashwood with his job on the line.'

'Shit, Alex . . .'

'Just tell me what you're going to be asking for.'

'Keep her on the CTO. She's only been out of hospital two months.'

We step back in to see faces popping up on the screen. I recognise the psychiatrist, Margaret McDonald, from a previous tribunal. Sixties, independent thinker, takes no shit from her colleagues. Good news for DJ, I'd say. Or at least for what DJ wants.

The legal rep and tribunal chair is a woman of about fifty, Tanya Ko, with short hair and a tailored suit, what I can see of it. The community representative is a man in his thirties: checked shirt and truckie's beard.

The fourth person on the screen is Rupert Emerson, late thirties: I'd pick him as a musician. Frodo waves to him.

Tanya does the introductions: Rupert is DJ's lawyer. She runs through a statement of purpose, addressing DJ directly: 'Celeste, this is your hearing and the tribunal needs to make a decision as to whether a community treatment order is still required.'

Tanya lays out the criteria for continuing the order: 'The person must have a mental illness, need treatment to prevent serious consequences, treatment will be provided, and there is no less restrictive means to provide this treatment.'

The tribunal directs their attention to DJ and Margaret McDonald does most of the questioning. DJ gives monosyllabic answers. I'm not sure if she's preoccupied – with music or voices – or intimidated.

Margaret finally asks, 'When you took off, do you think you might have risked putting yourself in danger?'

DJ, Frodo and Rupert all talk at the same time, and Tanya has to intervene.

Rupert takes over. 'Let me point out that Ms Boyce *escaped* from the institution –'

'The word we use is absconded,' says Tanya.

'I understand that. Ms Boyce's word reflects the *patient's* perspective and carries different connotations, which, I will argue, better characterise what happened. Regardless, we can accept that what she did required initiative, and was the right decision, as has been demonstrated by her ability to survive and prosper in a community setting. Going forward, we might want to bear that in mind, giving due weight to Ms Boyce's judgement about her ability to cope as opposed to that of those who got it wrong.'

This guy is going in way harder than I've seen at tribunals before.

Tanya asks DJ if she wants to add anything.

DJ takes a deep breath, looks at her mother, then Margaret and finally Tanya. 'What you need to know,' she says, 'is that your shitty CTO may be just a bit of paper to you. To me, it robs me of my dignity.'

Something in what DJ's saying or how she says it hits me in a way I wasn't expecting. I've been involved in quite a few community treatment orders. Issued without a lot of thought to make sure the patient does what's good for them. Without ever really thinking about how it must feel for that patient.

Margaret and Tanya thank her, and then I'm up.

I give a summary to support the shitty piece of paper. My conclusion – which Nash has agreed with – is that without a close eye being kept on her, DJ is likely to deteriorate. The mobile team are visiting and getting her off her feet. Whether those visits would continue if the CTO was lifted would be a matter for both parties. So probably not. Dignity versus survival.

I outline how unwell DJ was, the long period of time that she was non-compliant, the admissions. I conclude by saying that she is agreeing to take clozapine, is currently stable, but has a problem with lymphoedema that needs close management, and she isn't as compliant with that as she is with the medication. I look at DJ – can't read her expression.

Tanya asks me if I think DJ has deteriorated since leaving Extended Care 'so precipitously'.

Glances and smiles are exchanged around the room at the bland summary of *walked boldly out the door while recorded voices were screaming from behind the cupboards and patients were swarming up a rope ladder.*

'Not from a mental health point of view,' I say. 'But physically, yes.'

The community rep – Bilal Khan – asks how serious the lymphoedema is.

'It's the worst I've seen.'

'But,' says Bilal, 'what does it mean? Does it matter? I mean her legs may not look great – no offence intended – but so what?'

'The risk is that her skin breaks down. She'll get sores and infections that won't heal, and they could extend to involve her whole leg or cause septic shock. Which can be fatal.'

Mrs Boyce is clutching her husband's arm. DJ still doesn't look as if this is a conversation about her.

Tanya asks me: 'Dr Wright, can I confirm that it was Ms Boyce's partner who came to get her medication?'

'Yes, at her request.' I have to say it. 'He's been an important support. I've told DJ that I'd be worried if she didn't have him or someone similar around.'

'Are you concerned they might separate?' Tanya asks.

I don't have to answer, because Rupert interrupts.

'Your Honour, Dr Wright is not in a position to speculate on Ms Boyce's future personal arrangements. We will submit that her compliance is not reliant on having a housemate or carer, provided she can attend the outpatient clinic without threat of police harassment.'

Tanya looks up from her notes. 'We're in a tribunal, Mr Emerson, not a court of law. I'm Ms Ko, not "Your Honour". You'll have an opportunity to put your argument. But I understand the Service has seen fit to provide a second medical opinion. Dr Ashwood?'

Alex explains that he works in Extended Care, where DJ was being treated prior to absconding, and that he's representing the head of the unit, Dr Barnard. Then, in a voice so flat it's almost robotic: 'It is the strong view of Extended Care that Ms Boyce should, for her own safety, return to inpatient care.'

Frodo is on his feet; DJ is looking gobsmacked. Her parents are looking . . . concerned – worried, I'd guess, that there's disagreement about whether she's okay in the community. Rupert looks surprised, but not shaken.

Even before Frodo has sat down, Margaret McDonald is on it. 'Extended Care doesn't have an opinion. Is it *your* opinion that Ms Boyce requires inpatient treatment?'

'I'm advised –' begins Alex.

'I'm not interested in what you've been advised,' Margaret says. 'You've seen Ms Boyce?'

'Briefly. I'd only just started my rotation.' Alex glances apologetically at DJ but she isn't looking.

'Did you see enough to form the view you're presenting to us today?'

'I'm representing Dr Barnard's view.'

Rupert begins to speak but disappears from the screen: in his haste, he's stood up. By the time he's down again, Tanya is speaking.

'There's no written report from Dr Barnard?'

'No.'

'Then I think you've helped us as much as you can, Dr Ashwood.'

Alex looks like the robot he channelled. He's done the right thing for DJ but put another nail in the coffin of his career at the Menzies.

'Mr Emerson?' says Tanya.

Rupert takes a deliberate breath before beginning. 'If you'll permit an aside . . . Dr Barnard not having the time or inclination to join us says something about the process and his level of care, or of being – since this is a less formal setting than a courtroom, you'll perhaps allow me the expression – butthurt.'

'I think you've had your aside,' says Tanya, but all three tribunal members seem to be more amused than is dignified.

Rupert smiles and continues. 'I'd like to set the scene by describing for the tribunal how Ms Boyce is spending her time now. She is an internationally acclaimed electronic music star. She composes and creates music and videos seen around the world by . . .'

After a detailed history focusing on DJ's achievements, independence and sound decisions in the face of a debilitating illness, he summarises his case.

'Yes, she has a mental illness. We are not disputing that nor that she needs treatment. The treatment is being provided, but only through the initiative of my client, who had to send a friend to the clinic because she was under threat of being returned by police to a place where none of us would choose to be. Made worse by, I would submit, a paternalistic, petulant and punitive management, which had withdrawn her right to practise and perform – arguably the things that make her life worth living.

'Despite the risk of readmission, Ms Boyce showed up to the clinic. She recognised the importance of getting her medication – her *treatment*. And that is our simple point. There *is* a less restrictive way of ensuring she gets treatment. Which is to trust her to do what she's demonstrated she does: get it for herself. By all means monitor that and follow up if she's forgotten, as my dentist surely does if I forget to book an appointment.'

Rupert picks up on the smiles. 'You find the comparison amusing, because my teeth – or, if we want to raise the stakes, hypothetically my heart and liver – are physical. As, incidentally, is my brain, but I won't take us down that rabbit hole. What I will point out is that the only reason Dr Wright has given for the order to remain in place is Ms Boyce's lymphoedema – a physical disorder. As such, it should not be a consideration for this tribunal.'

Yes, it should, because the neglect is a result of her mental illness. But Rupert seems to have the tribunal where he wants them.

'Ms Boyce is attending a specialist and wearing the recommended stockings. Her mental illness is in remission. She would like her life back. To make her own choices without the draconian, and, in this case, unnecessary, powers of the Mental Health Act bearing down upon her. We can't be absolutely sure that she will be one hundred per cent compliant with what others think is best for her. But we need to afford her what I believe the tribunal calls the *dignity of risk*.'

Tanya nods and asks DJ's parents if they want to say anything.

'Just that we love our daughter and want her safe,' says Mr Boyce. 'It's all very well to talk about the dignity of risk, but . . . some of the choices she's made in the past . . .' He trails off. 'We respect that she wants to make her own life, but we just want someone watching out for her.' He's looking at Frodo.

While the tribunal members go into an online room to make their decision, I introduce myself to the Boyces.

'Oh yes. Are you the doctor who got into trouble for not telling Dr Barnard Celeste was planning to . . . leave?' asks Mrs Boyce.

I pick up concern rather than anger.

'No,' I say. 'I work in the outpatient clinic. You're thinking of Dr Ashwood.' I flash a look at Alex; I'm pretty sure he can hear.

Mr Boyce glances over. 'The poor bugger who just got hung out to dry?'

I nod.

'Dr Barnard suggested we should make a complaint.' He pauses. 'We relied on what he told us. If we've got the young bloke into strife, we're happy to tell your management that's what happened.' He smiles. 'Butthurt.'

When Tanya announces that they are taking DJ off the order, Rupert beams and DJ and Frodo high-five. I half-hope she doesn't leave him, sex wedge and all.

I spend fifteen minutes with the Boyces promising I'll do all I can to ensure DJ continues treatment.

DJ and Frodo are in the corridor, and I walk over to them.

'Hope your lawyer didn't charge you too much for that, but he made a good case. If it had been my call, I'd have kept her on it . . .' I realise I'm speaking to Frodo. I take a breath and turn to DJ. 'Sorry. Kept *you* on it. But maybe I was being too cautious. Please, *please* keep putting your legs up.'

'He didn't charge too much,' says DJ.

'Pro bono,' says Frodo. 'He's a fan.'

—

I have a few minutes to grab a coffee after the tribunal, and start thinking – again – about my upcoming date with Simon. And the look Alex gave me when he saw us together.

I wonder what the deal is with Alex's girlfriend. He can't have been dating her for long when he told me; maybe it hasn't lasted.

He's invited me to drinks twice – hasn't mentioned her. If it was over, would he tell me? He's not telling me how he feels about the trouble he's having at work; he walked away from our study group when he could have stayed and talked. I guess his girlfriend is his sounding board now. If she exists. I feel like texting him.

Hannah: stop. You're basically dating two other guys. Alex is your colleague. You'll see him at study group and in the registrars' room. Leave it alone. Are you paying attention, Hannah? Do not text him.

I text him, and suggest we get lunch at a sushi place over the road from the Oasis. Debrief about DJ. He's straight back to me: *Love to.* I can't stop the smile. Pathetic.

It's only a few minutes' walk and I need some fresh air, though today's weather is grim. A blustering wind sends dried leaves into whirlpools around my feet and the rain starts just as I get inside the restaurant.

Alex is there already, smiling. We order some miso and gyoza because they're hot.

'How was Keith?' I ask. 'About the tribunal?'

'Unsurprised.' He's trying to contain a grin. 'I told him what DJ's lawyer said about him.'

'What? Butthurt?'

'Said I thought he'd want to know. Just the messenger.'

'You didn't really?'

'I did. I've had enough. He has thirty-five patients locked up. Most – probably all of them – need to be there, but if it was up to him it'd be ten times that number. Better there than homeless or in prison or not looking after themselves is basically his attitude. So much for the dignity of risk. And he's not engaged. Too busy with his tribunals and legal opinions.'

'You know he encouraged DJ's parents to complain?'

'Not surprised.'

'They said they'd be prepared to –'

'Don't worry about it. Seriously. It's between me and Keith, and anything anyone else does will make it worse. And talking about him is only going to put me off my lunch. Have you found a therapist yet?'

'Not one I want to work with.' Laughing, I tell him about Adrian with the bike and the coffee and the patient ahead of me.

'So, did you choose therapists who were unsuitable, or did you decide that after you'd met them?'

'If you're saying I'm avoiding therapy . . .'

'That's what I'm saying. Nothing you told me sounded like a deal breaker. The older analyst you saw was a little unworldly. A lot of them are. This guy turns up late once. You've never been late for anything? So, what is it you *don't* want to talk to them about?'

'Guess.'

'Same as what you *do* want to talk to them about,' he says. 'Your family, right?'

I'm laughing. 'I suppose you'd be right ninety per cent of the time with that guess.'

'You're afraid that if you work through the stuff that happened around the suicide, you may not like what you find.'

'Maybe you and I have that in common,' I say.

'Very different circumstances. In your case, I think your concern is that you'll uncover buried anger at your family and become estranged from them. Like Lennon.'

‘Aren’t I supposed to work this out for myself, rather than you telling me?’

‘If I was your therapist. But we don’t see each other as often as you’d see a therapist. So I have to cut to the chase. What I’d suggest –’

I look at my watch.

Alex smiles. ‘Did I see avoidant behaviour?’

‘Don’t you have to go too?’

‘Keith can wait. In fact, Keith can get stuffed.’ He pulls out his phone and texts.

It’s pouring down outside. My 1 pm guy hardly ever shows up. I can be late. I text Mia. And Alex continues his non-therapist-like handing out of advice.

‘I think you need to let go of the idea of family reconciliation as the goal. If it happens, great. But deep down, you think the opposite might happen. That may be the price of insight; of facing the facts, of living honestly and authentically.’

‘Not sure I’m ready for that.’

‘And that might be a great starting point for your therapist. Why you’re not ready.’

I’m going to have to share some stuff I hadn’t intended to share. Not all of it though.

‘Before I do anything, I want to get a few things straight in my head. About what happened back then. Not just the suicide, but things that happened around it. I’ve got in touch with this guy who was there. He’s about the same age as me –’

‘Does he drive a black Porsche?’

That belongs to the stuff I wasn’t going to share. But I nod.

Alex goes quiet and I make an attempt at explaining. 'I'm seeing him because he's the one person who can help me make sense of something important that happened. I don't have any control over what kind of car he has. That's his choice.'

'Like the high heels were yours.'

I think he regrets that as soon as it comes out, but he's said it now. Time to close this one out.

'I dressed up because it was a date. And you told me you were seeing someone.'

He pauses. 'I did.'

This time he's silent for a lot longer and I let him sit with it.

'I am seeing someone,' he says. 'I really needed someone who wasn't involved in the stuff that happened around Xavier's suicide, who could be objective. I hope you find someone like that. Maybe it's Black Porsche Guy, but I'd be prepared to bet it isn't.'

'And I'll bet your girlfriend is a therapist of some kind.'

'Of course she is. Her name's Marla and, like I said, I think you'd love her almost as much as I do.'

I'm not sure I can hold my shit together for much longer, so I signal for the bill.

But before he leaves, Alex has one more piece of advice. 'Now that I've got a better idea of what you're looking for in a therapist, you might want to try this guy. Friend of my dad's – went to uni together. He just moved back from New Zealand and is building a practice. In case Black Porsche Guy doesn't have all the answers.'

I walk the long way back to the Oasis to cool off. I use the time to look up Alex's dad's buddy, online. His photo reeks of self-satisfied middle-aged businessman. He's in a private psychiatry centre close to the CBD, and is promoting some weekend meditation retreat that he seems to have a financial interest in. Looks like he'd drive a Porsche.

Alex can stick it. I'm still feeling bruised by his cavalier promotion of Marla over me as a confidante. I won't be having drinks with him anytime soon.

—

I arrive at the afternoon team meeting to sombre looks all round.

'Problem?' I ask.

'You didn't hear?' says Grace. 'It's on the news. When you didn't show up for your one pm, the guy cracked it and went on a rampage. If he'd only had his meds . . .'

'Oh shit.'

But Grace can't keep a straight face and then they're all laughing.

'Jan saw you at the sushi place with your boyfriend,' says Grace. 'Thought you deserved it.'

Luka is the real topic of today's team meeting, and a bit too close for comfort to Grace's version of my 1 pm patient, who in fact didn't show up.

I summarise the background we all know. Twenty-six, first diagnosed at sixteen with drug-induced psychosis, several admissions since, psychotic symptoms including delusions and auditory hallucinations even in the absence of drug use. Non-compliant with medication for most of those years, but recently been doing better on depot.

'The issue when we saw him,' Grace says when I finish, 'was that he was well medicated and not obviously psychotic, but he'd been using. Three times in a short space of time in increasing doses.'

I describe the assault and the aftermath. 'Has he seriously hurt his mother before?'

'Once, when he was very paranoid,' says Grace. 'We had about ten police at the home to get him out. Only good thing was he wasn't armed.'

'If he'd a gun they'd hae shot him,' says Louis. 'One of my patients back home strangled his ma.'

'Good to know,' says Grace, deadpan.

Mohammed, the fourth-year registrar, takes that as a cue to expand on Louis's contribution. 'Seventy per cent of men who kill their mothers have schizophrenia.'

So much for the official line that mental illness isn't associated with violence. Which doesn't sit too well anyway with the other line that a high proportion of people in prison have a mental illness. Great to destigmatise and break some of the stereotypes – but you wouldn't want to be Luka's mum.

'Surely, in this case,' Nash says, 'the issue is the drug use.'

'We've referred him to drug and alcohol services a million times,' says Jan. 'By the time he gets an appointment, he's back using.'

'We can't justify admission just for detox,' says Nash. 'You're telling me he's psychiatrically stable.'

'We could take him to the drug-counsellor appointment,' a nurse from the mobile team says. 'But we've tried before and he wasn't home.'

We conclude there are limits to how effective we can be if Rosalie wants to risk living with Luka. Jan will talk to her about other accommodation options. But we all know it's more about checking that box in case we have to answer to the coroner one day. There's no sense that Rosalie will act on Jan's advice.

—

This time I recognise Naomi's number. Brianna's friend's mother. Chloe's sister's friend's mother. The ripples of mental illness spread far and wide.

'Brianna got through the interview,' Naomi tells me. 'It was no picnic. When they found out I wasn't her mother . . . But I set them straight pretty quickly: over fourteen and she's seen a psychiatrist. Move on. Seems she's nearly fourteen weeks, so lucky that camp didn't go any longer.'

'She's okay?'

'As much as she can be. I mean, there was hell to pay with her father because she's back staying here overnight, but it seemed easiest as she'll have the procedure tomorrow and they don't need to know she missed a day of school.'

'You . . . Thank you,' I say. 'This is tough on Brianna and your support will make a huge difference.'

Naomi's tone softens. 'My mother had a child when she was sixteen. Before me. Adopted the baby out. Then the kid came to find her and totally rejected her. When Mum got cancer at forty-five she believed it was her punishment. I don't know if a termination or keeping the baby would have been better for her, but Brianna? She's got her whole life ahead of her. I'd like to see her move on from this and be happy.'

'I'm hopeful,' I say. 'She's a gutsy kid.'

—

Friday night, Jess catches me getting ready for my date with Simon – rescheduled to dinner after I had to cancel lunch.

'Hey, you didn't tell me you were going out,' she says, standing at the bathroom door.

'I didn't.'

'Because . . . shit.' She looks hard at me. 'It's Simon, isn't it? It is.'

As a doctor, you learn that people aren't always ready to hear the truth. 'No, it's Jason,' I say. I can see she doesn't believe me.

She groans. 'What about Jon?'

'Even if I was interested, he's not.'

'He told you that?'

'He said he's not looking.'

'Did he say why?'

'I didn't ask.'

'OMG, he can't tell you because . . . it's *you*.'

My turn to stare. But . . . no. Really, no. 'I don't get that vibe, Jess. Not at all.'

Jess, needless to say, doesn't believe me.

I'm in the Uber when Simon texts me to cancel. *Work crisis – sorry – but it goes with the territory.*

A lot to unpack there. I probably deserved it. But I'm surprised at how disappointed I'm feeling. On the other hand, I'm sort of enjoying the game. Thinking about what to do next.

But right now, I'm all dressed up. Which means calling Jon would send the wrong message. And Alex . . . *don't even think about it.* Which leaves Jason. I feel kind of bad using him as a last resort for a date – but we were supposed to be organising one anyway.

He's free and I meet him at the bar where I used to drink with Alex. No time to be original, and I'm comfortable there. And Jason is, despite his passion about documentary making, a comfortable sort of guy. Definitely more comfortable than Simon. Also keen enough to show up at short notice and not ask any awkward questions. Why would he when he's got the documentary to talk about?

'Your family have been fantastic,' he says. 'I'm shooting at their place next weekend. Will you be there?'

'I won't change my mind about being in your doco, no matter how much you sweet-talk me,' I say.

'I don't expect you to be on camera. Thought you might like to watch the interviews. Maybe give me some background.' He takes time out to eat a deep-fried prawn. 'I'm actually feeling a bit awkward meeting the parents of someone I've been out with . . . a couple of times. Especially without her being around.'

'If you don't tell them, neither will I.' I laugh. 'My mother does have a sixth sense though.'

'So, will you come? Help me navigate your family?'

'Sure.' And help them navigate Jason. I don't think he's naturally exploitative but he's working in a competitive world. I don't want them saying something they'll regret and having to endure all their friends watching it.

'I gather Kayla is being interviewed too?'

Jason nods.

'She's probably spending the day before in the hairdresser and won't need a make-up artist unless they need to peel some off.'

'I have a make-up artist who could manage the Kardashians. Your folks found me a couple of other ex-foster kids too.'

My mind goes through the few we see a lot. Most came from, and stayed in, the region. 'Who?'

Jason whips out a notebook. 'Jenny Pearson.'

'Foster Kid Twenty-Six. Quiet, maybe coming with her sister?'

'Good memory. She's going to ask her. Other one is Simon Trevallyan. Know him?'

He's one of the few that I know for sure my parents are *not* in touch with.

'Really?' I force a smile. How is it that the two men I've been out with in the last month are about to meet up? 'He's doing okay, I think. And he'll look good on screen. But white heterosexual male, I'm afraid. Very white hetero male.'

'As long as he looks good on screen.' Jason smiles. 'My co-producer is chasing down some stories in the African community. But you didn't like him?'

Acting isn't one of my strong suits apparently. But Jason has misread my expression.

'Don't worry, I didn't like him either.' He laughs. 'I'm a director, so I prefer to be the one directing things.'

I smile. I'm getting to like Jason. And I only promised myself I wouldn't sleep with *Simon* till I found a therapist.

—

When I get home the next morning, Jess is having breakfast. I don't have to ask what she's thinking but she tells me anyway.

'Oh my god, you did it! You had sex with your brother. I can't believe . . .'

She keeps going, and I'm laughing so hard, I'm crying.

'I swear, it was Jason. Like I told you.'

I finally fess up that though I really was with Jason, I had intended to see Simon. I find her visceral dislike of Simon both irritating . . . and disquieting.

I phone my family and get Dad. Ask if Simon has been in touch.

'Out of the blue,' says Dad. 'Asked after you.'

Bet he did. Before we went out.

—

When Mia tells me Luka is in the waiting room and isn't looking good – again – my immediate thought is that this time he's killed his mother.

He's crying, but he's not pacing or scratching, and his eyes aren't darting. I bring him into my office.

'She's back in hospital,' he says.

'What happened?'

'She just went down. Collapsed. I had to call the ambulance.'

'Luka, did you hit her? Push her?'

'No, no. Nothing like that. She's in ICU. They say it's from the first bleed. She bled again. She might die.'

'Oh Luka, I'm so sorry.'

'It's my fault,' he says.

I don't argue. Instead I say, 'What are you going to do to make sure it never happens again? With anyone?'

He knows what he has to say. 'Never ever use drugs again. I won't as long as she . . . makes it. If she doesn't . . .'

Nash is unavailable. I try Nicole, the person who wants to change the system. I explain I need an urgent drug and alcohol counsellor appointment. Like today.

'They don't work like that.'

'I know. But it might be the only chance of saving a patient's mother. From him. If she gets out of ICU that is. He's highly motivated right now.'

I let Luka hear this. He's nodding, tears streaming down his cheeks.

'Leave it with me,' Nicole says.

I send Luka to sit in the waiting room.

Nash is back to me an hour later. In the meantime, I've learned that Rosalie is in a coma and is scheduled for surgery to take the pressure off her brain.

'Good work ringing Nicole,' Nash says. *Really?* 'Get Jan to organise him a taxi voucher and get him to his appointment in an hour at ActNow.'

It's an appropriately named service for this situation; except there's normally a week's wait for an appointment.

On my way home, I go to ICU to see Rosalie post-surgery. She's unconscious but the treating team are positive. Luka is there.

'I have another appointment next week,' he says. 'I've promised God I will stop the ice.'

'Do you believe in God?'

'No. But my mother does.'

'Perhaps you could move out. What do you think?'

He considers this. 'When she's better? Maybe I'll go see my father for a while.'

'Good idea,' I say.

Luka beams, and engulfs me in a suffocating hug.

We don't get much gratitude in public psychiatry – let alone hugs. If anyone had told me the man who'd decked a security guard a few months ago and was restrained on a trolley would hug me and I'd welcome it . . . well, I guess I'd have been delighted.

—

When I get home, there's a bunch of irises on the table. Jess hasn't put them in a vase. No note, but I remember her story about Simon buying irises for the drama teacher.

It's an apology, right? For cancelling our date. That's the obvious, simple answer. But I have this weird feeling that he's sent them because of what I did instead of the date. I tell myself not to be ridiculous. How would he know?

But I thought he didn't know my address, either.

Time to find a therapist.

NINE

IDÉE FIXE

A woman sits in an armchair, unmoving, contemplating whether to lie down, take some more pills or kill herself.

Nobody understands constant, unremitting pain until they've lived it.

The well-meaning relatives and friends don't have a clue.

'Maybe try going for a walk, push through.'

'I'm not suggesting it's not real to you, but maybe it's . . . you know . . . psychological.'

'Have you tried meditation, or acupuncture, or reiki?' They'll offer to come with you, skipping with the joy of being pain-free, rubbing it in.

The lawyers who think that financial compensation will balance the books – they don't understand either.

And the doctors, the people you count on to help? They've got ideas, and theories, and suggestions. But none of them truly listen. None of them understand how the pain saps any desire to do anything.

It never should have happened. That's the cherry on top.

All the things she's thinking about feel too hard to do. But only one is a permanent solution.

I'm sitting in the tearoom at the Oasis reading the file for my first appointment after lunch. There are notices pinned over notices on the board – the puppies for sale are likely fully grown by now.

I've got takeaway from the mall. So has Nash. I grab him to get some help with my next patient and sneak in a gentle hint about some psychotherapy training that would help with Brianna and Taylah. Not for the first time, but I don't think I'm being heard.

'I hear you,' says Nash. 'Now tell me about this chronic pain patient.'

Valerie Caldecott: presented at ED with suicidal thoughts. According to CATT, who have been seeing her for the last two weeks, the acute crisis is over. She's on a waiting list for an assessment by a private psychiatrist. In the interim, she gets me.

In theory, I'm seeing her about her ED presentation, but reading between the lines of the notes, she's more likely to want to talk about the pain, which may have a psychological component. I know nothing about chronic pain, except that there are specialised clinics for it – which is why I know nothing about chronic pain.

She's been to the pain guys. Last seen by a trainee neurologist three months ago. On regular Panadeine. The trainee suggested pregabalin but Valerie refused; didn't want to even *try* an anti-anxiety drug. She seems committed to the pain having a physical cause.

'She may be doctor shopping,' says Nash. 'No-one is giving her an answer that makes sense to her, or that she wants to hear.'

'There's an ongoing workers' compensation claim.'

'So you're inclined to see her insistence that the pain is purely physical – and is as severe as she says – in that light?'

'I don't want to be naive,' I say. 'And I don't understand why she's having so much pain with so little injury. I mean, it was three years ago so it should have improved.'

According to the notes there was a soft tissue back injury, and a rotator cuff tear that needed surgery. But no broken bones or nerve involvement.

'Because you're thinking about acute pain,' says Nash. 'Chronic pain is another thing – nerves are acting differently. Just because we don't know how it works doesn't mean it doesn't exist. And we know certain genes make you more susceptible.'

As they do to just about everything, physical or psychological.

'Child abuse also makes you more vulnerable,' says Nash. 'Probably by altering your pain pathways.'

The mention of child abuse prompts a thought about Taylah.

Nash must catch something in my look. 'I sometimes think that child abuse to us is like smoking is to a physician: it's a risk factor for just about everything, and you're going to see the results of it all the time.'

'Except people choose to smoke,' I say.

Keith comes into the room munching a burger and Nash decides to brief him on Valerie's case.

'You're the medico-legal expert,' he says. 'Tell Hannah how to stay out of trouble.'

'Chronic pain . . . If you're in court you'll need to call it "somatic symptom disorder with predominant pain", but it's the same thing,' says Keith, apparently enjoying being asked about something other than chronic schizophrenia. 'When it comes to medical panels that review these cases for insurance and the courts, we end up tossing around a bunch of other diagnoses which are basically useless in the context of chronic pain: adjustment disorders, depression, you name it. If it's in the book, I've probably seen someone diagnosed with it.'

Keith takes a bite of his burger and I wait while he chews and swallows.

'I always ask, "Is there any part of your body that is free of pain?" You'd be surprised how many patients say, "I have pain everywhere".'

This isn't giving me any clues about how to help Valerie.

He sees my expression. 'The people I assess are trapped in needing to maintain their illness to support their claim while the system grinds on, quite often for years. Powerless and frustrated.'

He's basically saying that if there wasn't a psychological component there to start with, the system will create one.

'Your friend Alex would probably have them revisit the trauma; confront their employer or something.' He laughs. 'Their PTSD means they'd run a mile rather than do that. Not to mention the legal implications. Stick to medication.'

'Anti-anxiety drugs?'

'And antidepressants. If she's not on them, give her some. They'll help with mood and ability to manage the pain.'

Why do I just know Valerie is going to say she's not depressed?

—

'I'm not depressed,' says Valerie when I meet her in the waiting room. 'I'm very unhappy but that's because I'm *in pain*. If that was fixed, I wouldn't be unhappy. Am I making sense?'

Valerie is fifty-nine, but she walks hunched, like she's eighty-nine. It takes her a full two minutes to get to my office and the effort exhausts her.

She sits and relaxes a little. 'Today's a bad day. Even on the good days, I can only walk for twenty minutes.'

I let her settle in and get as comfortable as she can.

'I'm not a mental patient,' she tells me firmly. 'But my GP keeps badgering me to see someone and it was easier to give in. Maybe you can tell her that there's nothing wrong with me mentally.'

'You came to ED . . .'

'Because I was *in pain* and wanted to end it. I've talked to the CATT team. I'm managing at the moment. I'd manage better if doctors worked on the problem instead of telling me there isn't one.'

'You were injured, right? At work?'

'I was a disability support worker for twenty-two years. In a community residential unit. Loved it. Now what am I?'

She hasn't worked for three years. With Nash's comment about child abuse in mind, I ask about her early life.

She was brought up in a pull-up-your-socks-and-get-on-with-it farming family. Not abuse as such, but emotional neglect can also leave scars – and cause later vulnerabilities. No-one in the family has had anything like chronic pain, including a brother who lost an arm in a farm accident. Father died milking the cows, never missed a day, and mother is still going strong. Next question?

That'd be Keith's. 'Is there anywhere free of pain?'

'My knees and my ankles and my right eyelid . . . do you want me to go on? *Most* of me is free of pain, but that's not the point, is it? It's my back. Though I end up so tense, my shoulders and neck get pretty bad too.'

That half-joke, half-admonishment was a positive spark, and I can sense her trying to push through the pain. I search for something positive to keep it going.

'How do you spend your time?'

She's married with two children and three grandchildren.

'Waited hand and foot on my husband for years. He's having to pay it back now.' She moves uncomfortably in her chair and the wind goes out of her sails. 'I'm not up to going out. Used to belong to the local football club, lots of friends. Now I only go out to doctors' appointments.'

'Do you see your children and grandchildren?'

'They're great. We have the eldest after school a couple of nights a week when my daughter works. But it's not like I can get down on the floor and play. And Joel tipped the highchair and I had to catch him . . . You have no idea of the pain.'

This was the precipitant for the suicidal thoughts. She gets up, apologising that she can't sit still for long. And perhaps to hide the tears.

'Does it affect your sleep?' I ask, nudging the tissue box in her direction.

'Something shocking. Only get three or four hours, and even then it's broken.'

'How did the injury happen?'

She must have told this story a million times, but I want to hear it from her. She doesn't seem too put out.

'They moved me to a different unit, with more challenging kids. Even though I'd told them I wasn't up to it. A few months earlier, one of the kids had knocked me over. My back was sore but I was able to get back to work. I was supposed to be on light duties, but they were short-staffed and just kept pushing and pushing.'

She sits down, now openly wiping tears away. She reaches for a tissue. 'They're good kids, but they're big and they don't know their own strength. I asked for an aide, but . . . like I said, short-staffed.'

'Sounds tough.'

'Jude – that's the kid's name – just got frustrated. He grabbed my arm and pushed me. I fell over a chair. Haven't had a day without pain since.'

I nod and she elaborates. 'It's there all the time. Can't lift my arm up. Can't sit or stand for long, so I can't cook or do housework. Totally useless.'

During my surgical term I saw people walk again, pain-free or close to it, after car accidents that shattered their pelvis, femur and spine. In that context, it's hard to make sense of Valerie's experience – which means I need to do more homework.

Insurance claim or not, I feel she's genuine. Which is not the same as her knowing whether the underlying cause of her current pain is psychological, physical or a combination of the two.

I go back to what I sensed was bitterness toward her employer.

'It was a new manager,' she says, and the anger is definitely there. 'Thought he knew best. He really had it in for me. After the first injury, he'd belittle me in front of other staff and even the kids. Made it sound like I was whingeing. All I wanted was what was best for the children.'

'How did other workers find him?'

'Three left within the space of a few months. But he got away with it. Ruined my life. And got promoted.'

'You must be angry at him,' I say, thinking of what Keith told me. 'I don't suppose you ever had mediation?'

Valerie snorts. 'Lawyers wouldn't allow it. I'd like to tear him a new one, I can tell you.'

The expression sits oddly with Valerie's age and I can't help smiling. She smiles back, a moment of connection.

'So the . . . um . . . legal process . . . does that play on your mind?'

Valerie shakes her head, firmly. 'I leave it with the lawyers. They call me when they need me to do something. Otherwise I don't think about it. I've seen people get caught up in that sort of thing. It's only money. Not going to fix the pain.'

'I can understand how upsetting this all would be,' I say. 'No surprise you're unhappy. Have you felt it's more than that?'

'I don't have depression,' Valerie says. 'I told you. It's the pain.'

'I understand that. But as a consequence of having to live with the pain and not getting any sleep . . .'

Valerie gives me a look that basically says *I'm not mentally ill and don't try to make me say I am.*

'It would be hard to manage for the most stoic of people,' I say.

Valerie accepts this. Barely. 'They just need to fix my shoulder and spine.'

'Has anything helped?'

'The first surgery did, for a while.'

'What are your doctors suggesting is the next step?'

'The people at the pain clinic just feed me more pills. They constipate me and I don't want to get addicted. And my GP wanted to give me duloxetine. It's an antidepressant. See what I mean about her?'

I do. Her GP thinks that there are psychological consequences, if not causes. 'It might be worth a try. The pain is causing psychological reactions and at least the medication might help those.'

She ignores the suggestion. 'I've found a surgeon who thinks another operation might help. And I may need my bones fused.'

'Does anything help at the moment?'

'My dog. But then I feel bad I can't take him for a walk.'

'Can you try and do that if the suicidal thoughts are really strong?'

'I wouldn't do it to my husband and kids,' Valerie says. 'Kill myself, I mean. I took myself to the Emergency Department, didn't I?'

'But the thoughts are hard to manage. So maybe try some distraction?'

'Do you have any suggestions?' Valerie doesn't look like she's expecting any.

She's right. Parkrun isn't going to cut it. And time's up.

'I don't really know your life,' I say. 'But think about what might work. A psychologist could help you put together a list and try some different options.'

Her expression says, *Thanks for the platitude*, and I'm embarrassed. For just a moment during the interview there had been a connection and, as much for myself as for her, I want to finish on that note.

'If you see that psychologist, maybe tell them about tearing your old boss a new one. Could be a good place to start.'

Valerie nods and smiles. Grimly.

—

Taylah is late but only by a couple of minutes.

'Long line,' she says. She's got two cups of coffee in her hands and offers me one. 'I figure you're a skinny latte girl.'

Close enough.

'Me and Aleesha,' Taylah says as soon as we're seated in my office, 'we want to tell Mum. About what Ivan tried. And what Jimmy did.'

'Why do you want to tell her?'

'So she'll stop bringing these pieces of shit home.'

And Aleesha and I will have her to ourselves. I'm also wondering if Aleesha does want to tell Kelly, and if so, why? Or is Taylah including her because she still has a fantasy family in her mind?

'I get that,' I say. 'But . . .' How do I suggest that Kelly won't change her behaviour just because her daughter wants her to? When I told Brianna she couldn't change her mother, she heard me. But Taylah's need is deeper seated.

'How about you write a letter to her first?' I say. 'Not to send. But to get down all the things you'd like to say to her. Bring it next time and we can talk about what reactions your mother might have.'

This is a suggestion from Elena, who slipped in a swipe at the psychiatry training program: 'If you take the role of Kelly in reading the letter, you can put it in your case report and check off psychodrama.'

Taylah looks sceptical.

'It'll give you a chance to think about how to manage if your mother doesn't react the way you're hoping,' I say. 'We can talk about it, and then decide if you want to go ahead.'

Taylah's scepticism segues into incredulity with a dash of curiosity.

Before we finish the session I ask, 'So Aleesha wants to tell your mum too?'

'So we can be a team,' Taylah says.

She's Foster Kid Twenty aged eight, eyes shining. I feel enormously sorry for her and I'd like to give her a hug. But she's not Brianna; and Elena has warned me that if I get too close to Taylah she'll recreate the same dynamics with me as she has with her mother. There's a million ways I can let her down, even with the best intentions.

'Okay, we can keep that in mind too,' I say.

—

My place again for study group. It's actually Alex's turn, but apparently his apartment is a mess with the renovations. Ndidi said it'd be inconvenient for Torben – and told me privately that he'd arced up about cooking for us. Jon asked me if I could host it.

'See?' says Jess, as we're peeling potatoes. 'He wants to be with you.'

'He's going to be with me wherever we meet. Maybe it's you.'

I'm being flippant, but Jess turns away.

All five of us have patients we want to discuss.

Without thinking too much about it, I start with Brianna, and catch a look from Alex which I read as: *Here we go with your favourite patient, not the one you need the most help with.* And I have more supervision than these guys are getting.

Jess appears with her roast chicken, and joins us at the table. I take advantage of the interruption to cut my presentation short, and we switch to a patient Carey's dealing with in Acute.

When we've finished with our cases and the chicken, Jon asks Alex about the HR meeting – the one prompted by the complaint from DJ's parents.

Alex glances at Ndidi. 'I did what you said – had the union rep there. They were great. Pointed out that patients make threats all the time, that you wouldn't routinely report them, that DJ's threat lacked detail, and in the end her walking out was opportunistic.

'The rep didn't say it, but it was pretty clear to everyone that if Keith hadn't treated DJ like a child and locked her down, none of this would have happened. That was the media angle, and the HR guys must have known it. Don't think Keith did himself any favours with them.'

'So, a good outcome,' says Carey. 'If you ignore context.'

'Right. I have to keep working next to the guy. The union rep thought I should go him for bullying.'

'You should,' says Ndidi.

'Isn't going to happen,' Alex says. 'I'm the straight white male in this group. I'm just getting a taste of what the rest of you have had to deal with forever. It'll be over in a few months.'

I suspect Ndidi thinks he's perpetuating the system that keeps straight white males like Keith Barnard in power, but she lets it go.

And I let Alex go without offering support. I've avoided even looking at him for most of the evening.

When I see Jon hanging around after the others have left, I head to my room, leaving Jess to see him out.

—

I wasn't expecting to see Valerie again, but she's booked an appointment. I'm guessing she's not coming to tell me that our chat has cured her pain.

I've guessed right. Though it must be a good day – she's walking a lot better.

'I just wanted to tell you that it's definitely not psychological,' she says. 'I did what you suggested –'

'Found a way of distracting yourself?'

'Oh, I'd forgotten about that. No, what you said about my boss who made me work without an aide. About tearing him another one. I mean, my words, but you're the first person who's agreed with me.'

'I didn't –' No point. People hear what they want to hear.

'When the mediation broke down, I never got a chance to tell him what he'd done to me. And I thought, maybe you're right. Maybe confronting him will get me closure.'

Shit. 'Are you allowed –'

'I thought *to hell with the lawyers*. Like I told you, it's only money.'

I let her tell the story. Whatever she's done, it's done now.

'He's on LinkedIn. Would you believe, he's a *life coach*, for business people. I was just so angry at the idea that he'd be teaching other people . . . Did you know you can get pepper spray on the internet?'

'You ordered –'

'Didn't have time.' Valerie manages a laugh. 'It was a nice thing to think about for a while. Give him back a little of the pain he's given me. Anyway, I booked an appointment with him, face to face. Didn't use my real name, of course.'

Of course.

'He's living in this enormous property down on the peninsula. I knock on the door and, you know, I'm not scared at all.'

'Sounds like *he* needed to be.'

'I was just *consumed* with anger. He comes to the door and, you know, I wouldn't have recognised him. He's got a beard, and I thought he'd be in a suit, but he's more . . . alternative. Shorts and knobbly knees.'

I swap out my mental picture of Keith Barnard for one of my dad.

'He took a couple of moments to recognise me, and I put my foot out so he couldn't slam the door in my face . . . But then he started crying. Actually crying. Long story short, *he's* never been able to get closure because of the lawyers and everything, and he didn't want to stalk me. He got into disability because he wanted to do good, same as me, and then he got caught up in the management side of it and hated it. Now he's got this olive farm, and the coaching he does is to help people do what he's done: leave the corporate world.'

'So he offered you an olive branch.'

Valerie laughs. 'Actually, he offered me a joint. I haven't had one since I was in my twenties. And the pain went away.'

I hold my breath.

'Not for long. And I can't spend my life stoned. But when you think about it, it proves what I've been saying all along. Marijuana works on your nerves, right? It's *physical*. So's my pain.'

Keith's door is open when Valerie leaves and I can't resist telling him that my chronic pain patient didn't fit into his box.

'Because you didn't look beyond what she told you,' he says.

—

My next appointment is a Charles Dodgson. Carey arrives instead. Thought the name was familiar.

'The interviews for the training program are next week,' they say. 'You were going to coach me. It seems you were wrong about Mondays being a good day.'

'Sorry, I'd forgotten. You should have reminded me.'

'That's what I'm doing. But, on reflection, it's unlikely you can improve my general intuition in one session. So we should focus on interview technique.'

I laugh. 'Who are your referees?'

'Dr Sharma, and the oncologist from Tasmania. The one who pushed me into telling parents their children were dying. I figure he owes me.'

'Okay, lesson one. When you talk about him, he gave you the opportunity to learn about the process of giving terrible news to parents and helping them work through it.'

'I didn't help them work through it. I just told them and referred them to pastoral care.'

'But you learned about the working-through process, right?'

'Correct.'

'And telling them was part of that process, right?'

'It's hardly an honest answer.'

'It's not a lie. You have to sell yourself, Carey. Because that's what everybody else is doing. And not to do so would signal a lack of understanding of the unwritten rules, which is the last thing you want to do.'

'That's a reasonable observation. They'll know I'm autistic and be looking for me to screw up in that domain. Conversely, I suspect that if Jon's cultural background affected his interview performance, they'd cut him some slack.'

'Maybe, but I doubt it'd get you the training program unless you were going to make it anyway. And you asked me to coach you, not to change the world.'

Carey laughs. 'I'll say I'm a key member of the Acute Unit and a reference point for information. Which is an . . . embellishment. I have an excellent knowledge base, but I'm rarely asked about it.'

'That might come across as a bit too arrogant.' They're right. This isn't easy if you don't have the instincts for it.

'They're going to ask you why you want to be a psychiatrist,' I say.

'Really? That's so predictable.'

'They'll want to see that you did predict it and prepared an answer. The story about being asked to give bad news to the parents. The assumption that was made about you not having feelings. The way you tackled it, got good at it. The emotional impact on them and you. That's the story you tell if they ask about why you want to be a psychiatrist or what your strengths are.'

Carey nods. 'Obvious when you think about it. Also true, which is more comfortable for me.' They take a breath. 'I'm planning to be upfront about my autism. It's in my application anyway. I'll tell them that autism manifests itself in me as a respect for facts and ethical behaviour, an ability to focus on a task and to make connections that aren't obvious to others, which is useful in diagnosis. Plus a natural empathy for autistic people who comprise a significant number of our patients. Obviously, I'll paraphrase so as not to sound . . . arrogant. To people who think it's a disorder.'

'And the downside?'

'As an autistic person, my communication style is different from neurotypicals. In this imperfect world I acknowledge that I'm expected to do all the changing, and I'm prepared to do that. I'm a lot better than I was. I engaged a tutor.'

'What did you learn?'

'My focus used to be on precision in what I said. My tutor encouraged me to give equal attention to listening carefully.' They laugh. 'Rather than preparing what I was about to say next. These skills can be learned.'

'What if they ask about your gender status?'

'None of their fucking business.'

Carey sees my reaction and laughs out loud. 'You didn't expect me to use that adjective, did you? I like to mess with people's minds occasionally. Quid pro quo. No, I'll say being non-binary helps me relate to the LGBTQI community.'

'I think you're looking good. Seriously, you seem to be on top of it. But don't even think about messing with their minds.'

'No fucking way,' says Carey.

After they leave, I reflect on my own communication skills. How hard I've tried to get through to Valerie. What has she been saying to me?

—

Dawn lights up paddocks lush from the spring rain as I drive to my parents' home early Saturday morning. The mountains in the distance shimmer. The closer I get to them, the denser the foliage is, until I'm up against national park and roads twisting around narrow corners with rock faces and native bush. It'll make a good backdrop for the documentary.

My parents don't know I've been dating Jason. The only boyfriend I've brought home was Marcus, and they didn't hit it off with him: too establishment. I figure they'll like Jason – artistic is good – but go in the other direction and welcome him prematurely into the family. Not sure how they'd find Alex: establishment background, but not mainstream. Not going to happen now, anyway.

There's a crowd, maybe a little under twenty people. Jason waves from the verandah. He's talking to a woman who has to be his Sudanese co-producer – tall, lithe, with a ton of heavy bracelets. He pauses to introduce her – Inaya Bul – and kiss my cheek.

There's a guy with a camera and tripod; another setting up a reflector; another with headphones pointing a boom into space.

Kayla – Foster Kid Forty-Eight – looks like a reality TV contestant and she has two girlfriends with her who could be auditioning. My sister, Mel, and her partner, Jack, are hanging around talking while the kids play chasey and get in everyone's way. Like old times.

Kayla sees me and bounces over. 'Are you going to be in it too?' she asks.

'No. Just making sure you lot don't make idiots of yourselves.'

'That's so you. Telling everyone else what to do.' She's smiling, but there's a sting in it.

Inside, Dad is making pots of herbal tea. My parents don't drink coffee. Or even real tea.

'Are you sure about this, Dad?' I ask. 'It's not too late to pull out.'

'No harm in the truth,' he says. 'Fostering kids was the best thing we ever did.'

I force a smile. 'You helped a lot of kids.'

I go looking for Mum. She's painting, but the studio door's open. She's wearing a pale pink smock and her hair, long and thinning, is out loose. There are streaks of grey among the fairness, and it's always a shock to see her wrinkles because she should be ageless.

She smiles. 'Don't you look gorgeous. Am I right in thinking you've dressed up for someone?'

I'm just in jeans and a top. Nothing special, but I guess the jeans do fit me well. I'm still undecided about Jason.

I guess if my intuition comes from someone, it's Mum. Except she seems to use it randomly. Or ignores anything that doesn't fit her world view. Fine, until a kid shits in your dresser.

'It's nothing serious,' I say and take a breath. 'Mum, I believe Simon has been in touch?'

A slight cloud comes over her face. 'I've already told your father I won't talk about all of that.'

'Good,' I say. Meaning it. 'Just . . . I need to ask. In The Book . . . what did you draw for him? What did the words mean?'

'I haven't looked in The Book for a long time.'

'Can I show it to you?'

She sighs. 'Of all my children, Hannah, you are the one who puzzles me most.'

Big statement, because I suspect 'all my children' includes fifty-three foster kids.

'Why? Because I want to understand?'

My mother tilts her head and goes back to her painting. It's a landscape, all summer browns and vibrant banksia reds. Her therapy. She does a few dabs with the brush before answering.

'I don't know what you mean by "understand". It's like there's a whole world you see that I don't.' She stops and turns, the red-brown paint dripping off her brush onto the floor. 'Or perhaps I'm seeing a world you can't.'

I ask again. 'Will you look? Please?'

She sighs. It isn't an answer but I go to the 'library'. The Book is where I left it, with the others rather than in Lennon's hiding spot.

I'm careful to avoid showing her Aaron, and open it at Simon's picture: the animal I can't identify; the words I can't pinpoint. I read them again and still don't know what they mean. *He lives down in a ribcage in the dry leaves of a heart.*

Mum takes her time, then carefully puts her brushes down, wipes her hands and takes The Book from me.

'It's a chameleon,' she says. She looks at me. 'He wasn't sure who he was going to be.'

'And the words?'

'I met his mother. She was a very hard woman. There was no gentleness in her. The dry leaves of a heart refer to her. I felt . . . he was trapped by her coldness. I hope he managed to escape.'

'Where did the quote come from?' I ask.

My mother looks like she's about to say she doesn't remember, then thinks better of it. A bridge between our worlds.

'*The Silence of the Lambs.*'

—

I'm grateful that I'm not required to do anything for the documentary besides watch. I feel shaken. There is nothing concrete I can hold onto, and my mother has only offered me more unplaceable fragments of the twenty-four hours in which I went from being a child to an adult.

Jason films my father on the verandah. The wind comes up and down, creating problems with the sound, but Dad is a paragon of patience. Kayla and her friends get bored and cold in their miniskirts and wait inside in front of the fire.

I look with fresh eyes at the car bodies and caravans, the trailers and oil drums, and hope that their inevitable presence in the documentary doesn't take away from the solid core of who my father is and what he and my mother tried to do. They got some things right. A lot of things.

I listen to the cadence of Dad's voice and realise I can thank him for the inner sense of self I have. My safe haven. Both my parents would have loved me no matter what – in their own way, and at times not perhaps as I needed – but my father would also have fought for me.

It was Dad who held me after I found Aaron. Before we told my mother or anyone. But I never told him what happened with Simon. Whose black Porsche is now rolling up the driveway. Jason had told me they'd be filming him at his home.

He yells 'Cut!' when the engine sound interferes with the take.

From the far end of the verandah, I watch Simon, relaxed and confident, go over to Jason and introduce himself – I guess they've only spoken on the phone – say hi to my father and apologise for interrupting.

'Thought I'd come and have a look so I'd know what to expect when you film me.'

I watch my father. What does he think of the boy made good? Is he happy for Simon's success, whatever it looks like? Or disappointed in the kind of success that the car signifies? Unambiguously, it's the former: my dad's disdain for wealth runs deep, but not as deep as his care for the foster kids. He'd hold his own kids to a higher standard.

Simon sees me behind the film crew and squeezes onto the swing chair that's meant for one. His body is hard against me, lean and fit.

He kisses my cheek. 'I didn't know you'd be here,' he says.

I don't believe him.

'Let's go for a walk,' I say.

Simon raises an eyebrow as I head toward the caravan where I lost my virginity to him thirteen years ago. He isn't crass enough to suggest I might be interested in seeing if we can improve on what, at best, was some escape from the horror of Aaron's death, at worst a bad choice that could have landed me in the same situation as Brianna. No: at worst, an experience that would mess with my head for the next thirteen years. At least.

So now, like Valerie, I'm revisiting the trauma, with the instigator.

'What happened that night?' I ask him when we get there, well out of hearing range but still in sight of the film crew.

'You don't remember?'

'I don't mean the night we had sex. The night Aaron died.'

Simon leans against the caravan, expression kind.

'Aaron was with us. We were all drinking,' I say.

I open the caravan door and sit on the steps. Looking at the crumpled bed. I can see it all as if it was yesterday. It was summer. Hot. I was in skimpy shorts and a tank top, my skin tingling as Simon caressed my nipple.

Let's never grow old, I say, with a vodka and raspberry in hand. I'm laughing.

Take your shorts off, says Simon.

Aaron is looking scared.

Don't be a dick, I say.

Aaron'll help you, says Simon.

The three of us are on the bed and Simon's hand wanders lower. I push him away and get up, saying I need more to drink.

'I don't remember Aaron leaving,' I say. No matter how hard I try, the next memories I have are of me pushing Simon off and finally making my way back to my bedroom alone.

The Simon of thirteen years later smiles. 'Sorry, but I wasn't exactly focused on Aaron.'

'You said something to him.'

When I dream of that day – not so often now – I get to this point and wake. I sense that I saw Aaron again, after he left us. It would have been the last time.

I look at the bed. Go over to it and lie down. Turn my head. See the little window. *Yes.*

'He saw us,' I say. 'Maybe he was watching us.'

'Maybe. I would've at that age. Like I said, I've been traumatised by it – by what we found the next morning. But it wasn't anything we did. Kids don't kill themselves because they've watched other kids mucking around.'

I deflate. He's right of course. All we really did to Aaron that night was ignore him. If I was counselling a friend or relative of a patient that suicided, I'd say, *Lots of people get rejected socially, but they don't suicide. There was something else going on with them. It's not your fault.*

Except: if I hadn't been mucking around with Simon, Aaron wouldn't have slunk off. Maybe he'd have drunk himself into oblivion. But he would have had company and no chance to put a rope around his neck.

I remember even more vividly – I've been reliving it in nightmares – the night after Aaron died. Like I no longer had solid ground to stand on; like I no longer knew who I was. Does that explain why we ended up back in the caravan, having sex, dead sober, when the night before, drunk, I was sure it wasn't a good idea? Does he feel the guilt that I do? Or has he accepted, as I try to, that we were just kids trying to escape the pain, comforting each other?

'Sorry,' I say, getting up. And we leave the caravan, closing the door on the memories.

Simon smiles. 'You still owe me dinner.'

'Not now,' I say, meaning, *Now's not a great time to ask.*

I can tell he's not happy.

I watch them finish filming Dad while Simon chats to Kayla inside – she and her girlfriends have attached themselves to him. I don't think he and Kayla overlapped as foster kids.

'You're right about Simon being eye candy,' says Jason as the film crew set up inside in front of the fire, forcing Team Kayla to move to the kitchen. 'And this place is a director's dream. It's so rich with colour.'

The room is full of furniture my father's collected over the years from second-hand and bric-a-brac shops. The walls are covered in art – mostly my mother's, but some from when we were children and others that have taken her fancy. It's chaotic but vibrant.

'My family doesn't throw much away.'

Jason grins. 'Could do an art heist movie in here I reckon.'

He touches my arm gently as he heads off to talk to the cinematographer. There's still no electricity, but I feel comfortable around him.

I catch Simon watching from the doorway. Did he see Jason touch my arm? Did Jason do it because he saw Simon?

Simon points to his mug: *Do you want one?*

I shake my head. And as soon as Mum and Mel have been filmed, I head home. Simon can't have been far behind because his Porsche roars past me on the narrow road to the highway and I watch him disappear into the distance.

—

The next day I go for a long jog, have dinner with Jess at the pub next door to the Oasis, and try not to think about Simon or Aaron. Instead, I think about Valerie, and what Carey said about listening.

Thanks to Keith, I went into my first interview with Valerie expecting her to fit a certain mould – and it took me a while to realise that she didn't, even though she'd been telling me clearly enough. Maybe there was something else I didn't listen hard enough to: her insistence that her pain needed physical treatment.

I go to bed reading about chronic pain and about the role of antidepressants in treating it. I had a model in my mind: chronic pain causes depression, which exacerbates the pain; the antidepressants treat the depression, so the pain gets better. A neat answer tied up with a bow. Not much in psychiatry works like that. As it turns out, the real answer, or part of the real answer, is even neater. The drugs also treat the pain more or less directly. Depression or not.

I phone Valerie as soon as I get to the Oasis. We make an appointment for this morning.

'I've discussed your case with two specialists,' I tell her when she comes in. I don't tell her it was Nash and Keith, psychiatric specialists. 'You understand that if I prick you with a pin, it'll hurt and you'll pull away, and the pain goes away, right?'

'Of course.'

'Well, the problem you're having is that the nerve that causes you to feel pain isn't turning off, like it does with the pin.'

'Because there's still an injury.'

'Yes,' I say, though this may not be totally true in the way she means. 'The injury is to the nerve. It's stuck sending pain signals to your brain. It's an issue with serotonin transport. It happens that the drugs which work on serotonin are also antidepressants. You don't need pregabalin as an anti-anxiety agent or duloxetine as an antidepressant; you need them because they will alter how your brain reads the nerve signal.'

'Well, why didn't anyone explain that to me before?' Valerie says.

Probably because they didn't think it mattered. Or didn't have time. Same result.

It seems I've explained it so well that Valerie decides she doesn't need to see the private psychiatrist. I get a letter from her GP two weeks later saying the duloxetine has helped to, in Valerie's words 'dull the nerve endings'.

She isn't cured, writes the GP, *but she's definitely managing better and no longer reports suicidal thoughts*. She adds: *Based on discussions with her she may be a candidate for medicinal cannabis. I'd value your thoughts.*

Score one for the biological – neurological – approach. Except it wouldn't have got out of the gate if I hadn't found the right words to communicate it to Valerie. *Words*. And maybe, just maybe, the confrontation with her ex-boss helped unburden her of an ongoing trigger for the pain. More words.

Or maybe there was a depression, which the drugs are helping with as well, as per my original understanding. I guess we'll never know.

I want to share all this with Alex, add it to the tally of wins in our quest to be psychiatrists who do therapy. Not to mention that neat line about the olive branch, which nobody but a Freudian would care about. But I'm still pissed off with him.

TEN

RECALL

She's five years old. Out of place, dangerously out of place, surrounded by half a dozen middle-aged men. A couple of them are drinking beer. And talking about her.

'Who's a cute little girl? Ready to play? You like this, don't you?'

Then the room goes dark. Slowly her eyes adjust. The men are gone. But in the dim light, she can make out spiders. And now a snake. The stuff of nightmares.

But it's not a nightmare. It's so real that twenty-seven years later, she'll be able to recall it as if it was . . . today.

Stephanie Tapp is thirty-two, and my first thought is that if she wasn't a patient, I could see her as a friend. Short and curvy, with dimples. Some Asian heritage, I'd guess – maybe Thai. Long shiny black hair. A wicked smile. But the nine-month-old baby in the pusher puts her in a different world from me: mothers' groups, sleep deprivation and baby clothes rather than work, films and the latest cocktail bar. Or in my case, just work.

'You were in the Mother Baby Unit for a month,' I say. 'Just after you had Billie?'

Billie seems to recognise her name and smiles. She's cute. Even if the bread she's sucking on is going to end up shredded over my office floor.

'I went nuts,' says Stephanie.

Technically not, according to her notes. She wasn't psychotic, which is what I think of when laypeople refer to being 'nuts' or 'crazy' or 'going mad'. Her diagnosis was bipolar II, meaning her moods went up and down but mainly down. She was discharged on an antidepressant and a small dose of quetiapine – a does-everything drug – to alleviate her anxiety and possibly stabilise her mood. Possibly.

'But my GP is worried and wants another opinion,' says Stephanie. 'And I can't get into a private psych anytime soon.'

The clinic wasn't set up to fill in for private psychiatrists. Jan and Mia have some guidelines as to who we'll see and, in this case, the fact that Stephanie's been an inpatient in our service got her over the 'not serious enough' hurdle. Plus a baby potentially at risk.

'Can you tell me what your GP's worried about?' I say.

The referral letter is brief – he doesn't seem to like her psychologist and wants to restart from square one, including a review of medication. Which means a psychiatrist. Which, right now, means me.

'When I had Billie,' says Stephanie, 'I started getting these thoughts. Couldn't get rid of them. I completely unravelled.'

'Thoughts? Like obsessions?'

'No, memories. Just snippets.' Stephanie takes a breath and looks at Billie as she pulls herself together. 'Billie – just looking at her was terrifying. She was so little and vulnerable, and I was . . . I guess going back to when I was vulnerable too.'

I nod and let her go on.

'My childhood wasn't great. Mum and Dad broke up when I was five. They were in court for years fighting over me and my baby brother. Mum spent hundreds of thousands of dollars – literally – of her and my grandparents' money on lawyers because she wanted sole custody. Ended up half-half, and she went bankrupt and had to live with her parents. Still does.'

'How's your relationship with them now?'

'Okay with Mum. Having had Billie I get how tough she had it when I was growing up.'

'And your dad?'

'Haven't seen him since I was fifteen.'

Stephanie lapses into silence. I wait her out.

'We had an argument about what I was allowed to do and not allowed to do. Just never went back.'

'And the memories?' I ask.

'Were about being scared. Not much more than that. At first.'

'You're getting more now?'

'When I left the Mother Baby Unit,' says Stephanie, 'I took the meds, and did twelve sessions of cognitive behavioural therapy – which is what they suggested. But I wanted to understand what happened in my childhood. Why I get these moments of . . . not quite panic but really strong anxiety. I'm not even sure what triggers them. Even as a teenager I was anxious, and I felt it came from my parents separating.'

'And the psychologist couldn't help with that?'

'She referred me to the therapist I'm seeing now, who specialises in trauma.'

'And . . .'

'I'm doing EMDR.'

I have only the vaguest idea about EMDR therapy. The EM is 'eye movements'; not sure about DR. It's broadly about processing memories. Not something we do at the Oasis. I nod sagely. What Stephanie doesn't tell me, and the internet can't fill me in on, I'll get from Elena.

'I've had three sessions, but my GP wanted me to stop, at least until you saw me.'

'Do you want to keep doing it?'

'I think I have to. It's been amazing. It's just that it's also terrifying.' Stephanie falters, closes her eyes. 'Since I started it, I've been having the worst nightmares.'

She opens her eyes again. 'My husband wants me to stop. I'm more moody, erratic. Sometimes Billie . . . When she cries, I yell at her. It's not her fault and I feel terrible, but I'm not as patient as I was. All these thoughts . . . I need space, and a baby doesn't give you much of that.'

'Have you thought of delaying doing the EMDR? Waiting until you're more stable? Maybe even until Billie is in childcare or school, or you're back at work?'

'I won't have time then. And I want to have another child. Until I understand what happened, I feel I can't move on. I *have* to do this now or I'll never know who I really am. I'll feel like my life is a compromise.'

'Can you tell me about the therapy?'

'It's been unlocking memories. Horrible, awful memories. They're so vivid, I feel like I'm reliving them.' She starts to shake. Takes some breaths.

Billie whimpers, and Stephanie spends a moment settling her daughter as well as herself.

'My mum has Billie when I go to the appointments because I couldn't . . . I need an hour or two afterward to be able to even drive home.'

'The memories are of abuse?'

'Yes. Not just my father, other men too. I only get snippets, but with each session they're getting more vivid. Identifying images and labelling them. They . . . There's a lot of . . . I *feel* them. Sometimes I'm frozen.'

'As if you are there?'

'Yes. I feel like I'm five, maybe younger. There's spiders crawling over me, even into my mouth. And snakes.'

She starts to shake again, and it takes longer to calm herself and Billie this time.

'It sounds . . . unusual,' I say.

'I think my father was part of a satanic cult. My psychologist has seen this before. Even babies being sacrificed. I'm going to bring charges. It's wrong, so wrong, that they got away with it.'

I'm not sure where to go with this. I'll leave it until after I talk with Elena.

'It sounds like you've become a bit destabilised,' I say. 'Can you hold off on the EMDR while we increase your meds and see if that helps with the distress?'

It'll give me some time to read up too.

—

If Brianna had sent me an emoji today, I think it would have been a pensive face.

I suggest this and she sighs, shakes her head and says, 'A turtle. I just want to hide in a shell and not be bothered by anything.'

She tells me the termination – nearly three weeks ago now – was awful but that Naomi was great. The exams which have kept her from coming back to see me have helped distract her. 'I'm just glad it's over.'

'If, at your first appointment with me, you were at fifty per cent of your usual self, where are you now?'

'I was thirty per cent a month ago. Now?' She frowns. 'Hard to say because . . . I feel different. Not worse or better, just different. Maybe . . . eighty.'

'What part of you is doing okay and what's got a way to go?'

'During the camp, school just seemed kind of pointless. But now? I really want to work hard. I want to find a way out.'

Reflection, self-efficacy, planning. Things that Taylah would struggle with.

'Maddy and her mum are amazing, so I feel someone has my back.' Brianna pauses. 'You too. The emoji thing? It really helped. Going through the emojis for *how do I feel today* was something to do, to start getting through the day.'

'And . . .'

'I'm still angry. At Dad and the church. And I guess at Chloe, who's pissing away her life.'

And finally, the one that matters most.

'I can't bear to be in the same room as my mother. I know she's depressed, but I want to scream at her.'

'What are you angry at her for, Brianna?'

'She just does *nothing*. She doesn't care about anyone. Except herself. I don't think the church counsellor does much more than ask her to pray.'

Sue sounds like she needs to be in therapy with Elena. Or getting meds from Nash. Maybe leaving David.

'Have you thought about whether you want to talk to them about what you've been through?'

'No way do I want to tell them about the abortion, but I do want to tell them how I'm feeling and see if they can treat me like a normal teenager. Dad found I'd accessed a website on under-age sex – I just wanted to know what the law was – and went apeshit. Now I'm not allowed online except in the living room.'

'What's your mum say?'

'Just *whatever your dad says*.' Brianna sighs. 'Can you see if they'll come and meet with you? With me. I don't care if Chloe comes or not.'

'I'll do my best,' I say. 'But Dr Popa . . . or Elena . . . will be there.'

'Better not mention Elena,' says Brianna.

—

I review the session with Elena, as close to word for word as I can recall. Including Brianna's line about not mentioning her.

She looks hard at me. 'You want to do this yourself?'

'I can't juggle a family,' I say. 'Not this family. I've seen the complexity of the dynamics and how fast things happen.'

'Given it's the Youngs, I agree,' says Elena. 'I'll speak to Daniela.'

Before I go, I ask her about EMDR.

'Eye movement desensitisation and reprocessing,' she says.

'Does it work?'

'Like most things: yes, for the right person at the right time with the right therapist. Research shows people with PTSD do improve – it's now part of standard recommended treatment.'

I'm looking at her blankly. Should have googled first.

'The patient describes the trauma, watching it as if on a train going past,' Elena explains. 'They identify images and sensations and their negative beliefs about them. They focus on this while the therapist moves a finger back and forth or taps.'

'Sounds kind of weird.'

'There are weirder therapies. EMDR is based on the belief that the experience wasn't properly processed and integrated into memory at the time it occurred. The eye movement facilitates the process of integrating it. Look it up if you want to know how.

'In PTSD sufferers, the experience wasn't integrated because they were running from a bomb, or overwhelmed by the grief of a friend dying or whatever trauma triggered the stress. In your patient's case, it's because she was a very young child and couldn't make sense of what was happening to her. I've seen a few sessions really help break through fears so people can return to their lives.'

'Can EMDR make it worse?'

'All therapies can do that – wrong timing, wrong hands, or just not suitable for that client. The therapist may have pushed ahead too quickly in this case. Hypnotherapy is a great way to help relaxation and access to memories, but I would rarely, if ever, use it in a survivor of childhood abuse. There is a reason to forget sometimes.'

'Can you remember things wrongly? I mean, could she think she's remembering things that didn't happen?'

It's the sort of question people ask me when I tell them what I do. But this is the first time it's actually come up.

'Absolutely,' says Elena. 'The mind isn't a hard drive. People aren't reliable witnesses even in the best of circumstances. Her memories at, say, four or five were shaped by how she understood the world then.'

'Stephanie mentioned her therapist told her about other patients' experiences.'

'Not good practice. If in the next session Stephanie starts remembering babies being thrown into the fire . . . Well, I know what I'd be thinking.'

'And the satanic cult? Am I being naive thinking it sounds implausible?'

'No, but you're getting off track. We're not police or judges. Our concern isn't with the facts and the evidence; it's with the patient's distress.'

'But –'

'If everyone who recalled seeing these rituals actually had seen them, then there would be mass graves of dead babies. But go back to the problem – what was there before Stephanie saw this therapist?'

'Anxiety and mood symptoms – and some vague memories. She cut off her father at fifteen.'

'She may well have been abused,' says Elena. 'Having a baby often wakens the memories. But if she was that young when it happened, fear would translate into things young children are afraid of.'

'Spiders and snakes.'

Elena nods. 'If she wants to make sense of how her childhood has affected her current state, she should be doing long-term psychodynamic therapy, not EMDR.'

'Do you do that?'

'No. I trained in it, but I'm mainly doing short-term . . . up to a year. What about you? You found a therapist yet?'

I shake my head. But I'm thinking about what she's said about making sense of childhood. 'I suspect I'm going to need the long-haul option.'

Elena smiles. 'I think Barbara Quinlan has some availability.'

—

I book an appointment with long-haul Barbara for 10.30 am Friday, which I can just make if my first patient doesn't run over. Of course he does.

I run, tram and run, and, thanks to a lift that takes me straight to the twenty-second floor of the city office building, I'm only four minutes late – out of breath, sweaty and apologetic.

Barbara's waiting for me. She's about fifty, medium height, nondescript, middling in every way.

There's no receptionist or desk. But there's an umbrella stand and I recognise a parkrun Volly Brolly. Looks like she's a volunteer, which usually means a runner as well.

'Parkrunner?' I say and smile.

She doesn't respond, and I suspect she's making a mental note to get a plain umbrella.

I try again as she leads me into her office. 'Sorry I'm late.'

Nothing doing.

I'm not expecting her room to be a riot of colour, and I'm right. White walls, beige chairs and nondescript prints.

She still hasn't spoken. I'm sort of curious, in a professional way, as to how long she'll let the silence go on. Thirty seconds is about the most I've ever given a patient. It's a long time.

Turns out five minutes is a *really* long time. I'm paying for this.

But she cracks first. 'Why do you think you were late?'

'I think you know I'm a trainee psychiatrist,' I say. 'I had a guy who'd been non-compliant with his meds, and I needed to be sure he was going to be okay.' Common ground. Bonding.

'Is that the only reason?'

'If you're looking for something deeper, I don't think there was an unconscious motivation.'

She waits, so I give her what she's looking for.

'I guess I've been resisting therapy for a range of reasons. I mean, at a practical level, I've got the pressure of work and the training program, and I'm not sure I've got the headspace . . .'

I rabbit on for the full fifty minutes, minus the five minutes of silence at the beginning and of course the four minutes I was late. I talk about work providing an excuse for avoiding my family, but don't even mention the suicide or my issues with that. I think I get some insights, but . . .

'Will I be able to talk to you about why I came to see you?' I say as she opens the door to let me out.

'When you're ready.'

'And you'll offer me some . . . feedback? Interpretations?'

'We'll see.'

—

Jason calls me. 'Just looked at the rushes.' He has to explain to me that this is the raw footage shot at my parents' house. 'They're great, I mean *great*. I can't thank your family enough.'

'Just . . . make sure the doco is a force for good, okay?'

'I'll do my best. Want to come over and see some? Tomorrow night? Anything you don't eat?'

Jason lives in a one-bedroom apartment west of the city – funky and modern but small and no view. I sit on a stool at the kitchen bench while he cooks and tells stories and makes me laugh.

The pasta is good, and we move to the sofa to watch a selection of the footage on his large TV: my family as movie stars.

My dad's passion is there, and Jason captures it with a shot that stays on his gaze into the middle distance when he starts to get emotional about some of the situations he and Mum rescued kids from. I learn a bit. Realise how little I knew about what went on behind the scenes when I was a kid.

'We'd get calls that just broke your heart,' Dad says. 'One of the kids they found died of malnutrition. We got his older brother. Hardly surprising he stole food from the fridge.'

Foster Kid Seventeen. He didn't speak the whole time he was with us, which was about three months – the time it took Child Protection to locate his grandmother in Western Australia.

Mel comes across as shallow: 'We were all just one big family.'

'Love that,' says Jason. 'Took about ten takes to get the line right, and the cameraman didn't think we should go in so close, but I think it's really worked. What do you think?'

'I actually liked the one of my dad.'

'We probably won't use it. It's not obvious on the small screen, but there's a bit where he moves and the light changes. Looks a bit amateur.'

My mother is the surprise. She looks right at the camera with a calm conviction that makes me want to sign up to be a foster parent – almost – when she says, 'We wanted to give a few kids a chance to be what they could be. We probably made a lot of mistakes. But we only had to be good enough. And we're so proud of what they've become.'

'It's a positive perspective,' I say.

Jason frowns. 'Is there another one?'

'We're talking about kids taken from their families. There has to be an impact on trust, future relationships, personality.'

Jason's hit *play* again, and Kayla is filling the screen. 'She seems to be doing fine,' he says. 'I mean, we all have our issues. I reckon they're damn resilient.'

He doesn't get it – the whole sense of self being intertwined with our past. He's a visual man: reality is what you see. Or maybe he just doesn't automatically look for something deeper and try to tease it out. As I would. As Alex would.

I pull the conversation back to the here and now. 'When do you finish filming?'

'Next weekend. Hopefully.'

'Have you filmed . . . the investments guy. Simon?'

Jason looks at me. 'You don't have to pretend. He told me he's been seeing you.'

'Sorry. It was only once.'

'Well, you should know, there are some things about him that don't quite check out.'

'Yeah?' I can feel my heart beating.

'Can't find any record anywhere of his father being a mountaineer. Did he change his name?'

'You'd need to ask him. I think he had a tough background. Maybe he stretched the truth a little.'

If he did, so what? Jason's simplistic comment about resilience has reminded me how tough these kids' lives really were. Yet we want to hold them to the same standard of honesty about their past as those who have nothing to hide.

Jason sighs. 'There's something else. My co-producer has pulled out. When you're making low-budget docos, everybody pitches in with whatever they can do, and she was my right-hand person.'

'Shit. Wasn't she part of you getting funding?'

'Uh-huh. I'm going to have a battle to get the last instalment. Especially if she badmouths me.'

'What happened?'

'She told me I'm not someone she wants to work with and wouldn't tell me why.'

Though he's trying to play it down, he's shaken. And I can understand him being reluctant to share it with me. Hard not to wonder what he said to her or what she found out.

'Listen,' he says, 'I don't want to sound paranoid, but someone's got in her ear. There aren't many people who have an issue with me.'

He looks at me and I realise what he's saying.

'You're not thinking Simon?'

Yep, he's thinking Simon. And he was right – he's sounding paranoid.

I don't stay. I see enough paranoia at work.

—

It's 11 pm Sunday night and I'm in bed when my phone lights up. I'm thinking it might be Simon; he texted me yesterday night when I got home from Jason's. *Having fun?* I didn't reply. But it's Frodo.

Don't give your phone number out, said Nash. But Frodo hasn't abused it.

'You need to get here, right now,' he says. There's noise in the background. I'm guessing he's at a gig.

'What's the matter? Is DJ unwell?'

'I've never seen her like this.'

'Physical or mental?'

'Mental. That's why I called you.'

'You need to call the CATT team. Or an ambulance if she's in danger. I'll give you the number and you can explain –'

'Not calling either. You know what they'll do. And they'll have a reason now.'

'Frodo –'

'I'll bring her to the clinic. Tomorrow morning. Nine o'clock. Be there.'

He hangs up and I force myself not to over-function. There will be other people around; if she's in a really bad way, someone will call an ambulance.

I wake at 3 am, over-functioning. I text Frodo: *Is she OK?*

The answer is right back at me. *No. 9 am.*

—

I'm at work at 8.30 and tell Mia to make room in the appointment book. Days like these I need Zelda Fitzgerald to be holding a slot.

Frodo is on time, with DJ. Neither is in good shape. Frodo's hair is standing up and his clothes look like he slept in them. DJ is looking at me warily. She's so brittle she might break. I can't predict what she might do.

'I told her you're Keith Barnard's girlfriend, and you'll tell him to stop putting thoughts in her head,' Frodo whispers to me. 'Only way I could convince her to come.'

'I'm here to help,' I say softly to DJ. 'Remember, I didn't send you back to Extended Care?'

It's hard to know if this registers. DJ is staring ominously at Mia. The screen Mia sits behind is there for a reason. We're probably all part of DJ's delusional system.

I go to get a mobile alarm and see that there's a box of whistles beside them; apparently our duress system has been playing up. I clip an alarm to my skirt, put a whistle in my pocket and message the CATT team to be on standby.

I find a meeting room with more space than my office. DJ isn't tall, but if she thinks it's a matter of life and death – or being locked up again – she could make a mess of me. I get them seated on chairs opposite me.

'She's moved in with Ralph,' says Frodo. 'He's this . . . Doesn't matter. He's anti meds.'

DJ looks at Frodo as if he'll be the one she makes a mess of. 'Keith is spiking them,' she says suddenly. 'Get me addicted. Might not. Have to think. It's hard to. Can't. Might have to do something.'

She gets up and starts pacing, just as Keith walks past, stops and looks in. DJ has her back to him and I wave him away frantically.

'Are your voices louder?' I ask her.

'Louder. More. He's talking all the time. Can't hear the music.'

'I got her to take the clozapine last night,' says Frodo. 'Don't think she's had it for a few days. She started ranting at the gig last night. Ralph bailed.'

'DJ,' I say, 'stopping and starting the clozapine can be a real problem. For your health.' Both mental and physical. 'We need you back on it . . . but we'll need some bloods too.'

I see her expression. It's not a good idea to engage with people's delusions, but . . . 'It'll get Keith off your case.'

'It's not safe,' she says.

'No, it's not,' I agree. 'So how about we take you up to Acute to do the tests and get some clozapine that hasn't been tampered with?'

'Not going back to that cunt Barnard.' She looks at me hard, and I'm wondering what she might do with the 'Keith's girlfriend' thing. It's unlikely to be pretty. I jump in with a distraction.

'You'll be under Dr Sharma. The guy you like.'

'The hot one.'

I don't know if it's the prospect of being under Nash or the police she sights sitting in the waiting room that does it, but DJ makes no fuss about heading to the hospital in the car with Grace and George.

I call Ndidi in Acute. 'Need a bed. Do whatever you have to do.' If it had been Carey I was talking to, I'd have chosen my words more carefully.

Frodo's still in the waiting room, not allowed in the car and probably not wanted anyway.

'She said she didn't love me,' he tells me, looking like he might cry. 'When she was well.'

—

Mia summons me to reception: the police waiting there want to see me. Two officers, one male, one female, no appointment.

'We'd like to talk to you about a patient.'

Really? Didn't anyone tell them the rules? You don't walk into a mental health clinic expecting to get information about the clients. Not unless they've given you permission, which has happened exactly zero times in my career.

I tell them the rules.

They tell me they know the rules, and that the patient, Stephanie Tapp, has given her permission.

At which point Mia tells me there's a message from Stephanie. I retreat to my office to phone her.

'Just wanted to confirm you'll support what I said,' she says. 'About the paedophiles. You didn't think I was lying, did you? Or you'd have said something, right? I mean, I'm on the higher dose of meds, and I'm definitely feeling calmer, which is why I felt ready to go to the police. But feeling better doesn't change the facts, does it?'

I invite the police in. The male officer, Ewan, does the talking; the female officer takes notes. I'm guessing Stephanie will get to see what she writes if she asks or if it goes to court.

Stephanie's given them a detailed account of sexual abuse, complete with spiders and snakes and – sure enough – sacrifices.

'She's not certain about the sacrifices; seems that's still a work in progress. But she figures spiders and snakes should be enough.' Ewan's face is impassive; the disbelief is in his voice.

I play it equally straight. 'How can I help?'

'We want to know whether you think these things really happened.' And whether I'm a fool.

I'm getting into the therapist's habit of giving the other person space to talk, and, sure enough, he fills it.

'She's got a registered psychologist who says the memories are real. She – Ms Tapp – tells us that you'll back her up. If that's so, we don't really have much choice but to take your advice and investigate. But unless we discover some twenty-year-old video . . . it's not going to fly, and this is going to be a waste of effort for us and upsetting for her.'

I nod.

While he waits for me to speak, the female officer, Finola, chimes in.

'You know, this isn't the first report we've had of this kind. And . . . I'll tell you this in confidence: the psychologist has form. Ms Tapp's not the first patient of theirs who's reported . . . this type of abuse. There's also the issue that these memories can't be used in court if they're a result of hypnosis or this eye thing, which is basically the same, right? Which is why we wanted to hear from you.'

This is above my pay grade.

'Sorry,' I say. 'I've seen Stephanie once; I'm not a specialist in recovered memory; my job's to help her deal with the trauma.'

Finola smiles and puts her notebook in her pocket. 'And you don't believe it happened either. Don't worry – you didn't say it and I'm not writing it down. But I'll share something with you. When I was a kid . . . Well, there weren't any spiders and snakes, just the boring stuff we know that some men do. He's dead now, but I'd never have got a conviction. Maybe now they'd take my word. Things are improving, but people who come in with stories of babies being thrown on bonfires . . . They make it harder for everyone.'

'She's not doing it on purpose,' I say. 'I can't say if it happened or not, but I'm pretty certain she believes it did. And there's a good chance something bad did happen, just not as she remembers it.'

Finola nods slowly. 'I guess what I'm saying is that if you can persuade her that the world would be a better place – for her and for people who have a real story to tell – if she backed off . . .'

'I'm sorry, but as a therapist, I'm not about planting ideas in patients' heads.'

She just looks at me.

—

Keith bails me up in the reception area. 'Can I have a word?'

We go into one of the small meeting rooms – neutral territory. But he's all smiles.

'I gather you had to re-admit Celeste Boyce. Disappointing, but it happens.'

I nod.

'Tribunals get it wrong, often. And in the clinic, seeing a patient for the first time, you back your judgement . . . and learn a lesson.'

I'm thinking he's made his point, and will leave it there, but no.

'I think that Celeste needs some time back in Extended Care, probably just a few months. If you were to support that, I think you'd demonstrate to Nash and Prof that you've learned from the experience, rather than . . . digging in.'

And demonstrate to the media that he was right.

'I really don't think –'

'You know, Hannah, back in the day, a registrar – a first-year – wouldn't have thought of taking a position against a consultant. Especially a specialist who's known the patient far longer. This is the sort of thing that colours my perception in dealing with *all* of the registrars.'

His look says more than his words: *Do what I want, and I'll back off on Alex.*

I'm still pissed off with Alex and I've fobbed him off the last two times he's suggested drinks. But I need to give him a heads-up on this. And get over myself.

I suggest drinks at the usual bar and he's right back with a thumbs up.

It's after six by the time I leave. As I pass Nash's office, I hear what sounds like sobbing. I stop and listen. It is.

Maybe I should walk away. Men like Nash don't like to be seen crying. But then men like Nash don't talk to people and don't get help. And psychiatrists, who can recognise the subtle early warning signs – like a guy sobbing out loud in his office – should do better than they do. Our profession is right up there in the risk stakes.

I knock on the door. The noise stops.

'Nash, it's Hannah. Can I come in?'

The door finally opens. Nash looks a wreck. He waves for me to sit down.

'Sorry, I didn't realise you were around,' he says. Then, half-laughing, 'Nothing original, just a domestic crisis. My wife says she's leaving me. Taking the children to India.' He looks out the window. 'Usual reason.'

Jesus, I've been blind. 'Nicole?'

It's ambiguous enough that he could reply, *No, I haven't discussed it with management*. But that's not what he says.

'How did you know?'

'Just a sense.'

'It's . . . quite serious.'

He's on the brink of telling me things that are going to make our professional relationship difficult. I'm not his therapist or his friend.

'Have you got someone you can talk to?' I ask.

He laughs. 'Thanks, Hannah. You've done everything right. Yes, I'm okay, I promise you. These things happen to all of us. We're all human. And I'll make the right call.'

He doesn't ask me to keep it confidential, and I'm flattered by his trust. But as I walk to the bar, I'm struggling to vanquish an image of Nicole on Nash's desk, still in her stilettos. And the thought that goes with it: *Something like that has really happened.*

—

Alex looks like he thought he was being stood up.

'Minor work emergency,' I say. 'Is this my margarita?'

'Only because you arrived when you did,' Alex says. 'Another minute and I was starting on it.'

He's already had one. I give him the latest on DJ and Keith's offer to make life easier for Alex.

Alex shakes his head. 'Don't worry about it. I'm okay. But I bet DJ didn't tell her parents the biggest problem Keith had with her.'

'Go on.'

'Sex. Keith is in a permanent knot about segregating the men and women so they can't have sex.'

Not totally unreasonable: trying to prevent unwanted advances, unwanted pregnancies, unwanted sexually transmitted diseases. But that happens in the wider community too, and we deal with it.

'He's such a . . . bloke,' says Alex. 'He doesn't get that the only sex actually going on is between two of the guys.'

And, I think, *you're* such a bloke. The wannabe therapist who can't talk about his own feelings but expects me to talk about mine.

I'm in danger of getting wound up again, and excuse myself to go to the bathroom. On the way back, one of the women behind the bar calls to me.

I know her from somewhere . . . Amber Reed. A child-protection worker I dealt with when I was in Acute. One of a pair who were trying to separate my patient and her baby. We weren't happy with them, but she dismisses that. '*Everybody* hated us.' And now she's out of it, the training and experience wasted, because of that attitude.

We talk a bit, and I'm feeling chastened by the time I get back to find Alex on the phone. *My* phone.

He ends the call and passes the phone back. The call details are still on the screen. Fourteen minutes.

'What are you doing talking to my brother?'

'He called. You told me he was having some issues, so I thought it best to take the call.' He's grinning.

'What did you say to him?'

'Not sure he'd want me to share that.'

'You don't think you might have violated a boundary or two?'

'He's not my patient.'

'Alex, he's part of my *family*. Which you seem to think is dysfunctional. Like yours supposedly isn't. With me, it's *family trauma; see a therapist*. With you, it's the way you were brought up. So totally normal. Normal to share nothing, to treat your friends like you've got them on the couch. You know where that takes you? To being a therapist who doesn't have a life, old and alone, like Joan Drinkwater. And it's screwed up our relationship.'

'What? Who's the one who said it was never going to be anything?'

'Only after you told me you were seeing someone!'

I've had enough. We can pick up the pieces sometime between now and the next study group.

As I get up to leave, he fires a parting shot. 'Maybe you heard what you wanted to hear.'

I'm halfway home before the thought hits me. I stop, use my phone to google *Marla psychotherapist Melbourne*. There's only one. Marla Rudenski. The photo's professional; she's attractive – and about fifty-five.

I'm sure he said *girlfriend*. Or at least let it stand when I said it. But it's obvious the woman he's been *seeing* is not his girlfriend. She's his therapist.

—

Stephanie comes back to see me because the increase in the does-everything drug has made her too sleepy. But the antidepressant might be helping.

'I've taken a break from the EMDR, like you said,' she says. 'So nothing is triggering the memories in the same way.'

'Opening your past may cause you to deteriorate for a while, you know. Going to the police, you had to recount it all – and that will be worse if it goes to court. And you'll need to deal with your mother's and brother's reactions.'

'Yes.'

'You may even end up with another admission.'

'I know.'

'It'll put pressure on your marriage and Billie.'

Stephanie looks annoyed. 'Are you trying to talk me out of this? Because I need to know what happened, and I'm not going to let those bastards get away with it. We've been socialised as women into keeping the peace. I know it'll be hard. But my husband is right behind me.'

I think of the time a guy rubbed himself against me on a tram and I just moved away, embarrassed. She's being seriously brave.

She must sense my change of heart; she softens. 'But if you can help me not fall apart, that's good too.'

'Which is what I was getting to,' I say. 'Part of that is not letting the abuse cause you more distress. If you're going to pursue it, you need to be in the strongest possible place, which includes being clear on your memories.'

'Meaning?'

'EMDR memories probably can't be used in court. Plus, it's traumatic for you. You're not a war vet. You were a child, so your memories are fragile and easily . . . misconstrued. Maybe you want to come at them from another angle.'

'Such as?'

'You could try psychodynamic therapy. Once a week for an hour. Review after a year?'

'A year!'

'It'd probably go longer. There's a lot to unravel. But a lot can change in that time. A year ago you didn't have a baby.'

'What I liked about EMDR was the fast results – this has stuffed up enough of my life already. How does what you're recommending work?'

I think of Valerie and wonder what words I need here.

'Every patient and therapist – and their relationship – are different,' I say. 'The CBT you did was about dealing with symptoms. The right psychotherapy works by helping you understand why you get the symptoms in the first place.'

Stephanie looks at me. I think of how we could have been friends. There's something in her look that suggests she's thinking the same.

'And then?' she says.

'Then . . .' I take a breath. 'Then, if you're lucky, you get to choose, when you're ready, if you want to allow your past to have that much hold on you.'

'Sounds scary,' Stephanie says.

I nod. 'It can be.' But I'm thinking – and maybe she is too – that it's unlikely to be any scarier than spiders and snakes and babies on the bonfire.

She sits up a little straighter. 'I'm so over being scared. I'll give it a try. If it's a bit gentler, it'll get my husband's vote.'

I suggest Isaac Sandler. I know he deals with sexual abuse trauma. And maybe Prof will give me feedback on how Stephanie's going.

—

I can't sleep. One of my own memories is nagging at me.

I've been googling EMDR and found a DIY module. I ignore the 'don't try this at home' warnings. I've faced the tough stuff; this is just one last piece of the jigsaw that I'm after. And I'm a professional.

Safe space? Tick. It's a warm night. I sit in the courtyard in the dark, sipping a glass of herbal tea.

Target memory? Tick. While moving my eyes I focus on it, taking myself back thirteen years to the sweat and alcohol. It's not like I haven't relived the scene hundreds of times.

Let the memories and feelings come.

I see Aaron's expression through the caravan window. Simon is coming onto me and I'm intoxicated by alcohol, lying on the crumpled bed, laughing, full of a teenager's sense of knowing it all. Then Simon says something. But I can't hear the words.

I remember seeing fear in Aaron's eyes as he left, but I wonder now if it was something else. As I replay it, turning my head to see him watching us, I see it isn't fear. It's a mix of pain and . . .

Alex's story about Keith Barnard pops into my head. *He doesn't realise it's the male patients having sex.* At fifteen, gay sex wasn't on my radar, and why would it be with Simon? He'd made it very clear he was interested in me. But hadn't my sister remembered him as the 'gay' kid?

Aaron's look was jealousy, and pain that he had been used; that whatever had happened between Simon and him hadn't meant anything.

Fuck off, faggot. That's what Simon said to him to make him leave.

I start to shake. That was the final straw for Aaron. It's why he died, and why I had a role in it.

ELEVEN

POWERLESSNESS

She slips behind the wheel of the Camry – a suburban mum in a suburban car. Late thirties, unremarkable, jeans and jacket, no sense that she's dressed for a night out. She drives to a shopping strip, parks, walks into a bar and scans the room. Sees what she's looking for.

She's known here. The bartender acknowledges her as she takes a seat at the bar but doesn't move to serve her.

There's a man sitting by himself, and she gives him a big come-on smile. He smiles back, but it's a smile of 'if only' as his dining companion returns from the bathroom.

A guy at another table has seen the exchange. He walks up to the bar and the woman smiles, all but pats the seat beside her.

The bartender comes over and offers the guy the drinks list.

The early November weather is mild, and I'm eating my lunch in the untended garden by the Oasis car park when a psych nurse in Emergency calls me.

'I've got a guy who says his wife needs to see someone now. He says you know them.'

I need more than that.

'Apparently you were out with the CATT team,' she says.

She gives me their names and it takes a moment for me to place them. It's Ben of the Henry Cavill smile and Andrea who buys anchovies they don't eat. The presenting problem had been that she was 'not herself'. His way of dealing with that, and her response, had been loud enough for the neighbours to call the police.

'Does she need to be seen today?' I ask.

'Nothing acute or major, but . . . he says she's variable and right now she's agreeing to see someone. They had a private psych appointment last week and she was feeling great so she wouldn't go. And he couldn't see the point either because . . .'

'. . . she was feeling great. Got it. Send them over.'

Andrea is much the same as when I last saw her. Unconcerned. Ben is the one who's anxious. He hovers over her when she nearly trips over some upturned carpet, and she's dismissive of him. The hovering could be coercive control – but the dismissiveness doesn't fit so well.

'Please,' says Ben to me, 'I'm just asking you to take the time to work out what it is, so we can give her whatever she needs to sort her out. When she had postnatal depression, the antidepressants really helped. I'm not saying it's depression but it's definitely something.'

Andrea doesn't look fussed about her husband asking me to sort her out.

I ask Ben to step out and he's reluctant to leave. Looking at Andrea, then me, he says, 'I'm pretty sure she's having an affair.'

The statement is strange in Andrea's presence, but perhaps he wants it on the table for us to discuss. Her reaction is stranger. Her body language says, *Whatever.* Maybe she's already decided the marriage is over.

'Ben just overthinks things,' says Andrea after he's left. 'He's an engineer.'

'You're not having an affair then?'

'I go out at night sometimes. To get a break from the children.'

I decide not to pursue this. I need to build some trust if I want her to share the truth with me.

'It seems Ben is pushing you to get help,' I say. 'But today you agreed. Is there something *you* want help with?'

Andrea picks at a dried food stain on her jeans. For a moment I think she's trembling, but she sits on her hands, stretches her neck and looks at me. 'I do think sometimes . . . After my children, I got depressed. I'm a university timetable coordinator, and I'm working part-time. I'm trying to juggle school drop-offs and after-school activities and shopping and work calls.'

'How does the feeling compare to the postnatal depression?'

'Different. Less anxious, just flat. That's why I go out. It helps.'

I take Andrea through the symptoms of major depression, which would likely respond to medication.

She denies sleep or appetite change. Her mood is better in the evenings, but this seems related to the 'break from the children' excursions. 'I can just forget everything for a while.'

'What do you do when you're out?' I ask. When she isn't forthcoming, I add, 'This is confidential. You only have to tell Ben if you want to.'

'Ben used to be fun,' says Andrea. Here we go. To nowhere, it turns out. 'I just drive.'

'Why does Ben think you're having an affair?'

'You'll have to ask him.'

Okay, I've given that my best shot.

'I do get anxious sometimes,' Andrea suddenly says. 'Out of the blue. Not worrying about the kids like when I had the postnatal . . . just sudden anxiety.'

I take her through the anxiety checklist but find nothing to suggest that or panic disorder. Then OCD – I'm thinking about those tins of anchovies – but nothing shows up. I even search for PTSD, but again, she reports no trauma, no childhood abuse. I remember her saying she was adopted.

'As a baby,' she says. 'I always knew, and haven't felt any need to know my biological parents. Mum and Dad were great. Still are.'

I ask her if I can talk to Ben alone and they exchange places.

'She's fine a lot of the time, but then she isn't,' says Ben. 'Moody, irritable, anxious. Next day or a few days later she's back to normal.'

Bipolar II? But I'm leaning toward Ben being the problem or at least an unreliable witness.

'Why do you think she's having an affair?'

'Where do you drive at eight o'clock at night? I can't follow her because someone has to stay with the kids.' He's almost in tears. 'She . . . I just know . . . I can tell.'

His distress is real, but is it based in reality or not?

'Anything else you've noticed?' I ask.

'She forgets things sometimes,' Ben finally says.

Concentration can be poor in depression, and I didn't test this. I bring Andrea back in and do a mini mental state. It takes her a moment to remember today's date – she's not alone there – but she scores full points.

What I think I'm seeing is a normal woman showing the strain of multitasking and tension in her marriage – to an engineer who wants to find an external cause for their problems. *Scan the brain, see what lights up then sort her out.*

Cognitive therapy would be a more realistic option. Or changes to lifestyle, whether or not prompted by therapy.

I look at them both. 'How long since you've had a holiday? Time out to recharge?'

It's been a few years.

Is this really what I'm going to recommend? Take a holiday? I say she could try the antidepressant. Not much else I can suggest.

Andrea doesn't look surprised. Ben's shoulders sag.

As they leave, Andrea trips on the carpet again and her arm jerks out but . . . it's wrong. The outward movement would have done nothing to steady her or break her fall.

'Wait,' I say, and sit them back down. I'm remembering a Prof round – a weekly discussion of a patient with Prof Gordon presiding – where Alex presented a case and was torn to shreds because he'd forgotten he was a doctor first, psychiatrist second. Brain tumour was the diagnosis then, and it may be now.

'Have any weird things happened physically?' I ask.

Andrea shakes her head. So does Ben.

'Like losing vision in one eye? Loss of use of an arm or leg for a short period?' I'm thinking multiple sclerosis.

Again, they shake their heads.

Damn. I mean, good. But she does seem to have a disregard for her state, a bit like *la belle indifference* seen in some forms of dementia. Or the indifference that someone who is over their marriage is going to show to the doctor her husband is making her see.

'She's a bit clumsy though,' says Ben.

'Jerks?' I show a few options.

They frown. Andrea says no. Ben, predictably, thinks there could be something.

I take Andrea to the tack room and perform a full neurological examination. Nothing, other than her eye movements being a bit slow.

Back to my office.

'We could do some tests for neurological conditions,' I say, 'but they don't all have treatments.'

Ben nods vigorously, and Andrea's prepared to go along with it. I give them a pile of forms for pathology and X-rays, which will take a couple of weeks to get done.

Then I find some double-sided tape and stick the carpet down. Nice to do something useful.

—

Saturday, Ndidi and I are down to do a parkrun. Ndidi's organised it, which is the way it used to be but lately it's been me trying to get her to come along. And she wants to do a different course from our usual.

'Flatter and wider. We'll run a good time.'

So what? When we started, she wanted to beat me and then I needed to beat her. But we got over that. I figure she wants to talk about her upcoming presentation at the Prof round, but when I bring it up she's dismissive.

'Straightforward. Woman with schizophrenia.'

'So why are you presenting her?'

'Because she assaulted staff and a patient. My consultant listened to the consumer rep and stayed away from sedative antipsychotics – and we paid for it. I want to explore that.'

The parkrun is at a big open park. I recognise someone getting a pre-run coffee: it's Rupert, the lawyer who represented DJ at the tribunal. I point him out to Ndidi.

'What a coincidence,' she says.

'Shit, Ndidi. Is that why we're here?'

She smiles. 'He got in touch with a friend of mine who's a psych trainee – apparently he met *someone* interesting at a tribunal. C'mon. Age-appropriate, interested, not a doctor. At least go and say hello.'

'Jason told you it didn't work out with us?' I haven't seen him for a couple of weeks – since he started getting heavy about Simon. Haven't seen Simon either, though he's called and texted me a couple of times. Jason was over the top about him, but Jess was also less than encouraging with the *sleeping with your brother* stuff. And since my memory of what happened when I was fifteen has returned, I've been feeling wary.

'It happens,' says Ndidi. 'You keep looking. If you want to find someone.'

'You know I've been looking for a therapist as well?' I laugh. 'Someone accused me of avoiding finding one because . . . I guess because I didn't want to find one.'

'You're as bad as Jon. And Rupert didn't know you were coming. He hasn't seen you.'

'Ndidi . . . do you think maybe this is more about you fixing us – Jon and me – up with someone so you don't have to think about you and Torben?'

Ndidi looks away. 'Let's go listen to the briefing.'

She's right about the course, at least. I run a personal best, according to my watch. But as I cross the finish line and put out my hand to grab a token, a weird thing happens. The tokens volunteer turns away. A few seconds later, someone else gives me my token.

I won't be penalised; my time will have been recorded when I crossed the line. But I'm watching the original volunteer. Yep, it's Barbara Quinlan. My therapist.

I walk away and Barbara takes up her position again. Boundaries. But . . . give me a break.

—

Taylah has been doing well. Our deal to give her scheduled admissions at Short Stay in exchange for her working on her emotion-management skills seems to be working. No visits to ED. At team meetings, I've become a little smug.

Should have known better. Monday morning handover, Grace is her hyper self as she relates the weekend saga.

'Overdose of Panadol,' she says. 'Decent amount. Without the stomach pump and meds Taylah would have been in ICU for sure.'

Still a cry for help rather than really wanting to die – I hope.

'I'm seeing her mother today,' says Louis.

'No, you're not,' says Grace. 'She's in Short Stay.'

'And Taylah?' I ask.

'Still in ED, looking forward to popping in to see you this morning.'

Great.

When the appointment time comes, it isn't Taylah in the waiting room. It's her younger sister, Aleesha. She's looking slimmer but that may be because she's not in baggy clothes; she's wearing tight jeans, and her hair, which she usually wears pulled back, is loose around her face.

'If you want to see someone, Aleesha, it has to be Jan, at least initially,' I tell her.

Aleesha looks upset. 'Just for a few minutes? I'm feeling really bad about the weekend. About Mum and Taylah. I thought Mum was *meant* to see it and, honestly, I had no idea she'd have a meltdown.'

Right. I asked Taylah to write down the things she'd like to tell her mother. Looks like Aleesha, in an uncharacteristic rush of initiative, decided to play postie and deliver the letter.

I'm looking at Aleesha. I'm hearing her words. And I'm feeling a disturbing disconnect. My skin is tingling. It reminds me of a feeling I've had recently, but I can't place where or when or with whom.

'Maybe you should talk to Jan about this,' I say.

'I'm okay, I just want to help Taylah.'

There's an appeal in her eyes: *I'm telling the truth.* Because she's used to not being believed? Or not telling the truth? Or because she's honing her technique: *Can I fool the professional?*

No point judging her. She was abused too, like Taylah, and is trying to get by in a world that hasn't treated her well. But I'm not going to be sucked in.

'I need to hear this from Taylah,' I say. 'If you want to talk, Mia is at reception.'

I'm in the tearoom as Aleesha leaves. Through the window, I see Taylah coming up the path. She takes a run at Aleesha and gives her a shove. Aleesha falls against the trunk of the huge gum tree and there's a melodramatic wail as she holds her arm. There's a loud exchange between them and a passer-by gets their phone out.

Aleesha takes a quick look back at the Oasis, then barrels head-first into Taylah's stomach. Taylah doubles over and Aleesha walks away, giving her sister the finger and the audience a thumbs up.

I head for reception and get there in time to meet Taylah, who is distressed but apparently physically unhurt.

As soon as we're in my office, she turns her anger on me. 'It was a dumb idea to write things down.'

'I understand your mother saw what you wrote.'

'Aleesha showed her. And Mum went apeshit. Called me a vicious little liar and said I was trying to ruin any happiness she ever had.'

The barbs seem to have stuck. Taylah starts to cry.

'What happened then?'

'Ivan tells us – Aleesha and me – that we're lying cunts. About what he did, hitting on us. That he never touched us, and we're always coming onto him. Mum just loses it. Again. Throws things at him and he just fucks off out of there. Then she kind of dissolves. She's in Short Stay now. And it's totally your fault. I *need* to be there, but because of your stupid deal they said I couldn't.'

Where to start?

'Let's go back to the writing things down – we were meant to talk about it, remember?'

Taylah nods reluctantly.

'Did the writing down help at all? Clarify what or who you were angry at?'

This is apparently too long ago for Taylah to be able to tap into, at least while she's so agitated.

I try again. 'It wasn't the writing down but the fact that your mother saw it that was the issue, right?'

She hesitates, then lets me win this point.

'So how did she get to see it?'

'I told you. Aleesha goes through my stuff and finds it. Starts getting upset. Then Mum wants to know why.'

I consider what outcome Aleesha wanted. Just to stir the pot? Or to get rid of Ivan and not be blamed?

'What just happened out the front?'

'She's been on my case about upsetting Mum and I just wanted her to leave me alone.'

'What did she say?'

'That she'd spoken to you. That I broke the deal by taking an OD and she reckoned I wouldn't be allowed back into Short Stay. Like ever.'

It isn't hard to make Taylah doubt herself and other people. I think about Aleesha trying to see me. Unable to let Taylah have something for herself?

'I didn't go to Short Stay though,' Taylah says. 'So I've still got my three planned admissions, right?'

If I give an inch . . . But I can't be seen to reject her either.

'Let's review in a month, just before Christmas,' I say. 'No more overdoses before then and we'll talk about managing the festive season, okay?'

Taylah smiles. With real warmth.

'Have you spoken to your mum?' I ask.

'Not since she went in. She won't be home until Wednesday.'

'Let's talk about managing that interaction.'

I throw all the scenarios I can think of at Taylah.

Mum says sorry – Taylah loves this one.

Mum believes her, but blames Taylah and/or Aleesha for Ivan's and Jimmy's behaviour. Taylah struggles with this, even when I suggest Kelly might need time to process it, but agrees she can remain calm.

Mum doesn't believe her. Taylah will definitely not remain calm. Taylah still wants her mum to validate – and believe – her version of events before she can even attempt independence.

Maeve, her friend from Short Stay, is posting shots from the resort where she's working, but Taylah can't bring herself to go because she doesn't think she could stick at it. That unfinished business with her mother will pull her back.

'I want to visit Mum,' says Taylah. 'Will you come with me?'

More pushing of the boundaries, but I'm also aware that caring counts and no-one has cared much for Taylah when it mattered. I have time before the Prof round.

I check in with Louis, Kelly's therapist, and he thinks it's better to have the conversation while Kelly is still being supported rather than at home where other things – including Aleesha – are at play. He offers to join us but our diaries don't have any times that work.

Taylah and I walk over together and I help her rehearse her *Never meant to upset you*, and *I'm not trying to blame you, just working it out for myself.* I wish I could give her cue cards.

Kelly is relaxed, sitting in an armchair holding court when we arrive, dressed in jeans and a blouse that shows off her breasts – and making sure the male nurse gets a good look.

She looks at us with suspicion. 'What do you want?' she says to Taylah.

I ask if we can have a word in private. Kelly wants the nurse to stay. Fine by me.

'I just wanted to say I'm sorry that what I wrote upset you,' says Taylah.

She's nervous and it's contagious. Kelly looks as if she's judging us both: naughty schoolgirls in front of the headmistress.

'It was your idea, wasn't it?' Kelly says to me.

'Yes. But to write it down and not show anyone. I'm sure there are times you need some help sorting thoughts out.'

'You don't know anything about me,' says Kelly.

'It's a general statement.'

'What my daughter wrote wasn't general. It was very specific. She's responsible for breaking up my relationship.'

Kelly might have melted down on the weekend, but she comes across as tough now. Taylah, on the other hand, is in danger of melting down herself. Heads or tails on whether it's hysterical crying or she comes out punching.

'I don't think that's true,' I say quietly.

'What do you know? Just what my dipstick daughter tells you, and she lies. Always has, even when she was little.'

'It wasn't what was written that caused your partner to leave.'

'It pushed him into it,' says Kelly angrily. 'My daughter accused him of . . . molesting her.'

I want to let it sit. But I can see Taylah is about to lose it.

'Taylah, can you remember the second thing you wanted to say?'

Taylah looks at me blankly, eyes full of tears.

'About sorting yourself out?'

'Ah yeah.' Taylah takes a breath. 'I'm not trying to blame you, Mum. This is about me trying to get my head together. It wasn't really about Ivan anyway. It was about Jimmy.'

'I threw him out for you girls,' Kelly says. Her tone is sulky. 'I really loved him.'

As Taylah told the story, the first part isn't true. She went to live with her father to escape the abuse.

'Never knew he did things to you,' Kelly adds. 'You told whopping lies. How was I expected to know what was real and what wasn't?'

I intervene before Taylah can say anything. 'It's clear Taylah was abused. Children don't make sense of things in the same way adults can. She was scared of him, and also scared of upsetting you.'

Kelly opens her mouth then shuts it. 'Bugger off,' she says to us both. But as we're leaving, she yells out to Taylah: 'Get some dinner for Wednesday night.'

Probably as close to an acknowledgement as Taylah can expect from her.

Before I head back to the Oasis, I drop into Acute. DJ has been discharged after five days treatment.

'Just needed restabilising on clozapine,' Omar the nurse tells me. 'And her new man got a dose of reality.'

—

Alex and I arrive at the ivory tower – home of the Menzies' academic and research staff – at the same time for Ndidi's presentation at the Prof round. Her 'straightforward' patient with schizophrenia.

Prof's PA, Goldie the Goth, intercepts us. 'Have you two organised your act for the Christmas party? Last year the registrars did a scene out of *Mamma Mia* with changed lyrics. Genius.'

Seriously? They found time for that?

Jon has kept a seat for us, and we awkwardly manoeuvre our way over laps and backpacks to join him. Oscar, the senior registrar, has a slide up that gives us an indication of what we're in for: *You Knew the Job was Dangerous.*

Prof comes to the front and sits in one of the three chairs set up there. Oscar says a few words of introduction and Ndidi starts her summary. She's in wide-leg tailored trousers, matching purple vest, bare arms. Standing at the lectern, she looks cool and in control.

'Beiye is a twenty-eight-year-old single woman, ethnically Chinese, living in Australia since she was fifteen, who has a ten-year history of schizophrenia.'

Ndidi goes on to outline that the patient has had three admissions: two around the time of diagnosis, and the most recent in the setting of non-compliance with medication. Her delusions were paranoid in nature: she believed her flatmate was stealing ideas from her mind, enabling her to buy more things than Beiye could afford.

'Her depot medication ceased when she was taken off her community treatment order, and she stopped her oral olanzapine because of sedation. Her behaviour deteriorated over the last three months and she was admitted after stabbing her flatmate.'

The flatmate required stitches but didn't press charges.

We hear about Beiye's assault on another patient – fingernails scraped down the patient's face, narrowly missing her eye – and on a nurse, who wasn't so lucky and is off work for several weeks after an operation to repair eye damage.

'The third clinician injured at the Menzies this month,' says Ndidi. She steals a glance at Nicole – the admin director.

I doubt it's news to Nicole, but I get Ndidi wanting to make the point. The posters everywhere saying aggression will not be tolerated don't work with psychotic patients who aren't responsible for their actions. And they need treatment. Prof, as always, is inscrutable.

'Beiye had refused olanzapine and clozapine,' says Ndidi. 'And the asenapine, which is now resolving her psychosis, did not protect the staff as a more sedating agent may have.'

Wendy Li – who's in charge of Acute these days, so Ndidi's boss – is in the front row. She raises her hand and Prof nods.

'We had a team meeting about this and it was agreed that whatever we treated her with needed to be something she'd keep taking.'

'Shall we see the patient first and then discuss treatment?' Prof suggests mildly.

Beiye comes in with a nurse. Casually dressed in baggy trousers, she looks around the room and smiles at Ndidi. Prof seats her opposite Ndidi and himself.

There is something in Beiye's expression and smile that disturbs me, and Ndidi senses it too. She pushes her own chair slightly back.

Prof introduces himself and asks Beiye some questions about her psychosis – Beiye shrugs and says, 'That's all gone' – before doing his Freudian thing and cutting to her childhood.

'I was good at school,' says Beiye, her English barely accented.

'And friends?'

'Boring. Couldn't keep up with me.'

'Narcissistic?' I whisper to Alex.

'Prickly enough.'

Prickly makes me think of Kelly Keane, whose diagnosis is indeed narcissistic personality disorder. But this is different.

'Did that bother you?' asks Prof.

'Not really.' Beiye looks like she's sizing up Prof and finding him boring too, but then she gives him the smile and leans forward. 'So what do you think? Am I still crazy?'

Prof doesn't miss a beat. 'Is it crazy to assault people?'

Beiye narrows her eyes without the smile shifting. 'Some people deserve it.'

'I understand the staff member needed eye surgery.'

'She shouldn't have moved my things.' The smile. 'But the voices were louder then.'

Prof thanks her, and she leaves with the nurse.

Ndidi is still looking reasonably confident but I'm less comfortable. I'm back to Foster Kid Thirty-Five, who smiled at Mum and swore black and blue she hadn't punched Lennon even though I'd seen her do it.

'Does Beiye have a criminal record?' Prof asks Ndidi. 'Before the diagnosis of schizophrenia?'

Ndidi frowns. 'None I'm aware of.'

'That's by her account?'

Ndidi nods.

'Partners or friends?'

'None that lasted more than a few months.'

Psychosis can get in the way of relationships.

'Does her family visit her?'

'No. They're in China – and estranged.' Ndidi is sounding less certain and I'm thinking of the flatmate who didn't press charges. Maybe it wasn't out of love and understanding.

Prof turns to the audience. 'Dr Edozie has given us a clear outline of this patient's psychotic disorder. Would anyone care to comment on any comorbidity?'

Alex's hand is up. Looks like he plans to go down fighting, and Prof gives him his chance.

'I'd like to explore her personality structure in more depth,' says Alex.

Prof pauses. Creates some tension. 'Any personality structure in particular?'

'Cluster B.'

'More specifically?'

Don't say narcissistic.

'Possibly narcissistic.'

Prof turns to Ndidi. 'Do you think your patient is narcissistic?'

Ndidi senses the trap. 'I would see her behaviour as explained by her primary diagnosis of schizophrenia.'

'And would you consider any alternative explanation?'

'If there was evidence.' Ndidi is now on the defensive.

Wendy Li comes to her rescue.

'Professor Gordon,' she says, 'Dr Edozie has been trying hard to get collateral history but it hasn't been possible. I wouldn't want my registrars to diagnose personality disorders without that background information.'

'Quite,' says Prof. 'But a good psychiatrist will follow their intuition.'

As soon as he says the word, I know where he's going. His poster girl for intuition.

'Dr Wright,' says Prof. 'Your thoughts? Your *feelings*? How did you react to Beiye's presentation?'

As I collect my thoughts, the rest of me is dancing to another tune – and the nurse sitting on one side of me ends up with her cup of coffee over herself and the floor when I sit back abruptly. Alex pulls out a packet of tissues and leans over to help, and I end up with his hand under my foot as I pull away from the nurse and the mess I've caused.

Prof is waiting.

'I have a distinct reaction . . .' I'm not going to say *skin tingling* but that's what it is.

'Go on,' says Prof.

'It's the feeling of calculation, of being managed. That their emotional response isn't real.'

'Which you've experienced before?'

'I have.' Foster Kid Thirty-Five . . . and Aleesha.

Prof turns to Alex. 'Want to reconsider, Dr Ashwood?'

'You're suggesting antisocial personality disorder,' says Alex. 'On what we've heard, she wouldn't fit the DSM criteria: no criminal record, no evidence of lying . . .'

'On what we've heard. She may have lied about her criminal record. And I said "explore" not "definitively diagnose". In line with Dr Wright's intuition – her *countertransference* – if we looked harder, I'd be surprised if we didn't find sufficient evidence for antisocial personality disorder.' He smiles at the audience. 'Which, in common language, is to say that Hannah – and I – suspect our patient is a psychopath.'

It's a strong word, and I can see that Prof enjoyed using it.

He turns to Ndidi. 'Think about whether your patient has genuine remorse.'

To Wendy Li he adds, 'And where our responsibility to treat ends. Schizophrenia is ours. Criminal acts that result from psychopathy are for the police.'

There is more discussion, but I tune out. Because there's someone else who gives me this feeling of edginess in their company, of second-guessing myself. A Porsche-driving financial advisor. We've been circling each other, playing games . . . but now I wonder if there isn't more to it.

I'm still processing this, waiting for Ndidi, when Prof grabs me.

'Good work,' he says. 'Have you made an appointment with Isaac?'

His expression tells me he knows I haven't. Which is the problem. It's not something he should know unless I tell him.

'Unfortunately there was a conflict of interest: someone close to me who's seeing him,' I say. 'But I found someone.' Barbara Quinlan, who couldn't give me a parkrun token.

Ndidi has overheard, and on the way to the lifts she says, 'I hope it's not Jeff Turner.'

I shake my head, but she wants to tell me anyway.

'I've been seeing him for a year.'

So like Ndidi to tell me this in a situation where she won't have to go deep. I get this is hard for her but wish she wasn't so defended.

But when we're in the lift alone, she elaborates. 'Jeff came with a big rap, and that's why I've stuck with it, but all he wants to talk about is my family. Every time I bring up something current and important, it's back to my childhood. I'm not saying he's not insightful, but . . . fertility is a big deal in my family. Like a measure of worth. We end up talking about it *all the fucking time*. Which isn't going to change centuries of Nigerian culture. I terminated therapy this week.'

I want to say something helpful – of course I do – but Jeff has had a year at it. So I do what he couldn't. I give her a hug, and after the first second she softens and something shifts between us. The dampness her tears leave on my cheek is a sign of trust that I will hold on to every time she tries to keep me at bay. She won't be any more forthcoming, but she'll know she isn't alone.

—

At home that night, I go over the interactions I've had with Simon: the flowers and the texts after I saw Jason. The story about his father who might not have been a mountaineer. And a small moment I filed away: when he told me he had a commerce degree, then upgraded it to a master's. A bit of exaggeration on a first date doesn't make him a psychopath. But still. And I guess he'd check the criminal-history box – certainly the childhood-misconduct one.

I think back to when I was fifteen. He had seemed so smooth and smart. He'd made me nervous, and I thought that was normal, but now I'm wondering. Simon's callous disregard and harsh rejection might have been the final straws that led Aaron to throw a rope around a tree branch and hang himself. And, whatever he's tried to convey, I'm convinced Simon doesn't care.

When I've pulled myself together, more or less, I go for a short hard run, shower, and ring my father.

'Dad, I need your help.'

'Anything I can do.'

'I'm pretty sure you can. It's whether you will.' I let this sink in for a few moments. 'I asked you about Simon Trevallyan. I may be wrong, but I need to know as much as I can to decide what I'm dealing with.'

'I don't like the sound of this.'

'I'm just being cautious. Mum told me she met Simon's mother, and she was very cold. What I want to know about is his father.'

'He was in prison.'

'Do you know what for?'

'I'm not likely to forget.' There's a silence, then my father says, 'He tried to kill them both – mother and son. When Simon was three. Only succeeded in killing the good Samaritan who came to their aid.'

I guess I'd have made up a story too.

I do an internet search – *Trevallyan murder* – and there it is. Newspaper article from twenty-five years ago: not much more than what Dad told me. Except the headline: *Killer's Blind Rage.*

It's 8 pm and I can't eat. I google Inaya Bul, Jason's ex right-hand person. She's all over social media as a producer and activist. I message her saying it's about the film. Add my phone number and remind her we've met – *the doctor working in psychiatry.*

I'm surprised when she calls an hour later. I wasn't sure she would even respond.

'What's this about?' she asks. 'I've pulled out of the doco. I don't want anything to do with it.'

'I know,' I say. 'But I'm worried Jason might have been targeted. Because of me.'

Silence.

'Jason told me you didn't want to work with him. I just wanted to check it wasn't an anonymous tip, or something someone said when you were filming at my parents' place.'

'It wasn't anonymous, and it wasn't something anyone said when we were filming. I had an email. From a prominent Black woman. She alerted me to a short film Jason made.'

'Are you sure it was true?'

'I'm sure.'

'You know the woman?'

'Not personally. But she was concerned that I was associating with someone who gave a voice . . . He probably made a mistake, but it doesn't matter. Reputation is everything – you don't get a second chance in this industry. If *she* has a problem with it . . .'

'Could you check . . . that it really is her?'

'What are you . . . ?' There's silence, then, 'I won't give you her name, but I'll send you a link. The one she sent me.'

'Okay. But please check that it was really her.' And I was thinking Jason was being paranoid about Simon.

She hangs up and a few moments later a link comes through. It's an online conversation from eight years ago. Anger at a student video that featured a 'fascist' and his 'racist propaganda'. Jason defends it as 'needing to show both sides'. I think, perhaps unfairly, that the lighting might have been particularly good. The pile-on that follows is all about false balance.

I reply, thanking Inaya, then text Jason. It's six weeks since we've been in touch, but I want to know what's going on.

Did you film Simon?

Jason replies instantly. *He pulled out.*

Because?

He wanted a say in the final edit. Not how I work.

You were lucky. I know why your co-producer pulled out.

The student short, right?

You could have told me.

You could have told me you were seeing Simon.

—

The test results for Andrea have come in. Nothing. A couple are outstanding so I ring the lab. One is an oversight: all clear. The other: they'll get back to me.

They do, but won't discuss it over the phone. I give them my hospital email address.

I open the email and stare at my screen. I want to cry. I think of Carey giving bad news to parents of kids with cancer and call them for guidance.

'Kind and clear,' they say. 'They'll forget everything other than the fact that it's terminal, so write down some online links and set up some appointments to talk it through.'

Carey follows with a ten-minute briefing on the disease, drawing on their encyclopaedic knowledge of psychiatry, genetics and popular music. If they don't blitz the selection interview, there's something very wrong with the system.

—

I wonder if Ben and Andrea can tell, like when two cops arrive at the door. *No* is what I'm thinking from Ben's smile when they sit down.

I wait a few moments. 'I'm afraid the news isn't good.'

Andrea doesn't seem to be taking it in, and Ben's puzzled. 'What do you mean?'

'Andrea, your emotions have been all over the place. The tests were to check for physical causes. Our brain and nerves regulate our emotions, but they also regulate our thinking and our bodies. Everything.'

'So there's a . . . neurological problem?' asks Ben.

'Yes. It's a rare degenerative disease – Huntington's disease. About seven cases per hundred thousand people.'

You'd have to be unlucky. Just one famous sufferer according to Carey: folksinger Woody Guthrie was in its throes when a young Bob Dylan came to pay homage back in the 1960s.

Ben's eyes widen. He's heard of it. Harder to pick what Andrea's thinking – la belle indifference?

I let them sit with the information before continuing. 'The nerve cells break down and cause problems with thinking and emotions. Difficulties learning and concentrating, lack of energy . . . It's the reason for those jerks and clumsiness. It gets worse over time.'

'How much time?' asks Ben.

Andrea looks like she's still catching up.

'It varies. I've got you an appointment with a specialist – a neurologist – because this isn't my field.'

'But roughly?'

'Ten to twenty years.'

They look relieved, but in ten years Andrea isn't likely to be in as good shape as she is now. And in twenty years . . . Good chance she'll see her children graduate school, but she may be in full-time care by the time they have families. If she's alive.

'The movements will get worse. Getting around will become hard, swallowing will be a problem. I'm sorry . . . it's a tough disease.'

'There's treatment?' Andrea's caught up.

'For some of the symptoms.' But not for the symptoms like personality change. 'It's a lot to take in. I've printed some brochures for you, including for the support group – I strongly recommend you contact them.'

'Why?' Andrea asks. 'I mean, how did I get it?'

'It's genetic,' I say and Ben nods.

Andrea is adopted. I wonder if her mother was the carrier, or if her father was impregnating women randomly. One of the symptoms can be poor impulse control and random sex. As demonstrated.

'So, Andrea . . .' I say. 'Are you on some form of contraception?'

'I'm on the pill.'

Ben's already worked it out. 'We have two children. What are the chances they'll have it?'

I look away to ensure I've steeled myself adequately. Look back. 'Fifty per cent. Each of them.'

Which Ben the engineer will work out means a seventy-five per cent chance that at least one of them has a tragic timebomb ticking away inside.

—

I need to talk to Alex. At least the Alex I used to know.

He reads my mind. I'm still packing up for the day when the text comes: *You were right. I owe you an apology – two.*

I'm at the bar before him and order the margaritas. The server brings them as Alex arrives, looking better than he's been for a while.

'My turn to talk,' he says. 'Apology one is for letting you think Marla was my girlfriend. I told her last night, and she had to work very hard not to react. But I didn't realise you thought that until you were dating other guys, and . . . I didn't tell any lies . . .'

'But you deliberately let me go on thinking . . .'

'I really needed some space. The other apology is for everything else. Being closed. I should have told you – What's the matter?'

Suddenly I'm crying. Not about him or us; about Ben and Andrea. That's why I wanted to talk to him.

He gets up and puts his arms around me – awkwardly, because we're at a table in a bar. And in that moment, I just want to take him home. Our relationship has been more intellectual than sexual – the opposite of what's been happening with Simon. But right now . . . yeah.

Of course I don't take him home. We talk. I tell him about Ben and Andrea, and the issues it raises about their marriage – their lives, their kids' lives – for about an hour. He listens. He gets it. I feel heard. He makes me feel good about myself. He makes good suggestions about dealing with stuff.

He laughs. 'I came here determined to do my share of talking and . . .'

I laugh back. 'Tell me something. Something important about what's going on for you.'

He takes a breath. 'My mid-term assessment. Keith failed me. He'll probably fail me at the end.'

Fuck. It's not just about having to do an extra rotation to make up. *Nobody* fails their rotation assessments. Which is going to make it really stand out if it happens. It'll get talked about. *That guy.* On top of: *The guy whose psychotherapy patient suicided.* Maybe he'll get kicked out of the training program. Or pull out in shame.

'Shit, Alex.'

'Seriously, when Keith says I'm not applying myself to the job, I look at him and . . . I swear, half his day – more – he's on Zoom doing legal opinions. On our time.'

'Nice work if you can get it.'

'He came out of his office the other day and I just looked at him. Like: *You fail me, I'll take you down with me.*'

'Would you?'

'I want to get a job *somewhere.* I'll take the hit and move on.'

'Have you talked to anyone else about this?'

'Marla. Jon.' Then he laughs. 'But you want to talk about something else and you're trying not to because it's supposed to be my turn to talk. Go on.'

He's right. I'm happy to talk most of the time . . . just not all of it.

I tell him about Barbara Quinlan and the parkrun tokens.

Alex thinks she behaved reasonably within her way of working. 'Strict boundaries.'

'And no guidance. What if I just need some urgent help with a crisis? My family, or a patient . . .'

'Or a boyfriend . . .'

'All of the above.'

'If that's what you want from a therapist, maybe she's not what you're looking for.'

We have dinner. It's like old times. And, like old times, we go our separate ways when we're done. The rush of desire has receded: talking about work will do that.

On my way home I find myself thinking: who needs a therapist? And through the haze – or clarity – of a margarita and two glasses of wine, light dawns. Or at least I manage some self-insight. None of the therapists I've tried have measured up. Could that be because I wouldn't have these conversations with Alex anymore?

For his part, he hasn't exactly been encouraging about any of the candidates. Including his father's friend, who he must have known I'd reject.

What would Alex's and my conversations – Alex's and my *relationship* – look like if I was in therapy?

Next morning I phone Ndidi's therapist, Jeff Turner, the guy who wanted her to talk about family, and ask to take her slot.

—

Ben turns up in the waiting room at the end of the week. No appointment: they're in the hands of neurology now. I wonder how much help those guys are on the counselling side. I imagine, as with me, that it comes down to common sense and humanity rather than protocols and training. Or maybe the support organisations take that role.

'I won't keep you from your patients,' he says. 'But I wanted to thank you.'

Thank me for what? I want to cry, like I did when I lost my first patient and the family brought me a present. Now I know better the value to patients and families of spending time, of empathy and clarity and not shying away from the hard stuff. But I still want to have done more, and maybe he's sensed that. Or just wants to keep the connection with someone who was there at a critical moment.

'You know,' he says, 'I was pretty sure – *knew* – she was . . . being unfaithful. I was looking to you to find some cause other than the obvious. Careful what you wish for, eh?'

He manages a wry smile.

'We're going to make it work. Our marriage, the kids, what we tell them and when. I guess you know we can't get them tested till they're eighteen. There's research happening on gene therapies. Maybe something will come through. Regardless, we're going to make the most of the time we have. Make the best lives we can, together. Starting with your advice.'

'About?'

'We're taking that holiday.'

TWELVE

RUPTURE

Professor Gordon is not a natural manager or even a trained manager. Four months ago, when he lost his role as clinical director to Nash Sharma, he retained an 'overall governance' function. Whatever Nicole, the architect of the reorganisation, envisaged when she threw him that bone, it can't have been this.

It's she who arrives at his office first.

'You might as well tell me what you've decided,' she says.

'I'm afraid all I've decided is that you two will have to make a decision.'

'If you'll excuse me then, I'll do some work while I wait.'

Nicole stands up, makes a point of pulling out her phone, but Nash arrives. No apology.

'Sit down,' Prof says, but both remain standing.

If he was seeing Nicole and Nash in therapy, he'd ask them why they allowed themselves to be caught. Is that what they wanted – their hands forced?

'I'll keep this brief,' says Prof. 'The relationship ends, or one or both of you resign. Am I being reasonable?'

Nash nods. 'More than reasonable.'

Nicole looks at Nash. Reads his body language.

'That's a decision I've already made. I'm prepared to acknowledge an error of judgement on my part, and I'm sure Nash feels the same way. It's over. And thank you for allowing us that option.'

Nash is gutted. And relieved.

I'm having dinner with Alex. At his apartment. We've cleared the air, he's apologised, I'm optimistic I've found a therapist I'll stick with and it's almost Christmas. I don't know what plans he's made, but if I don't make a move, I could be waiting till next year to see if this is ever going anywhere. I throw an overnight bag in the Uber.

Alex has gone to a lot of trouble with dinner, which is nice, and has cleared away whatever tools he's been using for the renovations, but I wish it was just us.

Jon, Ndidi and I have made a start on the sashimi when Carey buzzes: uncharacteristically late. They've come straight from the selection interview for the psychiatric training program, and if they weren't autistic, I'd be diagnosing a manic episode.

'I screwed up I studied and I practised I did eight mock interviews with Amy and I screwed up I can't believe it.'

Unfortunately, I *can* believe it. The thing the selection people are looking for above everything else is sanity. Stability, judgement, perspective. Controllability. I've seen Carey get all of those wrong, but I've learned that in addition to being exceptionally knowledgeable, they're dedicated, perceptive and caring. And working effectively on their blind spots. Trouble is, it took me a while to see that, and the committee would be going by first impressions.

'Hold on,' says Alex, gesturing for them to sit down. 'Just tell us what happened. Slowly.'

Carey takes a few breaths but doesn't sit. 'They asked me to talk about a patient I'd seen recently. Obviously, I chose the most interesting and complex.'

'Okay.' I think even Alex would have chosen the simplest.

'Psychotic, brain injury, drug intolerant, query Lewy body dementia –'

This could be a long story, but Jon puts a hand on their shoulder. 'Where did it go wrong?'

'The chair of the panel was Dr McDonald.'

'Margaret McDonald?' I ask. 'I've seen her in tribunals. Wouldn't want her going after me.'

'She went after me. Asked questions – tough questions – not just about the patient but about the theory, the diagnostic criteria and the evidential base, what the controversies were. Which is supposed to be my strength. I knew about half, maybe sixty per cent.'

'Shit,' says Jon.

I remember the sort of clinical questions I got asked in my interview. Carey would have aced them.

Ndidi picks up on it too. 'No way you got a standard interview. There's got to be room to lodge some sort of protest.' But she's not sounding convinced.

I can only guess that the panel decided they didn't want Carey, for reasons which likely boiled down to 'doesn't fit the mould', but wanted to rationalise and justify the decision.

'Did they mention autism?' I ask.

Carey nods. 'Asked if I have difficulties working out what others are thinking. I told them I have a lifetime of experience dealing with people whose minds work differently from mine, which is surely an asset in a profession which is supposed to do exactly that.'

'Wait and see,' says Jon. 'And don't sweat it in the meantime.'

'Good advice,' says Carey. They're looking shattered, but when Alex passes them a glass of wine they manage a smile.

By the time we're done with the coq au vin, we've emptied three bottles and I'm sensing that's not just because it's nearly Christmas, with the end of our rotations in sight. We're all needing to de-stress.

Everyone moves to the sofas and Alex walks over to the piano. Looks like I'm going to find out whether he plays or not. The answer is yes. Jazz, which seems right for a guy who reads Freud and makes references to F Scott Fitzgerald. I've never really listened to jazz, but that could change.

Then he switches to the intro to 'Hallelujah', and I'm wondering what this is about.

'*I heard there was a magic drug*,' he sings. He's no Jeff Buckley, but he's in tune, and, as if I didn't know it already, a smart guy. The new lyrics are really good – *funny* – beating up on the biological model, the pharmaceutical companies and, not too subtly, Prof, Nash and Keith.

I'm tied up on the internet . . .

He's got the lyrics printed out, and I step up and harmonise. '*Hallelujah, we've found the cure.*'

It's a beautiful tune, I've drunk half a bottle of wine, and I wish that Ndidi, Carey and Jon would quietly fade away and leave us to sing all night. I may be in love with this guy. I'm definitely glad I packed my overnight bag.

We finish to applause and laughter.

'That's my contribution – Hannah's and my contribution,' Alex says, 'if she's up for it – for the registrars' revue at the Christmas party.'

'Brilliant,' says Ndidi.

But Jon is frowning. 'Don't get me wrong,' he says. 'It's great. But I wouldn't do it at the revue. Keith's got you pinned as a smartarse. Maybe not just Keith . . .'

Carey, who was clapping enthusiastically a moment ago, nods in agreement. 'One of my weaknesses – which caused me serious, possibly career-limiting problems a few hours ago – is to prioritise demonstrating my cleverness over the likely response to it. I think you're in danger of making the same mistake.'

I look at Alex. He's crestfallen. Called out for showing off – possibly to me in particular.

I'll be going home with my overnight bag. Wondering if Alex's need to be the smartest person in the room is ever going to work in a relationship.

—

Elena comes to see me, which seems ominous. It is.

'Daniela's not available for the Young family meeting tomorrow.'

I've continued to see Brianna regularly and we've scheduled a family meeting with Child and Adolescent consultant Daniela Popa.

'Could we delay it?' I ask.

'Daniela's seeing Chloe. And she doesn't want to do it.'

'Elena, this family is –'

'Read my lips. Daniela doesn't want to do it. You may be less experienced, but you know this family – and Brianna doesn't have a mental illness. I gather she's decided not to tell her family about the termination?'

I nod.

'You're not doing family therapy. It's a discussion about things that are already on the table. And I'll be there on the other side of the glass.'

I take a breath. In and out. This is the job I wanted to do. Maybe not on my own just yet but there isn't anyone else. Another breath. *Chill.*

'Are you okay?' says Elena.

I nod. 'You're comfortable with me doing it?'

'You're nervous because of what you saw me do with them in the context of Chloe's anorexia nervosa, and the emotions it triggered. You're not going to do anything like that.' Elena smiles. 'Better not. But you should always be ready to deal with anger.'

—

Inaya Bul, Jason's ex co-producer, calls me again. Angry.

'You were right. I phoned the woman who emailed me the link to that video – who I thought emailed me. Someone used her identity. You know who it is, right?'

I feel my heart pounding. 'Not that I can prove. But yes. You know what I do for work. This guy's a psychopath. But he's not interested in you.' And while I'm the target, I don't know what's going on in his head or how far he's prepared to go.

'It doesn't change the fact Jason gave oxygen to a racist,' says Inaya. 'I'm still out of the documentary.' She pauses. 'But I'll leave it there. Sounds like you guys have got enough problems.'

—

I arrive half an hour early to the Child and Adolescent Unit for the Young family meeting. I'm nervous – but Elena is waiting. She'll observe from the cupboard-sized room on the other side of the one-way mirror. It's the perfect way to assess the dynamics without worrying about any interaction with the patient or their family. Lucky her.

We've discussed how to start the session, but after that I'll be flying by the seat of my pants. We've run through a couple of the tougher scenarios: David threatening to throw Brianna out or threatening me with some sort of sanction. Been there. Coped.

'Chloe's coming,' I say. Apparently, she insisted. 'Do I need to be mindful of her?'

'Of course,' says Elena. 'But Daniela seems to think she's stable for the moment. If there's fallout . . . Daniela's seeing her tomorrow.'

Elena pauses and I can tell she's concerned – but not about Chloe.

'Have you considered that Brianna might be looking for a safe space to disclose?' she says. 'About the termination?'

'She's said she won't. I don't think she will.'

'She's fifteen.'

That's the reason I'm sure she won't disclose. I've never told my parents what happened with Simon when I was fifteen. Been there.

The Youngs arrive with a few minutes to spare. Elena's already in the observation room.

I greet them in the foyer. David, in suit and tie, nods with a tight smile as he shakes my hand. Sue is wearing what my grandmother would call a frock. Hair tidy, pulled back. She smiles at me: no obvious sign of the depression Brianna has talked about. If she's putting on a front, it's at least a sign that she's trying.

Chloe has gained weight but she doesn't look healthy. It seems to be all on her face and abdomen, and her arms and legs still look like sticks. Her colour is . . . hard to know, because she's wearing a lot of make-up. I suppose this is a step toward accepting she's an adult but she looks like the child who got into her mother's stuff.

Brianna looks nervous. She's in her school uniform, no make-up, and studs only in her ears. I want to give her a thumbs up and do my best to convey that with my smile.

They follow me into the room and I invite them all to sit. There are six seats – one spare – in a circle, as when Elena saw them in family therapy. Maybe I should have rearranged them. But I get to see how the dynamics have changed.

Chloe sits first, in the seat that was beside Elena in the prior session. David sits down next to Chloe. Sue hesitates. Previously she would have automatically sat on Chloe's other side – in what was Elena's seat. This time she elects to sit beside her husband, and Brianna takes Elena's seat next to Chloe. I sit beside Brianna.

'Thank you for coming today,' I say. 'This must be especially hard because this room has memories which I guess are mixed. But this isn't therapy. It's a meeting: a chance to share thoughts and find a path forward.'

They sit in silence. Waiting.

I tell them everyone will have a chance to speak without interruption. I mention the anonymous 'team' behind the mirror and offer them the opportunity to raise anything they think should be on the agenda.

No response.

'So,' I say, 'I've been seeing Brianna for a few months.' I look at her and smile. 'She's been struggling. Being fifteen is hard, and I think I can speak for her and say that there has been a lot of tension at home and that she's struggling to feel heard.'

Brianna nods, looking at her feet.

'So I suggested this session to allow her to talk to the rest of the family about her worries – and for you to explain your point of view without anyone feeling too stressed. Is that okay?'

They all nod. I'm not sure if this is worse or better than them all talking at once.

'So David, Sue, Chloe, before we hear from Brianna can I ask how you feel things are at home?'

'Brianna is uncommunicative,' says David. 'And disrespectful at times. Sometimes it appears she's deliberately goading us.'

I look at Chloe, beside him.

'I don't see much of her,' she says. 'I go out, and I've got friends. We all eat together on Sundays. It's okay.'

'Sue?'

'It's great to see Chloe bright and doing things. I still worry about her . . . but she's not out late or anything so that's good, and she's thinking of studying social work. Online.'

'So that's how Chloe is. How about otherwise?'

'I . . . Brianna's doing well at school. I'm not sure . . . I don't know how to get through to her anymore. I just don't know why she isn't happy.'

'Are *you*? Happy?' I ask.

Sue takes a few moments to answer. 'I still . . . That isn't really something I think about.'

I turn it over to Brianna, no clearer about what Sue's issues are or where her allegiance lies. I have a good view of David from where I'm sitting; I can see every twitch.

'Home feels unwelcoming,' says Brianna. 'Actually like I'm not welcome. I see the mat on the doorstep and feel it should say, *All welcome except Brianna*.'

'It's your home,' says David. His resentment of her not toeing the line, and of the process, is plain.

'Brianna,' I say, 'can you explain a little more why you feel like that? And then I'll get you all to comment on why Brianna might feel like that.'

This feels like therapy, not a family meeting. Clumsy therapy.

'Every interaction I have with Dad,' Brianna says quietly, 'is him yelling at me.'

Silence.

It drags on and I'm too nervous to not fill it. 'Does it seem like that to you, David?'

'As I said, she's disrespectful.'

Brianna looks at her father. 'It's little things like *Why haven't you unloaded the dishwasher*, and I get that, but if I'm running late or forget and Mum's home anyway . . .' She takes a breath. 'But it's also like you think I'm still eight. No-one, and I mean *no-one*, my age is not allowed the internet in their room. No-one I know doesn't have their own phone. I miss . . . It makes me the odd kid and I just want to be normal.'

David looks like he wants to jump in, and I indicate to him to wait.

'And Mum,' Brianna continues, 'you aren't there even when you are physically. It's like I don't seem to matter.'

'Do you have anything to say to Chloe before we hear from your family?' I ask Brianna.

She hesitates. 'Chloe, it's great seeing you do better, but I wish . . .'

David frowns and Sue maybe sits up a little – I'm not sure. Elena will have noted it.

'I wish you'd done normal teenage things. Then Mum and Dad might realise I'm not the devil because I read teenage magazines and want to be on TikTok.'

'Brianna is presenting us as though we don't care, when we care more than most parents of children her age,' says David.

'Can you say this to her?' I ask mildly.

'Teenagers are not adults,' David says to Brianna. 'It's our responsibility to protect you and that's what we're trying to do.'

Because it's your responsibility or because you love her?

'Your rules are from a hundred years ago,' says an increasingly truculent Brianna.

'*Two thousand* years ago,' says David. 'These are our rules and your rules if you want to be part of this family.'

A warning bell rings in my head. Brianna starts to tear up.

'Chloe,' I say before I can think through anything. 'Um . . . what was it like for you living with those rules?'

'I don't really think it was a problem,' says Chloe.

Fuck. I recall Elena using information she knew, and wonder if I can make that work for me.

'How about when you were younger?' I say. When teenagers usually try to separate from family. 'When you wanted to be a basketball player?'

'I was pretty popular then, but I was like only twelve. The whole Facebook thing . . .' Chloe screws up her twenty-nine-year-old face, wrinkled and aged by starvation and now looking puffy and too large for her body. 'It was scary – boys and that sort of thing. But I wanted to go to parties with the basketball girls so that was kind of annoying.'

As a vote of solidarity it's pretty half-hearted, but I do what I can with it.

'David, Sue, this is not about criticising your moral framework, but I'm hearing from both your daughters . . . Is it possible that your views *come across* as rigid and unreasonable to someone who's trying to work out the sort of person they want to be? If they get told "my way or the highway" most people would have an automatic defensiveness, even if they agreed with you.'

'I don't care what most people think or do,' David says. 'I care about what my family do.'

I try to send Brianna a hold-on-I-have-your-back look, but she's staring at her feet, more and more distraught.

David sees our distraction as a chance to push his point. 'Social media, magazines – they normalise immoral behaviour, they promote unhealthy ideals. You're the psychiatrist: you know the consequences of those images of thin women.'

He's sitting beside a daughter who almost died of anorexia nervosa, and may yet do so. We could disappear down this rabbit hole – and lose sight of Brianna. I simply nod as sagely as I can and take the spotlight off David.

'Sue,' I say, 'do you have any friends or family who maybe read these magazines, or watch some shows you disapprove of? And you still see them doing good things or being good people?'

Sue looks as Brianna described: a little vacant, not quite engaged. 'Oh . . . ah . . .'

'What about Naomi?' says Brianna. 'She took me in, cared for me.'

'It wasn't their responsibility,' says David. 'Or, frankly, their prerogative.'

Brianna keeps at her mother. 'But it was good they did it, wasn't it? You used to like Naomi.'

'Yes, yes, she's . . . I do like her. But, well . . . Maddy is a bit wild, isn't she?'

'What about Tina's mum? Or Julie who used to babysit?' Brianna is now crying.

I look to the mirror with a *Should I break this up?* question. In the absence of a knock, I ask myself what Elena would do.

'I'd like to pause this discussion to talk with the team,' I say. 'I think it's times like this that Brianna feels she isn't understood – and loved. But while I'm gone . . . Chloe and Brianna, I want you to see if you can remember a time when your parents were angry at one or ideally both of you, and how that got sorted out. David and Sue, can you think about . . .'

I have no idea how to finish this sentence. Because David isn't giving an inch. Brianna needs a crack in the armour; some hint of a capacity to forgive . . . anything.

My phone buzzes. 'Excuse me.'

It's a text from Elena. She gives me the sentence: *Ask them to think about a time when forgiveness gave them a way forward.*

I put my phone in my pocket, relay this to the parents, and escape before they can question or protest. I'm shaking when I arrive in the observation room.

'You're doing extremely well,' says Elena. 'Breathe.'

I breathe. 'Brianna is hearing that they will never love her if she tells them the truth.'

'I think you've read it right. David at least.' Elena looks less relaxed than I'd like her to be. 'You've done a great job of stopping that happening. Your break was inspired – I didn't knock earlier because I didn't want them left in the room to implode. You've done the best that could be done to prevent that.'

We're looking into the room. There's some conversation happening between the sisters, nothing between the parents.

'Okay,' says Elena. 'Understand that if David rejects Brianna, he was almost certainly going to do that anyway. It will not be your fault. Whatever else happens in that room, just hold firm that Brianna is being reasonable and that you are there for her.'

My heart is sinking. Every part of me wants to terminate the session. I know I won't. Brianna asked for this meeting because she knew her father was on the brink of rejecting her. She wanted me there to prevent it. Or to pick up the pieces when I couldn't.

'Get Chloe and Brianna to talk about the task you set them,' Elena says. 'Give them feedback, but it might be wise to finish up then and bring the family back for another session after the parents have had time to reflect. And at that point you make it clear to them that everyone mucks up, and if they keep this line they might lose another daughter because one day she *will* muck up, because no-one is perfect.'

I think about this and it feels right.

'What . . . what if I push ahead in the session?' I say. 'You would, wouldn't you?'

'Not necessarily. There's a big risk.'

'A risk of?'

'Brianna falling apart if it's clear they won't forgive her for her behaviour – and I'm talking about the behaviour they know about. Watching her . . .' Elena sighs. 'My best guess is that she had a fantasy that she'd disclose what happened, break the toxic dynamic between David and Sue, and – with Sue driving it – be forgiven.'

'You think that could happen?'

'Sue looks defeated,' says Elena. 'I'm surprised. She was ferocious over Chloe.'

Not anymore. Realising she couldn't save Chloe and needed to stop controlling her has been like pricking a balloon.

'That Sue is in there somewhere,' I say.

Elena is thoughtful for a moment. 'I can use texts if you like; also another knock. But if you see an opportunity with Sue . . . take it.'

'What I'm missing is a way of you saying, *Yes, keep going with this.*'

'I'll text if I think you should push ahead. You'll feel the buzz. I'll knock on the glass if I need to talk to you. If the phone actually rings, that's the signal to wrap up as fast as you can.'

Like I didn't have enough in my head already.

I return to the meeting and look to Brianna. 'How did you guys go?'

Brianna looks to Chloe, who giggles. 'Brianna found the Easter eggs before the Easter Bunny put them out. She was only three, I think.'

Brianna shrugs. 'I was pretty young.'

'And she offered me one. I was . . . Well, the anorexia was an issue. I just took it and ate it – I ate a few – and Mum and Dad walked in.'

I steal a look toward David and Sue. Sue has a half-smile on her face. David is unreadable.

'They both yelled,' says Chloe. 'I think I threw up . . . but they were upset that Brianna might realise the Easter Bunny wasn't real.'

'But you were both forgiven?'

'We just put the rest of the eggs away and it was okay,' Chloe says.

'Do you recall this?' I ask David and Sue.

'We were annoyed,' says David. 'Chloe obviously knew better, as she was older. It wasn't Brianna's fault.'

'And I was . . .' Sue pauses. 'I guess I was upset the secret was out and I couldn't have my baby for a little longer. But on Easter Sunday she seemed to have forgotten, so it was all okay.'

'Had you forgotten?' I ask Brianna.

She thinks, then shakes her head. 'I somehow knew that if I played along I'd get the chocolate.'

'Seems to me that you . . . kind of learned early to cover things up.' I have no idea where that came from, but the buzz in my pocket gives me the thumbs up.

I turn to Sue. 'I think the girls sensed you don't like conflict. Is that possible?'

Sue gives a little frown then looks down at her hands.

I let Brianna and Sue sit with that and get another thumbs-up buzz.

'You said, David, that you didn't blame Brianna then because she was too young, right?'

'Of course.'

'But you forgave Chloe too, though she would have been older than Brianna is now.'

'She was sick,' says Sue.

'Perhaps that was the only way she knew to get you to . . . forgive her?'

There's a moment when I think I might be sick myself in the ensuing silence, to just relieve the tension. My phone buzzes, but I'm sensing . . . something, and I'm not sure Elena will. This is visceral and in the room. It's not just David tensing. It's something from Sue and I don't know what it is.

'She didn't need forgiveness,' says David.

'Even though she . . . broke the rules?'

'She was thoughtless.'

It comes out before I can stop myself. 'Like browsing the internet might be seen as curious rather than immoral?' I put my hand up to stop him saying anything. 'Before we go to you guys, can I ask Brianna and Chloe how they feel about that incident with the Easter eggs now?'

'Kind of funny,' says Brianna. 'I'd hide the eggs better if –' She stops herself and looks at me in a way that suggests she's linked the aborted foetus with her future family – or that her parents would.

I shake my head slightly and ask Chloe how she feels about it.

'It was kind of cute seeing Brianna covered in chocolate.'

'Did you feel like your parents forgave you?'

She frowns. 'I don't . . . Well, I don't really think of them ever being mad at me. Just upset, wanting me to eat.'

I let them all sit with that. Sue's blanked a bit, but she's also looking into her lap. Thinking about . . . what?

'So, David and Sue?' I say. 'Did you come up with anything?'

'What you asked was ludicrous,' says David. 'We're Christians. We believe in forgiveness. We've forgiven a multitude of times. After the sinner – the person – has acknowledged their mistake and sought that forgiveness. Brianna hasn't done that.'

For a moment I realise I'm thinking about the abortion, because that's the tenor of David's words. They seem like massive overkill for teenage attitude.

'I guess the issue I need you both to think about,' I say, 'is that Brianna may want to genuinely ask forgiveness for some things, but still live her life not quite as you would like her to.'

A buzz in my pocket.

'I think we would need to tackle that in another session,' I add, forgetting that this is supposed to be a one-off.

David hasn't forgotten. 'No,' he says, so softly I can barely hear him.

'I'm sorry?'

'I said no. It was bad enough having to come here today. We let Brianna see you when she should be seeing a counsellor who shares our values, and what good has it done? Our rules are not up for negotiation.'

'Because you can't defend them. Because they're bullshit.' Brianna is on her feet, face suffused with anger.

'Brianna,' I say, nowhere near as calm as Elena was in similar circumstances. 'Remember respect. Could you sit and take a moment to calm down?'

Brianna does as I ask but turns to me. 'I need to do it now.'

Holy fucking shit.

'Brianna, this might not be –'

'If I don't tell them now, we'll all be living a lie.'

'There are ways of speaking and being heard, and I don't think now –'

'There's things I haven't told you either that they need to know.'

'Trust me, Brianna, for a moment. Please don't say another word.'

I am firmer than I have been before. I'm not going to wait for Elena. I have to call this and I can only hope whatever I sensed with Sue is something positive.

I look at each of them in turn before continuing. Brianna is looking scared and angry and determined at the same time. The others are giving me nothing except their attention. 'This is not where I wanted this session to go. But let me start by saying: all – and I mean all – fifteen-year-olds have secrets from their parents. I don't care what your moral code is; growing up forces you to try and think things out for yourself. And you make mistakes and learn from them. And that has to happen for you to become a responsible adult.'

Only Brianna knows exactly what I'm talking about, but the sense of impending doom is palpable. I try to lighten my tone, but it makes no difference.

'Just like Chloe was scared of your anger,' I say to David and Sue, 'Brianna has things she can't talk to you about because she fears your disapproval and losing your love.'

'I've always loved them,' says Sue.

'Sometimes it isn't enough to feel or even say that. You have to act on it. You've already done that once, with Chloe. It must have taken a great deal of courage.'

David is sitting bolt upright and Sue is looking hesitantly toward him.

'If you're sure,' I say to Brianna.

She gives me a brave tearful smile and says, 'I got pregnant and had an abortion.'

I'm pretty sure Elena is poised to burst into the room if mayhem ensues. The phone is silent.

Sue lets out a small gasp.

Chloe says, 'Shit. Shit, Brianna.'

There's a long silence before David says, 'And you are no longer our daughter.' He gives me a grim smile and adds, 'And don't lecture me about forgiveness. We don't answer to you.'

'What Brianna has been through at fifteen is more than most people manage well as adults,' I say, looking for a scrap of care or sympathy from him.

'She knew exactly what she was doing when she lay down like a whore.'

I want to punch him. Brianna might actually do it.

Sue is still sitting there expressionless, possibly numb, possibly still absent.

My phone rings – the signal to wrap it up – but I ignore it and go with my gut. Elena is wrong. It would be disastrous to break now. I'll deal with the consequences later.

'You hypocrite,' says Brianna to her father. What looked like anger is now unambiguously cold rage. 'You and your fucking church.'

Sue looks at her daughter, but I can't read it. 'Your father, he –'

Brianna stands up, chest heaving. 'Just so you both know. I got pregnant to Jordan.' She looks at me. 'The church babysitter. The youth *leader*.' She turns back to her father. 'You didn't trust me; you trusted him.'

Now her pregnancy makes sense. Her parents inadvertently pushed her to it.

'Don't be ridiculous,' David says, but his face has lost colour.

I say quietly, 'Brianna is fifteen. Below the legal age of consent. If this man is over seventeen, what he did was his responsibility, and it was illegal. And regardless, he was in a position of trust.'

'He's twenty,' says Brianna.

'I don't care about the law,' says David. 'He didn't rape you, did he?'

Brianna slowly shakes her head. The revelation hasn't had the impact she'd expected.

David's on firm ground now. 'We all know who calls the tune. Men are men. And he's not our problem. You want to be treated like an adult – well, now you can take the responsibility that goes with that. And this is nobody else's business.'

'I want Brianna to continue to see me,' I say. Firmly.

David opens his mouth, closes it. 'We're leaving. Now.'

He gets up and stands at the door. No-one else has moved.

Chloe looks at Sue and Brianna anxiously. 'Mum?'

Sue is looking at the floor. Chloe gets up and shuffles toward her father.

Sue looks up then, toward the door. 'David, she's our daughter. And you might choose to forget what happened when I was sixteen, but I haven't.'

She pauses and looks at me and Brianna. 'Brianna, I can't imagine what you've been through, and I'm not sure . . . I'm ready to hear. But I'm going to try.'

Arm around Chloe, David leaves the room without turning back.

Brianna crumples, drops to her mother's feet, puts her head in her lap, crying. Sue looks like she doesn't know what to do and I mime a stroking action. She looks discombobulated, but strokes Brianna's head.

It's a while before Sue and Brianna leave together. Sue is talking about going to stay with her mother. I give her my work number and say they're both welcome to see me.

As the door closes, I fall in a heap in my chair in the empty room.

Elena joins me and sits in the chair that had been David's. 'Are you okay?' she says.

I nod. 'Sorry I didn't take your call, but I –'

'Call? I didn't call,' says Elena.

I check my phone. Unknown number. Probably a scammer. I start laughing. 'So . . . okay?'

'Okay? Holy Mother of God, I've seen therapists with years of experience do a lot worse. We'll go over it later – you won't have many sessions like this, so you should learn as much as you can. And one day I'll ask you what you went through as a teenager.'

It comes out before I can think if it's a good idea to tell a work colleague – one who is my hero – stuff that doesn't belong at work.

'At fifteen, I lost my virginity to a guy who'd been doing it with a thirteen-year-old boy who I later found dead at the end of a rope. My parents only know the last bit.'

'Jesus, Mary and Joseph. Do you want a drink? I sure as hell need one.'

—

By the time I get to my 7 pm appointment with Jeff Turner, I'm two vesper martinis deep and am feeling the need for someone to help me make sense of my life.

His office is in the front room of what is probably his house. A similar set-up to Joan Drinkwater, the woman who didn't know what Facebook was, but who would likely have been fine if I'd been in the right frame of mind.

I'm buzzed in, and there's an empty waiting room. No secretary. Jeff appears exactly on time; neat but unremarkable, maybe fifty. Kind brown eyes and a firm but soft voice and smile.

The office is tidy and elegant. Nothing personal. The couch is soft black leather. I take one of the matching chairs – he's in the other one, desk to the side.

'Tell me why you're here,' he says.

My reasons – or rather my understanding of the reasons for coming to therapy – have changed. At the start it was Prof's concern that my experience of suicide would affect my clinical judgement, which was my concern too. Now it's about the underlying problems of wanting to sort out how I feel about my family and deal with the unresolved trauma in my life. But the starting point is always the same.

'When I was fifteen, we had a foster kid who hanged himself.'

Maybe it's the martinis and the disclosure to Elena, but I skip all the stuff about finding Aaron, and what my father said, and how the Child Protection people took the kids away, and what it all meant to my family and my feelings toward them.

'I think he did it because he saw me and another kid . . . fooling around and was jealous – hurt. The other kid . . . We didn't actually have sex then. I've told myself that I couldn't have known that seeing us would affect Aaron so badly, and I think I believe it.'

Jeff nods. I doubt he's convinced, because I'm not, not completely.

'But . . . the next night, on the day I found Aaron dead, I *did* have sex – for the first time. With . . . the other kid.'

Jeff nods like he's following my convoluted account.

'I think what I'm really feeling guilty about is that while everyone was in shock and grieving . . . he and I were having fun.'

'That's how you remember it? As fun?'

I laugh, inappropriately. 'It was fun for him. And he won't have felt guilty for a second. But for me, I guess it was more . . . distraction. Comfort. A way of smothering the pain.'

Jeff just sits. And I'm thinking about what I've said.

'I guess the obvious question is whether it's affected the way I feel about sex now. I'd have said it doesn't, but . . . I recently got stood up on a date, and went and slept with another guy for the first time. I'd have said it was just that the time was right, and my flatmate would say it was revenge, but . . .'

'Comfort?'

I let my breath out. 'I'm going to walk out of here and start reviewing every time I've had sex.'

And the other night when I wanted to, after crying on Alex's shoulder about my Huntington's patient. Maybe I'll tell Jeff that next week. Along with a bunch of other things I haven't told anyone else.

But there's something I want to ask him now. 'Have you ever had a patient stalk you?'

He waits while I remember that I'm the one who's supposed to be telling him stuff.

'I reconnected with the guy I had sex with when I was fifteen. And I'm worried he's not going to leave me alone.'

Jeff nods. 'Which one of you got back in touch?'

I don't have to answer.

'You said earlier you didn't think he was carrying any feelings about what happened back then. He may not have the same interest as you in pursuing it.'

'You think I'm projecting my need to make sense of what happened onto him?'

He smiles. 'I think you're the one who's started a journey.'

—

When I was a kid, the lead-up to Christmas seemed to go forever. Now, it's upon me almost unheralded. Several hundred Menzies Mental Health staff and a smattering of partners are gathered in the town hall to share low-budget catering and homemade entertainment.

I spot Nash and look around for Nicole. They're solo, at different tables.

Jon has his cousin on one arm and on the other . . . Jess. The two women are in hot pink pantsuits; some coordination has gone on.

Carey is in all red and Amy in all green. 'Christmas colours,' Amy says in case we hadn't picked it.

Ndidi is solo.

I've resurrected the dress I bought to show Alex what he was missing after he turned me down last rotation and which he didn't ever see. I'm still thinking about the times I sought out sex when I was feeling down and avoided it when I was feeling good.

As we're about to take our seats, Prof comes over and extends his hand to Carey. 'Congratulations,' he says. 'You're in.'

Carey looks gobsmacked. 'I thought . . .'

'Then,' says Prof, smiling, 'you need to work on your ability to read a situation. I suspect that's an ongoing learning process for you, so at some point I'll contribute by telling you what happened in the interview.'

'You can tell me now,' Carey says. 'These are my friends, and I've annoyed them by telling them how certain I was that I'd failed.'

'Out of deference to your friends,' says Prof, 'I'll keep it brief. Margaret McDonald told me the story. She was concerned that her colleagues on the panel might not respond positively to your . . . atypicality, which I gather you were a little superior about.'

'Surely not,' says Alex.

Prof smiles. 'Margaret recognised that you knew your theory. So she went hard at that – basically gave you a final-year-written-exam-level grilling. I'm not saying you'd have passed at that level, but you impressed them enough that they couldn't say no. So, as I said, congratulations. And remember, it's the beginning of the journey, not the end.'

Prof turns to me. 'Nash has been leaning on me to address some gaps in psychotherapy training. I'll be starting a group for interested trainees next year. I expect you to join.'

He leaves without looking at Alex.

—

I take a bathroom break and as I cross the foyer on the way back to my table, I see Carey, standing alone near the vacant reception desk. They turn away, but not before I see there are tears running – streaming – down their face.

'You okay?' I say.

They nod and wipe their face with a red sleeve. 'She didn't even know me. We'd never met. She could see I wasn't going to be accepted and she could have just gone with it, but she contrived an amazing plan . . . and she's changed my life.'

As Carey and I return, my colleague at the Oasis, Lian, is bouncing onto the stage. She's dressed in a rainbow of colours that even Sandra Byrd, head of the Mother Baby Unit, would blanch at. Of course, it's Sandra she's channelling.

She introduces the end-of-year revue with a few nods to Dr Byrd's mannerisms and an 'any resemblance to consultants we know and respect is purely coincidental', but the clothes have done the work. I find Sandra in the audience – she's easy to spot – and she's laughing her head off.

I feel Jon move behind me. 'The play's the thing,' he says.

I've no idea what he's talking about. I look to Alex, but he doesn't seem to know any more than I do, and now Jon has headed off.

Oscar, the senior registrar and Prof's protégé, comes on, sporting a stuck-on beard, and does an impression of his mentor. Not so much physically – his Coke-bottle glasses are just too defining – but he's got the speech down pat. And is using it to offer one-line analyses of the consultants, as though they were patients sitting opposite. No names, but none are required.

'Perhaps your phone phobia is a rejection of the connected but not connected connectedness that technology offers, and symptomatic of a search for a gentler life, with fewer patients and registrars.'

That'd be Daniela Popa, and, in case any of us have doubts, Oscar is looking toward her as he offers his analysis. He must have located her before he started; no way his eyesight's good enough to see her. She joins in the general laughter and Oscar lines up his next target.

'I'm fascinated by the fake Scottish accent, which I see as a manifestation of a desire to continually escape yourself, and wonder if, as a child, you were subjected to some esoteric trauma such as being forced to wear a girl's skirt and eat offal in the freezing cold.' Louis the Locum, who's arrived late and taken the vacant seat beside Ndidi.

Then he lines up Nash. 'Have you considered that your focus on the biological rather than the psychological might be a response to constant rejection by women . . .'

Oh shit. He can't know that Nash, whose movie-star good looks are the joke here, is in the midst of what may turn out to be a marriage break-up, with the other woman sitting a couple of tables away.

Nash is pushing back his chair. Oscar won't be able to see it.

I check Nicole. She's doing the same as me, willing Nash to stay there, to just go with it.

Then I look back up at Oscar, and somehow he's sensed it. Has he heard the scrape of the chair? A gasp from someone in the know? I can only admire his speed of thought. He looks away from

Nash and adds, 'I mean, *climbing a wall* to escape you. It doesn't get much more hurtful than that.'

I'm not sure if it's the deftness of the save, the joke about DJ's escape, or the fact that nobody much likes Keith Barnard, but there's a roar of laughter.

Keith, looking like he's had a few drinks, laughs along. But when I look over to where Nash was sitting, he's gone.

Then Jon comes on. We first-years weren't going to do anything after abandoning Alex's 'Hallelujah'. But there he is: shabby suit, white shirt hanging out, loose tie. Unmistakably Keith Barnard – who's copping a double whammy.

Jon doesn't need to say anything. But he does. He makes as if to launch into an impression, then stops. 'Sorry. I've got to take a Zoom call.' And walks off.

'Fucking *clap*.' It's Ndidi, who's already clapping, grabbing Louis's hands to get him to join in.

Our table claps, laughs, hoots and the room goes with it. On and on. Until Keith, who *everybody* knows does private tele-psychiatry during office hours, has had enough and walks out.

—

I'm not sure what to expect the next morning but it isn't a text from Alex to the whole group: *Registrars room 1 pm*.

I'm on my way when my phone rings. Goldie the Goth, Prof's PA.

'Putting Prof through.'

'A quick in-confidence query,' Prof says. 'Your patient Celeste Boyce.'

DJ? This I was definitely not expecting. 'How can I help?'

'Her parents complained about Alex Ashwood.'

I have a chance, and I take it. 'Yes. They told me. But Dr Barnard encouraged them to. They felt pushed.'

'That's more or less what I wanted to know. Do you happen to know anything else about Dr Barnard's treatment of Dr Ashwood?'

I begin to tell him – the rejection of conference leave, the negative mid-rotation report – but he stops me short.

'Why didn't Dr Ashwood put in a complaint?'

'He felt strongly that he should take his med— take it on the chin and use it to grow. He's been doing a lot of self-examination after what happened last term.'

'Seems I was right with my initial assessment of him,' Prof says. 'It would have been a shame to lose one of the few trainees who has an interest in psychotherapy. Make sure he comes with you to the group next year.'

—

I arrive at the registrars' room five minutes early, and only Jon and Carey are there. Carey thanks me for the coaching – a little prepared speech I suspect.

'I hope you didn't interpret my gratitude to Dr McDonald as supplanting my appreciation for your help.'

I shake my head. 'Any thoughts about your first rotation as a trainee?'

'Hopefully it won't be my first. I'm applying to get my time in Acute accredited, retrospectively. I did all the tasks a trainee is required to do.' I don't need to ask if they've checked the rules. In forensic detail.

'Unfortunately,' they continue, 'it's uncommon for it to be granted. But from a legal argument of natural justice . . .'

Ndidi has arrived and picked up the thread. 'Do it.' She turns to me. 'You did an unaccredited term in Acute, too, didn't you?'

'I'll organise the paperwork for you,' says Carey. 'Tangible appreciation.'

Alex, who called the meeting, is last to arrive.

'Well?' says Ndidi.

'He's gone,' says Alex.

After the conversation with Prof, I can make a guess. 'Keith?'

'Dr Barnard is no longer running Extended Care. He spent the morning screaming blue murder – about how Prof hasn't shown him respect for all his years of service. And people in glass houses. But he's walked.'

'Slow down,' I say. 'You're saying Prof fired him? Because of last night?'

'Asked him to resign,' says Alex. 'Prof must have known about the tele-psychiatry. But what last night showed was that everybody did. With Nicole sitting there listening, Prof had no choice.'

Jon's been silent. Alex is looking at him with something like awe. *The play's the thing* is what Jon said before he got up to do his fatal impression of Keith. *Hamlet.*

But there's still something that doesn't fit.

'You say *Prof* fired him,' I say to Alex. 'Keith reports to Nash.'

'Nash resigned this morning,' says Carey. 'I thought that was what Alex was going to tell us.'

'No!' says Ndidi. 'This place is his life.'

'Maybe,' I say, 'that was the problem.'

THIRTEEN

CLOSURE

Christmas is the worst time. Having to deal with family or not having family to deal with. Joy to the world; if you can't be joyful, please be invisible. Everything closed but the police station and the hospital. And now there's an email from the mental health clinic, an oasis in this time of despair, probably advising that they'll be closed too.

Every year, Jan the case worker organises a Christmas lunch for the Oasis patients; anyone who's had an appointment is invited. It's outside, in the park, so they can smoke. She takes up a collection and brings a gas barbecue. Leans on the butcher and seafood vendor at the local market to give her what they have left when they close on Christmas Eve. 'For some people who are struggling.'

It's a lot of effort for something that isn't meeting any KPIs and that management doesn't support, at least not enough to count it as hours worked. But Jan takes some satisfaction in knowing she's doing it for different reasons: because she cares about the patients and has faith that, at least for some, it will be a stepping stone to healing.

Louis the Locum, now acting head of the clinic, sheikh of the Oasis, presides over the barbecue while Jan thaws a batch of frozen prawns in a bucket of water. Scott Glover, history teacher and colleague of a cold-war spy, is helping her.

A middle-aged woman is looking after some of the patients who have trouble getting plate, cutlery and food together. It's Valerie, the disability worker whose chronic pain drove her to the brink of suicide. She accepted the invitation, but has come to work. Which she can do now, in small bites, thanks to the drugs she finally agreed to take. And the prospect of a joint when she gets home.

—

Kelly Keane has also made an effort. The living room is festooned with tinsel, streamers and a Christmas tree that took an hour to assemble. There's a chicken and roast vegetables on the kitchen table. She'd have bought a turkey, but the butcher told her they don't make them small enough for three people. That'd be a turkey *chick*.

She and the butcher had both laughed at the picture it conjured up. He may have been flirting. Anyway, the chicken's fine. What's not fine is Aleesha's can of rum and Coke.

'Get a glass, Aleesha,' Kelly says.

'Get off my case.'

'It's Christmas. I've cooked the chicken and I've done all these vegetables. All I'm asking is that you put your drink in a glass.'

'Don't start, please,' says Taylah.

Then she does something that surprises everyone, even herself. She walks to the dish drainer, gets a glass and puts it beside Aleesha's plate.

'Are you going to thank your sister?' says Kelly to Aleesha.

'She's just sucking up. Because of that letter she wrote.'

Taylah steadies herself. This is her family Christmas, as good as it gets. She so much doesn't want it to descend into squabbling, then abuse, and, finally, driven to absolute despair, saying, 'You know what you've made me do,' before she takes an overdose and Aleesha calls the CATT team.

What she needs to do is turn the anger outward, to a common enemy. It's not conscious; it's not something she's learned in therapy; it's instinctive. And, thanks to that letter, she has a better target than fucking Centrelink or fucking Ivan or the fucking bitch in the Emergency Department.

'I'm glad I wrote the letter,' Taylah says, adapting the script she practised with Hannah. *Focus on what you did do, not on what you failed to do.* 'You didn't know Ivan was hitting on us, and when you did, you chucked him out.'

'Too right,' says Kelly. 'Nobody touches my daughters. Jimmy the same. But you two have to –'

Taylah cuts her off before she can turn it back on her and her sister. 'My psychiatrist says a lot of the shit that's happened in our lives is basically Jimmy's fault. Childhood abuse fucks you right up.'

'Well, I don't think he knew that at the time –'

Aleesha isn't having this. 'Fuck, Mum, he messed with little kids. Everyone knows that's wrong. You go to jail for it and the guys in there cut your balls off. If he doesn't know that, believe me, I'd be happy to get in his face and tell him.'

'Well,' says Kelly, 'you know where he lives.'

—

Nash Sharma is having Christmas with his family. It could easily have been otherwise. Samira and their three children could have been flying to India without him, which is what Samira had threatened to do. He couldn't have lived with that. If he could have left the marriage but continued seeing his children, it would have been different. But that would have meant asking Nicole to come to India.

He'd been prepared to do that, right up to the moment in Prof's office when she announced it was over. He'd believed that she might have accepted the offer, though it meant throwing in both of their jobs and moving to a place that for her would be foreign, and for him, at best, problematic. He hasn't yet reached the stage of feeling a fool; he's still mourning the love that couldn't be.

And Samira. He's wronged her, but she's won. It wasn't enough that he broke off the relationship. She wouldn't have him working with that woman. One of them had to resign, and he was the one whose wife was demanding it. No choice.

Keeping the children he loves has meant losing the woman he loves, the job he loved and living in a loveless marriage. The only choice.

—

Nicole is having Christmas dinner with her parents, brothers and their families. They're working-class people: Nicole's interest in social work had its roots in the neighbourhood where she grew up. Now, she's the prodigal daughter.

Her mother pulls her out to the kitchen. 'You okay?'

'He resigned.'

Her mother nods slowly. 'I won't say it . . .'

'Married men. I know. No winners.'

'That too. I was going to say it might have been too soon for you, but what would I know? You took a chance, but you have to live your life.'

'I'd have gone to India if he'd asked me.'

'We'd have missed you.'

A two-year-old totters into the kitchen and Nicole picks him up.

'We'd have missed you too, Lucas,' says her mum.

—

Sue Young and her daughter Brianna are at Sue's parents' home. It's a big family gathering, with tables placed end to end in the living room and the air conditioning blasting to deal with the Australian weather, the people and the steam rising from the turkey.

The awkwardness of Sue's separation from David and the splitting of their two daughters has been overtaken by everyone's delight at seeing her and Brianna. They hardly came along to anything for years because of Chloe, and when they did, everyone was on edge about saying the wrong thing. And Chloe's anorexia nervosa was confronting. As for David . . . well, he was Sue's choice, but nobody misses the dirty looks he'd give you when you poured yourself a second drink.

Sue's dad is a few sheets to the wind when he stands to propose the traditional toast.

'Absent friends,' he says, and when Sue squeezes Brianna's hand, the tears rolling down her daughter's face are not of sadness, but relief.

—

David Young is spending Christmas with Chloe. His estranged wife and – as he sees it – disgraced daughter are still living in the family home, but today they're with Sue's family. Sue's changed. Maybe he should have looked more closely at the way her family lived before choosing her as a wife.

In the last days people will be disobedient to their parents, ungrateful, without self-control, treacherous, rash, conceited, lovers of pleasure rather than lovers of God. Have nothing to do with such people.

Young men will do what young men do, but it was a breach of trust. And there was the pastor, shamelessly asking David to withdraw his complaint against Elena Karras, and not to make one against the younger woman, Hannah Wright, because he was afraid it would come out that his son had sex with an underage girl in his care. David complied, but he's looking for another congregation.

It's a strange Christmas dinner, just the two of them. Chloe has put on weight since last year, but it's in the wrong places. She doesn't look healthy and David knows why. Sue has let her eat whatever she wants. Now that she's better, it's time to get her diet back on track.

He's bought a takeaway roast chicken: he's never been the cook and he's not planning to start now. But it's solid food. Meat and veg.

Chloe has taken the tiniest bit of breast.

'Come on,' says David. 'Take a decent piece.'

Chloe doesn't move.

'Do it for me, baby,' he says.

And Chloe helps herself to a steaming, fat-laden drumstick.

—

At Ben and Andrea's the meal's going to be a bit late: Andrea forgot to turn the oven on.

They're hosting Christmas for their extended families. It's the first time they've done it – but if not now, when? They've got a big bucket list to get through. Now that they know what's going on with Andrea, they've been able to deal with her occasional odd behaviours without disturbing the neighbours – or the kids.

Hungry relatives are milling in the living room and garden. Ben appears from the kitchen, smiling, carrying a big platter of anchovy toasts.

One day at a time.

—

For Max the barrister and his partner, Lillian, every good day is a gift now. He's had to put physical survival ahead of his mental health and can no longer take the lithium that kept him stable.

But today he's in the sweet spot between mania and depression – maybe slightly on the manic side. The ten-course meal he's spent all day creating may be just a little too much for the two of them.

—

Kelly, Aleesha and Taylah have taken an Uber to Jimmy's place, the house where they lived a decade ago. They've had a few drinks and the Uber driver's going to give them a shitty rating. Won't be the first, and Kelly gives him one star in anticipation.

The house is unchanged. Crappy weatherboard that needs a paint. Kelly wonders if Jimmy's fixed all the things she broke on the way out.

He's home, or somebody is. Plenty of noise but no answer at the door. It's unlocked and they walk through to the backyard, where a barbecue is in full swing, maybe twenty people drinking from glasses and cans. Including Jimmy in shorts and singlet. Not looking too bad, Kelly thinks.

He's talking to another bloke and doesn't see the Keanes until they're almost on top of him. He's surprised but makes a quick recovery.

'Give me a minute, buddy.'

He looks at Kelly, appraises the girls. 'What do you want?'

It's a good question. A fucking good question, Taylah thinks. What can he give them now? How can he change anything? Undo the damage he's done?

Her mother's apparently contemplating the same issue.

Fortunately, Aleesha has an answer. 'I want you to get down on your knees, you fucking dog, and tell us you're sorry for what you did, and then I'm going to kick you in the fucking head, you piece of shit.'

Taylah thinks that's a pretty good answer under pressure. 'Piece. Of. Shit,' she adds to confirm it.

A woman with a couple of primary-school-aged kids in tow comes over. Jimmy's partner, Stacey. Kelly smiles: she's put on weight.

'What are you doing here?' Stacey says.

It's basically the same question that Jimmy asked, and he saves Aleesha from having to repeat her answer.

'Making trouble. I'm just asking them to leave.' He turns to Kelly. 'Politely.'

'We're not leaving,' says Aleesha. 'Not till he's said sorry.'

'Okay, sorry,' Jimmy says. 'Shit happens, it didn't work out, we all moved on. Now, if you could just move on.'

He smiles at the neat turn of phrase. *Grins* at Stacey.

'Tell us what you're sorry for and we'll leave,' says Taylah. That's the best she can hope for and maybe it'll give her some sort of closure.

'Sorry I left you and your slutty old lady,' he says. 'That do?'

Wrong move.

'How about sorry you screwed my daughters,' says Kelly.

'That's enough. I told you nicely. Now, fuck off.'

A solid guy in his thirties, a tad better dressed than Jimmy, comes over. 'Jimmy giving you ladies grief?' he asks, lightly.

'We're not leaving until he apologises for fucking my daughters,' says Kelly, having settled on a righteous ultimatum.

Solid Guy smiles, looks at Taylah and Aleesha, then at Jimmy. 'Can't say I blame him,' he says, and puts a casual arm around Taylah.

'Fuck off,' she says, moving away, and he puts his other arm around Aleesha, who lets him keep it there when she sees him eyeing Kelly as a third option.

'You know how old I was?' says Taylah. 'I was fucking eight. *Eight.*'

'Ooh,' says Solid Guy. 'That's not on. That true, Jimmy?'

Jimmy seems unaware of Stacey's gaze on him. 'Mate, I don't know how old they were. Eight? No way. But I'll tell you this: whatever age they were, they never said no.' He looks at Aleesha. 'Until this one got too big for her boots and tells her mum, and . . .' He laughs. 'Well, she wasn't happy.'

'Tell him,' says Taylah to Aleesha, 'how old you were.'

'Hey, hey,' says Solid Guy. 'It's Christmas. Goodwill to all *men*. This must've all been a long time ago . . . and it doesn't look like it's done this young lady any harm.' He gives Aleesha a squeeze.

Suddenly, Taylah feels detached, like she's been smoking weed. Her mother and Aleesha are now competing for the attention of Solid Guy, their love for her so shallow that they can't even focus on the man who abused her, who's standing just a few metres away with his partner and their kids, sucking on a beer.

That's not what does it – not by itself. It's not the sessions with Dr Wright or the time in Short Stay, or the encouragement from the friend she met there – Maeve, who's escaped to that resort in Queensland. It's all of those things, and in that moment of clarity, Taylah finally realises that her mother will never give her the love she's been holding out for.

This time when she says, 'You know what you've made me do,' it's only to herself.

—

Jon is hosting Christmas with his family, or at least the five now living in the city. And Jess, who of course has cooked. His cousin Tarni, who accompanied him to the Mental Health Service Christmas party, is telling a story, planting the seeds of a legend.

'And Jon, he's dressed totally like this guy – who's *sitting there watching* – who's crapped on Jon's mate like he craps on the psychos –'

'Watch your language,' says Jon. 'That's mental health patients. Say it.'

'*Mental health patients*, and Jon just stands there, totally cool, and says like five words, but everyone knows what it means – that this guy's been ripping off the hospital. And next day – *pow*! Fired. Out of there. After like fifty years.'

Jess nods vigorously to confirm the story, or at least its spirit, and they all pause to take it in.

It's one thing for Jon to have made it into medical school, to have qualified as a doctor and to be on the path to being one of a handful of First Nations psychiatrists. It's another for him to have spoken truth to power. And won.

—

Keith Barnard is holding court, a glass of port in hand, while his wife and daughter clear the dishes. His audience of one is his daughter's husband, Travis, who has just been appointed Assistant Minister for Health in the State Government.

'The system is at breaking point,' says Keith. 'I gave it forty years, but trying to care for patients, handle the politics and do tribunal work at the same time . . .'

'What do you think needs to be done?' asks Travis. 'I mean, mental health is like the Indigenous situation: we all know there's a problem, but throwing money at it doesn't do much good.'

Keith smiles. 'It'd be a start. And I'd throw a good bit of it at some long-stay beds. Get the mentally ill off the streets. Everyone will thank you. Including the patients who are homeless or being exploited.'

'Like the woman you were telling me about?' Travis says. 'Who climbed the wall.'

'She's basically being kept as a sex slave. Last straw for me. And there's the crime aspect. Prisons full of people who wouldn't have done what they did if they were being treated.'

Travis nods. 'Timely argument.'

'That one's always timely.'

'You'd be available to give us your input? As a consultant?'

'I'm pretty flat out. The tribunal work has ramped up. But it'd be a paid engagement?'

—

The Santa hats on Frodo's garden gnomes have been nicked, but there's an inflatable Father Christmas in the living room fireplace and a decorated plastic tree. And dinner: turkey breast and roast potatoes. He's cooked a load of broccoli because it's healthy, and DJ needs healthy stuff.

She pulls a cracker with him and puts the silly paper hat on her head.

'Crazy year,' Frodo says. 'And more gigs next year.'

'Only if you can get me to them. And keep me out of jail.'

'Have I done that this year?' Frodo is beaming.

'Yeah, but I won't be living here next year.' Living with Ralph hasn't worked for DJ, but she's not planning to stay with Frodo.

'What would it take for you to stay here?' he asks.

DJ thinks for a moment. 'I need my own bed.'

'Bed?' says Frodo. 'You don't like sleeping in a bed.'

DJ shakes her head slowly. 'No, I don't like sleeping in a bed with someone else in it.'

Frodo's eyes widen. 'You mean . . . if I put a bed in the basement . . .'

DJ smiles. 'That'd be amazing. How soon can you do that?'

—

Jozef and Capeka Dulka are spending Christmas Day at home, just the two of them. They had their Christmas celebrations at Capeka's mother's the night before, according to tradition.

They didn't tell Maria that the IVF failed, or that they're planning to try again. Jozef's thought processes are slow and his communication slower, but he's figured it's best to surprise Capeka's mother with the baby to join its brother and sister rather than give her a chance to stop them. Capeka's schizophrenia isn't so disabling as to prevent her from following the plan.

Today is a day of recovery and rest, away from the stress of the two children, who are getting a bit feral. Jozef sometimes wonders if it's all a good idea. The kids don't seem to love their parents; if anything, they fear them. Because of things he and Capeka can do nothing about.

They're watching the soap opera that prompted their desire for a third child. There's no TV baby on the horizon now though – no birth scene to bring a moment of shared feelings. Maybe that's what they need to renew their commitment to the IVF.

Jozef switches to the menu, searches 'baby'. A movie from 1968 comes up. *Rosemary's Baby*. He hits play.

—

Another house, another family Christmas, this one in a leafy private-school suburb, the lunch a genuine feast of exotic dishes, not a turkey in sight.

'I know it's been tough on you,' says Torben.

Ndidi keeps quiet, watches her mother across the room fussing over her sister's baby, who hasn't coped with the jetlag, or at least isn't accommodating her parents' exhaustion.

'I get the biological clock thing.'

Ndidi doubts it. The crying is getting on her nerves; her mum takes the baby and walks outside.

'Listen,' says Torben, 'if we did IVF, nobody else would need to know. So it's up to you.'

'Thing is,' she says. 'It's not just about having a baby. Or babies. It's about who's going to look after them. Mum's going to be in Canada half the year.'

'There's childcare just around the corner.'

'I'd need to go part-time to make it work,' she says. 'We can't afford that.'

'We could wait until the next round of grants is announced. We're in with a chance.'

'No, Torben, we can't.'

It's been increasingly difficult to live with the string of failed funding applications, and projects which have been fulfilling for Torben and his fellow filmmakers but brought in no income.

'You want me to go back to teaching,' he says.

'I'm sorry,' says Ndidi. 'I think we've passed that point.'

They're both silent as Torben takes in what Ndidi has said – and her expression. 'You've found someone else.'

It isn't a question and Ndidi doesn't answer.

'Fuck. He's a doctor, isn't he?'

—

It's an hour after Taylah's departure when Aleesha and Kelly finally leave Jimmy's, having found other company to amuse them and to fuel an argument which is now in full flight. It's not a dignified exit.

Stacey, Jimmy's partner, mother of his two children, watches them leave, then goes indoors and finds Jimmy pulling beers from the fridge.

'Need a word,' she says.

'Bit busy right now, love.'

'Don't "love" me. You screw those girls or not?'

'What's it matter? You weren't around.'

'How old were they?'

'Give me a break. I don't know, they were young, but you better believe they were up for it. I'm not a fucking rapist.'

'Under or over twelve? Simple question.'

'Fuck, it was a long –'

And Stacey is gone. With the kids. For good.

—

Carey has taken Amy to Tasmania to present her to their family, having just completed a secret project. Secret because to the casual observer, the research component may have looked a bit like stalking.

They're still overwhelmed with the joy of being accepted into the psychiatry training program. For an autistic person who struggled for so long with their gender identity, acceptance has been an ever-present obstacle – socially, professionally, personally.

Without Margaret McDonald, who had faith in them, and found a solution to get them past people who didn't, they would, once again, have been on the outside, isolated and self-doubting, wondering where they would find the strength to try again.

—

This is Margaret McDonald's first Christmas alone . . . ever. She escaped to Melbourne less than a year ago and has thrown herself into work – private patients, tribunals, interview panels. Her patients are largely at the hard end and there aren't any easy days. She's told herself it's what she needs.

She's yet to make friends in Melbourne: her only social outings have been lunches with her peer-review group. She's toyed with asking Isaac Sandler to dinner, or at least a drink. He's recently widowed and there's a connection, but . . . boundaries.

So, Christmas Day, she's doing a locum in Menzies Extended Care, covering for the head who resigned suddenly. It's quiet: skeleton staff, a lot of patients on leave. She has to open the door to the delivery guy herself.

It's a huge white box, and the accompanying card is addressed to her. Just two words. *Thank you*. She bursts into tears, thankful that someone, somewhere, appreciates what she's doing.

—

Professor Gordon has volunteered to be on call over the Christian holiday, but he's found time to have a seasonal drink in his office with Isaac Sandler, a longstanding member of his peer-review group. As always, they're talking about patients.

'You'll be amused to know,' says Isaac, 'that I actually directed a patient – or at least suggested a course of action. Under, as you'd imagine, unusual circumstances.'

'Risk of harm,' says Prof.

Isaac shakes his head. 'No, the harm had already been done. By a quack psychologist planting false memories. EMDR.'

Prof nods. Not the first time he's heard of eye-movement therapy being misused.

'The patient – Stephanie is her name – young mother, thirties, had these very unlikely memories of childhood sexual abuse: spiders and snakes and sacrifices, all of which had arisen in the EMDR sessions. Prior to that she did have some less vivid stories consistent with abuse, which I certainly wasn't discounting. In fact –'

'No need to explain,' Prof says. 'I'm assuming she wasn't prepared to question the new memories – or accept any interpretation.'

'Exactly. In the past, I'd probably have worked with what we had for a couple of years. But the referring doctor was at pains to point out that her current trauma was causing distress to her family, including a young child. To cut a long story short, I suggested the patient talk to her mother.'

'And . . . ?'

'Her mother knew all about it. It had been the impetus for her divorce. There was a group of men involved, a couple of whom have been successfully prosecuted – relatively recently – using the historical offences provisions. It all came out then, with the details. Which were pretty horrific and have now displaced the spiders and snakes in my patient's memories.'

'The father?' Prof asks.

'Apparently died before he could be called to account.'

'And the patient was unaware of all this?'

'The mother hadn't told her because she didn't want to traumatise her.'

'Had more sense than the psychologist.'

'To be fair, there was a reason the patient sought therapy, and the psychologist's intervention brought things to a head. We still have a lot of work to do, but knowing there was some measure of justice done has been therapeutic in itself.'

Prof nods. 'There's always work to do when our colleagues are done with their medication and machines and' – he searches for an apt word beginning with M but can't find one – 'snake oil.'

'Incidentally,' says Isaac, 'the referring doctor was the trainee with the teenage-suicide trauma who you wanted me to see. Hannah White.'

'Wright. I mean, you're wrong – her name's Wright. I mean, you're not right . . .' Prof has tied himself in Abbott and Costello knots and begins laughing. Sometimes you have to.

They are still laughing when there's a knock on the door. Their peer-group colleague, Margaret McDonald, enters pushing a hospital trolley: on it, a bottle of champagne and an enormous platter of food: an eclectic – even bizarre – array of crayfish, doughnuts, caviar, cheesecake, oysters, jamon, sashimi, chocolates, guacamole, liquorice allsorts and a vanilla slice.

She smiles, sheepishly. 'All my favourite foods.'

—

A year ago, if someone had told Alex Ashwood he'd spend Christmas Day working in a soup kitchen, he might have been surprised. He saw his future – his place – as a psychotherapist, working with people who could afford to pay for his services.

He might still have brushed the idea off even if they'd added that he would have been pulled up short by the suicide of a man of similar privilege; a family man who embodied many of Alex's own ambitions and values. Doctors do lose patients – sometimes, despite their best intentions, through their own mistakes. But when the suicide happened, Alex, like many budding psychiatrists and indeed fully-fledged psychiatrists, couldn't brush it off.

It's been a tough six months. He's come through it, no small thanks to a colleague from a far less privileged background who put himself on the line. And Hannah, who championed him to Prof. And never said no to a catch-up, despite him giving nothing of himself in return for the confidences she shared with him.

He's wondered if he was punishing himself by denying himself a relationship he wanted but thought he didn't deserve.

Or was it simply that he was too fragile to risk a rejection? Jon had suggested the latter last week. Forcefully.

Now Alex is going to do something to settle things one way or the other.

—

Simon Trevallyan is in Noosa. The girl he hooked up with last night has gone back to wherever she came from, so he's sitting alone at the window table that affords views past the boutiques and restaurants to the sand beyond, the blue ocean gleaming, white caps in the distance. He toyed with asking her to stay for the champagne Christmas dinner he'd booked at the hotel, but he can do better.

His mind goes back to Hannah. He hadn't thought of her for years and when she'd contacted him out of the blue . . . it had seemed like a sign. It had felt good going back to the hillbillies, still in the same house, to show them how well he'd done. They were impressed by the car and his business. And him. Especially the ex-foster kid and her friends. But the film guy hanging off Hannah had soured things. Touching her, just to make a point.

He smiles. *Piss me off and pay the price.*

And what about Hannah? He's lost in thought, considering whether to continue that adventure, almost at the point of formulating his next move – until he realises there's a young woman a table away smiling at him. The man she's with is talking earnestly but she's bored. His phone goes off and he takes it, apologetically: *I'm on call, sorry.* Might be a doctor. Poetic. And she is very pretty.

He returns the smile. He's forgetting Hannah already.

—

I'm on the periphery of Jan's barbecue. I'm not really needed and yet . . . here I am, feeling way more self-assured than when I started at the Menzies nearly a year ago, but still avoiding my family.

Yuusuf, the professor of philosophy who only months ago was housebound, brings his dirty plate and puts it in the bin beside me.

'Thank you,' he says.

'Thank the TMS people.'

Yuusuf shakes his head. 'Without the hazmat suit I would never have got there. Too many doctors think only in one dimension. But you thought more broadly. You will make a very good psychiatrist.'

He's still thanking the wrong person, but I text his endorsement to Carey.

Grace appears with a paper cup in one hand and a prawn roll in the other. 'Look who's here,' she says.

Walking toward us across the park is Luka, with a man almost as big and twice as scary: beard, biker jacket, biker attitude. Biker *boss* attitude. I'm guessing it's Luka's father, who he's been living with since assaulting his mother in an ice-fuelled rage.

'We're not staying,' says Luka before Grace or I can speak. 'This is my dad. He wants to thank you.'

Luka's father offers a handshake; my hand looks like a child's in his massive mitt.

'Luka's still struggling,' he says. 'But he's made a commitment. That's what he had to do. I've been down that path, and it can't start until you make a commitment. He tells me you're the one who got him there.'

'I think he got there because he was ready,' I say. After seeing his mother in a coma in intensive care.

'Tell me,' says Luka's father, 'once he's clean, will it be easier to do something about the other thing?'

'The schizophrenia? The symptoms won't be as bad, and yes, we'll have a better shot at dealing with it.'

'Good. We'll get there.'

'Couldn't bring my mum,' says Luka, 'because she and my dad don't get on, but you've met her. She says thank you too.'

His father nods. 'Dangerous job you people do, dealing with people like Luka when they're not right.'

'Goes with the territory,' says Grace.

'Well, if you ever have anyone giving you trouble . . .' He nods curtly in Luka's direction and they head off.

I laugh. I have a flash of Luka's dad leaning on Simon's Porsche.

'Good day to have ADHD,' says Grace. 'The hits keep on coming.' She points across the park. 'Keane family alert. Taylah, so it's an overdose.'

Except overdoses don't usually present at a barbecue with a backpack and wheelie bag.

'Came to say goodbye,' Taylah says. 'Just to you two, so it's good you're together. Not to Fergus McFuckface, who did fuck all for my mum, or Bitchface Jan who let my sister . . . Doesn't matter. Nobody else has done any better. But I think you guys tried, and . . . I'm out of here. Getting the bus north. Said to myself, "That's what I'm going to do," and I'm doing it. I'm getting a bus. Out of here.'

She's only just holding it together. Before I can think too hard, I quickly hug her and whisper in her ear, 'One day at a time.'

'Amazing,' says Grace. 'Gutsy call, but I'd say the right one. Want a lift?'

'To the bus station?'

'That's where you said you were going. You've got cash, somewhere to go?'

'Yeah, I'm not that fucking useless. Got a job at a resort.'

'Amazing again. You want the lift?'

'Yeah. Thanks.'

I watch them walk away. With Luka and Yuusuf that makes three resolutions – as much as anything gets resolved with drug addiction, people with borderline personality disorders in dysfunctional families, or with mental illness in general. Or maybe life in general.

I see Ndidi's car drive up. She gets out and I watch her stand awkwardly by it. What's she doing here? For a moment I wonder if she wants to talk to me, but then I see Louis – Fergus McFuckface – wave and walk over to her. And kiss her.

I look back at the Christmas picnic; Jan, karate-kid-racer Grace, and some of the people I've lost sleep over. I feel as if I belong. Not much more than a year ago, I saw my future in the Emergency Department. Or maybe even as a GP in the country, where my mother wanted me. If I'd chosen either of those, many of my patients would have come in with well-defined problems that I could treat and perhaps completely resolve.

Mr Smith, you've contracted syphilis and this penicillin will fix it right up. You'd better send Mrs Smith in, and use a condom next time.

In psychiatry it's always complex, the treatments are almost never completely effective and, especially with six-month rotations, you don't always see the outcome.

Taylah could be back in a week; her mother and sister presenting at the Emergency Department tomorrow. Actually, given what Taylah's done, this evening. But you keep the faith. There will be setbacks, but things will be better than they would have been.

I've never received flowers or chocolates from mental health patients or their relatives, as I did in general medicine. But today will do.

'You who now will bless the poor shall yourselves find blessing.'

It's Alex's voice behind me. My chest constricts.

I turn and stare at him, trying to think of a smart reply. 'You want to help me clean up?'

'Good metaphor.'

We walk around in silence collecting paper plates and cups – a comfortable silence that I don't have with anyone else.

'So,' I say, 'what was it in your family that gave you this need to be the smartest person in the room?'

'I thought I was the one who asked these questions.' But he's smiling. 'You calling me narcissistic?'

'More controlling. When it comes to who's analysing whom. That I've noticed.'

'It'd take a long time to explain.'

'But you will, right?'

He smiles and nods. 'If you want to listen. Do normal people have these conversations? I mean, outside the therapy room?'

'I think we all talk about what's going on in our lives, using the language we have.'

'Wise words. Do you have plans after this?' he asks, making the big question as casual as he can.

'Next rotation isn't out yet.' I know this isn't what Alex is asking, but I'm not going to make it easy.

'I meant this evening,' Alex says. 'I'm guessing you're not going to see your family.'

'Actually, I am seeing them,' I say, making an instant change to my plans. 'Going up tomorrow. Nothing on tonight.'

'I hope we're speaking the same language.'

I smile. I'm happy he's here. Happy he feels the same way about the world we've chosen to work in. Happy he understands what's gone on between us and is going to try to do something about it. Happy. Not needing comfort.

'We could be,' I say. 'And after that . . . it's a bit of a journey. Be good to have someone to talk to.'

ACKNOWLEDGEMENTS

The Oasis is a novel, its characters and cases fictional. But, as with *The Glass House*, we wanted it to be as accurate as possible a portrayal of mental illness and its treatment, and of the mental health system – not as we might wish them to be, but as they are.

So, again, we supplemented Anne's experience in the field with input from specialist clinicians and people with lived experience. Our aim was to check that the cases and their treatment were realistic, which is not the same as being typical – or stereotypical. Everyone's experience is different.

Our team of beta readers checked that the medical descriptions were intelligible, the personal stories believable and the prose readable.

Thanks, then, to Tania Chandler, Dr Eamonn Cooke, Robert Eames, Dr Michael Epstein, Heidi Everett, Dr Justine Hoey-Thompson, Rod Miller, Elizabeth Quinn, Dominique Simsion, Donna Stolzenberg, Prof Dennis Velakoulis, Dr Beth Whitehouse, Janifer Willis and a number who have chosen to remain anonymous.

We would also like to thank Rebecca Saunders and the team at Hachette Australia, in particular Kate Taperell and Georgina Harrison, for their continued enthusiasm for the Menzies Mental Health series and for building a strong base with their support for *The Glass House*. Editors Rebecca Allen, Vanessa Lanaway, Nicola O'Shea and Pam Dunne demonstrated again that good writing is rewriting and set us on the path to doing that as productively as possible.

These books have been inspired by the courage of patients and the dedication of mental health workers. There are those who argue that mental health stories should be told only from the perspective of lived experience, rather than by clinicians like Hannah Wright. We believe that if we are to improve our attitudes, approaches and systems, we need a better understanding of the needs and experiences of all parties. We hope that *The Oasis* will contribute to that understanding.

BOOK CLUB QUESTIONS

1. Did any of the patients or cases in *The Oasis* particularly resonate with you? Why?
2. Hannah often finds herself relying on 'common sense' and her life experience as a 28-year-old rather than her textbook knowledge. Do you see this as a problem or true of most jobs?
3. How well do you think Hannah handled the situation with Brianna's pregnancy?
4. On page 33, Professor Gordon, considering Hannah's request to see Brianna in therapy, says 'therapists are not mentors'. And it seems that Brianna does not have a mental illness. With this in mind, what do you think of Brianna seeing a publicly funded therapist?
5. On page 63, Kelly Keene says she's 'Doing what you tell us to do – check if people are okay. If not, get help, right? My daughter is *not* okay, so I try to get help . . . I wait half the night in the Emergency Department . . .' Is Kelly's complaint reasonable? Are we given advice that isn't supported by our

mental health system? Have you had experience in trying to get help for someone with mental health problems?

6. On page 66, Hannah comments that Taylah is not getting the 'best practice' care for her personality disorder compared to the care she'd get if she had a physical illness – and Hannah implies that mental health is seen as less worthy of attention and funding. What do you think?
7. In the past, many of the patients living in the community and being treated at the Oasis would have been in long-term institutional care. Those facilities have been drastically cut back. Keith Barnard believes that we've gone too far. What do you think?
8. On pages 288 and 289, Professor Gordon suggests Ndidi's patient Beiye has an antisocial personality disorder ('in common language . . . a psychopath') and says, 'Schizophrenia is ours. Criminal acts that result from psychopathy are for the police.' Where do you think society should draw the line between mental illness and criminal responsibility?
9. DJ Voices argues that the community treatment order requiring her to have treatment for her illness robs her of her dignity. On page 201, in arguing that the order be revoked, DJ's lawyer talks of 'the dignity of risk', but DJ's parents are worried that their daughter will come to harm – and indeed she has a relapse due to not taking her medication. Did the tribunal get it wrong?
10. Capeka gets IVF when there's little chance she'll be able to care for the baby. If Andrea has another child, it'll have a fifty percent chance of having a debilitating illness. Naomi says that girls of Brianna's age should have to go through hoops to have

a baby rather than an abortion. Should medical practitioners and the law get involved in the right to have children?

11. Carey seems to face some discrimination in getting into the psychiatry training program. What do you think of a selection committee considering attributes such as autism and gender fluidity when choosing future psychiatrists?
12. The narrative gives us a close-up view of Hannah and her colleagues as human beings who make mistakes and have messy personal lives. How does this portrayal relate to the way we think of doctors? Do we have unrealistic expectations of them?
13. 'Humans often fail to see what is close to them and obvious to others,' says Don Tillman in *The Rosie Project*. How do you think this applies to Hannah's assessment of Simon?
14. Dating a colleague is much less common than it once was. What do you think of Hannah's choice? Do you think Hannah's relationship with Alex will last through her next rotation?
15. What advice would you give Hannah?

Professor Anne Buist is chair of Women's Mental Health at the University of Melbourne and the architect of the national screening program for perinatal depression. She began writing at eight but medicine intervened until 2015 when she wrote *Medea's Curse*, the first of five psychological crime novels. The internationally bestselling *Two Steps Forward*, co-authored with her husband, Graeme Simsion, was optioned to Fox Searchlight / Disney, along with its sequel, *Two Steps Onward*. She is co-author of the Menzies Mental Health series with Graeme.

You can find Anne at annebuist.com, on Facebook @annebuistauthor and on Instagram @anneebuist

Dr Graeme Simsion is the author of the widely acclaimed novel *The Rosie Project*, which spent 65 weeks on the *New York Times* bestseller list, and, with its two sequels, has sold seven million copies in forty languages. A film is in development with Sony Pictures. *The Best of Adam Sharp*, also an international bestseller, is in development with New Sparta Pictures and *Creative Differences* was optioned to Truce Films. Graeme is co-author of the Menzies Mental Health series with his wife, Anne Buist.

You can find Graeme at graemesimsion.com and on Facebook @graemesimsionauthor

BOOK ONE IN THE
MENZIES MENTAL HEALTH SERIES

Psychiatry registrar **Doctor Hannah Wright**, a country girl with a chaotic history, thought she had seen it all in the emergency room. But that was nothing compared to the psychiatric ward at Menzies Hospital.

Hannah must learn on the job as she and her fellow trainees deal with the common and the bizarre, the hilarious and the tragic, the treatable and the confronting. Each day brings new patients: **Chloe**, who has a life-threatening eating disorder; **Sian**, suffering postpartum psychosis and fighting to keep her baby; and **Xavier**, the MP whose suicide attempt masks an explosive story.

With intelligence, frankness and humour, eminent psychiatrist Anne Buist tells it like it is, while Graeme Simsion brings the light touch that made *The Rosie Project* an international bestseller.

hachette
AUSTRALIA

If you would like to find out more about Hachette Australia, our authors, upcoming events and new releases, you can visit our website or our social media channels:

hachette.com.au

HachetteAustralia

HachetteAus